THE ASSASSIN'S KEEPER

By

John McClements

Prologue

He scanned the street for the slightest evidence that anything was out of place. All was as it should be, but still something was gnawing at him. There was no time for hesitation here. Pedro drew his Beretta and slowly began to place pressure on the brass door handle with his gloved hand. It wouldn't do to leave any evidence. He moved it from the three o'clock position down to five, and then it released without so much as a click. Pedro pulled the door toward him and swung it flat against the side of the building. In the silence of the room, Pedro's eyes darted to the jumbled pile of papers on the table which were preaching anti-government propaganda. He knew that the communists were about to put their revolutionary plans into action.

His orders were to arrest the family who lived at the address. He cast his eyes around the dark kitchen. It looked like an ordinary family home, but then they always did. Family homes could be hotbeds of dissidents. Children made the most effective soldiers: no one expected them to have guns or explosives. No one stopped them joining crowds. There could be no mercy.

Pedro heard a noise in the back. They must have been tipped off. Maria Zaffaroni and her ten-year old boy got out just in time and hid in the alleyway behind the house. Her husband Jorge escaped, evaporating into the night. Pedro saw her in the shadows, pulling the collar of her black coat around her neck to ward off the bite of the cold evening.

"They're coming," the boy beside her hissed, almost inaudibly.

She looked as tough as they came, but Maria was finding it very difficult to walk. She was heavily pregnant – she looked like she might go into labour at any time. That part of Pedro that was still human frowned. This was no place for a woman or child. At that moment, all hell broke loose: lights flashed on and off, shouts and crashes emanated from every point of the alley.

The boy had made a run for it. Maria whirled, finding herself face to face with Pedro and a large group of armed police.

"No! No!" she screamed, desperately. "He's just a boy!"

It was too late. Astiz would later congratulate his men on their efficiency. Her son was shot in the back of his head. Maria watched him fall, dropping to her knees in time with him, unable to stop the scream that forced its way out of her throat. Pedro saw her stare wildly around, pale and terrified, blinking blindly into their flashlights. He almost reached out to her, to offer some comfort, but he stopped himself. It wasn't his place. Leave comfort for the men who still had souls.

"Please, please – my baby," she pleaded.

Astiz stepped forward and pulled Maria up from the ground. He said to another officer, "Put the filth in the van with the others."

"Where are you taking them?" Pedro asked, catching a glimpse of Maria's terrified, grief-stricken face as she was pushed past him.

"They're going to Batallón de Inteligencia for questioning; if they are innocent they will be free to go," Astiz barked. "As you will see, it's my job to rid the country of this scum. Now get out of my way!"

He slammed the van doors shut and banged the back of it, waving the driver away. The woman and her unborn child were as good as dead. Pedro knew that once they were in that place, they would never get out. It had become a detention centre for dissidents and suspected terrorists. For them, it had become the end of the world.

***

Uneasy, unpleasant feelings lingered in the air. Some of it was her own fear, but some of it was just part of the room, as if so much pain and cruelty had happened inside it that it had infused into the walls; become a part of the atmosphere. She licked her dry lips, struggling to know what to do. If it weren't for the child growing in her stomach Maria would have killed herself there and then. The cold, creeping fingers of despair had closed around her heart.

Her husband had been captured trying to board a ship. He, too, had been sent to the Batallón de Inteligencia. Knowing that he was here, somewhere in this dreadful maze of cells, had almost broken her – which was exactly why they had told her.

She was taken from her cell roughly. The corridor beyond the stairwell door was long and featureless. Spaced at regular intervals were numbered doors, each with a spy hole. The guard pulled open one of the cell doors and motioned Maria inside: sitting at one side of the table was Jorge. Her heart leapt – he was alive. A moment later, her joy evaporated. In this place, in this room, simply being alive wasn't enough. Neither of them would leave this complex alive. She bit back a sob. Jorge met her eyes, the same desperate conflict written across his face.

He motioned for her to sit down. The guard locked the door, leaving them together for a moment. Aware that they were probably under surveillance, they did not speak, only pressed one another's hands. They were alive in this moment, but in this place it would only be a matter of time. Would they be tortured in front of one another, the better to extract information? Maria couldn't tell. She clung to her husband's fingers like a lifeline, unable to express the depth of her despair. He whispered the name of their son, and she knew that they had told him. Maria closed her eyes, momentarily surrendering to the depth of her despair. They snapped open again as the door opened.

An officer walked in and sat in front of them, glancing between them. His uniform was prim and perfect, a credit to the Inteligencia. The rest of him, however; his mouth looked dry from smoking too many cigarettes. The officer started to explain that his role was to help select people to become sleeper agents and hide them across the world until they were needed. Zaffaroni, the person in question, worried increasingly about Marie's safety. Maria laughed – a lonely, hollow sound. They had killed her boy for this? No. To leave here with Jorge and her unborn child she would agree to anything that kept them safe and living. She was determined – almost recklessly so.

He even asked her if she was sure she wanted to spend the rest of her life looking over her shoulder – without a moment's hesitation she said 'yes'. She knew that she and Jorge would die unless they agreed – and with one son dead they had to think of the baby. There was really only one avenue open to them. By the end of the day, a deal had been made which would assure their freedom. They swore a solemn oath and would stick by it, not letting anyone or anything to get in their way. Fulfilling their final obligation was all that mattered now.

Jorge Zaffaroni had been a member of the Uruguayan resistance group, known as OPR-33. A trained foot soldier, and a trained killer. He was tall, but no giant, a man somewhere in his mid-thirties. The only notable thing about him was his slight limp – a war injury – and he favoured his right leg over the left. This was the path he and Maria had chosen. The officer walked them back to their cells to wait for transport, much more gently this time.

Maria sat alone, unobserved, in the darkness of her cell. Finally, she allowed herself to grieve for her son, the sobs wracking her swollen body until the first streaks of silver were staining the eastern sky, just visible through the grill that served as a window. She scrubbed the tears from her face, then, and washed in the water they had given her once she agreed to work for them. Free or not, she would not allow them to see her pain.

They were together again at first light. A car whisked them off to Essen, the Argentine intelligence agency that was the equivalent of America's CIA. It all happened so quickly. Within a day, Jorge and Maria had a new identity and a new life, sworn and indebted to the organisation. They would travel – as far as the organisation needed them to. They could be anywhere, wanting and waiting to unleash mayhem on the enemy. Coming from obscurity to threaten the very foundation of their enemies. They would go to any lengths to protect their identities.

Chapter 1

Buenos Aires, 1975

The morning was cold and dark, the approaching dawn only beginning to tinge the eastern sky with colour. Pedro Garcia was in the heart of Buenos Aires, in the midst of a neighbourhood of narrow avenues and twisting side streets. The alleyway was dark – there were no overlooking windows – but Pedro still took a moment to check that nobody had observed him. He was waiting for the drop, standing still as a statue in the shadows of a doorway. When it finally arrived – and Pedro was satisfied he was alone – he squatted down. Using his left hand, he unzipped the leather case and pulled out a long envelope embossed with the seal of the Battallón de Inteligencia. As expected, the contents instructed him only to answer to Alfredo Astiz and no one else. He smiled grimly to himself: everything was beginning to fall into place. He vanished back into the shadows and hurried home, ready to slip back into his everyday life – his cover, now.

In the usual way, a message materialized – passed by hands unseen: an order to attend a secret meeting that night. Pedro burned the paper when he had a chance, feeling that strange mixture of excitement and fear that kept him coming back for more. At the appointed time he slipped a jacket over his clothes and made his way outside. As expected, there was a car waiting for him. The men in the car acted as though he didn't exist, and he stared out of the window as they drove through the gathering darkness. They knew the drill, these men of darkness. It was as if they felt that if they didn't look at him they could pretend never to have seen him, should they be questioned.

He ran over things in his mind: the endless rounding up of dissenters, the black work he carried out for the Inteligencia, the restless nights where people's pleading voices chased slumber away. Pedro was a man committed to the cause, fervent and inviolate in his belief, but he had begun his life as a man. These days he wasn't sure what he was anymore. You couldn't get to be the legend he was in the secret police without losing some of yourself. If it furthered the cause he was prepared to continue; real lives were for civilians. Some days, Pedro was almost human.

He looked up at the building – the crumbling confection of bureaucratic architecture from the days of an older regime. It seemed appropriate that this should be the place. Pedro climbed out of the car without a word or second glance at the driver and ran through the cold rain up the stone steps of the building. Inside, three anonymous looking men sat in the round, marble foyer of the building, waiting. Pedro dropped the envelope on the desk, pulled off his damp jacket and slung it over his arm. The rusty hinges on the inner door squealed as it was pushed open, the sound making all four men wince. Pedro took a series of deep breaths, confident that the other men wouldn't see him, pulling air into the very bottom of his lungs and holding it to a count of four before exhaling. He needed to be calm tonight. He needed to focus.

Astiz stood in the doorway. As usual, he was dressed smartly in his officer's uniform. His hair was cut short and neat, like his personality. Casting his deep-set eyes across the waiting men, Astiz marched up and down the room, flapping the long vicuña overcoat, cracking the bones of his knuckles and displaying that kind of restless energy that some claim was part of his process of reasoning. Now his face was taut with anger. When he spoke, his voice sounded loud, vulgar and obtrusive.

"Today's meeting pertains to national secrets of the highest order," he declared. "And so I must insist that you all raise your right hand and swear that, for the rest of your lives, you will never divulge what you are about to learn – not to your wives, fellow soldiers, nor your children."

The words were powerful and the emotions high as Astiz's voice increased in volume.

The room was quiet in the wake of the oath. It seemed that each man was consumed by his own thoughts, united in contemplation of what they might learn and how these details could change their lives. Pedro watched the faces of his fellows. They were gaunt, focused. He wasn't totally sure of their methods, though he recognized their features from the files, but he was certain of their allegiance to the cause. Like him, when the time came, they would get the job done – whatever the job turned out to be.

The lantern light was extinguished with a rush of silence and someone at the back of the room started the projector. As it began whirring, Astiz gestured sternly for them to stop jabbering. There was a feral look in his slightly crossed eyes, and it warned the men not to mess with him tonight. Pedro leaned on the table, gazing at the screen.

They sat, quiet and attentive, smoking with a fierce kind of concentration. Ten minutes into the film, Pedro understood why they had been instructed to conceal the information they were receiving. If something of this magnitude got out, all hell would break loose. As the film drew to a close, it became clear that the present course of action included a long-term plan to hide operatives around the world until they were needed. Pedro knew, without asking, that he would be one to pave the way, and when the time is right, he will ensure they inflict as much damage as possible. He would be leaving everything he knew behind. He felt a glimmer of reluctance. His loyalty to the cause was born out of his love for his country, after all, and leaving wasn't a thing he would ever take lightly. He compressed his lips, thoughtfully. He would do what it took. They all would.

Astiz paced around the table. Pedro could tell by his posture that he wanted to say something meaningful, something that would have a lasting impact on his men. He was wound like a spring tonight; this operation was his baby. Nothing could be allowed to jeopardise it. He spread his arms out wide in a strangely inclusive gesture, trying to make his point.

"We need a commensurate attack to show our commitment to killing those who have caused our people such long-lasting pain."

Pedro glances at his fellow guests. They were all trained killers. Both he and Astiz knew they could pull off such an operation with relative ease. Gustavo, the leader of the three, grunted, and stubbed out his cigarette in the ashtray in the middle of the table.

"I am tired of sitting around here, doing nothing," he complained.

Astiz let out a sigh and held up his hand to stop him talking. Pedro knew that he liked his fierce determination and commitment to the cause, but his intrinsic lack of patience was not good for the purposes of morale or planning. The other two men said nothing. They were afraid to make eye contact with Astiz, let alone speak. Neither offered any indication, any body language or facial tells, that might tell the others how they felt.

Pedro watched them, calmly. One of them glanced up at him and then looked away again, just as afraid of making eye contact with him as he was with Astiz. Pedro kept his gaze on him, exploiting the man's anxiety. With a little more time he would be able to make the man – who had assassinated more than his share of marks – sweat like a schoolboy who'd forgotten his books. It was childish, perhaps, but the temptation to use his position for a little harmless entertainment was sometimes overwhelming. Besides, if he was going to be giving up the life of privilege and respect he had carved for himself, he might as well have a bit of fun before he left.

The contract killer fingered his collar in a rare show of discomfort. Pedro smiled quietly to himself and looked away. Power was the consolation for his line of work. They lived in a world that had been broken by corruption.

Corruption led to situations that would attract power, but this was something that some of the secret police aspired to: announcing the discovery of incriminating files, 'proving' that the communists were on the brink of a long-planned revolution. Women and children were sent in front of the terrorist groups.

It scarcely mattered that there was no proof of such allegations. Suspects were rounded up in military-style trucks. The last barrier had been broken, and now anything might happen to anyone, at any time. The people felt it. No one wasted time on goodbyes that no longer had any meaning. There was no longer any need for pockets, or large suitcases, or fashionable clothing. They had given up.

Surveillance was crucial: people wanted order. The threat of violence or simple non-compliance always lurked in the background, threatening the life of one brittle government after another.

Today was no ordinary day: it was the culmination of five years of planning. Pedro watched his superior carefully. They had worked together before, and Pedro respected the man, but there was something in his defiant intensity that irked him. Astiz was the kind of man, he felt, whose zeal would have found a home in whatever cause had presented itself. He reminded him of that particular kind of revolutionary that had cast themselves upon the barricades of Paris in centuries past. There was an edge to him: sharp and unforgiving. Pedro gained satisfaction from knowing that he was making the world a better place, fashioning it in the shape of the cause. He had a shrewd suspicion that Astiz got his satisfaction in other ways.

Keeping one eye on Astiz, he asked him, "Have you read the file?"

"Yes… and would you care to know how you ended up on that list?"

Pedro nodded.

"I put you there. I told Milan you are a man we can trust to get the job done."

Astiz reached across the desk and took the envelope. He removed two typewritten pages and two photographs, and slid them across the desk.

"Have a look."

Pedro inhaled sharply and straightened his back. He examined the photographs: one was of a young man and the other a pregnant woman. His eyes widened in astonishment – he recognized that face. For a split second he didn't know what to say.

He had thought that she was dead.

Only two weeks previously, Pedro had led the police squad to a safe house in the city.

"What is it that you want me to do?" asked Pedro, remembering her tear-stained face.

"His name is Zaffaroni," Astiz grunted. "Your job is to protect him, whenever and wherever he needs it."

Pedro recognised the name and the words he had been about to speak died in his throat. He took a moment to absorb what he had learnt. He didn't know much about where Zaffaroni had come from, nor how he had secured his freedom with the organisation. Nevertheless, it was widely agreed that he was possessed with unusual powers; instead of seeing the dead, he created them.

Pedro's mind was ruffled. This could take years – was he prepared to take on such a long-term project? He nodded to himself. He could. He was loyal to the organisation. The other thought that chased around his brain was far more perplexing: how had he earned this honour? Why him?

"How do I find him?" he asked.

"You will be contacted. I've arranged for you to leave first thing in the morning. I don't want any glitches. Have I made myself clear?" Astiz asked, giving him a hard look.

"Yes."

Astiz was never anything other than clear.

Driving home again in the car that had simply appeared from the bureaucratic ether, Pedro felt a strange surge of relief. Although the life of a sleeper agent's keeper wasn't exactly one of rest and relaxation, he could be undercover for years. No one to answer to, no particular place to be, no more night raids, or sweating palms, or dreams shaken by remembered screams. He could use the time to recharge, to prepare for a time when he would be required to be less than human once more. He bit his lip, surprised: for the first time in years he felt excited – almost hopeful.

He wasn't nervous or fearful, though he knew that that time may come, eventually. He went over the plan in his mind, from start to finish. Astiz had been thorough. This was it. There was no sense in delaying what had to be done. He left the official car at the kerb, assessing all the things he would need to achieve in the coming weeks in order to fully disappear.

**

The first undisturbed night's sleep in two decades had left him feeling refreshed and ready to begin. He eyed his reflection in the mirror above the sink in his hot, meticulously clean bathroom. Eyes, so dark they were almost black, peered back at him from out of a bronzed olive face. His thick, black hair and beard, uncombed and wild, gave him a sort of rugged look that he used to his advantage in the field. Looking like a beast of a man helped put the fear of God into people, and a beast of a man he had remained for the better part of his career. It was part of his aura of authority. He wouldn't need it where he was heading, however. There, he would need to fit in, be unobtrusive.

Steam from the washbasin curled around him as he worked, wreathing him like a shroud. He worked methodically, carefully trimming and shaving his beard. He left a moustache, trimming it neatly. His motions were slow, careful; with every stroke he contemplated his changing face. When he had finished he looked noticeably different: much more the clean-cut man about town than the Inteligencia loyalist. It was possible that no one he knew would recognise him now. Even if he wanted to, there would be no walking away from this.

Pedro stubbed out his cigarette in a metal ashtray on the side table. It glinted in the morning light as he sucked in his cheeks, turning his face this way and that to inspect his profile. It would suffice.

He looked around the apartment he had called home for the past five years. It was really more a place to sleep than anything else. He felt no lasting attachment to it. It wasn't as if he had friends or family to miss. Pedro trusted no one. To stay alive in the secret police he had learned to be vigilant, to keep people at arm's length. He'd seen what had happened to operatives who had let people get too close. Pedro wouldn't let that happen to him: he was a lone wolf.

He considered himself to be of above-average intelligent; a person with a very good understanding of what motivated people – and, more importantly – what they feared. He could read body language like a book, and he was aware that if he could do it, there would be others out there who could do it to him. If the last twenty years had taught him anything it was that out of chaos came great opportunities, especially for those who were bold and ruthless.

He would need to disappear. It was common enough for members of the Inteligencia to be called away at short notice. People would wonder, but no one would ask. He would need money, though, and lots of it. It wasn't the kind of thing a devout follower of the cause could easily put his hands on, but he would need just enough to take him across the border. From there, it would be easy.

***

The instructions Astiz had laid down had been very clear. Pedro had made his way to the appointed place, dressed in workman's clothes. He had insinuated himself into the sometimes grumpy, sometimes garrulous crowd of labourers, gathered at the end of the street hoping to be picked up by the work crews that roamed the area, even at this late hour. Short notice work, and no guarantee of it. These were some of Argentina's hardest and poorest men, doing anything they could to keep their wives and families fed. He lounged against the hot stucco wall, smoking, scanning the road in both directions. There was still no sign of any vehicle, only the halos of light cast by the scattered street lamps.

Two hours passed slowly, measured in cigarette lengths. His breathing accelerated when he saw the truck swing around the corner. Around him, the eyes of the job-hungry men snapped to the back of the van in anticipation, and then slid away, sensing trouble. A slender young man in a white overcoat and black fedora stepped from the back of the truck. He was followed by two brawny men. Enforcers. The first was bald, his right hand wedged into his pocket of his black leather jacket. Pedro accepted this, grimly. They were armed, so they were expecting trouble. The other specimen was tall and heavy-set, with a dark, scraggly beard and an unwieldy jacket.

Pedro's gaze shifted to the young man, who seemed puzzled for an instant. He gestured at Pedro and pointed to the back of the truck. The men of the work crews looked away, wanting no part of what they thought was an arrest. That suited Pedro. These things happened with such frequency that he would be quickly forgotten. He gave him a little grin and nodded, climbing in the back between the two thugs, who were a little more friendly now they had their cargo safely aboard. The slender fellow offered him a cigarette and they spoke of inconsequential things until Pedro fell asleep, lulled unconscious by the enforcers' snores.

***

Bruised and tired from the journey, Pedro stepped out of the vehicle and into the early morning light. He wasn't exactly sure where he was. In the long, dark night he had lost all sense of place. As he stepped off the bumper, stretching his aching limbs, his eyes lighted on a young captain who saluted, crisply.

Silently, they marched in step down a curved staircase, along an echoing corridor and into the briefing rooms in the bowels of the building. Pedro heard the door close behind him, unconcerned. Two men stood warming the backs of their legs against an open fire, and they greeted Pedro with the usual lack of warmth displayed by officers of the Inteligencia.

"Juan Ramón," said the first, with a perfunctory nod. "Assistant director at Essen. I think you know Milan Silva."

The chief adviser, slightly younger than his colleague, nodded; he shook Pedro's hand.

"Come and sit by the fire," said Ramón; Pedro was aware that it wasn't a request. The man spoke softly, inviting the listener to move closer, creating an atmosphere of secrecy. He indicated a chair. "Pull it up. Take off your coat."

Pedro perched, poised in expectation on the edge of his seat: his body bent forwards, his hands clasped, forearms resting on his knees.

Ramón's smug smile dropped as the men made themselves comfortable and his lips pressed into a hard, unforgiving line. He was absolutely frank with Pedro.

"Whatever paperwork we file will be falsified to cover our tracks."

"I understand," said Pedro. There was no other way for this to work. He would be completely on his own; he preferred it that way.

"Jorge Zaffaroni is not a man to be taken lightly."

Pedro kept his features carefully impassive when he said, "Right."

"So you are familiar with his activities?"

"I have heard rumours," Pedro admitted, "but they are only rumours."

"Well," said Ramón, sagely, nodding his head, "you can believe at least half of them. He is a natural-born killer." After a slight pause, he added, "I want you to make sure he doesn't fail."

Pedro eyed his superior suspiciously, wanting to ask him for more detail, but Ramón didn't give him a chance. He retrieved a slim dossier from his jacket pocket, containing cash and the papers of his new identity, and handed them over to Pedro. He took it, and frowned, wrestling with an unexpected flicker of doubt that had flared through his mind. He pushed his hesitance back into the deepest recesses of his brain. Now was not the time for second thoughts.

Wordlessly, Pedro looked at Ramón and made a gesture with two of the fingers of his left hand. The man fumbled in his shirt pocket for a moment and fished out a packet of cigarettes. He offered one to Pedro who lit it and inhaled the smoke with satisfaction. It calmed his fraying nerves, and some of this new contentment must have shown on his face, because Ramón and Silva Milan chuckled and lit up themselves.

"You need to be ready in two hours, go and rest," Ramón ordered, his own match flaring.

Pedro left Milan and Ramón talking in low voices. He encountered another man, tall and well-dressed in a black uniform, outside the door. This new officer escorted him down the long hallway to the penultimate door on the right. He left him, mutely, to his own devices. Pedro stepped into the small bedroom, pausing for a moment before flicking on the light. The room was quiet, except for the electrical buzz of the lightbulb, which was easily silenced again. Pedro slid the deadbolt back on the door with a click and slipped into the uncomfortable bed. He stared, wide-eyed at the ceiling for a moment; something here was a little off. He had been born with a great sense of awareness that had been honed over years of having to survive in a hostile environment. That awareness had been taken to a new level, and now he lay awake, certain – without even having to search for a camera or microphone – that he was being observed.

A long, black car was waiting to drive him to the 18arbor in the noonday gloom. Pedro could hear the engine, even this deep inside the complex. He took up his pack, his new papers tucked safely within, and headed to the courtyard. A thickset man in his forties with stringy black hair was leaning against the car, looking quite out of place in a dark jumper and scruffy jeans. Pedro met his unflinching gaze with an uneasy stare. The man's face was shrouded in his hair as he bent to light a cigarette. A match flared in the deep shade of the clouds, lighting up his expressionless face.

The man nodded at Pedro and pointed to the car. He pulled open the door and slid into the leather seat, pleased to find that his present transportation was infinitely more comfortable than the van of the night before. He settled in as the car set off in a screech of tyres. Pedro slept, aware that there was nothing he could do, now, until he handed over his documents at the 19arbor gates and boarded the ship.

Chapter 2

Drinda stared, hollow-eyed, at her own reflection. Her skin was taut and drawn with worry, paler now than she had ever been with grey-blue shadows of sleeplessness beneath her dark eyes. Her dark hair hung lank around her shoulders, unwashed for several days now. It looked lifeless, like the rest of her, slumped on the frame of her bed. The police had been through here, too, and everything had been overturned.

Exhausted, Drinda let out a great sigh, staring at her scattered possessions, and wondered how the hell it had come to this.

***

She had met Lee on a crisp winter evening in 1982. It had been the kind of night with potential – she and the girls had been out for someone's birthday in Ashton, Idaho, the small town of small towns. The seed potato capital of the world. Population: one thousand. It was one of the few places on earth where poultry outnumbered humans. She had been intending to get pleasantly merry with her girlfriends and have a night to remember – and maybe a hangover to regret. Hooking up had been the furthest thing from her mind.

The atmosphere in the local dance club had been electric – you could almost taste it in the air, over the jug of beer and hot bodies. She'd felt his eyes on her for a while as she danced with the birthday girl, enjoying the music and showing off her assets. She'd turned to see a dark looking man leaning against the bar: dark hair, dark eyes, dark suede jacket. He was the epitome of cool, and for a small town like Ashton, that was saying something. At six feet tall he had towered over her, her very own tall dark stranger.

Drinda had shaken out her shoulder-length shiny black hair, adjusted her tight black leather pants and made sure her low-cut white blouse showed her to her best advantage before sauntering over to the bar. Lee had bought her a drink and complemented her ass, which made her laugh. By the time they stumbled back to her apartment she was already halfway in love with him – and he with her, or so he said.

He'd had a bad first marriage, he told her, when they'd gone for breakfast the next morning, and had decided that marriage was not an institution he should participate in further. Otherwise, he'd said, he would have asked her to marry him on the spot. Charmed and a little dazed by the fairytale nature of the night and morning, Drinda had allowed herself to be carried along by Lee's natural self-possession and exuberance. It was a great feeling, having someone who cared about her, having someone there she could rely on.

Before long they had moved in together in an okay part of town just off Willow Creek. You had to go up a steep hill to get to it, through a driveway and to the left was the old church. Further along to the right was the recently refurbished block of townhouses that they called home. Drinda and Lee occupied the third floor.

Their friends had helped them to move in on a sunny spring day in return for pizza and beer. They'd waved them off and then tumbled into bed – the only piece of furniture they'd put together – where they'd stayed until the following afternoon. They'd shared so many happy times in this apartment. It was spacious and nicely furnished, with a separate dining room to the side of the kitchen where they'd entertained their friends.

***

She couldn't quite pinpoint the moment when things had begun to change between them. It was present in the little things, the tiny moments on which their relationship turned. They had lived together for nearly two years when she 21ealized that they'd stopped eating together. One of them would cook and they'd intend to sit down at the dining table together, but somehow it just never seemed to happen. There would be a late shift at the salon where she worked, or Lee would be out later than he expected.

She talked to him about it, and he was as surprised as she had been. They decided to work on it, and for three weeks they were the happy, affectionate couple they had been when they first moved in. Then something had slipped again and Drinda had found herself eating alone four nights out of seven. The dining room seemed so cold and lonely without Lee, so she ate her dinners on her lap in front of the TV. These days they barely used the dining room. Friends rarely came over. Lee saw his friends almost every night, but only Drinda went out with her girls – most of them settled now and beginning to raise families – on Saturday nights.

The next change was in Lee's 22ealized. He became grumpy and aloof, spending most of his time out of the house or drinking with his buddies. He became utterly unreliable. She never knew when he would be home, or what state he would be in when he did turn up. Drinda had taken to cancelling plans made with friends, telling them one or the other of them was sick rather than admit that her partner had simply failed to come home. She only tried to talk to him about it once. There had been a look of such venom on his face that she hadn't brought it up again.

She found herself pulling away from him. Signs of affection that had once been ready and quick to call to mind became harder to find. Instead of curling up together on the couch she would fold herself up at one end while he dozed at the other. Farewells that used to be kisses became awkward waves or nods of the head. She 22ealized, one morning, that they hadn't been intimate with one another for two whole months without noticing.

Some days he was the same old Lee who had danced the night away and made her laugh. He would surprise her with flowers when she was sure he had no time for her at all. It made her feel so guilty, thinking the worst of him. A hundred times she had decided to leave, only to convince herself that this was just a phase. Arguments became their only means of communication.

***

It was so quiet in the flat without him. She had even muted the TV today, she had a headache leftover from work and it was pounding inside her skull like a steel drum. It had taken three attempts to get the budget alarm system to let her in the apartment. It didn't seem to matter how many times you put in the right code, 8989, it just didn't seem to recognise it. As usual, just at the point when she had been ready to call an electrician it had accepted the code. Drinda occasionally wondered whether it had a mind of its own. It always seemed to know when she was about to give up. Lee had promised to get it fixed, but Lee was no longer in the habit of keeping his promises.

He'd promised to stop gambling, too, and look how well that had gone.

She'd showered, washing the day's work out of her hair and sank gratefully onto the couch. The phone had rung and she flinched at the overloud tone in the sullen silence of the empty apartment. Lee was supposed to be home soon and she hoped the call was from him.

Recognising her mother's number she sighed.

"Hey," she said, fighting to keep the weariness out of her voice.

"Hey Drinda, just wanted to check what time you're coming tomorrow, honey."

"About six o'clock," she said, and listened while her mother chatted away about her day and what her brother's kids were up to.

Everyone seemed to be doing just fine, she thought bitterly, putting down the phone. Everyone except for me. She tried Lee's number, feeling tremendously low. It went straight to voicemail. He'd switched it off, probably to prevent her from reminding her that

Page 24

he had somewhere to be – somewhere, it seemed, that he didn't want to be.

Drinda went into the kitchen and made herself a coffee. She took her time. After all, he might have been stuck in an area with no cell signal, or somewhere it had to be turned off. He could be home any moment. She settled back down on the couch and glared at the phone, willing it to ring. She just wanted to hear Lee's voice. Tears began to well up in her eyes. She blinked them away angrily, hating herself for feeling so weak.

She was so focused on the phone that she didn't notice it growing darker. The lights of a car passing by caught her eye and she shook herself. She had been sitting there for an hour and a half. Annoyed at herself, Drinda went to make dinner. She turned on all the lights in the apartment and switched on the radio. Loneliness is often easier to deal with in the light. She ate alone, as she had dreaded, though she found that she no longer had much of an appetite. Chasing the mac'n'cheese around the plate with her fork, she tried to remember the last time he had come home on time.

In the end, she put her dinner to one side, keeping Lee's hot for him in the oven. She flicked aimlessly through the channels on the TV, not taking anything in. Really, she knew, she should get up and do some housework, or call one of her friends and see if they wanted to meet up, but she felt so emotionally drained that staying on the couch was more or less the only option.

She heard his key turn in the lock at a quarter to midnight. Early, for him.

"Why the fuck didn't you call me?" she demanded, not even bothering to turn around and look at him.

"I know sweetheart, I know." He didn't sound particularly apologetic, more sort of peremptorily annoyed, as if he knew she was going to be upset. "You just can't imagine – it's been a nightmare."

Drinda sighed.

"I was worried about you, Lee," she said, turning the TV off. "I've had a shit day – the alarm was playing up again, the outside lights keep going on and off. Can you imagine how freaked out I was? And you didn't even try to call me."

"I called you."

"You did not, I've been here by the phone the whole time!"

He huffed, annoyed to have been caught out in such a stupid lie. He put the bottle of chardonnay – his peace offering – down on the coffee table with a thump.

"I had to stop off to collect something."

Drinda knew what he meant. She rubbed frustrated hands across her face.

"So, now you're telling me that we don't have any money," she said, nearly in tears. "Again! What is going on with you?"

She knocked the edge of her fork and it clinked against the plate, which still had most of her food on it. Lee seized the opportunity to change the subject.

"You've got to be starving," he said, concerned evident in his voice. It sounded insincere to Drinda. "But you're only picking at your food as if you're weight-conscious."

"Why didn't you tell me?" she asked, ignoring him.

"Because I knew it would upset you."

"This upset me!" she snapped. "I'm sick to death of being messed around."

"I'm sorry, I truly am," said Lee, his voice already hardening, closing her out. "That's just the way things are."

He slumped into the seat next to her, not even bothering to take his shoes or coat off. He slid the remote out of her hand and switched the TV back on to a car show that Drinda had no interest in whatsoever. Why couldn't he tell that he was hurting her?

After a while she asked, "Got any more little secrets you want to share? I'd like to know all of them now."

She didn't get a response.

"Have you gambled away all our money?"

She gave him five full minutes to come up with an answer, but he didn't even turn his head. Drinda sighed and stalked into their bedroom. She was a little afraid that Lee night get violent. She had seen him break a guy's nose just for looking at her. He'd kicked him in the groin, too, and for a moment Drinda had seen him look down at the man, wanting to carry on. There had been something dark in his eyes, a spark of malevolence that she had never seen before.

She rubbed her stomach where the last bruise he had given her was still healing. This hadn't been the first souvenir of their damaged relationship and it wouldn't be the last. Lee's fists would often be pressed into her flesh, reminding her who was boss. He was always so precise with the way he hurt her – never leaving a mark anywhere anyone could see – and he was always sorry.

He looked guilty and vulnerable, like a small boy caught with his hands in the cookie jar. There was disgust there, too, and she would be lying to herself if she thought it was all directed at him. A part of him hated her, hated that he had brought her here, hated the stress he was under trying to keep her. He'd always thought of himself as the breadwinner, though she worked just as hard as he did – and all her money was sucked up by the rent and his gambling habit.

Sometimes he was nice to her, and she knew that he felt the stress of their situation, too. She was a physical girl. She needed to be touched, held. She was prone to running her fingers through his hair or down his back in a friendly scratch. She received reassurance and comfort from touch. Lee, it seemed, did not.

***

In the other room, Lee poured himself a drink and considered calling an old girlfriend. He even got as far as picking up the phone, but after listening to the dial tone for a few seconds he changed his mind and carefully replaced the receiver. He didn't want Drinda to hear. He knocked back the contents of his glass in seconds.

Page 27

He left Drinda to her own devices and stamped down to the parking lot. She could be so difficult sometimes. They'd been together for three years now and he'd always promised to look after her. Somehow he needed to get back the money he'd lost – but first he needed another drink.

Bubbling with rage, he parked his car outside a gas station club, the neon lights above the door casting a sickly glow over the parking lot. He walked through to the main part of the club and shook his head. The place seemed brighter somehow, shinier – everything was covered in a dazzling mass of tinsel that refracted the light and hurt his eyes. The festive decorations had gone up, lending the bar a gaudy level of glitz that it usually couldn't achieve.

It was a busy, lively night – one of those nights when everyone seemed to have come in after a good day, intending to have a good night. Pretty girls were nice to homely guys, homely guys were nice to homely girls. People were buying rounds for strangers just because. It was festive and festival. It was coming to the end of the night, now, nearly closing. He knew he would have to be quick.

He knew that Frankie came in sometimes and he searched the crowd for her, but she was nowhere to be seen among the club's usual hotch-potch of patrons. Frowning, he leaned against the bar and called over the bartender.

"Is Frankie West around?" he asked, after ordering a beer. "The redhead – the boss's daughter."

"No."

"Thanks," Lee said. "I appreciate the help."

He had been about to leave but the bartender glanced furtively around and beckoned him back.

"I might be able to help," he said, confidingly.

Lee stared at him suspiciously.

"Oh, yeah?"

"What's it worth?" asked the bartender.

"Give me her number and I'll give you twenty."

"Fifty and it's yours."

Lee nodded and handed over a pen.

***

He knocked on the door and forced his way past Frankie as soon as she opened it. He pushed straight past her before she had a chance to say anything and kicked the door shut behind him.

"Please, Frankie – I need to talk to you," he insisted.

"Leave me alone!" she cried.

"Please – I need the money I loaned you back."

"You're not getting anything from me!" she cried, backing into a corner of the room. She was shivering now and Lee couldn't tell if it was from fear or from the cold blast of air that had followed him into her apartment.

"Frankie…"

Lee shook his head, despairing. He never should have got involved with her – he'd been with Drinda at the time, and drink had got the better of him. Drinda didn't know and Lee wanted to keep it that way. It had been nothing, really, and it had meant nothing to him at all. Those five months had been an aberration.

"You stay away from me, Lee, or I'll tell Drinda everything!"

Lee raised his eyes to the ceiling, trying to keep his cool.

"You will do no such thing!" he hissed, taking another step forwards.

Frankie shrank back, visibly wincing.

"I'm not going to hurt you, you stupid woman."

He sighed. He wasn't getting anywhere here.

"I need the money, Frankie. You're going to have to pay me back sometime," he warned her.

Lee left her trembling in a corner of her kitchen and went home.

Drinda was curled up in the bedroom, crying. He rubbed her back, muttering soothing words into her ear – words he really meant, and would continue to mean right up to the moment when they became inconvenient.

"I can't live like this, Lee," she sobbed, exhaustedly into his shoulder. "I just can't."

"I've been an idiot," he said, and she readily agreed. "Are we okay?"

"What did you talk about?" she asked, sniffing. Lee rolled his eyes. Drinda always came back to this, though he was sure she'd never found out about Frankie, or any of the others. "What is she like? I mean, really like? Was she like the girls in the magazines?"

"You're wrong," he lied, soothingly. "I never went to see any girls. Sweetheart, what we're dealing with right now is – look, I just need to make sure we're okay. That's all I need," he insisted, steering the conversation away.

Drinda shook her head – he wasn't sure if she believed him this time, but she pressed herself up against him, almost desperately, all warm and lush.

"That's all I need, too," she purred. "Please, Lee, I'm freaked out. I know you – I know you don't want to talk right now and that's fine, but I need you. I need you to be with me. I feel so stupid," she added, though it was barely more than a whisper. Lee wasn't sure he was supposed to hear it. "I love you." Her voice was oddly hollow, as if she was trying to will him to love her back.

Lee did care, deep down. He did love her, really, but at any opportunity he would cheat. He couldn't help it – it was simply a part of his nature. He thought of Drinda as an escape from everything else, an easy option. He liked to know that she would be there when he got home, waiting for him. She would be cold at first, staring at the wall, waiting for him to say the first word. It had become a mental challenge to get her to open up to him – his own personal, human crossword puzzle.

***

Page 30

Time passed, as is the nature of things, and Drinda held their relationship together with sheer grit. Lee was grateful, she tried hard. He was determined to find the money to make it work.

He still worked for Frankie's father – it was how they had met in the first place. Apart from the bar he owned a factory down on fifty-seventh street. The company had a new contract with some big steel storage house and Lee's job was to ensure that it had enough electrical equipment in stock at all times. He was responsible for purchasing and organising maintenance, and his immediate manager, Michael West, trusted him to write the cheques on the company's behalf. It was easy enough to produce a fictitious invoice and write out a cheque for himself. $2000 dollars would make a dent in their debts. He wrote out the cheque for cash.

Drinda drove him to the bank that day on her way to work, but he didn't tell her about the cheque. What she didn't know couldn't hurt her.

Lee didn't notice the man on the corner, watching him proceed into the bank and back out again. He didn't see him take a photograph of him, or notice when he followed him along the street.

***

The feeling of impending doom crept up on Drinda when she showered that morning and followed her all day, through work at the hair studio. Working with other people's hair usually relaxed her, but today it didn't do a thing for her. The worst feeling in the world is when you know someone is going to lie to you and you have to wait for them to do it. Lee needed his freedom. He didn't like to explain himself, especially not to her.

He'd had plans to meet the guys for days, but he still didn't tell her until an hour before.

"Hey, I thought I'd join the guys for cards tonight," he said, nonchalantly. "If that's okay with you."

Drinda didn't even bother to sigh. It wasn't okay with her and it didn't matter to him at all. She was used to it now. She had even grown numb to the drugs he occasionally brought home from the guys who were doing brisk business in a secret spot by the river. She had seen him. These days she simply turned a blind eye to it. It was simpler, and it meant he didn't give her any more bruises.

He had the car that night so the next afternoon she walked to her mother's house. She was exhausted, and out on the street, with no one else around, she didn't need to pretend to be strong. She didn't even bother to look up until she got to the house. To her astonishment, two suits from the FBI were standing guard outside the front door of her mother's house.

Drinda stared at them, blinking. She looked around, as one coming out of a dream. Their black Ford Crown Victory was parked directly in front of the drive, almost blocking it. They seemed to have kicked the door in. Her mother, wide eyed and terrified, was just inside the door, explaining that Drinda wasn't due home from the hair salon yet.

"Mom?" she said, but got no further as the men who had been looming over her mother immediately handcuffed Drinda and escorted her firmly to their car.

***

They waited until she was at the Sheriff's Office to tell her that Lee was dead.

He had been found in the trunk of his car with the pointed end of a metal comb shoved through his throat on the old road that ran by the canal. Drinda had been so shocked that she couldn't even speak – she could barely hear the agents' voices. It sounded like they were coming from a long way away, or as if she were underwater. Someone released her handcuffs and she fell to her knees, the world spinning around her. They dragged her roughly to her feet and processed her.

It wasn't until she was thrust into the cell that she realised she had been charged with his murder.

Eventually, shock turned to fury. She was sick of being treated like a criminal. They hadn't even bothered to interview her, they'd just decided she must have done it. She pummelled her pillow in rage. She loved Lee. He wasn't perfect, but that didn't matter to her. Finally, she burst into big, noisy tears and wept into the bed until they came to get her.

***

She stared at the detective sitting across the interrogation room table. Detective Potts was a hardworking impatient policeman in his forties. His suit jacket was permanently crinkled because the moment he no longer had to wear it he would toss if over the back of the seat in his car. He had already decided that she was guilty. She wondered why he was even bothering.

"This is your lawyer," Detective Potts explained, shortly.

"Please let me talk to my client in private," the lawyer requested, but Potts ignored him.

"Drinda Tanner, you have been charged with murder in the first degree," said the detective. "Do you understand?"

Drinda burst into tears. She couldn't help it – nothing made any sense anymore. Her lawyer sat very still, remaining silent as he and the detective waited for her answer. She looked up at him after a long, tense minute where she tried to come up with an answer that didn't call the detective's parentage into question.

She wiped angry, helpless tears away with the backs of her fingers and glared at the man.

"Look, if you'd just let me tell you, I did not kill Lee."

"Do you know why you are here?" the detective asked, somewhat patronisingly.

"Yes, you just told me I am here because you believe I killed Lee. I did not. I have no idea why you think that I did."

"If you could stick to answering the questions I ask you, Miss, that would be a great help," said the detective, smarmily. "Did you kill your boyfriend?"

"No."

"You cashed a stolen cheque with him, but it wasn't enough, was it, Miss?" he accused. "So you planned and calculated the murder of your boyfriend. He was found dead with the pointed end of a metal comb forced through his carotid artery."

Drinda gaped at him. No one had told her how Lee had died. The image of that handsome neck, bloodied and torn swam in front of her eyes. God, what a horrible way to die, she thought.

"No!" she gasped. "Wait – what cheque?"

"We have evidence that puts you in the car at the time of the murder," Detective Potts insisted.

Drinda broke down and sobbed.

"You can't have, I wasn't there!" she cried. "I have done nothing wrong! I drove Lee to the bank on Thursday and then he took my car after he dropped me off at the salon – he was going out to meet some of his friends."

She stared hopelessly at this man who wanted her to go to prison. He poured her a glass of water, which she greedily gulped down.

"What happened next?" he asked, though he didn't sound like he believed her.

"I was going to meet him at my mother's house yesterday, when you picked me up."

The detective sighed, and told Drinda that she was just making things worse for herself by not confessing right away. He pulled out a small evidence bundle from the case box at his feet.

"These are your fingerprints," he said. "All over the car your boyfriend's body was found in."

"It's my car!" she said, exasperated. "Of course my prints are on it!"

"This," he said, pulling out a second bundle, "is your handkerchief, found in the footwell of the car. It has blood all over it. Can you explain that?"

"No, I can't. I must have dropped it in the car when Lee took me to the salon.

"I think you murdered your boyfriend, jammed a metal comb into his neck and wiped your hands clean on your handkerchief."

"No, you are wrong!" she snapped. "How stupid do you think I am? Who in their right mind would wipe their hands on their own handkerchief and leaves it at the scene of the crime?"

Potts glared at her suspiciously.

"Drinda," he said, trying to build a rapport. "I have been a detective for over twenty years now, and I know when a person is lying. I have an ear for it. It's why I have such a high case closure rate. You are one of the best liars I have ever met – but you are lying to me. We have more than enough to convict you of this crime."

"I am not lying!" she shouted, distressed. "Someone has murdered my partner and instead of going out there and doing something about it you're wasting your time in here with me! Nothing you have said puts me at the scene of the crime at the time Lee was killed. I know that because I wasn't there! This is purely circumstantial!"

"I would like my client to have a break now," said the lawyer.

Both Drinda and the detective stared at him; they had all but forgotten he was there.

Detective Potts sighed.

"For the record, this interview is being suspended for one hour."

***

Detective Potts watched the woman across the table. She had gone way beyond tears now. She was holding her head in her hands, looking as though she thought the entire world had gone insane. He had been interviewing her, on and off now, for three days, but she was sticking to her story like glue.

He curled his lip, feeling the familiar pull of the scar between his lip and his nose, hidden by his moustache. He was a hard individual and his inability to break Drinda Tanner was beginning to irk him – and it was beginning to show.

"Were you provoked?" he asked, the anger evident in his voice.

Drinda glared at him.

"I didn't kill Lee."

Remorselessly, he snarled at her that she would suffer a harder sentence if she refused to confess, but his remonstrations fell on deaf ears.

Her lawyer seemed intent on assuring him that it was all an innocent mistake – self-defence – but Drinda had other ideas.

"Will you stop telling him that?" she exploded, after his latest attempt. "I didn't kill Lee – are neither of you fucking idiots listening to me? You have no fucking evidence!"

It came as no surprise to Potts that she had fired the man the next day.

"You have a right not to speak to me without representation," he informed her, when he saw her next.

"What's the fucking point?" she asked him. "You've already made your mind up – nothing I say is going to change your mind."

"No, it isn't. I don't listen to murderers."

She put her head in her hands.

***

Trying to prove her innocence was the most degrading thing she had ever done. It had taken three days to persuade Detective Potts to let her call her mother and another two days before her mother had managed to find her a willing lawyer. She had, Drinda felt, finally come up trumps.

Milan Silva swept into the interrogation room like an icy wind, dislodging the recalcitrant detective and giving Drinda the first particle of hope she'd had in days.

"I believe you," he said.

I believe you. Those three words had been enough. He had looked at the evidence and he believed her. Finally, someone useful was on her side.

Milan Silva was practically a household name. He thought of himself as a grim necessity. He was on almost every network channel these days – the face of the real crime shows. He worked on both sides – prosecution and defence – but only where he felt that justice needed a hand. He was a sort of lawyer and private detective all rolled into one and had been known to pick up investigations where the police had left off. His commercial could be seen on almost every channel.

Business had been good for him in the last two years. He had worked to find the evidence that exonerated a well-known celebrity doctor who had been charged with murdering his wife. Silva had proved that the 'irrefutable evidence' was anything but and saved the doctor from the lethal injection that would otherwise have been waiting for him. He had about a fifty-percent success rate, which in terms of the work he took on wasn't half bad.

He went in with her mother, who was tiny and ferocious. He couldn't help but like her, and from what he saw of Drinda, who by rights should have been a trembling mess after a week of intense interrogation, he liked her, too. She was pale, drawn, with dark circles beneath her eyes and she didn't seem to have slept for some time – but she was holding her own. She hadn't let them trick her into saying anything other than what he believed was the gospel truth.

"Right," he said, when he was sure he had her attention. "I've looked over the evidence and as I said, I believe you, but now you have to listen to me. I need total honesty from you – it won't work any other way. So, tell me everything about your relationship – tell me the worst. If I know the worst then I can plan to encounter it in court, but if I'm surprised by it then you're in trouble."

The abuse had come as a surprise, but she was insistent that she loved Lee and that he loved her. Silva wasn't sure that that was entirely true, but Drinda clearly believed it. He assured her that he would work on her case and told her to try to get some sleep. He rather doubted that she would.

He took her mother to one side after the agents escorted her back to her cell.

"I don't want to lie to you," he said, fairly. "It's a tough one. They were having money troubles and a bumpy relationship. People have killed for less. The media have turned on her, and with them, the public."

"There must be something we can do," he mother had cried, aghast.

"Well," he said, "the cops think she did it and they let the media know. The media tell the public what to think and the public is outraged, demanding arrests and charges. So, first off we have to prove that Drinda was nowhere near the car when Lee died. If we can find someone who was, then so much the better. Two, you've got to keep supporting her. If the media sees you abandon her they'll think you believe that she'd guilty. Three – if this goes to trial we've got to fix her image. Right now she looks guilty, even though she'd not. We want them to pity her, and that can directly influence the jury. The only thing I can tell you is that I cannot put my hand on my heart and swear that everything will be okay. I believe that Drinda is innocent, but I can't promise to clear her name. Making rash promises like that just wouldn't be fair. I will, however, do my best."

"Thank you, Mr Silva," the tiny woman said. "That's all anyone could ask."

***

Page 38

They had let him look at all the evidence, which suggested that they felt they had an airtight case against Miss Tanner. The more he saw of it, the more he suspected that they did not.

Thoughtfully, he took the crime scene photos down to Detective Potts' office.

"If you have any information, come out and say it," said Potts, recognising the expression on his face. "There isn't anything you can say that will alter my decision. Drinda Tanner murdered her boyfriend and that's the end of it. Everything that has transpired so far proves she is guilty."

Calmly and without uttering a word, Milan handed the crime scene photograph to the detective. The man flicked his jaded gaze across it. He froze for a moment and Silva saw his eyes widen. Slowly, his complexion began to colour, turning ruddy. His jaw clenched, his nostrils flared and he turned away from Silva to glare at the wall.

Silva knew he had him. If his team had missed that, then what else had they missed?

"Let me look into it," said Detective Potts, tersely.

Silva simply nodded. Once pricked, the detective would make sure the investigation was done properly this time. It was a matter of honour.

***

"Miss Tanner, how are you feeling this morning?" Silva asked, sliding into his seat in the interrogation room.

"I slept," she said, her voice gravelly and underused. "Which is an improvement. Do you have any news?"

"Quite a bit," he said, with a smile. Detective Potts, while not overtly apologetic, had actually made Drinda a coffee and told Silva to give it to her. He pushed it across the table. "From the good detective. I think it's by way of an apology, but it's difficult to tell."

Drinda picked up the coffee, puzzled.

"An apology? Then…" she met his gaze. "What happened?"

"Do you know a woman named Frankie West?" Silva asked, as delicately as he could.

Drinda nodded.

"She's Lee's boss's daughter," she said, and then her face darkened. "I'm assuming from your expression that she was one of the women Lee was seeing behind my back."

"I'm afraid so," Silva nodded, and watched the resilient woman in front of him tip her head back in resignation. "It seems they were seeing one another for about five months last year."

Drinda's face whitened and her lips grew taut, but she motioned for Silva to continue.

"They were both involved in drugs and during an argument about drugs and money, Lee assaulted Frankie," he explained. Drinda closed her eyes, possibly remembering all the bruises Lee had given her. "She didn't go to the police, but her father, Michael West, found out. He couldn't fire Lee without everyone finding out that Frankie was involved in drugs, but he vowed revenge."

"He killed Lee?" Drinda gasped, pressing her fingers to her mouth. "Oh God…"

"Eventually, yes," Silva told her. "But first he wanted to ruin him. He made it look like Lee had been embezzling money from the factory – not least by cheque fraud. He had the Federal Fraud Squad following both of you. I don't think he expected that Lee actually would forge a cheque and cash it. It was bad luck for you that he did it the day he died. Bad luck for you, but good luck for West. He knew that the police wouldn't look into the murder further if they had an easy suspect, so when he set up the cheque fraud scam he made sure to implicate you."

"Me?" Drinda looked appalled, lost. "Why? What had I ever done to Michael West? Or Frankie?"

"Absolutely nothing," Silva assured her, with brisk sympathy. "He needed a scapegoat. Perhaps he chose you because you were convenient – he knew how Lee had treated Frankie, it wouldn't be a great stretch to imagine that he would be the same with you – or perhaps he didn't like you because you loved the man he loathed. Either way, he made sure you would be caught up in the middle of it. That's why he used a hairdressing comb to kill Lee – he knew the police would come directly to you."

He paused.

"Ironically, if he hadn't been so intent on involving the Federal Fraud Squad, then the case against you might have been stronger," he reflected. "There were two agents watching you all day on the day of the murder, and sitting outside the apartment all night. They confirmed that you didn't leave until you walked to your mother's house the next day."

He watched the hope kindle in Drinda's face, blossoming through her pale face and lending her lips a healthier colour. He smiled. This was the part of the job that he lived for.

"West was also pretty careless," he continued. "He waited until Lee finished gambling with his friends and then made sure that Lee would see him. He was too drunk to drive, so West took his keys and offered to drive him home safely. Lee trusted his boss, and they think he fell asleep in the car – that's why he didn't notice they were driving to the opposite end of Ashton, and why he didn't put up a fight when West killed him. He didn't feel a thing," he added, conscious that that might mean more to Drinda than her innocence.

She pressed her eyelids closed for a moment and a single tear leaked out of the corner. She nodded for him to continue.

"When he dragged the body from the front seat to the trunk of the car his wallet fell out, putting him at the scene of the crime," Silva explained. "He reported it missing the next day, but he had no reason at all to be in that car – unlike you."

There was a short silence when Silva finished speaking, time he knew his client would need to digest this information. She frowned up at him.

"So, they know I'm innocent?"

"Yes," he said, simply, and she burst into tears of sheer relief. "They're just going through the paperwork now. The charges are being expunged from your record and I should be able to take you home in about an hour. Shit happens, Drinda. The world is full of whack jobs."

Drinda raised tearful eyes to his face and managed a smile.

***

She wasn't sure how long she had been sitting there, in the chaos of her upturned bedroom, simply staring at her own reflection. In two weeks, her entire life had been turned upside down. Lee was dead. She had been arrested for murder and exonerated. She had done an awful lot of growing up in the past two weeks. Now, though, she was simply exhausted.

Milan Silva had taken her for lunch on their way back from the penitentiary, which wasn't strictly in his job description, but Drinda was grateful. The food they had had in before she'd been dragged away from her life had all gone off, and she would have been starving by now if he hadn't. She had called her mother, who had been under the weather since her arrest, and promised to go over first thing in the morning. Tonight, though, Drinda wanted to be alone. Privacy had been the first thing to go out of the window after her arrest.

It wasn't until she'd sat down on the edge of the bed, her possessions in disarray around her that the shock had really set in.

Unsteadily, she got to her feet and undressed herself with shaking hands. The zip on her jeans was broken, so she kicked off her trainers and stumbled out of them. She pulled her dressing gown out from under the desk where the ham fisted detectives had left it and wrapped it tightly around her. Slowly, she cleared a space around the couch and coffee table and switched on the lamp so that a small, cosy circle of warm light spilled out around it. She didn't want to see the chaos that lay beyond it – not yet. Suddenly freezing, she found a blanket hanging over the back of a chair in the dining room and wrapped herself in that too.

There was no way she could sleep in their bed tonight, not without Lee. While she had been fighting for her freedom she had little time for anything else, but now... now it felt like all the grief she had been holding at bay for her lover's murder was threatening to overwhelm her. Wearily, she lay down on the couch, wrapped the blanket around her, and slept.

Chapter 3

San Francisco, 1982

Today, as on most days, Pedro was wearing his long, black jacket. It flapped when he walked, making an impression on anyone who saw him. He didn't wear the jacket for warmth; he wore the jacket because he liked to make sure he had everything he needed to hand and a long coat full of pockets was far more convenient than a briefcase – and far less obtrusive.

He had taken a job as an outside contractor for the CIA, an organisation which prided itself on knowing every part of their agents' history. The thought that they'd missed a great deal of his entertained him greatly. As far as they were concerned he had defected from Argentina, which was about as far from the truth as you could get.

Pedro's line of work meant that he was never without the various little tools and tricks that allowed him to gain entry to places he shouldn't, make copies of things that ought to remain secret and allowed him to escape detection. He always had several forms of identification on him, along with several bundles of cash, all concealed in secret pockets of his greatcoat.

He strolled up the stairs to his office – not in the best part of town, but not in the worst, either. It was comfortably between those two worlds, as he was, and it suited him perfectly. He heard his office phone ringing as he turned to start up the next set of stairs. Pedro raced up the rest of the steps and unlocked the door, picking up the receiver just in time.

"Hello?"

"This is Gustavo," said a smooth, assured voice. "We need to meet."

Gustavo? Pedro went silent for a moment, before he realised who he was speaking to.

"Oh, right."

"Meet me at Green's Bar on Main Street. Do you know it?"

"I do. What time?"

"One."

Gustavo hung up and Pedro replaced his receiver thoughtfully. Today had just become interesting.

***

Gustavo was waiting at a small table outside when Pedro pulled into the parking lot. Pedro watched him for a moment, looking entirely at his ease. He was sipping a beer and eating peanuts from a dish he must have swiped from the bar. Pedro shook his head. There was just something about the man that annoyed him.

"I appreciate you meeting with me," said Gustavo, catching sight of Pedro. "Can I buy you a drink or something?"

Pedro shook his head and joined him at the table, flipping his sunglasses down from the top of his head.

"Very well," said Gustavo. "Let's get started, Pedro. Here is the new file. He lives in the UK."

Pedro lifted the cover, but only enough that he could see inside. Pedro nodded, thoughtfully, recognising the photograph within.

"Okay, leave it with me," he said, keeping his micro-expressions carefully blank.

Pedro slid the file into the briefcase he had brought along entirely for this purpose. He didn't want to say too much, not with Gustavo watching him. Instead, he shifted on his barstool, like he was rearranging his weight. Gustavo got up and shuffled his feet. Absently, he scratched his head and held his hand out to Pedro, who shook it, surprised.

"Yeah, we probably won't meet again," said Gustavo.

Pedro cocked his head curiously. This was more detail than he had come to expect from Gustavo.

"Okay," he said, guardedly.

He took the briefcase he rarely used and made his way back to the car, recognising this as a dismissal. Every step of the way he could feel Gustavo's eyes boring into the back of his head, making the hair on the back of his neck stand up.

***

Back at the office, Pedro slumped into his desk chair. For a few minutes he simply gazed out of the window at the city he had come to call home. He sighed, pushing the air out of his cheeks with an audible huff. He was putting off the inevitable.

With some reluctance he pulled the file Gustavo had given him out of the briefcase and laid it flat on the desk. He flipped through the file, his mind hundreds of miles and several years away. It had all happened such a long time ago. He had begun to dream that he could simply walk away, that no one would worry about an old renegade like him. He could vanish and no one would ever know anything – except for Gustavo and the people he worked for. He would have to do as he was instructed, all those years ago.

The trouble was that he had never really believed that this day would come, and the longer he had lived in America, far from the tensions and certainties of his home, the more he had come to believe that perhaps that day shouldn't come.

For years now, Pedro had fantasised about retiring, about trying to make a normal life for himself.

A fool's hope.

It had been so long that his contacts in the government were not what they once had been. Almost all of them were either dead or retired now. There had been a time when he had known exactly who among them he could trust, but time changes many things and he couldn't say for sure that he could trust any of the few still left. He knew now that he was on his own.

His thoughts turned to an old associate: Silva Milan.

Milan had been working in Essen when they met, as an intelligence adviser. The two of them formed a ruthless partnership, working together on several seemingly impossible projects since. Pedro liked Milan because he was the mirror image of himself; intelligent and pragmatic, he never got caught up in the emotional component of things. This and the way they viewed the world had fostered a deep, mutual respect between the both of them. They made the perfect team: Milan's quick mind and Pedro's heartless, crush-the-enemy-at-any-cost attitude.

There were plenty of people who didn't like Silva Milan. For all his keen sense of justice, sometimes he played dirty. He wasn't one of those men who had to do everything by the book. The last time they had met, having taken the measure of one another, they had obliquely admitted that they were each aware of the other's part in the coming action. Milan had told him – and he could see for himself – that the revenge Astiz had in mind for the enemy was not far away. Zaffaroni must be found, wherever he was, and protected.

That was Pedro's purpose: to keep the man alive until he could complete his mission.

With a practiced eye, Pedro ran through his current caseload, making adjustments that would allow him to work out a workable timeline. He needed to make sure that when the time came he wouldn't be missed.

His mind full of calculations, he fumbled for a cigarette, lit it and took a deep, soothing drag. The rush of nicotine calmed his nerves. He held the smoke in his lungs longer than normal before exhaling, running through all the possible pitfalls in his mind. A gulp of scotch burned his throat before picking up the phone to talk to Milan.

"We need to meet, now," he said, when he was sure he had the right man.

Pedro felt a strange rush of adrenaline as he slammed the receiver down. For years he had hoped that this day would never come, but now that it had he was itching to get started. He slid his chair back with an unpleasant screech. He grabbed his keys and unlocked the door of his car and climbed inside. His foot was itching to push the engine as hard as he could. The Ford squealed through a hard left, drifted slightly and came to a controlled stop. Driving – and driving well – was one of Pedro's passions. He switched off the engine and strode across the dark gravel expanse of the parking lot, heading towards the main entrance of the Sixty-One Club.

The familiar din greeted his ears as he stepped inside, took a sharp right and moved at a brisk stride up two short flights of marble stairs.

Silva Milan stood in the doorway, a look on his face that suggested he, too, had been contacted and that he was struggling to wrap his head around it. His hair was cut short and neat, as was his moustache. His slim, fashionable glasses and sharply cut suit gave him an air of unassailable dignity. The dark pinstripes and highly polished shoes got him in and out of all manner of institutions without the need of Pedro's series of fake IDs.

Together, they went into Milan's office and flipped through the file together. There was a moment of silence as he digested the information, then he groaned. Every part of his body language screamed 'You have got to be kidding me'. This Zaffaroni thing had put Milan in a foul mood – not that he was known for a bubbly personality at the best of times. Today, though, he was unusually stand-offish.

Pedro dropped his chin against his chest, thinking hard. He began pacing from one end of the room to the other, turning quickly to face Milan. He wagged a thoughtful finger.

"We need to recruit," he said, sharply. "Are you in?"

Milan's expression tightened. Suddenly, his focus shifted to some distant point in the past, hidden from Pedro's gaze. He nodded and cleared his throat. He knew exactly how badly this could turn out, and he was tempted to say so. He knew, however, the less said the better, even to an old friend. Pedro watched these emotions chase one another across the man's face.

Now almost sixty years old, Milan worked for one of the city's top law firms and had been looking forward to a relaxing early retirement. He knew he'd lost the focus of his cause.

Pedro read it in his eyes.

"You know we can't avoid this," he said, irritably. "You need to consider your options carefully."

"As do you, old friend."

Pedro let out a tense chuckle, conceding the truth of this. They had known one another for twenty-five years and trusted his judgement. Sometimes, probably because of his legal training, he could be a little officious.

Together, they stood on the second-storey balcony and talked cautiously for hours. Pedro leaned lightly against the metal rail, his leg bouncing impatiently. He was anxious, now, to get the belated operation underway.

The conversation kept turning back to the importance of Milan's part in the coming operation and how fortunate he was to be in his position. Pedro was careful not to sound like he was threatening his old friend, which Milan appreciated. He didn't give anything away, however.

Pedro reached into his pocket and retrieved a small roll of film, no bigger than his fingernail. He told him it was the only photograph they had of their mark.

Pedro rubbed his head and asked the most basic question, "How in hell do we find him? He will have changed in the last few years – this is an old image."

Milan nodded.

From his pained expression, Pedro could guess the direction of his thoughts. Milan had never liked being the centre of attention. He was far more used to being a man working behind the scenes than taking part of a central operation. He knew that their chances of success were remote. This man had proven extremely elusive over the years; up to this moment, very few people even knew he existed. Chances were, sleeper agents all over the place were waking up to the knowledge that Zaffaroni was a person of interest for their operation.

Their best starting point would be London. It was an easy place to disappear in. Locating him might be one of those operations that quickly became tedious and drawn out. They could take months or even years. Every so often, though, a shortcut might present itself. The trick was to recognise it and to know when to take advantage of it.

If there was a chance here, they couldn't waste it. Pedro knew there wouldn't be a second. He closed his eyes for a moment.

"It will change everything," he said. "Years of work and we would be the ones who make it happen."

Milan gritted his teeth. He knew that Pedro was quite correct.

"I will do what I can," he promised. "But now I must check on my client. I got her acquitted, but she relocated to San Francisco and she's not coping very well. I get the impression I'm the only person she talks to now other than her mother."

Pedro chuckled.

"You always did have a soft spot for a damsel in distress," he said. "I'm heading south myself to Miami. The CIA have me assigned to a cruise ship."

"We will speak soon, my friend," said Milan, and shook his hand.

"I'll make sure of it."

Chapter 4

"Hello?"

She winced as her voice rasped. Gone were the days when her voice had bubbled out of her mouth as though she hadn't a care in the world.

"Drinda, it's Milan." There was a pause, and she could almost see him contemplating how to phrase his next words. "Are you okay?"

"I'm fine," she replied, almost managing to keep the bite from her tone. It wasn't his fault that she'd had her mother on the phone earlier asking her the same question every three minutes. Drinda shoved a hand through her hair, grimacing as her fingers snagged on a knot. "Sorry, it's been a trying day."

"I understand. Listen, I'm heading out your way – I was thinking I'd drop by and see you."

There was nothing but the sound of their breathing for a moment as her brain struggled to figure out why he would come all this way to see her.

"Sure… I mean, it's not as though you're crashing any plans…"

"Wonderful…"

***

Three days had passed since Milan had called her; three days since he said he was coming to see her. Drinda moved agitatedly around the confines of her apartment as she waited for him to arrive. She'd heard people say that time healed any wound, but she still felt the suffocating pressure of not being believed – of being framed for something that she'd never even contemplated despite all of her troubles with Lee.

She was startled out of her reverie by the doorbell. It was hopeless to think that the buzzer from the street door would go – there were so many people coming and going from the block that it would be simpler to just have a revolving door.

Casting one last glance around in the dim light of her kitchen, she moved to open the door. Checking briefly that it was, indeed, Milan, she opened the door. Her smile was brittle, but polite. He stepped forward to give the air near her cheek a kiss.

Drinda eyed him up and down until he offered his hand. Taking it, she responded with another smile – this time slightly friendlier - and opened the door wider for him to come in. Belatedly, she realized that she was still holding on to the dish towel she'd picked up in the kitchen, and began twisting it nervously in her hands. It was disconcerting how little he'd changed over the last seven years.

She raised her eyebrows and lifted her chin as he remained silent, causing her earrings to jingle. "Why are you here?"

"I'm here because I think your life will soon get better."

"What?" Her eyes followed him as he moved around her apartment, trying to convince herself that he wasn't judging her on the piles of random crap that had accumulated.

Milan moved towards the window and pulled the shades open.

"It's like a cave in here. You need light, woman."

Drinda flinched, closing her eyes against the sudden infiltration of bright light, making a small noise in the back of her throat as her lips settled in a moue of rebuke. Blinking her eyes carefully open, she watched as Milan stalked to the kitchen and – pulling the blind in there up as well – picked up two glasses from the draining board and set them on the small kitchen table. He pulled out a chair, and folded himself gracefully into it before eyeing the bottles she had collected there. Picking up a bottle of vodka, he poured a measure into each glass before flicking his steely eyes back up to her and leaning his elbows on the table.

"Sit down with me," he said, nudging the chair opposite him out from under the table.

Slowly, hesitantly, she moved towards him, wondering just how much her life would change – it already had in the five minutes that he had been in her apartment. Drinda watched with apprehension as his gaze moved over her, coming to rest on the dish towel that was still wrapped around her hands. Her breath caught as he reached towards her and yanked it from her grasp.

"Drink," he said, his tone brooking no argument, as he raised his glass to his lips and tipped his head back to swallow the measure in one.

Her hands shook as she raised the glass to her lips and shuddered as she forced herself to swallow. The vodka was neat; it had been a while since she'd touched neat vodka.

"Things have been tough for you, Drinda... am I right?"

"I..." She watched him pour himself another measure.

"The thing is..." he swirled the liquid in the glass, "you can't keep on like this. All this hiding and pretending that you're fine."

There was a pause as he sipped at the vodka this time.

"It's not been easy you know," Drinda snapped in the momentary silence. "I'm constantly on alert – I feel like I've been damned even though you got my name cleared. My mother..."

"Loves you too much to let you wallow," Milan interrupted. "But that's no reason to shut yourself away from everyone – everything. I came because I have a proposition."

"Proposition?" Drinda suddenly wished her hands weren't shaking as much as they were – that they would be steady enough to let her down her vodka at the calculating measure of his words.

Milan quirked his lips and dropped his eyes back to his glass. "I've decided that you deserve a vacation."

"A... what?"

She snapped her eyes from his fingers that were tracing the rim of the glass to his face, searching for a hint that he was joking.

"You've been cooped up here too long. There's a cruise ship leaving at the end of the month. I think you should be on it when it sails."

Suddenly she was far away in her thoughts, remembering a dinner conversation that she'd had early in her relationship. "Lee always did say that he'd take me on a cruise one day…"

"Let's discuss details over a drink,' he suggested smoothly, as though this was how he'd planned it all the way. "There's someone I want you to meet, first. I'll just make a quick call, then I'll explain in the car."

***

Milan picked up the phone as he watched Drinda walking unsteadily to her bedroom to change. It was shocking really, he thought as he dialed, how much she'd let herself go since she'd been accused of murder.

After the third ring, the call was answered.

"Yes?" The sound of a pen tapping against a table top carried over the line, and Milan felt an eyebrow rise at the sign of agitation.

"Pedro, that cruise ship you're going on – I need you to travel with someone for me." Milan said, turning away from Drinda's bedroom door, talking quickly and precisely.

"Who?"

"My damsel in distress, as you so wonderfully dubbed her."

"Her? Why?

"She needs to remember how to live. Look, her boyfriend was murdered – stabbed in the neck by someone who wanted him out of their lives – and she ended up being framed for it. No-one believed she was innocent until I came in, and got her acquitted. She's never moved past what happened. At least meet her."

Milan could hear Pedro's pen stop its tapping and the line crackled momentarily. He imagined Pedro scrubbing a hand over his face.

"Fine," Pedro grumbled eventually, "but you owe me."

***

When she emerged from her bedroom, Drinda wore a dark red sweater and a black pantsuit that hugged her curvy hips and fell straight down over her long, thin legs. She was momentarily conscious that she wasn't wearing any make-up and that her hair which she wore tied back, was probably sticking up somewhere. She was nowhere near the refined elegance of Milan, but she was at least out of the over-large, slouchy jumper and leggings that had been her refuge for so long. They spoke little as she locked her apartment door and they made their way out of her building – some of her neighbours looking curiously at the man accompanying her.

Outside in the car park, Milan led her over to a silver Mercedes and opened the passenger door for her; she slid into the leather seat.

They were silent as they travelled. Drinda stared out of the passenger window at the setting sun, the street lights flickering into life as the darkness swept along the road. It was strange, seeing Milan so soon. Clasping her hands tighter around the seatbelt, Drinda tried to ignore the wave of memories that threatened to crash across her consciousness. She could still remember the hard bed and sense of frustration and disbelief that no-one believed her.

***

She glared at Milan with a tear-streaked face.

"You need to stick to your guns; relay the facts and refuse to be intimidated."

"I can't even think what we'd argued about. Just stuff." She said, bewildered.

"Do something. Whatever it is, do something," he told her frankly, as he shuffled some papers into his briefcase. "Make the most of the situation. Don't sit and wait for someone to fix everything for you. You've got to snap out of it."

She arched an eyebrow through her tears.

***

After a short drive, they parked behind the local drug store and walked to the nearby bar. Milan swiftly ushered her in and settled her in a booth with a view through the window whilst he went to the bar and procured them drinks.

Drinda stayed quiet, even as Milan returned with the two scotches. She didn't really know what to expect, staring at each car as it flashed past the window in the pooling dusk. Pressing her right hand against her forehead, she willed the world to stitch itself back together in some semblance of order. She raised her head after a few minutes.

"Will he be long?" Her voice raised a couple of octaves.

"He shouldn't be too long," Milan replied, as Drinda spotted a black Ford parked in the lot, noticeable only because of the light glinting off the driver's side door as it opened.

The man that got out was tall and slender, but his frame was clearly muscular as he moved to the door of the bar with an easy grace. Even in the dark, she could see that he had dark hair and a neatly trimmed moustache. The two men locked eyes and before she knew it the men were shaking hands whilst some kind of rapid, fluent, non-verbal messaging passed between them.

Milan turned to her then, and introduced her to Pedro, who smiled mirthlessly.

"No need to look so pleased to see me," she joked weakly before ducking her head in apology, almost missing the stranger's wince.

"He must have treated you badly." The stranger said matter-of-factly.

Her eyes widened with surprise and she gave him a long, hard look.

"What?"

An uncomfortable silence settled as Milan maneuvered the man into the other side of the booth, and signaled to a waiter. The staff at the bar buzzed around preparing for the dinner crowd, setting tables and serving drinks over the bar. Drinda realized that Milan must have set up a command with the staff earlier, as a waiter manoeuvred his way through the crowd to the bar and returned with three glasses of champagne and a dish of olives on a circular tray..

"Now then – Drinda, this is Pedro Garcia. He's your ticket out of San Francisco." Milan rested his hands on the table top, clearly feeling satisfied with himself at the introduction, and Drinda felt her tension ease as she studied Pedro.

They sat there talking of small, inconsequential things, each sipping at their champagne. Across from her, Milan smiled, the corners of his eyes crinkling into little lines.

Drinda took a deep breath and reached for an olive while she thought of what to say next. She watched Pedro scratch the corner of his finely sculptured mouth with his index finger and found herself strangely mesmerized. So much so, that he made her momentarily forget all the horrendous things that had happened to her.

"I've heard some impressive stories about you, Pedro," she said.

Pedro traced the stem of his champagne glass slowly before bringing his hands together on the table in front of him. As he opened his mouth to respond, one of the waitresses came over and whispered something in his ear. Grimacing, Pedro pushed back his chair and stood up.

Page 59

"I've been called back to the office," he said apologetically, draining the rest of his champagne, before giving a grim smile and nodding. "See you on the cruise in one week."

Drinda smiled at him approvingly and shook his extended hand. As he walked away, she watched as he tossed his keys up and caught them in the same hand. She felt a great sense of relief as she watched him leave the room, but then within a few seconds, asked herself why he was leaving so quickly. Something didn't feel right.

She turned and gave a single twist of her head to tell Milan that it was time to go. As they pulled away in the car, Drinda spoke.

"That was an… interesting meeting."

Milan agreed mildly, but underneath his bland façade was a cunning mind.

Chapter 5

As always on a Friday night, Pedro headed to the gym. He found that whenever he needed to think, having his body busy doing something else freed his mind. The night was calm, utterly silent except for the mellow whine of his Ford engine, newly tuned and sensitive to the slightest touch of his fingers. Pedro drew a deep breath and pushed his head back into the leather-head rest before putting his foot more firmly on the gas pedal. The Ford leapt forward, hitting eighty, and pulling up to the gym's main gate with its tires screeching.

The gym was almost empty. As he started his workout and looked out of the gym's windows to the streetlights illuminated below, Pedro reflected on the task that the CIA had assigned to him. All he knew so far that he was to observe a Wallace Wilkinson who would be on the same cruise ship that they had assigned him to. He didn't have the official file as yet – his handler had that and would be meeting him in the morning to hand it over. Breathing hard as he finished his workout, Pedro wiped the sweat from his forehead using the back of his hand and wondered what exactly the CIA wanted with Wilkinson.

Once he was back at home, Pedro flipped through the dossier he had been compiling, looking at a series of photos. On the second page, a spread of photos of Wilkinson's various homes caught his attention and he briefly wondered how anyone could get that rich. Scanning his eyes over the latest information from the CIA, it seemed that Wilkinson was into everything from petty theft to major fraud. It wasn't only that that he was into either –at least a third of the file dealt with his proclivity for prostitutes. At least Wilkinson's wife had left him years ago and taken the kids, and got the hell out of his sad life.

The man was clever, Pedro grudgingly admitted; he knew how to make money through whatever means he came across. The CIA wanted him behind bars, and under twenty-four-hour surveillance. Pedro closed the file thoughtfully – the timing on this was crucial. His mind raced through all the possible alternatives at his disposal – he didn't really want to spend too much time on this. One thing was certain, however: he needed to pick his team sooner rather than later.   He glanced at his watch. It was 8.10 a.m. and he had a growing list of priorities that needed his attention. Firstly, he needed to talk to Milan.

***

They'd agreed to meet at André's that afternoon. Pedro arrived early and slouched down low in his seat, sipping at the glass of red wine promptly delivered by one of the bar staff. He looked around as he overheard the Maître d' welcoming Milan and directing him over to the table.

"What would you like to drink?" Pedro asked as Milan settled at the table.

"Water," Milan said, hoarsely.

Pedro frowned as he nodded at the Maître d'; he seemed very off-balance, as if his emotions couldn't decide where to settle. There was a kind of tension in the air between them – one that said they had been friends all those years ago, but were pretending they hadn't.

After a few more moments of tense silence, Pedro crossed his arms and shot Milan a pointed look.

"Are we going to do this?"

Milan sat back, rolling his eyes, and held up a cautionary finger.

"Yes, alright."

"You need to make the arrangements with London, let them know of my arrival," Pedro said.

"Consider it done. You may be lucky; you can always find a Brit on a ship."

He stared at Milan in disbelief. "You want me to work with a civilian?"

"Yes. A Brit would be ideal. We need an outsider; someone who no-one knows."

"That won't be easy." Pedro fired back, struggling to grasp the significance of Milan's words.

Milan smiled and handed him a letter. "Have a look."

It was background information on a young British man who worked onboard the ship. Milan had done his homework and discovered that the man had a rather long criminal record as a thief, and potentially useful friends in London's underworld.

"There's plenty of information here he wouldn't want you to reveal to the authorities once he starts working for us. He won't be able to back out even he figures out our plans."

"You're sure about this guy? You can't make a mistake here." Pedro stared doubtfully at Milan.

"Yes, and Drinda will be useful as well – she could be a good asset. Just don't tell her too much."

"Do you think we can trust her? And how do we know that she has her facts straight?" said Pedro. He'd heard she was smart, but he had yet to see.

"She was perhaps the only person who had me fooled," Milan replied.

"What do you mean?"

"When I started to represent her, I was convinced that she was telling the truth – that she'd had nothing to do with her boyfriend's death. She demonstrated none of the telltale signs. She could lie without blinking if it served the moment. The only thing that I realized was safe to assume was that when her mouth was moving, she was lying."

"So are you saying she did kill him?"

"Without a doubt," Milan said, flippantly.

"So how the heck did you get her off?"

"You know as well as I do that there's always ways to tamper with evidence – as long as you're willing to pay," Milan gave Pedro a lopsided grin. "And I was sure she'd repay me in one way or another."

Pedro swirled the red wine around in his glass, thoughtfully. "Milan, we've always been straight with each other. There can't be any mistakes. I need to know about her. The more information I have the smoother this whole business will go."

Milan held up his glass of water and, with a reassuring smile, said, "I'll get her to call you."

Pedro was under no illusions that he could trust her, but Milan's points were valid. Pedro would never be able to share everything, but maybe he could give her just enough to help point her in the right direction. And see what might come of it.

*** *

Two days later, Pedro arrived home from a meeting to find his answering machine blinking. Two missed calls, neither of which left any form of message. He was contemplating who had his number but wouldn't leave a message when the phone rang again.

"Hello, who is this?"

"Hey, where are you?" Drinda's voice sounded nervous and tinny on the line. "Milan gave me your number; said you wanted to talk to me."

"How about we go for a drink tonight."

"Hmm, alright."

The answer brought a smile to Pedro's face. She was cute, he supposed. He made quick arrangements to meet her at her apartment block before heading to the beach club. She was waiting outside when Pedro pulled up in his Ford. He pushed open the door and she slid into the seat. She smelled showered and fresh, her hair styled perfectly. They made small talk as he drove, pausing momentarily as they arrived, the familiar sounds of a bar reaching out to greet them as Pedro helped Drinda out of the car.

"Does a booth sound alright?" he asked as they made their way inside.

Drinda nodded, and she followed as Pedro rushed to claim a recently vacated booth. They both sank back into the cushions of the booth. She was turned on by the fact that he was a good-looking, smart man who made her laugh.

"I am looking forward to being on the ship." Drinda said, straightening in her seat.

"Did Milan tell you I need to recruit?" Pedro replied.

"Yes he did; though, aren't you supposed to be there to observe somebody?"

"Milan informed you well."

Pedro smiled and signaled to a waiter; he already knew what he was going to order. "Two glasses of champagne, please."

Pedro was enjoying her company, and clearly the feeling was mutual, as she invited him back to her place when he offered her a lift home.

Inside, he took his jacket off and felt himself freeze as a piece of notebook paper fell from his pocket.

"What's this?"

She leaned forward, her voice raised by curiosity squinting as she made out that it was a name of a ship's crew member. Pedro lunged for the paper, but she got there first, holding it in a tight grip and laughing. She eyed him suspiciously, looking like she wanted to ask for a little more detail, but Pedro didn't give her the chance. After enduring another few seconds of scrutiny, he gripped her arm and led her to the bedroom. Sliding into bed, Pedro was caught off guard by a wave of loneliness.

He wished he could open up to Drinda and tell her about his life. It would be nice to have the freedom to be with someone for more than a night. Pedro had never before stayed up and talked and got to know a woman he was attracted to; his history was sprinkled with clandestine meetings, hurried sex and rushed orgasms. It had never been about companionship, or love because that was a risk to his work. Drinda was the biggest risk he'd ever had, but her natural sympathetic attitude and Milan's assessment of her convinced Pedro that she was apparently very good at keeping her lips zipped.

Chapter 6

Pedro did not expect to find him until he was on board, this Wilkinson. He knew where he was booked in first class: en suite on A deck, with his stateroom just around the corner. In the jostle of the crowd, he was content to not even think about him for the moment. The ship security was tight, and he was content to be frisked and passed along, but it turned out that the strong lavender smell behind him was the pomade slicking down the black, centre-parted hair of none other than Wilkinson. He recognized him from the photos: faintly jowled, dense eyebrows, wide in the shoulders and short in the legs.

He stayed just ahead of him through the whole process with the purser and the baggage steward, and then lingered at the foot of the grand staircase. He saw him in his periphery and he moved away and up the plush, ruby red carpet of the staircase. He passed what he knew to be Wilkinson's en suite rooms, A20 and A21, and then he moved on down the corridor and turned into a passageway. A few steps later, beyond a short, forward-heading corridor, he arrived at the door of his own single-room cabin, A4. Still conscious of him, from around the corner, he distantly heard Wilkinson shutting his door.

Pedro looked at himself in the mirror over the cabin's wash basin. He washed and dried his face, rubbing hard at it, and put his jacket, shirt and tie back on, before leaving his cabin and passing Wilkinson's suite. He checked the stairs quickly and then started up them two at a time. Stopping just short of the top, he listened. From the door straight ahead and to the left came passionate purrs of a young woman moaning. He stepped out onto B deck promenade, and there, quite near, leaning at the railing with his back turned towards the dock and an air of casual indifference, was Wilkinson. He watched him holding a cigarette rather effetely between the tips of thumb and forefinger with his little finger lifted. He looked content.

Pedro needed to focus on his assignment. He knew how to move quickly. He went to Wilkinson's en suite and, using his picklock, opened the door. He needed to find Wilkinson's notebook, which would reveal amounts, dates, and names. His mind began to move fast. In the corner, on the floor, he saw a black suitcase; he forced it open. In between the numerous crisp white shirts, he could see the black leather book. He grabbed it and stuffed it into his jacket pocket. He checked the rest of the case to confirm there was nothing else he should know about. He pulled the door shut and quickly slipped out of the cabin. Taking a deep breath, he decided to go for a walk.

He'd arranged to meet Drinda later at the grand lobby bar. The place was full of tuxedoed men and bejeweled women who were milling about with cocktails in their hands and murmuring to each other as they were trying to find a seat at one of the glass tables with their cream sofas. There was a stage, framed with spotlights above and big speakers at either side. In the centre of the room, an expensive-looking chandelier hung proudly from the ceiling. The bar was shiny aluminum and there was every optic known to mankind behind it.

Drinda sat at one of the tables and met his eyes as he came in. He walked over to her, then leant down and kissed her on the cheek. He sat in one of the luxurious armchairs and angled it so he could watch the main entrance. He signaled to the waiter to bring a bottle of champagne. Draining half the glass in two mouthfuls, she smiled, before draining the rest. She took her time with the second drink, talking excitedly about the people she had seen and the views from the upper decks. She threw her head back when she laughed, her face animated by joy, her moves fuelled by the surge of alcohol in her blood.

After the second bottle, he took a deep breath and said, "Remember, you need to get him to come to San Francisco."

She smiled and squeezed his hand. "I know."

He reminded himself that this was nothing more than a business relationship.

When she raised her hand to touch her dark hair, a tiny strip of tanned and toned navel showed. He pulled her from her chair. "My cabin's right over here."

He extracted the key from his pocket and slid it into the metal lock with a steady hand. She pursed those full, glossy lips and looked deep into his eyes with a big, sincere smile. He pressed her against the hard surface of the cabin wall as his tongue explored her mouth. He undressed her slowly, his warm hands fondling her gently. He was kissing parts of her body that had nothing to do with sex – her shoulder, her ear. She delicately guided him away from her wrist and ankles.

"Just fuck me, for Christ's sake," she said.

He began pumping gently, pausing for kisses, until she grabbed him by the buttocks and began pushing him into her.

"Fuck me hard," she cried out. Her insides fluttered with the feel of him. She arched, moaned. She gasped as he entered her more deeply. A minute passed. Then another. His expression tightened as a small noise caught his attention. The door was slightly ajar. A man stood there, gawking in disbelief, clearly caught between the desire to stay and watch and the common decency of leaving quickly. Suddenly, Drinda's eyes, which had been screwed shut, opened slightly in ecstasy only to fly wide upon seeing the man. Pedro barked a warning, and the rhythmic bouncing of the bed ceased.

"Can we have some privacy?" He stretched out his long arm and pushed the door closed.

Chapter 7

At six feet in height, John Scott's dark hair was closely cropped, and his moustache neatly trimmed. Last year in London, he'd got into trouble after conning some of his friends from the underworld out of money and run off to sea, where he was now serving successfully as a galley cook.

It was supposed to be his morning lie-in, but when he opened his eyes and looked at the clock, he couldn't believe that it said only five o'clock. He quickly reached over and punched off the alarm before it went off and woke his cabin mate.

Tony Lester was short and fat and sported an American GI haircut.

"Morning, John." His voice floated across the room.

John wasn't really sure how to take him. Most people, you either liked them or you didn't. Tony was a bit strange. He'd told John that before he signed on the ship, he'd graduated from the N.Y.U. School of Law. And yet he felt like a loser, such a sorry chump. His stories could drone on, seamlessly, forever. They went on for so long that they became genuinely annoying and then swung back around to being hilarious.

He'd found that out the first night they'd met. Tony was moving on to another story about something or other.

"Stop there, I'm going to sleep."

"You want a tab?" said Tony. 'My brother was a great believer in the easiest way. Pop a pill, get unconscious."

"No."

"They're in my case if you change your mind. Are you sure?"

This guy is a complicated character, thought John. He grasped Tony's shoulder and gave him a gentle shake.

"Tony, listen to me. Are you listening?" It took a moment, but he eventually murmured an affirmative. "The best thing you can do is leave me alone." A lot of people lacked that gift: knowing when to fuck off.

Tony raised his arms to interlock his fingers behind his head for a moment before taking his diary from his briefcase. He was like clockwork; he always kept a log of what he had done each day. After a moment of staring at the blank page he gave a small shrug, his head still bent down. He wrote in neat, small capitals that ran along like hieroglyphics. John couldn't decipher them upside down.

He finished the sentence he was working on and put a full stop on the page as if he was stubbing out a cigarette, twisting the pen so it almost broke through the paper. John resisted the urge to lean forward to look. Tony ran his finger along the sentence, reading it to himself, tapping along the words as if they didn't make sense; then, he leant forward.

"Washington?" he asked.

John didn't know how to react to this.

"Tony, what are you writing?"

Tony jerked his head up and squinted. He opened his mouth to speak. Slowly his mouth started to move, but no words came out; then he started to stammer as if he was back in grade school.

"I'm ... I'm sorry," he began. "Oh ... it's about a group of people who live in past-time ... Washington." His words then came out in a string of furious spittle. "Writing is my passion." He paused, as if searching for something else to say.

John laughed, covering his mouth with his hand. Tony lifted a shoulder as if saying he had plenty more where that came from. That was the trouble with Tony – you just didn't know what to expect. He would say things like, "Trust me, you wouldn't want to know," which would get up most people's noses. "Nothing wrong with his brain," they'd say. "He's sharp as a tack."

John believed he just pretended to be that way.

Later that day, John had to report to the dining room to discuss a menu for a VIP. Fifteen minutes later, he found himself sitting at a corner table in the massive restaurant. The blur of activity from the breakfast waiters made it look like a beehive, the maître d' barking orders as he moved across to John, a file tucked under his arm.

"Honestly," he grumbled as he thumped the file down on the table, "you'd think half of these guys had never bussed tables before…."

After the meeting, John wandered back to one of the main foyers, settled himself on the plush sofa and gazed around, thinking that life was good. No, life was great! He couldn't help but feel a little bit mystified as to how well everything had worked out. His eyes kept flickering to the other side of the room.

The black and white checked marble floors were immaculate, the moldings on the wall exquisite. But it was neither of these that had caught his attention. She was totally still, wearing a red blouse and a string of pearls around her neck. Her hair was sleek, and cut to the level of her jawbone. With high cheekbones and an angular face, she was one of those striking women you would notice in any room. Her knees were clamped tightly together, and she stared at her hands the whole time, in a way that made it obvious she was trying not to look at him. But she was.

A waiter arrived with a trolley to serve late breakfast. She poured maple syrup all over her pancakes; after the first bite, he saw her lick her top lip. Shortly after, another woman joined her. She had a sort of bottom-of-the-well voice, a deep and strangled resonance, and was heavily pregnant. She seemed to be having a tough time in the weather; her movements were sluggish and her ankles and feet so swollen that she had to wear rubber flip flops.

On his way back to the galley, he saw her waiting by the elevator. She was dressed for the cameras: a snug black sweater and even tighter white jeans. He looked at her and smiled. He asked her name and said he couldn't fathom how she had possibly got into those pants. A sharp ripple shot down her spine at the words. She clenched her fingers around the cord of her handbag as she fought the urge to whirl and swing her body.

Had she seen him watching her? Of course. She closed her eyes briefly, mentally kicking herself for being so obvious. But it wasn't like she had planned it.

Her figure was incredible and John had to make a conscious effort to stare at her face rather than her body during their conversation.

Later that evening, John stood at the back of the crowd in the bar area, searching for the woman who'd distracted him for the whole day. Almost everyone on the ship was in here tonight, thanks to the art auction that was taking place. When he finally spotted her, she was bidding against someone for an art piece that he thought looked like a cat had vomited on the canvas. Making his way across to her once the bidding ceased, he quietly asked if he could join her.

"Can I get you a drink?"

"A glass of Chardonnay would be nice." Drinda responded, a coy smile forming on her lips.

***

They were on their second glass of wine when they spotted the auctioneer's assistant talking to people at the next table. He was asking for help to start the bidding, promising free art in exchange for their help in driving up prices. There were a couple of Filipino helpers who called out loudly every time someone made a bid and offered a false bid. John felt excited. He and Drinda sat together just observing the rest of the auction.

"So, what made you come on a cruise?"

"It's not important," she replied. "I had some personal problems."

Before John could say anything else, she smiled and began wiping her tearful eyes.

"Not to mention that my gran left me a little money," she explained, "so I thought I should splash out a bit."

She shook her head like she was sorry. He looked in her sweet, tear-stained face and told her it was okay. She leant in close to him.

"I do apologize," she said, embarrassment lacing her tone.

"Tell me what happened," he asked. She flared at that: she didn't really need a man's help.

"Really, it's okay," said John, sensing her discomfort, and pushing his chair back to stand up. "Let's go to the champagne bar."

Smiling, she took his extended hand and let him lead her to the bar. There was a big silver wine bucket at the bar with about ten or so different bottles of champagne pressed into crushed ice.

"Why don't we just grab a bottle and go and relax?" John said.

" I think the barman is watching us."

The barman had the look of a tall, handsome movie star, his beard trimmed with a sort of military precision. He stood a good head taller than John as he glared down at them.

"I hope he is capable of smiling," said Drinda quietly as they moved closer.

The barman had overheard her and grinned. He picked up a bottle of champagne and offered John and Drinda a glass each, placing on their table some little salty nibbles.

It was cool and quiet in the bar. John took his time, enjoying every minute with her. Her eyes zeroed in on the tiny white Band-Aid on John's finger.

"What happened?" She asked.

"I accidentally cut myself while slicing vegetables."

She moved closer and slowly reached out. Her soft fingers touched the skin around the Band-Aid and John felt a small shock of

Page 75

electricity run through his upper body. She had softest, most feminine hands he'd ever encountered.

He glanced at his watch. Best not be late, he thought. He had to be back in the galley to help with dinner. They both stood up and he put down some money, ready to go. He leant forward and kissed her on the cheek. On the way back to her cabin, she glanced over her shoulder and gave him a wave, arched an eyebrow, and was gone.

The next day, the ship began to make its way back to Miami. It was the last night of the cruise. Drinda had a relaxing day in the ship's spa, enjoying one of its special pamper packages. John tiptoed in and had a peep. He left a note for Drinda to meet him at the captain's farewell party.

Later that evening, John couldn't help smiling when he saw her standing by the entrance to the Manhattan Room, an elegant bar at the ship's stern. Around the room, waitresses stood like soldiers, all holding trays of champagne and cocktails. The guests had begun gorging on canapés and sloshing down champagne that quickly went to their heads.

"Let's go next door." Drinda suggested – the band was loud and all she really wanted to do was have a real drink and talk. John nodded and walked to the bar. He was gone and back in record time with their drinks; he gulped down a little hoping it would soften the edge of his nerves. She was staring at the corner of the bar, chewing on her lip, clearly lost in thought.

"What are you thinking?"

"You should come and visit me in San Francisco," she said, her eyes still unfocussed in the distance. "You could even find a job in a restaurant."

He huffed a laugh. "Come on, you can't be serious."

"Just catch a flight." Her eyes focused on him, finally.

"I don't know." He stared into the distance for a long moment trying to decide if she was serious.

"There are some really good restaurants in San Francisco. When I go out to eat with friends, I often go to a little place called Prego – it's just halfway down the hill from where I live." She blushed and smiled at him, flicking her hair over her shoulder in a way she must have thought was alluring.

"Look, Drinda ..."

She stood up and pressed a thick cream-colored card into his hands. "Let me know."

John took the card with a smile, thinking how good it would be to live with her. You could tell just by looking into her eyes that there was something very sincere about her.

They said their goodbyes and as he walked away, she called out:

"See you soon."

Chapter 8

It was an incredibly hot day. Members of the crew were rushing around getting ready for the turnaround. Decks were being hosed, cabins cleaned, and a cranky looking Korean guy, who was probably a lawyer or something like that in his own country, pushed past John while carrying some boxes. Why do people do that? thought John. Do they have some kind of mental deficiency when it comes to personal distances?

He squinted over at the man to check for signs of this, but was surprised to find the complete opposite as a Filipino man, dressed in a white boiler suit, called out to the guy in question and addressed him as 'Sir'. John was soon to learn he was the chief engineer.

The captain then made an announcement over the tannoy that all passengers could disembark, and a man dressed in an officer's uniform stood to the side of the deck, smiling politely and saying goodbye to each of the passengers as they went past.

John watched Drinda as she left the ship, taking particular interest in the dark-haired man she was talking to. With his charcoal suit, white cotton shirt and black tie, he looked every inch the respectable gentleman. Drinda smiled at the man, resting her hand on his arm, and John thought it a bit strange how they were acting – as if they had known each other for years. As she was walking down the gangway exit he noticed that she gave this person a small brown paper parcel. The man then shook hands with her and John overheard him say, "See you soon". She nodded, smiling.

He began to wonder who this guy was. Could he just be a new friend she'd met, or maybe an old boyfriend? Whatever it was, it was intriguing the hell out of him, and he frowned as he watched her turn away from the man.

That very moment, Tony came along. John watched as he trudged along the deck with his shoulders hunched, his hands deep in his pockets and his head down as he made his way over. Looking up briefly, Tony nodded at him in acknowledgement.

"What's wrong?" John asked.

"Do you know who that woman was?" replied Tony.

"Who?"

His gaze flickered to where Drinda had been just moments before. "The one you were talking to earlier? Just thought you'd like to know she spent a lot of time with another man."

"What do you mean?" asked John, stepping closer as he lowered his voice.

Tony raised his eyebrows. "She went to his cabin, and let me tell you, they weren't just talking."

John paused for a moment, taking this in. "Really, is that so?"

"I also remembered them sitting in the champagne bar," muttered Tony. "I saw them having a deep conversation, and she did more listening than speaking. I assumed he was her boyfriend by the way they had their lips locked together."

"What?"

"I saw you and the girl standing together by the elevator doors," Tony explained. "After you left, he appeared. He put his hand on her shoulder, then kissed her on the cheek. It was interesting, he got in the elevator and his mouth opened to speak as he reached to stop the doors from shutting, but he was too late."

"And?" John asked, now more intrigued than ever.

"Well, I managed to read the first words on his lips before the doors closed."

John rolled his eyes; was Tony ever going to spit it out? "So what did he say?"

"He said 'he would be perfect' . . ."

"What does that mean? Who would be perfect? Do you know?" John continued to shoot questions at Tony but Tony wasn't having any of it.

His cheeks flushed as he muttered, "See you later," shaking his head before John could get another word in. "Uh, I've got to go. I don't have time to talk right now, but I'll see you when I see you." With that he walked off, head down and shoulders hunched once again, like he was trying to blend into the crowd.

Strange man, thought John.

At last, an opportunity was about to present itself to him. In two

weeks' time, the ship was due to go up the coast of Mexico and sail into San Francisco Bay. A wicked glint rose in John's eyes as he exchanged his previously grim expression for one of superiority.

When he was in the crew bar a few days later, he saw a newspaper on one of the tables. It was a few days old, but he grabbed it anyway, and continued to scan through it, paying particular interest to the employment section. Upon looking at the adverts, John realized he would need a new identity if he were to stay in the States, but how?

After a couple of drinks, he started to formulate a plan: he could steal the personal information of his cabin mate, using his name and details to do whatever he needed to do while staying off the radar. This, however, was where things got tricky: in order to 'become' Tony Lester, he would need to gain his Social Security number, which was easier said than done. He knew he would be committing identity theft by stealing the man's name and papers, and there would be serious consequences if he got caught. He knew the dangers and the risks, but he was willing to take that chance. What other option did he have?

His mind made up, John went back down to his cabin; he needed to at least try to get some sleep.

On his way down, John's attention was grabbed by an Asian man dressed in a white boiler suit. He sat on the steps of a narrow metal staircase, enjoying the last few puffs of his cigarette, looking out at the night. Down below, there were three decks below the waterline, the lowest of which was for the water tanks and the engines. The other two hid the crew cabins in an insane labyrinth of metal corridors and steps.

As John continued along the corridor, he saw two men, talking and laughing with each other. They both looked wiry-strong, their muscular arms rivered with popping blue veins. One man shook the other's hand – John could tell he liked him – while the other man continued his conversation. John never stopped to talk; instead, he carried on walking, and before he knew it, he found his own cabin, which was right at the bottom of the ship. He extracted the key from his pocket and slid it into the metal lock with a steady hand. Turning it, he pushed and stepped into the cabin. Home sweet home.

He lay on his back on the sagging mattress and stared at the ceiling, his thoughts unfocused. After ten minutes or so, he realized it wasn't his own thoughts that were stopping him from sleeping, however, but instead a feeling, like he was being watched. But that was ridiculous, wasn't it? He was the only one in here!

Sitting up, he looked around the room, sensing that something was wrong. A few quiet sounds caught his attention, and his gaze moved over to the door. Was someone waiting on the other side?

As if in response, there was a sudden, instant movement – the sound of a key being jabbed in the lock.

"Who's there?" he called out, his voice raspy. He got up to open the door, but it was too late. Whoever it was had gone.

Now completely unable to sleep, John thought he'd make the most of his time alone in the cabin (Tony was working his shift). He had a look through some of his papers and personal files, searching for anything that would give more information on his background. He had to make sure he had enough information about him as possible, even including his family members. For instance, his brother's birthday was 20 March 1957.

Every little detail was important, and John needed to know everything. After a while of rummaging around, he had enough data to open a bank account in his name, and even borrow money from his bank. It really was quite easy. Deep down, he found it quite amusing that he could use a different identity. He pictured himself in San Francisco, walking around with this huge secret. It appealed to him.

He felt excited, and the best part was, he knew that as long as Tony stayed on the ship, he wouldn't need any of his papers, freeing up John to use them as he wished.

He did feel a little guilty, however; Tony wasn't very popular, and he didn't have many friends, so John started to make an extra effort to be friendly towards Tony whenever he could. Of course, this also helped John out too – by talking to him as much as he could, he could find out more things about him, about his identity.

He'd offer to walk with him to his shift, talking the whole time about his past and getting Tony to open up about his. John would ask questions about his family, what he did before working on the ship, whether he had any scars or any secrets. He offered up information about himself too – otherwise he'd never have got much out of Tony – but most of what he revealed were lies, or at least a vast embellishment of the truth.

It was clear that Tony had confined himself to his own little world, and it was only now that he started to feel like he had a friend whom he could trust. It was hard sometimes, as John didn't want to hurt his feelings, but he knew this was the only chance he had of staying in the US.

So he continued to befriend him, talking and laughing with him as he learned all about his new pal.

He was ready.

It was early February when the ship sailed under the Golden Gate Bridge and into San Francisco Bay. By now John was ready to leave the ship, and as he gazed out at the iconic bridge, he felt like he was sailing into a new life. He didn't have that much money – only $200 – but he was sure he would find work. It would be enough. He had the one small suitcase, which was good, as it would not make him look too conspicuous when he departed. The rest of what he needed – the information about Tony – was safe and sound, all locked up in his brain.

It was a misty morning, the slight breeze making John shiver slightly as he tugged his baseball cap lower over his eyes. A bit different to Miami, he thought to himself as he walked along, holding his head down so he wouldn't be recognized.

A wave of panic hit him as he wondered if she might be there to meet him, or was that just a quick romantic thought? Maybe he was going to be surprised. Sailing under the Golden Gate Bridge and seeing the hills in the background and the spectacular view, this city looked like his kind of place. There was something different yet appealing about all of it. Despite his fears, he felt excited.

As he walked down the gangway, John thought he could see her, and as he made his way down the harbor, he started to wonder if he'd done the right thing. He noticed some crew members and Captain Bowman walking towards him, and he smiled and nodded at them as he passed – the walkway was very narrow and it would have been difficult to avoid them.

Moments later he heard a honk, and as his head whipped around, he couldn't help but smile when he saw Drinda in a taxi. He opened the passenger door and when Drinda got out, she opened her arms to hug him.

"I'm really sorry I'm late," she said, looking up at him and smiling.

He responded with a kiss. "That's okay. It was worth the wait."

"Did you have a nice trip from Miami? Was the weather nice?" She held his hand, beaming at him as she waited for him to answer.

"Yes, yes," he said, looking around him. "I'm glad to be here now though!"

"Oh, me too," she said. "I've been counting down the hours! It's come around quickly, though, don't you think?" She couldn't stop talking. She had really looked forward to him coming, she'd been waiting for this moment, it was so good to see him… but something about her words sounded hollow to John. He had a strange feeling in his gut. Was she really happy to see him? Something felt wrong, but he wasn't sure what.

A traffic accident meant that it took a while to get out of the harbor, and John kept sneaking looks at Drinda as they slowly got onto the freeway. She seemed very excited, pointing at things out the window and explaining when they passed a landmark of interest. Eventually, he started to relax and enjoy the scenery.

Taking a break from her tourist role, she noticed John staring at her and returned his gaze with a smile. "Are you OK?" she asked, seeming genuinely concerned.

His suspicions of her lessened a little. "I'm fine, it's just a little weird being here, with you."

She laughed. "Weird but good, right?"

He nodded, laughing with her. Talking to her – just being with her even – was easy. Really easy.

Eventually the taxi pulled up on a quiet street, and Drinda paid the driver before getting out. She lived in a nice part of town above a little bakery, on the corner of Union Street.

"I want to show you around," she said, once the taxi had driven off. "But first, would you like to unpack?"

"I haven't brought much," he told her, gesturing at his single suitcase as she let him in to her place.

It was neat and tidy, and on the roughly plastered wall in the corner, John recognized the framed photographs of the cruise ship. He smiled, before noticing that Drinda was watching him intently. She'd clearly expected him to spot the photographs. John smiled back approvingly.

"And the other photograph?" he asked, pointing at a picture of a man, who was staring at the camera with only a hint of a smile on his face.

"That's my dad."

"Seriously? You look a lot like him," replied John, still staring at the image on the wall.

"He's got wavy hair," she said, "but it used to be pitch black, like mine. I also have his eyes and a lot of other stuff, like his weird super pointy elbows."

John laughed, moving his gaze to Drinda. "Your elbows look fine to me."

After John had been given a tour of the house, they sat down at the kitchen table for a 'quick coffee' and ended up talking for hours on end. So much for Drinda showing me around the neighborhood, thought John, although he didn't mind really. He was having fun.

"John, you look so tired!" Drinda suddenly announced, before standing up and guiding him to the bedroom.

Next morning, Drinda was up early. "Sorry, I didn't mean to wake you, John," she whispered. "After breakfast, I have to go to work."

She changed into a red and black low-cut top with a black skirt. John smiled; she looked a sight.

"Just make yourself at home," she said, smiling at him.

"I will," said John. "But I may venture outside and have a look around too. Lots to do. Maybe we could meet later?"

"Of course, but find some time to relax!" she purred, as she brought him in for a hug.

John frowned as he pulled back from her. "I will, it's just that all of this is a little too much for me," he said. "I need to find a job, and fast."

Drinda nodded, before grabbing a paper from the table and thrusting it into his hands. "Try these places here," she replied, showing him the restaurant guide in the San Francisco Chronicle.

She had one of those square handbags and, like most women, she crammed as much as she could into it, far more than it looked like it could actually hold.

He walked downstairs with her and waited at the tram stop, peering down the hill in fascination. He could hear the tram bell ringing at the bottom of the hill, and as it slowly climbed, he wondered if it was going to make it. Maybe it's just going to roll back, John thought.

"They usually get really full and most of the time you have to stand," she said as the tram pulled up. "Just for once, this one looks empty."

John smiled and gave her a quick kiss before she hopped on and looked out at him. "Good luck with the job hunt!"

He smiled back, and when she was gone he looked at his surroundings. With the newspaper in his hand, he set off down the hill.

That night, John got a call to go for an interview the next day on a moored seafood boat, and the next morning, he arrived early and waited at a small table.

"Tony?" the man approaching him asked, extending a hand.

"Yeah, that's me," he replied, slowly rising to his feet and returning the handshake. It felt a little strange to be called Tony, but he was sure he'd soon get used to it.

"I appreciate you coming today," said the man. "Can I get you a drink or anything?"

John shook his head. "No, thank you."

After a few questions, the boss appeared to be impressed. He was smiling at John anyway, and nodded quite a few times as he gave his answers.

"Tony, thank you for coming," he said after the main part of the interview was over. "Can you start tomorrow?"

John breathed a huge sigh of relief. "Yes, I can," he replied, smiling. "Thank you for the opportunity."

As John walked away from the boat, he started thinking about his new identity. One day soon he hoped to blend in, but for now he still felt like a fraud. The law of averages told him that he should tread carefully as, sooner or later, something could go wrong, and he would end up in a jam. That thought was now at the back of his mind, and it was going to stay there for a long time to come.

Now that he had a job sorted, John realized he needed to find his own space, and an apartment down Pope Street had just become available. On Thursday – his first day off – he moved into the place, which was small with a simple floor plan. Beyond the tiny bedroom, the living room was furnished in Salvation Army chic. There was a cigarette-scarred table, and the room's sole hint of architectural charm came from the shallow bay window facing the street.

For the remainder of the week, John kept up his routine, and on Monday, he arranged to meet Drinda. He glanced at his watch and saw that it was almost lunchtime, so he passed the old ferry building clock tower before making his way up the hill. He was a little early and, as he was walking towards her, he could see Drinda talking to someone. This guy was in his late forties, with sleek jet-black hair and large sunglasses – the same guy John had seen her with on the cruise ship. Another man, dark-suited with extremely glamorous blond hair, was sitting with them. She looked as if she had been poured into her pink-creamy dress.

John stopped for a moment and watched, and to his embarrassment, the pinprick of tears suddenly formed in his eyes. It really made him wonder what was going on. They all seemed very friendly, as if they knew one another well.

He waited until their meeting was over and then casually went over to meet Drinda. He asked her how her day had been.

"Really nice," she replied. "So, how do you like San Fran? What have you seen? Have you bought a road map of the streets yet?"

"Mostly I've just seen the inside of bars," he replied, still thinking of the mystery men Drinda had been with.

"Well, that's just sad. Makes me glad I've met you today. You shouldn't sit in bars without me."

John slung his bag over his shoulder and suggested they walk for a while.

As they walked down the hill, she asked how his new job was going. "Do you enjoy it?"

John shrugged. "It's okay, it's work. I'm just glad to be earning some money."

"I must come for lunch one day," she said, as she linked her arm through his. "But today we can lunch in the park."

They found a suitable patch of grass and sat down. Once they got comfortable, he decided to ask about the two men she'd been talking to. "So I saw you talking to two guys before," he said as casually as he could. "They friends of yours? Who are they?"

She suddenly went quiet, and after a few seconds, she whispered, "No one. Actually, it's a long story… and now's not the time."

John gave her a meaningful look and her mouth snapped shut. He clearly wanted to pursue the topic, as he said, "I've got time now."

He picked up his bag again and glanced around at the groups of people nearby as he waited for her answer. He didn't want to put her in an awkward situation, but he couldn't quite shrug off the uneasiness he felt.

He could see she was nervous, so he suggested they get a drink – he'd spotted a bar on the other side of the street. She agreed, and after walking over to the building, he pulled back on one of the doors and held it open for her. When they were seated at the corner table, he called the waiter over and ordered a bottle of Chardonnay. The waiter promptly returned with the ice bucket containing the bottle.

Reacting purely on instinct, he brought up the topic again. "I've seen this guy twice now – first on the ship, and then again half an hour ago, so you'd better give me an answer."

Her eyes were shrewd and assessing, and they bored right into him as she made him wait. "Okay," she said. "The man's name is Pedro and he is from Argentina."

John frowned. He knew next to nothing about the country, apart from the fact that it was currently at war with his own – fighting over a handful of rocky, rain-drenched islands somewhere in the South Atlantic. Not that John cared. He felt no particular loyalty to 'Blighty', never had.

"So," said John. "How do you know this 'Pedro'?"

"He's… he's a work friend."

John stared long and hard into Drinda's eyes, making her squirm uncomfortably. He could tell that she was lying, but what was she trying to hide?

"What?" she said finally. "Why are you looking at me like that?"

John merely shook his head and reached for the wine bottle. Drinda put her hand over her glass, so John refilled his own nearly to the brim. Maybe she was worried about getting tipsy and letting something slip. Whatever, thought John. It was an effort for him to even look at her.

"Perhaps we can talk later?" She said after a few moments of silence. "I've got to get back to the office."

"Of course," replied John, the usual warmth in his voice gone.

"Why don't you wait for me at my place?" she said, smiling, as she stood up. After a brief hesitation, she leaned over and kissed him, and then she was gone.

God, he was so stupid. Tossing his keys onto the table, he went straight to the fridge and pulled out a beer, twisting off the cap and guzzling half of it before collapsing into a chair at the table. He didn't want to make excuses or apologize. He wasn't even sure he had anything to apologize for. Lots of thoughts were going through John's mind and, if he was being honest, he was actually exhausted and could do with some sleep. He had a lot of questions to ask her, but they could wait. He went to bed.

Drinda woke John up early the next morning. She brought him a coffee and sat on the end of his bed. They were both quiet, and a tension was beginning to grow that John didn't like. Not at all.

All things considered, this probably wasn't the best way to initiate their relationship, or whatever it was they had going on.

"I feel guilty," she said eventually.

He paused for a moment, before replying with, "Just tell me."

"Well…" she stared at the floor, unable to even look at him.

John was starting to feel a little uneasy and out of his depth. "So, my suspicions were right," he said. "There was something between you and him?"

"Look, it's not what you think," she replied quietly.

"So what is it?"

"Pedro was in the Argentine army, a long time ago. He defected because he didn't agree with the way things were." Of course, It was a well calculated lie.

"And what didn't he agree with?" asked John, curious despite himself.

Drinda bit her lip as she thought the answer through.

"Was he a spy or something?"

"No," said Drinda. "Well, I don't think so. Just let me explain."

And that she did. She went on to tell him that this was the time of the dirty war, and that tens of thousands of Argentines had disappeared or were killed. The army tried to involve Pedro in a plot to overthrow the Argentine government.

"How do you know all this?" asked John, completely bewildered. He hadn't expected any of this.

"Pedro is a very open person," she replied.

"What!" John was shocked by what he was hearing. "But that still doesn't explain your connection."

"Pedro now works for an agency here and does specialized work," she continued.

"Such as?" John asked.

"It's a sort of keep-the-peace, or set-up situation."

John asked her again, "So why were the two of you together on the ship?"

"I was there because a friend of mine introduced me to Pedro and we became friends," replied Drinda. "Pedro was there because of Wallace Wilkinson, the former Governor of Kentucky. Pedro was undercover, gathering information regarding an investigation into fraudulent investments."

John had to clear his throat to speak. "Why was he under an investigation?"

"Wallace Wilkinson was operating a Ponzi scheme."

"Right."

"Why don't I introduce you to Pedro?" she suggested. "We can all meet and have a chat."

John looked at her. "To be honest, I would rather stay in bed," he said. However, he knew he couldn't put the confrontation off forever. Better get it over and done with, he thought to himself.

"Tomorrow then," she said.

He nodded, not trusting himself to say anything else.

John went for a long walk just to clear his head. He was beginning to wonder what it was they wanted to talk to him about. For the first time he was feeling content with himself: was it getting to know people, and making new friends that helped? He toyed with the idea of going out for a few drinks, but he shrugged the notion away. He had to be up early the next morning and he needed to keep his wits about him.

John arrived at Drinda's apartment early, as requested. He didn't know how he should feel: excited, afraid? After all this time, he was finally going to meet the stranger. What with all the build-up, this cloak-and-dagger expedition was beginning to feel very intriguing. Why not be bold? he thought. Be open-minded.

It appeared that Pedro had committed his life and energy to his cause. From what Drinda had told John about him, he guessed he was a very stubborn man. His nightmares, he imagined, would not be filled with beauty, but with looming images of death and horror.

Pedro arrived five minutes after John, and Drinda introduced the two men. As she did, John found his hand trembling. Pedro's grip was tight and he greeted John with a smile. He was dressed impeccably in a decent suit that looked like it cost at least five hundred dollars. In fact, Pedro looked the way John had always wanted to look: like a very handsome, very decent fellow. Yet, there was something about him...

"Nice to meet you," said Pedro, who was studying John with great interest.

John's face lit up in a half-smile, half-grimace as he thought how to respond.

Pedro's black hair gleamed. He was bigger and even more impressive close up. However, he looked a little different from how John had remembered: he'd shaved off his moustache, and it completely changed the shape of his face.

He'd recently turned 49, but he worked hard at staying in shape, just as Drinda had told John. He was a firm-jawed, impressive-looking man, with broad shoulders and sharp eyes. To say he was intimating would be an understatement.

They had their meeting in the dining room, and suddenly the whole thing seemed imposingly formal. Glasses of water had been poured, and a bottle of chilled vodka and plates of sliced salami and little pickled vegetables were placed on the cabinet. The atmosphere crackled with tension as he took all this in.

Before they started in on the meats, Drinda wondered out loud whether the tray of sushi that had been ordered that morning had arrived. That moment, the doorbell rang, and the delivery man handed over a large flat box which resembled a pizza. Drinda held it just below her breast as she walked over, then placed it onto the middle of the table.

John stood staring at the box – ominous-looking in this new setting – and a sense of dread began to descend on him as he opened it. The thought of eating raw fish was making him feel cranky.

Drinda brought out a little china bottle then, which contained a rice-flavored wine. "Would you like to try it?" she asked John as she held it up for him to see.

"Sorry, what is it?" He put a hand across his mouth and rubbed upward, the flesh of his cheeks bunching up around his eyes.

"It's just sake," she answered, giggling at his expression. "It won't kill you."

"Of course, just a little then," he answered nervously. He realized how sweaty his palms were as he took the bottle off her.

She smiled and rearranged her legs delicately. "Don't worry if you don't like it."

Pedro smiled. "You will love it."

Drinda watched John as he drank straight from the bottle, then placed it back on to the table. She stood up and sat beside him, her leg pressed against his. She discreetly picked up the bottle and poured a little of the wine into his glass. "So, that's how they do it in London!"

She did that thing where she tossed her hair over one shoulder and threw her head back to laugh at a joke.

John was curious as to why they wanted to meet him, and he had a lot of questions to ask. Maybe it was all a ploy to get him drunk so he would be less alert. Was he being set up for something? He felt as if this meeting was a test of his character, to see whether he was committed no matter what the personal risk might be.

Even with all his worries, however, John started to chat with Pedro and Drinda, and he eventually started to relax. In fact, he was surprised to find he was having quite a good time.

After an enjoyable few hours, Pedro eventually got to the point. "Listen, John," he said in a voice barely above a whisper. "It would be good if you could join us."

John sat up. "What d'you mean?" He swallowed the lump in his throat.

"I would like you to work for me."

He was caught off-guard and he couldn't say anything for quite a few moments. "Yeah, why not?" He eventually said, before sucking in a deep breath. Ha! Was this the hidden agenda? "But why me?"

John tended to see everything in black and white, and in this case, it was very clear that there was much more going on. He stole a glance at Pedro and was surprised to see that he looked sincere. No smirking, anyway.

Pedro raised his glass to John in a salute. "As you have shown a lot of interest in the work we do," he said, "and as we are really busy, it would be a good opportunity to have you on board."

"What is it you want from me?" John asked as he leaned forward, his voice going up an octave with his curiosity.

"The world is a dangerous place, John. Not because of the people who are evil, but because of the people who don't do anything about it."

"That's not really an answer," John said out loud. He caught the look in Pedro's eye and knew it was probably all he was going to get. "So, I'm going to sit here and quietly listen to the two of you share state secrets?"

Pedro laughed.

They seemed keen to impress him, and John suspected they wanted to keep him interested. He was enjoying the warm rice wine, but he still wasn't sure about the raw fish – it took him a few seconds to get his taste buds back. Although he was nervous about what was happening, all the attention was now making him feel quite special.

"Don't drink too much of the sake," Pedro said.

"Why?"

"You won't be able to walk down the stairs."

John placed the glass on the side table, holding the stem between the thumb and forefinger of his right hand. They were running out of things to say.

They both watched him, inattentively, congenially.

"So, what do you think?" asked Pedro as he got up to leave.

"You'll have to excuse me," replied John. "It's all a bit too much to take in right now."

Pedro's eyes slid to the clock. "Look, let's meet tomorrow," he suggested. "This is my address."

He handed John a card before heading for the door. Turning the brass handle, he shouted back at John over his shoulder, "See you tomorrow. About 11 a.m."

Ten minutes later, John's taxi arrived, and he stood up to leave, a little wobbly from the sake. Pedro had been right.

"See you soon," said Drinda. "Don't leave it so long next time, John."

"Bye," he managed, as he swayed out of the apartment.

Once he was back at his new place, he went into the kitchen, tossed his wallet and wilted dollars on the coffee table, then crumpled a series of credit card receipts and threw them in the trash. He couldn't sleep; instead, he dropped into a chair to think. He was toying with the idea of meeting Pedro again.

"It still could be some kind of trick," he said out loud to himself, making him jump. The sake had really got to him. However, his curiosity got the better of him and he decided he would meet him. What did he have to lose?

By now, John was more than a little intrigued, and while every instinct told him not to go, he ignored his inner voice.

The following morning, John shot a quick look at his watch and winced. He gently pulled the door closed behind him, leaving early as he still didn't know his way around the city very well.

He walked down Pacific Heights, and then found himself strolling down Pier 39, next to Fisherman's Wharf, with its shops and seafood restaurants. He stopped at the shop to buy a newspaper and a coffee, furtively glancing at the attractive woman behind the counter. Instead of responding, she just stared at him with a curious expression on her face. Though young and still pretty, the woman seemed despondent, as if her life somehow lacked the magic she had expected. Everyone looked disgruntled, as people always do at 10.30 in the morning, hurrying along with heads bent, full of domestic cares and worries.

Pedro's office was above a Chinese supermarket at the top of the hill in Chinatown.

As he walked along the street, John wondered if it was safe – he thought it looked strange to see a Westerner walking through Chinatown.

When he reached the entrance to Pedro's office, he could just barely make out the sign on the door. In the entryway of the shop next door, a man was huddled under a few blankets, his hair wet with sweat.

"The fuck you want?" the man asked. He was emaciated; his face thin, his hair tangled to his shoulders.

John gave him a lopsided grin and flipped a dollar onto his chest.

The man gave a toothless smile. "Thanks, man."

John peered into the gloomy window. The place looked empty. Even so, he pushed open the door and went up the narrow staircase, covering his nose with his hand – the place had an unpleasant smell. It had clearly been painted the same cream color over and over again to cover up the scuff marks from furniture, luggage, dust bins and whatever else people had hauled in and out of the service door.

His rubber-soled shoes made no sound as he walked towards the hall, and due to the lack of light he couldn't see where he was going. At the top of the stairs and along a short corridor was a metal door which had a small box attached to it. Connected to that was a bell, which John pressed. He could just make out the spy hole in the door. The door opened.

"Nice to see you, John," said Pedro. "Please come in."

John apologized for being late, but after a few minutes talking with Pedro, he started to relax; he could now see a different person to the one he'd first seen back on the ship.

Pedro was extremely suave, and he seemed to have all the credentials; he looked kind of world-weary and was very pleasant and soft-spoken. He went on to tell John that his profession, like older ones, had its own rigid entrance requirements and, like others, required proficiency and offered areas of intense specialization. People worked at it until they were numb because they loved it, and because the rewards were those of professional accomplishment.

"John, intelligence today is not merely a profession. But, like most professions, it has taken on the aspects of a discipline. It has a recognized methodology; it has developed a vocabulary; it has developed a body of theory and doctrine; it has elaborated and refined techniques."

The phone rang, and Pedro answered it without a word to John. He sank down onto his couch, talking to the person on the other end.

"It's impressive," he said into the phone, "how expertly you fucked this one up, and in record time." His voice, with only a trace of a Latin American accent, had a hard edge to it. "Listen carefully – as far as I'm concerned, there is no such thing as no." He slammed down the phone. "Sorry, John," he said, smiling. "Look, I'll show you some stuff in a sec."

John stared wide-eyed at the wall for a moment, deep in thought. "But who are you? What side are you really on?" he asked eventually.

"You have to trust me," Pedro said, though John wasn't sure at all if he did.

For one thing, Pedro was very careful with his answers. For most people, it would have been a fairly easy question to answer. For Pedro, however, his life had become far more complicated. He had so many different identities he could use.

"The type of work we do is very detailed," he said curtly, clearly anxious to move on.

"What do you mean?" asked John, not wanting to let it go.

"It requires a certain way of doing things. But don't worry; it will come to you as we go along. If you're ever alone, the best way to protect yourself is not to sit around and answer questions. You need to turn the tables and be the one who is asking the questions."

Pedro went on to explain how the work was bespoke and, for most of the time, there would be no record of what they did.

"We only have one hit," he carried on. "If we don't succeed, we don't continue any more. If anything happens to any of us, we cannot help each other – or, at least, we cannot be seen to help."

After pressing him for more details, John asked Pedro how all of this could happen. "It can't be that simple," he said. "What you say, it isn't done these days."

"Well, I did it. And I'm good at it," replied Pedro with a smug smile.

"Okay, I understand," said John. "But what if we really need help?"

"Don't worry, I will find you if you need help."

There was a small safe attached to the desk, which Pedro opened, taking out a blue metal tin from which he pulled out a bundle of cash. He counted out the fifties, one by one. Fifty, one hundred, one hundred and fifty, and so on. He handed John an advance of $300.

"This is for you. But remember – we are only paid for performance and I expect full cooperation from you at all times."

"Do you need me to sign something for the money?" asked John.

"No," said Pedro. "All you need to do for me is to be loyal. That's all I ask."

They talked some more, and John was pleased to find that Pedro was frank and straightforward now. It seemed that he'd developed an inability to demonstrate any negative emotions, but there were plenty of positive ones; he told John some stories of his profession with pride, for he considered it an art.

After a while, John became curious enough – and brave enough – to ask him whether he'd ever killed anyone.

"Well, I'm not going to lie to you, John. There's a risk to this. People do get hurt. I've seen it done so many times. A dossier would be put together, a price would be determined, and then the right man for the job found. But that type of stuff is usually handled by outside contractors."

John nodded. He was beginning to take to him, something he never would have imagined would happen.

"We need guys who are willing to bend the rules..." continued Pedro. "Guys who will do certain things that your average mentally stable individual would never consider."

He showed John his gun and said he would have to feel comfortable with holding one. "It's a weighty thing, and it has to feel right in the hand. It took me a few weeks to find the right one, but to be honest, I don't really carry it."

Pedro told John that he had access to virtually any gun he wanted. In general, though, he found them to be a pain in the butt; they were bulky, and they made his suits look lopsided. He spent a lot on his suits and it wouldn't do to have them look off. He was a man of style. John liked that about him.

Pedro's training had covered the nasty hazards of his business, including how to stay alive should he fall victim to a gunshot, or a variety of other attacks that were meant to kill him. Now, more than ever, he understood why they'd trained him to shoot with both hands, and while Pedro was a lefty with a natural eye, it had taken a good deal of work to get his right hand up to snuff.

"You can trust me," said Pedro, staring at John levelly. "But you can't trust anyone else."

John thought about this for a moment, before replying with, "I wouldn't have come here today if I'd never trusted people."

Pedro smirked, continuing to stare at John in that calm way of his. He was very clearly a professional; John knew straight off that he was way ahead of him. It was also obvious that Pedro had been trained to think ahead, and to always cover the gamut of possibilities in any one situation.

"Your job may require long periods of sitting and watching while trying to act as if you aren't watching," he said after a while, breaking the silence.

"Does that mean I'll become the worthless sort of man who hangs out at cafés for long hours?" replied John with a smirk. "Drinking and working on crossword puzzles, and reading important-looking books."

"If you want to fit in, if you want to pass the time without looking like a private eye, or a policeman, you have to look busy," said Pedro, nodding.

"So, would my look be okay?"

John hadn't shaved for a few days and his face was covered with thick black stubble. Pedro thought that might help.

"We could assume you had adopted some kind of disguise," Pedro smiled. "Look, John, here's the bottom line. I'm easy to deal with, as long as you don't try to fuck with me."

John leant on the table and looked directly into Pedro's eyes.

"This is serious business," he said.

"And it's best to know right now where we stand," replied Pedro.

"That's fine," John said.

Pedro suggested they take a walk, as there was a problem with sewers in the building, hence the smell. As they walked down the stairs, the stench made John want to gag.

Pedro screwed up his face. "Let's just get out of here and grab a glass of wine," he suggested.

"That sounds good. I can barely stand the smell myself," John replied, grateful. He hadn't eaten and his stomach was seriously protesting at the lack of food. Maybe they could grab a bite as well as the wine.

Chapter 9

It was a bright, crisp afternoon and the sidewalk was heavy with a blend of locals and tourists. The Americans were easily identified by their girth, their bulky clothes, fanny, back, or otherwise. Europeans were a little more difficult to pick out, but they all shared the same interest: eating.

Pedro took him to a high-end restaurant for lunch. The waiter raced forward but John got there first, sliding out the chair from underneath the table and sitting down. After glancing only briefly at the wine list, Pedro chose the Chateau Cissac 1978.

The waiter wheeled a trolley around the room displaying cuts of meat, and when he stopped at their table, John chose the two fat entrecôte steaks. Pedro actually cracked a smile and then wiped it away with a grimace as he tasted the wine. He gave the waiter a sideways glance as he set the glass down. The waiter arrived with a fresh glass and a new bottle. He poured a little for Pedro to taste. After it was approved, he poured more into the glass, set the bottle down, and retreated.

"It's something I enjoy, eating fine food while working undercover," Pedro said. "Over the years, I've spent many hours sitting in restaurants. I know I'm good at it, that's why I still do it."

"I think that you still being alive is proof that you're good at it."

"Okay," Pedro said, sounding more serious now. "I need an honest answer from you. I need a verbal commitment. You need to look me in the eye and swear that you are going to answer this question honestly."

John hated being penned in like that, but he didn't have much choice. "Fine."

"I won't bullshit you, John. Ask away and I'll always tell you the truth. But first, are you in? All I ask, John," he continued, "is that if our relationship is going to work, I need you to understand certain things. When I tell you I want something to happen immediately, it needs to happen."

"I understand."

The dark red liquid that he swirled around in his glass was helping him to focus, and he looked at John with his deep, sharp eyes. "Listen, John. I'm very busy and I don't always have time for the smaller cases. I've got a lot of jobs I'm trying to tie up right now. That's why I need help."

All of a sudden – and after only two big gulps of wine – Pedro called the waiter over and asked for the check. "We gotta go, let's move. Come on," he spoke so quickly that the words tripped off his tongue as one. They both stood, and Pedro dropped a fifty dollar note on the table. The waiter eyed him and held open the door.

They walked out of the building, Pedro murmuring something about the quality of the wine as a reason for why they'd left so abruptly.

They continued walking, their faces stunned by the sudden chill. John still hadn't got used to the fact that even after a hot, sunny day in San Francisco, temperatures could suddenly drop once the fog rolled in. Pedro suggested they go for a drive, and John nodded towards Pedro's '76 Ford. They slid into the leather seats and drove back to town. John was deep in thought, taking mental notes; he was also trying to decipher a sheet of paper that had fallen on the floor. What the hell does that say? Is it a ten?

"John, there's a really nice bar which I go to occasionally. I sometimes bring my newspaper and sit and have a glass or two."

They stopped and parked the car. Pedro swung open the bar door and they walked in. It was a noisy place, but it had a great feel to it. There was a line of men sitting at the bar, all eyes aimed at their drinks, shoulders tense. A lethal-looking bottle of pure vodka caught John's eye. He saw a clump of men in the corner drinking and playing cards. He nudged his way through to the bar, hoping to get a shot. Pedro stared at him, opening his eyes wide. He flicked his fingers to get his attention.

"John, do you know that I really enjoy good wine and I consider myself a wine expert? It's an interesting fact, isn't it, John? Ask a dozen winemakers how they know their grapes are ripe enough to harvest and chances are you'll get a dozen different answers. Try this glass of wine – it's a Chardonnay." John hadn't even noticed him order it.

Pedro scanned his face as John's left eyelid drooped slightly. "I must admit, I really am a vodka drinker." Though it never mattered to John if he drank fancy wines, as long as they were cold he didn't care. He just needed to hear the clink of glasses. However, John got the impression that Pedro had another reason for stopping here; his eyes were everywhere, darting from one group of men to another. Apart from the regular glances he gave John, he kept checking the door as though he was expecting someone.

One guy walked in with a cigarette dangling from his lips. The man loitered for a moment before exchanging glances with Pedro and giving him a knowing nod. He looked Latin American.

"Please excuse me, John," said Pedro. "There's someone I know. I just want to say hi." John wasn't sure why, but Pedro's words sent a shiver down his spine; his tone had been more than a little off.

The guy had a small briefcase which he left on the floor next to him. He showed very little emotion. The body language of both men told John they didn't seem to know each other. The guy was tapping his hand against his leg while he was talking to Pedro. They stood with their shoulders hunched, their faces towards each other. The guy looked impatient, as if he was in a hurry. They talked for a moment and the guy then turned around.

"I know," he said with an easy smile.

"It's been a long time," Pedro responded. "Your reputation was far beyond mine back then."

A few minutes later, the man pushed away from the corner of the bar and headed towards the door; he slid out but left his briefcase behind. Pedro remained tight-lipped as he looked around suspiciously, and, as he picked up the briefcase from the floor, he turned his back to John as if he was trying to hide something. He shrugged indifferently.

"My friend has forgotten his case," he said.

Sure, John thought to himself as he stared at him, waiting for the info.

John noticed that the case was made of brown leather, and it featured a metal badge on it with the letter T engraved onto the metal. A few moments later, two police officers came into the bar.

"Not to worry," said Pedro calmly. "They're just checking out the bar."

John, however, overheard the officers questioning a couple of guys, asking if they had seen a tall, dark male in a black leather jacket and blue trousers. The description definitely sounded like the person Pedro had been talking to just moments earlier. After a few more questions, the police left. Pedro was quite cool and calm and did not seem at all disturbed by the police asking questions.

Suddenly, quarrelling seemed to break out amongst the men in the bar, as if they were continuing with some argument.

"I think we should be on our way now," said Pedro, suddenly sounding anxious. "Drink up." He glanced at his watch and set the half-empty glass of wine back on the bar, leaving some money – including a generous tip – under the glass. John swallowed the last drop.

Outside, Pedro started his car and cranked up the heater while John dropped his head back onto the headrest and groaned. He wanted to ask, What the hell was that all about? but he stopped himself.

They drove on for a while. It was a rainy day and they were getting low on gas. "Let's stop here," said Pedro. While he was filling the car with gas, John noticed in the wing mirror the man he'd seen at the bar earlier. He had a feeling that the man was following them. John thought he should keep it to himself and just see what happened; he knew he was dealing with a meticulous and observant personality. They parked the car outside Pedro's office, and he suggested they should meet up again tomorrow.

"By the way, I keep meaning to ask you. Why me?" John was fidgeting from one foot to the other, feeling uneasy. He wondered how on earth he would be able to do this. Maybe he should just stop now and move on.

"John," Pedro replied, "you are a very observant person, and quick to notice things. We like that." This compliment made John feel good. Pedro really knew what to say and when it mattered. "We first noticed the suspicion you showed on the ship," continued Pedro. "There aren't many who would have guessed what you did."

"To be honest, I don't intend to stay here for too long."

"That's okay," Pedro said. "One day, I will come to London to see you. I need to go now – I have some reports I need to write up. Goodnight." As Pedro turned and left, John crossed the road and went into a coffee shop, choosing a seat at a table from where he had a good view of the entire length of the street. He could clearly see Pedro's office. A plump, amber-eyed waitress took his order, returning moments later with a black coffee.

He began hearing worried murmurs, upset-sounding exclamations and gentle reassurances from other people with their own problems. He felt a burst of anger inside him, making him wonder. He was just halfway through his coffee when he accidentally spilled a little on the table, and he flicked his fingers out as if he was trying to rid himself of something sticky. At that moment, the man who had been following them appeared. John could see him looking around the outside of Pedro's office, and then he went inside.

John waited, eventually checking his Timex: the man had gone through the door nearly fifteen minutes ago. Finally, he saw some movement and the man came out with a small paper parcel under his arm. Even in the light of the hazy street lamps, he was easy to make out. This really got John thinking. He thought back to when he was in the bar – had he witnessed a drop off? Or was it something more sinister? Things settled into a slow pattern as John slowly realized what had just happened.

As he was about to jump onto the moving tram to take him home, he noticed another person enter the building. A tall, dark-haired woman.

***

The next day was another crisp, bright sunny morning, but John was feeling a surge of angst. He thought about the night before. What a fucking day that had been! He went down to the North Park and, standing in the middle of the piazza, he gazed up at the pale blue sky while he pondered on the wisdom of what he was getting involved in. He'd dropped about ten pounds in the last week and had got a new haircut in an effort to feel good. He had tried all night to find an alternative explanation for what he was doing, but had come up with nothing. Well, not exactly nothing; for a while, John had toyed with the notion of catching the next flight back to the UK, or maybe to one of those hot islands. He had hoped it would all turn out for the best, but now he wasn't so sure.

He was just about to call Pedro when he remembered he'd mentioned to John he was taking some time off with Annabel. He needed at least one day out of the month to step away from it all and try to gain some perspective.

Annabel was a refined woman who oozed confidence, and was older than the smooth-talking Pedro. They'd met a few years ago when Annabel was running around doing all kinds of bad things for the CIA. There were days when Pedro's job sucked, but this was not one of them. Tonight he seemed to be a happy man, which was hardly surprising: this woman was beautiful and classy, and he was proud to have her at his side. Her long, black, wavy hair was shorter than he remembered it, cut to just below the ears. A few wrinkles had appeared around the eyes and mouth, but in a strange way it made her look even sexier. That a woman could age so gracefully was something that turned Pedro on. Whether it was due to genetics or some daily regimen, he didn't care. The end result was all that interested him, and the end result was a gorgeous 45-year-old woman who had never tried to place any constraints on him. Annabel was a married woman now and they only met two or three times a year. For Pedro, it was just business and he was only focused on one thing: his cause. His love life would have to take second place.

Chapter 10

The next day, John didn't want to go in too early: someone might notice him hanging around. It was nine o' clock, and he was waiting in the parking lot, leaning against a car door with his eyes trained on the entrance to the office. John's only real worry at this point was whether anyone would show up. Pedro was not due in until later.

John opened the office door. The light blinked on and, taking a deep breath, he walked inside. He began pacing, his hands on his hips. Then, as quickly as he'd begun, he stopped. His senses were a little off-balance. A slowly rotating ceiling fan cast its shadows across dingy white walls, and his eyes drifted across the room to the big plate glass window framing the rear wall. After a moment or two he walked over to a small table in the far corner of the room, upon which sat a small box. Inside were a variety of transmitters, some as big as a pack of playing cards, others as small as a dollar. The reason why he carried them was that many of his subjects were under extreme pressure, the kind of pressure that could cause certain men to do stupid things. He could not help but notice a sheet of paper with a handwritten text in Spanish. He paused. It was a long pause that grew longer. With the morning already half gone, John decided to push the letter into his pocket.

Later that day, Pedro arrived. He unbuttoned his black jacket, took it off, and draped it over the back of the corner leather chair in his office, before lighting his cigarette and popping his head round the doorway. He told John he didn't want to be disturbed.

Over the plastic pitter-patter of John's computed keystrokes, he heard a phone receiver slam into its cradle. He stopped typing and strained to listen. Pedro called out to John. He knew he was in trouble. "Can you come here?" Pedro barked, pointing at the uncomfortable chair. "Sit!" John did so without hesitation. Pedro grabbed a small stool by the wall and dragged it over, placing it in front of John.

"Have you taken any papers from my desk?"

"No," said John, but he knew Pedro didn't believe him: he was eyeing him with what could only be suspicion. He was very quick to blame, and did so without evidence. It was amazing how he'd eliminated any other options. John flashed him a smile and told him that the many long years of his pouring over paper files had probably made him forgetful. A touch of anger crept into Pedro's voice. "You seem to be confused about something, John. I'm your boss. I'm your superior. I'm the one who gives the orders."

John wondered what he had stumbled onto. His mind was racing. This might be an opportunity to get a better insight into Pedro's state of mind, he thought, if he kept pushing for answers. He then realized that Pedro was ahead of the game. Way ahead. In retrospect, John believed he had wanted him to see the document. If he had known the devastating impact it was going to have on his life, John would have left the damned thing there.

"John, let's stop wasting each other's time," Pedro said, without turning to look. John just smiled and gave a nod. Pedro was excellent at reading people.

It was Friday afternoon and it had been a long week; he just wanted to get on with things. Reaching into his back pocket, he pulled out an envelope which he then handed over to John. It contained three $100 bills, which he said took care of business for the last week. John got the feeling that he was keen for him to stay interested. John considered this for a moment, though. He wasn't sure how precarious things had become. He wanted some separation in case luck turned against him. What worried him more was the thought that he could be hauled off to jail if all this should go wrong.

"Look, John, so far we've made a deal that you will do things my way, and I expect you to honor our deal." Pedro softened his hard stare. "I'm someone who can make you a lot of money. All I need to know is, are you in or are you out?"

They were both quiet as the tension began to build around them – a tension that John didn't like at all. All things considered, this was not an ideal partnership, or whatever it may become.

"So, what's your answer?"
John didn't reply right away. He thought about it carefully; he wasn't really sure why Pedro was keen for him to be a part of his operation, or what role he wanted him to play. John regarded Pedro for a long moment before nodding. A twinge of pain came with the question and John couldn't help but think of how he'd pictured this conversation going a few days before.

"Fine," he replied. "I'm in. But I'm warning you – don't mess me around, and don't make me do anything I'm not happy doing." John started to think about the last few days then, and he simply had to ask the question.

"It wasn't a coincidence, was it? That guy showing up at the bar the other day."

"Here we go." Pedro rolled his eyes, but the corners of his mouth twitched in amusement.

"Okay. What was in the briefcase?"

Again, Pedro refused to answer. They both went quiet for a moment.

Pedro could never share everything, but maybe he could just give him enough. He was the first to break the ice. "Look, John, there are things that I can't tell you and this is one of them." Pedro reached behind him for his wallet. "Considering the trouble I'm causing you by dragging you into my chaos..."

John waved away the offer. "No, seriously. You don't have to do that."

They both agreed to meet later at Drinda's apartment and have a few drinks, and a few minutes later, John's cab arrived. As soon as he entered his apartment, he mixed himself two stiff drinks, which he drank as he watched TV, waiting until it was time. He dozed fitfully for a while, constantly going over what he had discovered in his mind.

Checking his Timex, he realized he was running late, and he telephoned Pedro to say that he was on his way.

When he arrived at the apartment, Pedro offered him a drink and told him to sit down. He didn't seem too concerned.

"Right."

"John, you have no idea what kind of paperwork and red tape you have to go through just to follow up these reports. Do you know there are a lot of people in this town who are jealous of me?" he asked. "Because unlike others, I never underestimate my enemies."

"I understand." John started to feel like he was being tested. Pedro brought out two more lowballs, tossed in a few ice cubes, and filled them to the rim with vodka. Although he liked it before, John was definitely beginning to get the taste for vodka, as he was drinking so much of it – some days, a bottle a night. Just then, Drinda phoned. She was on her way. She liked the sound of a few drinks.

Later that night, he dragged himself up from the armchair he'd collapsed in; he must have fallen asleep after one too many vodkas. His stomach was aching, his head spinning. Basically, he felt like shit. It took five minutes to raise himself from the chair and cross the hall to the bathroom, and then he stared at himself in the mirror over the sink. He looked as bad as he felt. Cupping his hands beneath the cold running water, he rinsed out his mouth and then washed his face.

He was disturbed by the memory of a conversation that Pedro had had with Drinda earlier. He'd overheard Pedro saying that he knew John had stolen the identity of a person he'd been working with on the ship. The name of the person was Tony. Pedro then went on to say that John would do what they wanted him to do.

Then the tone of the conversation changed.

"I'm not sure how to put this," he'd heard Pedro say, "so I'm just going to come out and say it. Is there something between you and John you haven't told me about?" Pedro stared while waiting for an answer.

"Alright, okay ..." Drinda seemed not to have taken in anything that Pedro had said. Her face went blank and it took a few seconds, but he sensed the exact moment when the pin dropped. She shifted until she was facing him, one leg curled up beneath her on the sofa.

"I'm sorry, but haven't you listened to anything I've said about him?" he asked impatiently.

"Shit. What are you talking about? I was answering your question," she murmured. "I've listened to everything, but you've given me too much to think about." She got up and walked into the kitchen to get a glass of water. "Just trust me." She knew what Pedro was getting at.

"You've fallen for him, haven't you?"

The look she gave him grudgingly confirmed that she had, but her mouth said otherwise. "What are you talking about?" she said in a disbelieving tone, following him outside.

"Drinda! Take it easy. I'm not saying anything. Sorry, I shouldn't have teased you."

She ignored his apology, too distracted by the multitude of thoughts running through her mind. She walked over to the window, wiping her tears away and trying to pull herself together. Drinda liked John, and beneath her embarrassment, she was scared of what Pedro would think.

"Stop playing fucking games. You're acting like a prick," she said with a full-on scowl. "You and I both know there's no love lost between John and me, but what you're doing is messing with his mind. Take away all this craziness and he's a really nice guy. Down to earth."

She jumped up and darted aimlessly about the tiny room, changing directions every few steps. She was right about one thing: he certainly didn't want to spend the next few days feeling miserable.

"I didn't make him any promises," Pedro mumbled.

"Oh, he's well aware of that," she replied. "He saw us both on the ship together. He's not stupid. Look, I didn't sleep with him. I guess I just wanted to reach out to someone who sort of knew what I might be feeling."

Pedro turned his back stubbornly. "And sure, I'll be totally mortified if we all can't get on."

"I'm not talking about this anymore."

He said they would talk later. He had a meeting with the CIA – they wanted to talk to him about the Wilkinson trail. He paused to take a deep breath and his earnest expression softened.

"Okay. See you shortly." She smiled approvingly and waved him off.

John was feeling a little worried after overhearing their conversation and decided he should be more careful. In fact, maybe he should just quit right now. This can't be happening, he thought. And what the hell was this? His curiosity… or sudden obsession… or whatever was going on here. He felt an overwhelming urge to march back into the room and force them to tell him what the hell was going on. He frowned and rubbed his hands over his face, knowing that he had to get a move on. He pulled the curtain over the bath and had a lukewarm shower, then pulled on his jeans and a denim shirt. He went over to the kitchen door and stuck his head in.

For a while, John just stood there, his arms folded across his chest. He was about to say something, but he stopped himself. He was infuriated, and he didn't know what to do with himself; he unfolded his arms, dragged his fingers through his hair, folded them again. He made a valiant effort to box the thought back up, but it wasn't budging. What if – okay – what if, maybe, it's all a trick?

He tried his best to look uncomfortable after what he heard. He stared at his own shoes for a moment and then at her. When he thought the proper amount of embarrassment had been conveyed, he looked her straight in the eyes and smiled. She blushed back.

Drinda was putting on her make-up, including a really deep red lipstick, and when she blushed it was almost the same color as her lips.

John decided he needed a drink, so he poured two large brandies and placed them on the living room table. She plopped down in one chair and he took the other. She had been thinking about how much she should tell him. They both sat motionless for a few moments, then John reached out and downed his drink in one go. She took a sip and shook her head. She was a little dizzy and had tears in her eyes.

"Why are you crying?" he asked, intrigued despite himself.

"John, you are just a nice guy. There are lots of things I would love to tell you, but you know I can't."

Emotion was playing in her eyes as she sat there, idly scratching the side of her face with her long fingernails. He asked her what she had meant by her comment.

"What things would you love to tell me?" He looked her straight in the eye, so that she could see he was sincere. The thing with Drinda was that he never could tell if she was going to slap him or let him kiss her – he kind of liked that unpredictability. John wiped her eyes.

She was clearly annoyed with herself for letting the words come out before considering the consequences, and her face turned pale as she tried to change the subject. Taking a tube of hand cream from her bag, she squeezed it, and began to slowly massage the cream into her fingers. "You know," she said, "I can't remember now. I think it's just too much brandy. Gone to my head."

She stood, then slumped herself down on the beige sofa, suddenly realizing that she was actually drunk. She leant forward, slapped her hands on her knees and cackled. "There!" Then she

Page 119

started to cry again and began to tell him about her boyfriend, who'd been murdered.

"He only got what he deserved," she sobbed. "That bastard wrecked my life. I hate it. I hate it," she said. "Sometimes I can't get it out of my mind. I used to believe love could fix damn near anything – love and brandy, that is. I just need larger doses of both of them."

John put his arm around her. "It's all over now," he told her. "You have to get over it and keep focused." He poured her a small brandy. She looked down, swirling the brandy around the glass. Then she sat up straight and composed herself, gently squeezing his hand. She was trying as hard as she could to stay calm, but it wasn't easy. A crazy mixture of dread and elation was flooding through her body.

"Listen," he said. "I know last year has sucked for you and I know how hard it is to get back to normal, but you can't just give up." More tears fell. "It doesn't have to be that way."

As they were both tired, they decided to call it a day, and John made himself comfortable on the sofa. He found it difficult to sleep as so much was going through his mind, but eventually, he nodded off.

In the morning, he met Drinda coming out of her bedroom, still fully-dressed.

"What the heck?" she mumbled, rubbing her temples with both hands as it all started coming back to her. She shook her head, and in a voice filled with desperation said, "This just keeps getting worse."

"Take it easy," he told her.

"I'm sorry," she replied. "I just need a drink to calm me down. Actually, I don't normally drink this much. You sure everything's cool? What did I say last night?"
John blushed and his eyes darted away. "Yeah…" he sighed.

"Listen, I'm not sure what you might've heard…" she said.

Page 120

He quickly thought about his answer. "I didn't hear anything," he reassured her. "Although… are you sure Pedro wasn't telling you to stay away from me?" he asked.

"No, no. That's not it," she rasped. "He's just been keeping an eye on me after what happened. He's my friend, like you're my friend."

He bit himself on the side of his cheek to keep himself in check. Who knew what would come out his mouth if he opened it now?

Drinda swiveled around, the blood draining from her face as she looked at him. He knew, yes, but he wasn't going to let on. He noticed how upset she was and grabbed her shoulder for a quick squeeze.

"Oh, that makes me feel much better," she said. John blinked, wanting to believe it, but he was seeing way too many holes in her story, way too many potential lies.

The trust was now gone.

* * *

Realizing that he'd left his keys in the office, John went back there; he knew that Pedro was away at some meeting in a hotel, so he knew he wouldn't be running into him.

As soon as he arrived, John noticed that something was wrong: papers had been moved and drawers had been opened, but there was no sign of forced entry. It just seemed odd. John phoned Pedro, who was held up in the hotel and being scrutinised by the CIA. After what seemed like an eternity, he phoned him back.

"I think we're getting too close on the Wilkinson trial," Pedro said.

"What shall I do?" asked John.

Initially, Pedro hadn't thought that the case had anything to do with this break-in. But he was wrong: it had everything to do with it.

After some more searching, John noticed the Wilkinson file had gone. He was still worried. They must have had a key.

"It's unbelievable. I don't get it. If I didn't know any better I'd say it was a set-up." His words tumbled over each other; he knew it wasn't making any sense. John shook his head.

"You need to change the locks," said Pedro. "I'll see you later in the red bar."

"Y-yeah. No problem," John answered, trying to hide his irritation.

The line went dead. John stared at the phone for a second, every instinct telling him there was more to all of this. Why couldn't people leave well enough alone? He had to tread very carefully here. He wondered if it had been the CIA, but he couldn't reveal that until he had some solid evidence – if this investigation turned out the way he feared it would.

He took a deep breath to steady himself and to get the sudden tumult of questions in his head in order. Why would someone need these papers? And why make it look like an inside job? John agreed and disagreed at the same time. Why would it matter, though?

"I don't know," he said out loud to himself, while pondering what to do next. But there were always orders to follow, and Pedro had made his intentions clear: he needed to change the locks.

That night, after securing the new locks on the door, John had a quick rummage through the file cabinets, looking for some – any – background information. He was wondering if there was anything to what Pedro was telling him. So far, not much. He didn't like where this was headed, and he hoped there weren't any surprises in store.

On the way home he stopped at the red bar, and after two big mouthfuls of wine, he called the waiter over and asked for a cold, neat vodka. He took a big gulp. He was trying to sort through the different possibilities so he could put this thing out of his mind when just then, Pedro walked into the bar. John stood and held up his glass as a salute.

"Sit," Pedro commanded. He flagged down a waiter and asked for a glass of white and a full bottle to follow. He fumbled in his shirt pocket and retrieved a three quarters empty pack of cigarettes, then paused as he tapped one out.

"I get the feeling you have some things you'd like to discuss," said John.

"John, men like us can always find something useful to talk about," replied Pedro, staring at his cigarette instead of at John.

"I'm sure that's true, but I know you're not telling me everything. There's more to this Wilkinson thing than you're letting on." He let the words hang in the air, willing Pedro to fill the silence.

After a while, Pedro just shrugged as if to say "guilty as charged."

"Listen, John," continued Pedro, "we are going to have to be careful. Someone doesn't want this Wilkinson thing to go to trial." He started sorting through the possibilities, quickly realizing that it wasn't what, but who.

John slowly turned his head to say something.

"Shut up," snapped Pedro. "I'm thinking ... It has to be someone high up. Perhaps another intelligence agency is involved."

"What makes you think that?" asked John, intrigued but annoyed at how Pedro was talking to him. It made him feel so inferior.

"Too many questions from the department. And isn't it a coincidence that the file has gone missing?"

While he was talking, Pedro had been keeping an eye on his car through the window, and he now angled his chair to the right so he could see down the length of the street.

"How do you know these people won't just show up at our apartments?" asked John, watching Pedro look out the window.

Pedro swirled the wine around in his glass and said, "Trust me, it's a little bit more complicated than that. They have what they want. Maybe we have to let this one go."

Pedro sighed angrily; he had more important things on his mind than to worry about this. He'd been waiting for years for someone like John to come along and he sure as hell wasn't going to change his plan now. He stood and stabbed out his cigarette in the foil ashtray, then neatly folded his newspaper and left it on the table top with his empty glass and a five-dollars tip under the glass. Watching him do his usual paying routine, John suddenly realized they were spending far more time in the bar than they needed to; it was becoming a bad habit, especially as Pedro hardly ever finished the drinks he ordered. He didn't stay in one place long enough.

Pedro started walking off. "John, I'll see you tomorrow."

It was late, so John called a cab to take him home. He didn't want to be anywhere else right now.

Chapter 11

John wanted to throw open one of the windows and suck in a deep breath of cold, fresh air, but he knew he couldn't; the recent break-in had prompted Pedro to fit locks on all the windows, and now it was stuffy and uncomfortable. In the corner of the office room, John could see him sitting in an armchair reading.

Pedro looked up and smiled, then shut the file. He reminded himself that it was time to move on to the next phase of the operation, so leaning forward in a businesslike manner, he cleared his throat, as if preparing to deliver a well-rehearsed speech.

"It's that Wilkinson case. It won't go away. I just heard that a man who goes by the name of Rimier intends to trade information."

"About what?"

"The truth about the Wilkinson trial."

John, who was more focused now, was making copious notes. Pedro reached into his jacket pocket and withdrew a cassette tape, which he passed over to John.

"When you get a moment, have a listen. We don't know what Rimier looks like, but we know what he sounds like. We also know that he is a tall person: about six foot four and built like a bull, right down to his big, rounded, heavy-rimmed glasses and doughy complexion. But that's all we know. Listen, I need you to watch their office."

"What I am looking for?"

"Anything strange. Look, you have to be well prepared for tomorrow's operation; it's important you follow Rimier. We need that package; those papers are important."

Pedro gave him a little smile, then handed him a scrap of paper with the address of the office in Parks Street. He went over everything with John and answered his questions as patiently as he could, of which he had many.

Eventually, it was time to get down to business. "Here's what I want you to do. There's an alley about a hundred feet ahead, on your right as you step out of here. Take it and stop at the third door on your left. Open the door and head all the way down the hallway, last door on your right. It should be unlocked. I just want you to check that it is unlocked."

"Why?"

Pedro cleared his throat before speaking again. "I'll put a man in there. The window overlooks the courtyard – it's a perfect viewpoint."

John shot him a suspicious look but nodded, eager to show he was going along with it.

Pedro pushed his chair back a few inches. He sensed uncertainty. "Just do what I say. Are you in?"

John was in, even though he never answered. Pedro lit a cigarette, then uttered a small but heartfelt, "Are you?"

"Yeah, yeah," John said, scratching his moustache.

"Okay."

Pedro picked up the ice bucket that he always kept on a small side table, went out, and was back in a minute with a fresh batch of ice cubes.

"Got some white rum," Pedro said. "I've been drinking nothing but the stuff –apart from wine, of course – and it's good, but it ain't vodka."

"Alright," said John.

Pedro found two glasses, scooped some ice into them, and poured two large shots, holding both glasses in one hand and his cigarette in the other. Putting his cigarette between his lips, he held out one of the glasses towards John. "Cheers."

As he spoke, smoke came out of his nose and mouth. They downed the shots, then he checked his watch, looked at John, and nodded. "Back to business."

He pulled out two relatively small devices from his pocket. He handed one to John and kept the other.

"These are the latest in microphone technology. As soon as you know something, I want to know."

***

If he'd had a brain in his head, he'd have used the cover of the darkness to scoot out of there, but every time he'd flexed his legs to move, he'd talked himself out of it.

Using his left hand, John turned up the collar of his jacket and stepped out. He walked with a moderate pace – purposefully, but not frightened – and he checked often to make sure no one was following him.

After a few moments of silence, a noise from down the block froze John in his tracks. Logic said it was impossible that he'd been followed – he'd been careful – but still he paused, his ears straining for any hint of pursuit. Nothing. It was all in his imagination.

Pulling himself together, he located the building and went inside. Quietly, he walked down the hallway until he found himself in front of the door. A few seconds passed. He slowly turned the knob and slid through the door without making a sound. He was in.

His job was pretty simple, with one primary directive: scan the room, nothing else. Even though he wasn't certain why or what he was looking for, he had done exactly what he was told to do. Silently, he closed the door and walked back down the hallway, quickly slipping out before anyone could see him.

As arranged, the next day, his checklist complete, John moved down the sidewalk towards Park Avenue at a casual pace. As he turned the corner onto the busy street that fronted the office block, he caught a glimpse of a tall dark man walking towards their office. A speeding car almost collided with him, but the man dodged out of the way just in time.

Pedro had told John to call him if he saw anyone trying to enter or leave the building. He then saw someone who looked like Rimier walk past the window, and, seconds later, a man emerged carrying a suitcase. Another man was standing in the courtyard of one of the larger buildings in the block. His left leg was straight and firmly planted on the pavement and the other was bent up behind him and placed against the side of the building. He looked casual, a little too casual. He wore blue jeans, was nearly bald, and was sweating profusely, his big frame resting against the building while he took a long drag of his cigarette.

"This is a go!" John barked into the microphone attached to his shirt collar, and from his vantage point he had a perfect view of the next few minutes of action.

"Looks like he's headed for the door," he said. "Yep, he's in the front hallway and headed straight for the door. What do you want me to do?"

"Sit tight." This was an opportunity Pedro couldn't pass up. If he did, he'd kick himself in the ass for it for the rest of his life.

"Repeat the last order," said John.

"I said sit tight," replied Pedro. "We don't want to spook him, just be ready to follow him."

John heard footsteps echoing down the block – two men moving quickly –and suddenly, police were everywhere. The men worked quickly and efficiently, as the sunlight was fading fast. The two men were seen exchanging their packages, unaware that any moment now, twenty or more agents were about to ruin their day. They looked particularly ghoulish, all wearing black bulletproof vests and Kevlar helmets, and each armed with a 9mm MP5 submachine gun.

"Freeze!" No shots had been fired, and the leader of the team ordered the men to lie on their stomachs. Officers dragged both men to their feet and into the awaiting police van.

John looked around him wildly; he'd found himself in the middle of an FBI sting operation.

Pedro broke from his cover, and John looked up at him. He seemed surprised. The plan had been to grab him when he was leaving. Pedro frowned at the officer in command: hard-faced Special Agent Luke Black.

Pedro stood there, anxiety nagging at him. "This is bullshit. Something is not right," he said. He ran his fingers through his black hair then pursed his lips, wondering what the hell was going on. He cursed under his breath. His nervous system began sending alarm signals to his brain, each one more frantic than the previous one.

"This is getting stupid," said Pedro. "We get close, then this happens. Someone just doesn't want justice."

They stood in silence for what seemed like an eternity, but that in reality was only a brief moment. By the look on Pedro's face, John could tell he was none too happy about what had just transpired. He looked on with irritation. To his right, he heard Pedro muttering to himself.

"What's just happened, shouldn't have," Pedro shook his head.

With obvious displeasure on his face, Pedro pushed his way past Agent Black and said something that sounded like, "You ass..."

Black shot him a look.

John held up his hands. "Commander... what he's trying to say is that it has been a very busy day."

John kept his eyes on Pedro as he called the deputy director of operations from a nearby phone booth. Over an unsecured line, it was impossible to give all the details of what had happened, but he got the gist. Pedro wanted to know what the hell was going on. John, who'd followed Pedro to the booth, wondered as well. Pedro shook his head vigorously.

"This is such a fucked-up mess," he whispered in a heated rush.

It had been a long day, and although he thought he had a fairly good idea of what had gone wrong, Pedro wanted answers.

"So, what did they say?"

"I asked him why he was interfering in my investigation," said Pedro. "He just said they had no idea. The police were handling the investigations and the deputy director isn't exactly known for his cooperation. He knew what was going on here, he just wasn't saying."

There was too much bad blood between the director and Pedro, and what the deputy director wanted, he almost always got; the deputy director had never trusted Pedro, not since something that had happened a long time ago. He should never have let it get this far. What he needed to show was that the deputy director had no place in this investigation. They were interfering and had to stop, as simple as that. It could start a turf battle and people might get pushed back. It was the kind of juicy governmental tidbit that the press would fall over themselves for. It was at times like these that Pedro Garcia wanted to throttle the deputy director for not being more cooperative. He'd never liked the man and he still couldn't bring himself to do so.

Exhausted, Pedro leant his head on top of the phone. He couldn't allow his personal bias to interfere. The phone rang, and after he answered, he listened intently and breathed a sigh of relief. The caller told him that the evidence was still at Rimier's office.

"So, what did the police recover?" asked John.

"Drugs."

John felt guilty for instantly doubting Pedro. Nothing was as it seemed. John didn't even consider that all of this could be a set-up. At that moment, he became aware of a man, looming two or three feet behind him. He was missing several teeth, his face covered in a patchy rash.

"It's okay," said Pedro.

The man held out his hand and said something in his gruff native Mexican tongue. Pedro didn't understand his dialect, but he didn't need to. They had an agreement and the man wanted to be paid. The dirty mutt handed Pedro the key for the safe, and as Pedro had already counted the money, he handed over two hundred dollars before turning to John.

"It's back on again. The package is in Rimier's safe." Pedro glanced quickly at his watch, then breathed a sigh of relief. "One step closer to wrapping this thing up." He shook his head as if he could still barely believe it. He told John he'd call him tomorrow.

John could tell by the wide-eyed expression on his face that the case was about to take another turn. He watched Pedro walk off. He seemed to pause and hover, as if he was considering turning back. Suddenly, he rushed off in a hurry.

The next day, Pedro's feet glided along the pavement as he marched back to Rimier's office. He had timed it in his head, and he knew he could be in and out in less than five minutes. He stopped at the payphone and called John, telling him to wait outside the back of the building by the window and that a parcel would be handed to him through it.

Pressing the phone to his ear, John thought Pedro sounded a little off. He sat up. "You alright? You sound weird." There was a sound like a throat clearing.

"I'm fine," replied Pedro. "Great. Yeah." John didn't buy it. "Don't worry," Pedro continued, "I'll make sure you're compensated. You get your head back in the game and get me what I need."

Pedro was so aware of John's every move, he was already sure of the outcome. There was no place for compassion or feelings; fulfilling his obligation was all that mattered now. Pedro had sworn an oath, and he would stick to that oath. He wouldn't allow anything or anyone to get in his way. He knew that if it was successful, he could finally relax.

"That's right, John," he continued. "Stay by the phone and await my next call." Pedro placed the phone back into the cradle and walked back to his car, reaching into his pocket and fishing out a pack of Marlboros. Turning away from the street and facing the blank façade of the building behind him, he flicked his lighter. After a deep pull of the cigarette he continued. Drinda was waiting inside the car, her eyes concealed by stylish, oversized Chanel sunglasses that nearly covered a third of her face. He climbed behind the wheel and turned round to look at her.

"Sorry I'm late." His voice was a deep basso, developed from years of smoking and drinking.

Drinda looked up. She took off her sunglasses and placed them in her purse before giving him an icy stare. After studying him for a moment she asked, "Why?"

"What does it matter? You know the plan. They will think he stole the papers, and he will run back to the UK. I will find him and he'll do exactly what he's told."

"What if it goes wrong? He could get killed." Her thin, pursed lips told Pedro she wasn't following his line of reasoning. She shook her head abruptly.

"You're overreacting, he won't hurt him, just rough him up a little."

She stared at him for a long moment. "I thought you said this was going to be easy."

"Don't... worry."

There were some very good reasons why Pedro had chosen John a few years ago in London. He was like a child who simply couldn't resist touching the paint when the sign clearly said: 'Wet paint. Do not touch.' Milan discovered he'd run off with some important documents, not once, but twice, and furthermore, he'd managed to sell them on the black market. Pedro knew that John couldn't resist an opportunity like this.

For Pedro, it was the biggest roll of the dice. Everything depended on it, and if it didn't go perfectly, his entire operation and everything he had risked would be for naught.

"I disabled the lock," he said. "Here's what I want you to do." He walked her through the next move, which was pretty easy. "It's not too late to back out."

Drinda didn't bother looking at him. "Let's just get it over and done with," she replied.

Pedro drove for a few minutes, maneuvering the car through the narrow streets, before applying the brakes so hard they screeched loudly. He parked the vehicle a block from the meeting place, then he and Drinda got out. He kissed her on the cheek.

"Are you ready?" he asked. She just headed off without a word.

Pedro watched her walk away and then found a phone booth. He'd previously timed how long it would take for her to get to the final meeting place. Pedro then called John and told him each turn he wanted him to make. His timing had been perfect. He flicked his cigarette into the gutter and watched it bob and swirl its way into the sewer. He felt not even the tiniest bit of remorse over what he had just set in motion.

"When you get there, there's an alley about a hundred feet ahead, on your right. Take it and stop at the second window."

By this time it was late and getting dark. The night was especially chilly, with a brisk wind blowing and whistling through the branches of the trees. Hidden in the darkness, bits of litter skittered across the roadside.

By now, John had arrived and Drinda was in position. A number of police were around, so he took his time and walked to the back of the building, where he waited like he'd been told.

The window opened and John could just make out the figure of a woman inside. She had very short, slightly curly hair, and she tried to pass the parcel out to him while trying to hide her face. John grabbed the parcel from her and, turning, began to walk away.

Suddenly, and without warning, John felt a sharp, piercing pain on the back of his head. While he didn't immediately realize what was happening, the force of the object on his skull forced his legs to collapse from under him, and he started falling to the ground.

As John fell, he pulled his attacker down with him and managed to get away. He could see the man had a knife, and in the following struggle he was cut in the back of his neck with a sharp object.

After a few more seconds of wrestling with the unknown assailant, he somehow managed to pull the knife from his assailant's hand before realizing that the knife had cut into the other person. John levered himself clumsily up onto one knee, and he could see that the man was writhing in pain. John got close to his face, and when he looked into his eyes, he saw genuine fear. After what seemed like an eternity but was probably only a few moments, the man stopped moving. John took a deep breath and stood up. He recognized the man: he looked like the Mexican.

John stuffed the package into his jacket and ran towards Main Street, but on noticing that the police were everywhere, he found refuge behind a large rubbish bin. He held his breath, concentrating, trying to figure out the noises. Someone was approaching. He must have crouched there, silently and shivering, for what seemed like hours. A trickle of sweat ran from his forehead and into one eye.

John suddenly felt that his time was up, that this was it. He was deeply upset about what was happening, not to mention confused – there were seemingly a million crazy thoughts going through his head. He slammed his hand against the wall in anger. The sirens were growing louder, and just then, a police car came skidding around the corner.

He was starting to lose a lot of blood from the cut on his neck, but at least he was still alive; he suspected that the other person was dead, as he never saw him come out of the side street. He told himself to snap out of it and calm down. He couldn't make himself think straight, and was barely able to breathe.

Realizing that his only chance was to wait until the police had gone, he checked again until the street was clear. When he heard nothing, he got to his feet, his jaw tightening as he inched forward. He tried to stop a taxi so he could get to hospital, but when the driver saw he was covered in blood, he drove away. John dragged the back of his sleeve across his eyes to wipe the blood from his face.

He kept on walking, desperate to get as far away from the area as possible. He was feeling very weak by now, but he managed to walk to a telephone box and call 911. Once the call was done, he waited by the roadside, willing them to hurry. It was all so hard to comprehend. He needed to get his head screwed on, but first, he needed some medical attention.

The pain in his neck was excruciating and he was starting to feel more than a little dizzy. He had to grab the edge of the post to keep himself from vomiting. His lungs tightened, and even though he was trying to maintain some sort of composure, he couldn't draw in any air. It soon became clear that the abrupt pain and emptiness was too difficult to bear, and he collapsed, closing his eyes as he fell backwards. The memory of the day was flashing in his mind, going in and out of focus as he rolled around on the ground.
A few seconds later, the memories stopped, and everything went blank.

Chapter 12

In his blurred consciousness, John was aware of a woman's soft, concerned voice coming from next to him, and as time went on, he realized he must be in hospital. As he opened and closed his eyes – letting the bright light of the room flicker into focus – images flashed through his mind. As his throat constricted, his mind shot back to that moment as the memory formed fully in his brain. Tears unexpectedly filled his eyes and he fought back a hysterical sob. He hurt all over, and the constant pain in his neck was excruciating.

As if that wasn't enough, his throat was dry and he could barely speak. As soon as he'd woken up the nurse had brought him some water and strong painkillers, and while they had just about taken the edge off, every jostle sent ripples of pain through his neck. Slowly, the thought began to occur to him that someone had laid a trap for him, and he'd walked right into it. It was all a set-up, he thought to himself.

He decided this was not for him anymore; after such a lucky escape, this time he'd had enough. He knew Pedro would be looking for him by now as he would want his parcel, but his first concern was to get out of hospital. The doctor had told him there was a police officer coming to interview him, and he couldn't afford to be around when that happened.

He sat up too quickly and immediately regretted it – his neck screamed with pain. Trying to ignore it, he lunged to his feet and staggered across the floor, looking around him wildly. Where were his shoes? After a few more moments of panic he found them in the side locker. He then quickly got dressed, put his shoes on, and walked towards the door. Peeping out of the door first to make sure no one was there, he then crossed the hall and opened the fire escape door. After he'd walked down two flights of stairs and across another hall, he was out of the hospital.

Once outside, he came upon two employees who were smoking by the back door, and ignoring them, he pushed past and turned left, into the bright afternoon sunlight. He was glad for the fresh air, but he was still in a lot of pain – his neck had been stitched, his finger had had to be reconstructed, and generally, he felt like shit.

Seeing a cab up ahead, John hailed it and waited for it to pull over. When it did, he jumped in and told the driver he didn't have much money, and could he just drive him to a cheap, nearby hotel. After a few minutes, they arrived outside a shabby-looking motel and John tried to get out. The cab door, however, had a lock on it and would not open until he had paid the $5 fee. He stayed quiet for a while, thinking, and eventually, he nervously wiped a hand over his mouth and sat up straighter. He thought to himself that the cab driver might recognize him if later questioned, and that it probably wouldn't make sense to actually check in to this motel. He didn't need his whereabouts getting out.

John paid the $5 and waited until the cab had disappeared before deciding to walk to another hotel. He stumbled along the sidewalk, with no idea where he was, and as he continued onwards and saw each new unfamiliar street, a sense of terror grew inside him. Just when he was feeling what could potentially be the start of a panic attack, he saw a doorway with a sign above it saying 'Hotel'. He breathed a sigh of relief.

Slowly finding his bearings, John remembered there was a shop there that sold wines and spirits and, on the other side of the doorway, there was a Vietnamese restaurant. Well, it was more of a takeaway really, with some bench stools at the bar. Looking around him and seeing no one he recognized, he walked into the hotel and checked in for two nights. His heart was pounding as he did it, but the man at the reception desk didn't seem too fussy; he just asked him to fill in the register, which he did by giving a false name.

He had to pay for one day, there and then, and pay the balance of $18 when he checked out. John was happy to do that, as he knew he needed at least two days before he would be well enough to get around.

Once he'd got the key, he traipsed to his room and let himself in. It was dark in there and he could smell the damp everywhere. All the wood was rotting. The toilet was covered with shit. It was an awful place, but John didn't exactly have any choice – he had to hide somewhere.

Within minutes John was sitting on the edge of the bed, transfixed by the TV. The murder was the hot topic on the local channel, and even Fox News had picked up the story. This was big. He resisted the urge to call Drinda – though he wanted to, he was still trying to figure out if he could trust her or not. On the face of it, John thought he could, but the reality of their curious profession was that he didn't really know, and his instincts told him she was a professional liar. John didn't want to believe that she had betrayed him, but it was a possibility he had to face. In the end, he knew he'd been played. He felt incredibly stupid.

Sighing, he popped some painkillers he had left over from the hospital, and turning to one side, he craned his stiff neck as far as he could, catching the reflection of the back of his neck in the mirror. He could see a mass of purple and black bruising, but the stitches were still intact. He supposed he should see that as one tiny silver lining in this whole big mess. Dragging himself off the bed and over to the foul-smelling bathroom, he took a shower before cleaning and dressing his wound with some cotton wool he found in the cabinet.

With the pain temporarily numbed, he drew the curtains and climbed under the covers. The discomfort was making sleep almost impossible, but after about thirty minutes, the drugs kicked in. He just lay there, staring up at the ceiling, until eventually he fell into a restless sleep.

He slept fitfully, his head full of nightmares of hospitals and blood. When he finally woke up his mind was still wrestling with all the implications of the recent events, and he sat up and swung his feet onto the floor in one swift motion, a motion which sent bolts of pain shooting up his neck. After gritting his teeth for several seconds, he glanced at the bandage on his hand and was pleased to see no sign of blood.

He sat there for a few minutes, analyzing the various paths he could take. Disappearing was still an option. Whether he had the skills to pull it off was another matter, but would they bother to look for him? The way the press were reporting the incident suggested they seemed to think John had killed the man.

Slowly, he realized there was only one option open to him – get the hell out of the country, fast.

Chapter 13

A crime scene had been set up and the police had cordoned off the entire block. Officers stood to one side, ready to start processing the site once it had been thoroughly photographed. Forensic techs were everywhere. Curious neighbors and reporters pressed against the barricades. The bottom of the street was closed.

A sound of sirens approaching caused confusion and fear – suddenly, the crowd started talking all at once, asking questions and yelling at the officers. Trying to get control of the situation before it got out of hand, a young uniformed cop told everyone to stand back, and despite his obvious youth and lack of experience, the people – on the whole – obeyed.

Pedro entered the scene and looked down at the body while behind him, Detective Mann called, "Sir, this is a crime scene!" A man was on all fours near the window, squirrelling along the floor, searching. A tense female police officer stood next to him, her lips wet with gloss. She stared at him, not cottoning on in the least that he wasn't interested.

"Who found the body?" he asked.
Detective Mann was short, with a swarthy complexion, a fleshy nose, and a neat little soul patch that actually looked good on him. He grunted as if he had something stuck in his throat. "The guy has been stabbed."

"Detective Davies is a friend of mine," Pedro said. "Can you give him my card in case I can be of assistance?"

For now, Pedro had work to do, and the first thing he did was glance around the scene and documented what he could see. He looked up at the surrounding buildings, taking careful account of the potential witnesses. He saw that four buildings had views of the alley. He took another look at the body and shook his head – it was the same futile gesture he'd seen every cop make when they saw something so revolting. Pedro gave a quick nod to the detective and left.

Detective Davies was the officer in charge of the crime scene. He wore a fine-looking suit and seemed a little out of place in this scene of death and destruction. He frowned at what he'd been hearing, and as he approached, the officers moved aside, letting the body came into view. "Keep 'em back," Davies commanded as he moved through the crowd. It was a large crowd, but it was nothing in comparison to the numbers that would show up when the story really got out.

Even after twenty years on the force – and after many crime scene investigations, due to his meticulous nature and sharp eye making him an asset – Davies had not once spoken to the press. Years ago, he thought that eventually they would realize he would never comment, but they still sidled up to him, throwing questions.

Ignoring them, he looked up and started directing his men. "Has the evidence been touched?"

Detective Mann mentioned that a man had checked out the crime scene. He pulled Pedro's business card from his pocket. Davies stared at the card, frowning.

The next day, Davies contacted Pedro, asking him to come down to the station, and Pedro had agreed.

An hour later, Pedro jerked the wheel of his car into the parking lot, located an empty spot, and parked. After shutting off the engine, he stared grimly at the building, determined to wait another minute before confronting Detective Davies. He looked into the mirror and wiped the perspiration off his forehead with his sleeve. Then, tightening the knot in his tie, he took a deep breath, opened the car door, and walked off towards a pair of uniforms who had just arrived.

He asked to talk to Detective Davies, and both men met at the bottom of the stairs. The two greeted each other with solid handshakes and warm smiles. Well, they were warm on the surface, anyway.

"Come this way," said Davies, in an authoritative voice.

Davies punched a code into a cipher lock and they entered the main precinct. He greeted a man behind the desk but didn't bother with introductions. They continued down a long hall with ugly cream walls and linoleum floors; unlike the rest of the station, this area had missed out on what looked like recent remodeling. Davies opened the door and motioned for Pedro to sit down on the corner chair. Pedro did so, before lighting a cigarette.

"Can I get you a coffee?" Davies offered politely, still smiling at his guest. Then, not even waiting for Pedro's answer, he poured two cups of thick, overcooked coffee, and brought them to the table. He sat down opposite Pedro and pushed one of the cups over to him.

"Hope you don't mind," the detective said, getting right down to business, "but I need to ask you some questions." Davies brushed a wisp of thin brown hair from his forehead, opened the file on his lap, and extracted a few sheets of paper. He paused for a moment as he glanced through the first sheet, then he looked up. "Why was it that you happened to be at the scene of the crime last night?"

"I don't mind telling you that," replied Pedro. "I was working close to the scene. In fact, I may have even witnessed the crime."

"So tell me," said Detective Davies, leaning forwards.

"Well, I was investigating a fraud when I noticed movement outside."

"Movement? That could mean anything," suggested the detective.

Pedro studied Davies for a few seconds, sensing something he didn't like: Davies was fishing. Pedro cleared his throat and then added, "Yes, I notice details, it's my job." Then, after a brief pause, "I could see a person, a young male, turning right into one of the passages that linked the buildings."

"So, did you see the murder?"

Pedro shook his head, drumming his fingers on the table for a moment. "But I would know the person if I saw him again." He flicked his ash onto the floor, smirking to himself. Pedro knew he was by far the smartest man in the room.

Just then, Detective Davies got a call on his radio, and when he'd finished speaking to the caller, he turned back to Pedro. "We had confirmation from a paramedic that a young British man came into the hospital two days ago with a knife injury. When we went to interview him this morning, he'd left the hospital."

Detective Davies wondered to himself why a man would do such a thing. There were only two possible reasons. Either he'd done something seriously wrong, or he'd almost been killed for what he'd seen. Davies took a moment to measure what he had just learnt before asking the most obvious question. "Was it just a robbery gone wrong?"

Pedro shrugged. "Probably."

Davies paused for a second and then shook his head. "Probably is the best we can do at the moment." He pulled a card out of his wallet and passed it over. "If you think of anything or hear anything that you think might help, call me. Thanks again for taking the time to meet with me."

Pedro nodded, recovering his smoldering cigarette from an otherwise empty ashtray. He couldn't help the look of relief on his face when the interview ended, and he took the card with a smile. He had played out every conceivable development in his mind, the key being to keep the police confused, and only telling them what he wanted them to know. He found them incredibly easy to manipulate. As he stood up and shook hands with the detective, a broad grin spread across his leathery face. He was sure that he'd covered all his tracks. This was a delicate business, where patience was every bit the virtue. There was no way anyone would know the whole thing was a set-up. No one was meant to die, it just happened that way. All Pedro had to do now was wait.

Chapter 14

The knock on the door pulled John from his thoughts of retribution, and he froze, staring blankly ahead of him for a few seconds. Then, pushing himself up against the headboard, he flipped on the light. Finally, he pulled himself up and stepped softly to the door, leaning against it and peering through the peephole. It was a woman. John watched her purse her lips, and then she reached out to knock again.

"Hello, it's the maid..." she said, before going on to ask if she could empty the rubbish.

Without hesitation, he called out to her, "No!"

The maid frowned and walked away. John breathed a sigh of relief.

He had slept for nearly twelve hours, and that was after napping for six hours the previous afternoon. He remembered waking once during the night to use the bathroom, when he took another handful of painkillers, but apart from that, he was out like a light.

Making sure the maid was gone, John opened his door and stepped out into the hotel corridor. Two doors down from his room stood a girl in her mid-twenties. Her hair was a bright artificial blonde, and she was wearing a short red skirt, a black sleeveless T-shirt and a pair of sequined flip flops. Her legs were long, bare and ivory white. A cigarette hung between the fingers of her left hand.

John had started talking to her the previous evening. He couldn't remember her name, but it could have been Cindy. Something like that. It didn't matter to him, as he was feeling a bit down and didn't care who she was. He just needed some help. Walking over to her, John said hi, then told her that he didn't want to leave the hotel before asking whether she could fetch him some things.

"Rather not," she said shortly, before heading back into her room.

Frustrated, but knowing he had to go, John wandered downstairs to the shop. He felt very nervous, but he needed to buy antiseptics for his wound.

"Where's your first aid stuff?" he asked the shopkeeper once he was inside. "Do you have any creams and plasters?"

"Band aids?" the shopkeeper mumbled. "Yeah, over there."

"What's the sticker price?" John asked.

"Like, three-twenty," the shopkeeper replied.

John rummaged in the pockets of his pants and came up with just three and a cent. That wouldn't even get the plasters let alone any antiseptics. "I'm a little short of cash right now. I guess I'll have to borrow some money from you," he said jokingly.

The shopkeeper's mouth hung open in disbelief, but then his face took on a cynical smirk. "This is some kind of joke, right?" he said as he took the money from John.

Ignoring the question, John said thank you and went back into the hotel, walking quickly up to his room before anyone could spot him. Once inside, he rolled up his sleeves to wash his hands; his fingers were still covered in dried blood. He'd brought some ibuprofen with him from the hospital, so they would have to do. Should help with the swelling, he thought, as he filled a glass with water and dropped the pills into his hand, hoping they would kick in fast.

He spent the day watching bad TV, and before he knew it, evening had come around again. In the middle of the night, he occasionally heard the odd gunfire, a screech of tires, the banging of car doors. He could even just about make out someone saying, "Hands up!"

He thought of the woman he thought was called Cindy. She was from the south, but he wasn't sure where exactly. There'd been no sounds out in the hall, so it seemed that she wasn't that worried by the gunfire.

Intrigued, John climbed out of bed and walked over to the window, gently pulling back the tattered curtain and looking down at the street. At first he could see nothing outside, but he definitely heard some yelling and the sounds of someone running.

Just then, there was a knocking on his door, and he opened it to find Cindy there, staring in at him, her eyes wide. Perhaps she was worried about the gunfire. She walked into the room without a word and sat down on the bed.

The girl had that vacuous look of a drug addict, with empty eyes and a mouth that had no joy in it. Her face was filthy and bruised, her lips unevenly swollen from a slapping.

"Who did that to you?" he asked.

She jerked her hand in the air as if to say it didn't matter. She wore no make-up and her hair looked as if it were purposely messed up.

Not knowing what else to do, John turned the TV on, and while he was watching it, the young girl suddenly started to shake. He watched as she pulled out a needle and a spoon and started to melt down what he presumed was heroin. She started to look for a vein, but was unable to find one. The poor girl had so many holes in her body, how she ever found what she needed was beyond him.

He watched in morbid fascination, only vaguely aware that he was starting to feel sick. He should have seen the signs: even though he'd only met her a couple of times, whenever he asked her questions, she wouldn't answer. It had made him think that something was wrong. She was probably a runaway.

Suddenly, she stuck the needle into a vein in her neck, then promptly passed out.

Shit, John thought, what should I do now?

He checked her pulse – which he couldn't find – then tried to wake her, but she wasn't responding. She was dead. He just stood there for a moment, shocked. What the hell have I got myself into? Why now? he thought desperately.

He glared at the clock on the wall and watched as the minutes moved past midnight. He didn't know what to do. He kept picturing the girl injecting herself over and over again, but it was so quick there was nothing he could have done. He knew he'd better get himself together and quick.

John decided that the best thing for him to do was to get out of there. The girl was lying there with her mouth wide open, and he picked her up and carried her back to her bedroom before going back for her needle and her belongings.

He wiped the needle carefully with a piece of toilet paper and then laid it down on the floor next to her. He checked to make sure there was nothing in the room that might connect him in any way to what had happened, but he didn't think there was.

He couldn't help but notice a picture of her with two children, who he supposed were her kids. He really felt sad for this poor girl – her whole life had now ended, and for what? On the side cabinet he found a torn black handbag, in which was a key with stuck-on tape with the number '45' printed on it. He noticed on her arm a tattoo of a butterfly and a name engraved next to it, which said "Forever". John said to himself, "Forever what?"

John imagined that this girl had a lot of secrets and that her story was a long one. He supposed no one would care about her anymore, and she would probably just be one of the many casualties that happened every day in this city. If he called the police, they would be looking for him, and he couldn't take that chance.

He cleaned her room again, making sure there were no fingerprints, then hurried down the corridor to check no one was around. He then went back into her room once more, just for a final check, nearly busting the doorjamb as he opened the door. Once he was satisfied, he went back to his room and cleaned it from top to bottom. He put anything he could find with his name on into the little metal waste bin and set fire to the contents. He even washed the window with water from the tap and dried it with some old newspaper, before tossing the used newspaper into the fire.

When he was done, John drummed his fingers on the table, trying to think. Then he realized what he'd just done – by drumming on the table, he had left more prints.

"Get a hold of yourself," he told himself, cursing under his breath. He was no good to himself in this state.

Although the police would probably treat it as just another dead junkie in a city battling an insidious wave of drug abuse, he didn't intend to stay around long enough to find out. The staircase was right next to his door, and John took the steps two at a time, as fast as he could. By the time he reached the bottom, his heart was pumping, but he knew he would recover within seconds. He stopped just inside the fire door and took a couple of deep breaths. Then he used his elbow on the door handle so he wouldn't leave any fingerprints. There, at the opposite end of the hall, was the desk. John leant over it to call the man over quickly.

"How can I help you?" he asked, smiling.

"I'd like to check out early, please,"

John gave his details, handed back his key, and paid the $18 which he still owed.

As he stepped outside, his heart began to pound, but there was nothing else he could do. Threading his way through the crowd of people, John realized that he had checked into what was a really bad area, as the street was full of drunks.

He tried to think. At this precise moment, he didn't know if the police were looking for him, because he didn't know if the person who'd attacked him was still alive. Or whether the police had connected him with a burglary and attack, or maybe neither. He picked up the pace, afraid to look over his shoulder, weighing up his options. He knew one thing for certain: he couldn't chance going to his apartment. They were guaranteed to be waiting for him. So, he kept right on moving. Rows of semis formed long alleyways, each one a potential escape route. It all felt so impossible.

He had walked more than two blocks before he collapsed and the ambulance found him, so there probably wasn't a connection to the burglary as far as they were concerned. His instincts were no good to him now, though: he had to get back to Miami, as his open return air ticket was from Miami to London. Considering his next move, his heart began to pound. There was nothing else for him to do, nowhere else for him to go. The urge to run was overwhelming. He couldn't fight it any longer.

The safest way was not to fly down to Miami, as he suspected the police would be looking for him at the airport, and it would only be a matter of time before they found out that the name he was using was not his.

John decided to take a chance. He would just have to pray for the best.

He was just looking through his wallet to check how much money he had left when he pulled out a business card – the one his friend Jerry had given him on board the cruise ship. He quickly found a telephone and called the Irish bar where he worked. Jerry answered.

"I'm in trouble, Jerry," he said, getting straight to the point. "I need to get back to Miami, but I need to buy a coach ticket."

Jerry could tell by John's voice that something was wrong; he could hear the panic in it.

"Okay, John," he replied. "If you need a little money, I'll meet you in one hour at the Greyhound coach station."

"I need one more favor from you, Jerry," added John. "Could you please check out flights from London to Miami and book me on the next available one in three days' time?"

Jerry reluctantly agreed, and John breathed another sigh of relief.

After saying bye to Jerry, John started walking again. Traffic was light, but as he'd guessed, the police were everywhere. He had his hands shoved deep in the pockets of his jacket, keeping his chin tucked in and his eyes uninterested as if he were just another person heading off to work.

When he was near the coach station, he waited in the doorway of a shop, watching for Jerry, and after a few minutes, a cab pulled up and Jerry got out. They both made eye contact and then walked to the corner of the coach terminal. Jerry handed him $40.

"Jerry, I really appreciate this. Thank you."

"Good luck," Jerry replied, patting him on the shoulder before walking off again.

A coach was leaving in one hour. He bought a ticket and sat in the waiting room, looking around to make sure no one suspected anything.

Finally, after what seemed like forever – which didn't bode well, as the trip to Miami would take three days – he stepped onto the waiting bus. As the coach rolled across the bay bridge, he wondered to himself whether he should just get off and try to start a new life for himself. He supposed it was a possibility.

He could see his reflection in the driver's mirror, and John looked like he felt, which was like crap. His dense black hair was sticking out in various directions, though that was hardly the worst of it: his neck was hurting again, and it was worse now. After a few tears and a lot of time feeling sorry for himself, he began to realize that he could go downhill quickly if he didn't practice some mental discipline. He leaned back in his seat and stared out of the window while he tried to think.

Into the second day, they drove through San Antonio on the Mexican border. It looked like a good place to hide out for a while; analyzing the various paths he could take, he thought disappearing was still an option. Would they bother to look for him? If they knew the whole story, probably not, but the way the press were reporting things, he knew he didn't stand a chance. He cracked a smile and shook his head as he realized how close he had come to spending the rest of his life behind bars.

He hadn't eaten or had anything to drink since getting on the coach, and when they stopped at a bus station, he spotted a large TV hanging from the ceiling in a shop. He went in to find food and saw a woman standing behind the counter; she reeked of cheap perfume and cigarettes. A man was sitting at the counter. He shook his head and mumbled something, and it seemed to John that he pointed to the refreshment room opposite.

Gathering his things together, he hurried, hoping to find more reliable assistance, but there was no one there except a fat man in a white apron who was clearing the counter.

The restaurant was dimly lit and not very inviting, but John seated himself at the small counter and drank a coffee. The coach was due to depart in ten minutes so he had to be quick. When he was finished, he nudged past the fat man and looked up and down the street before getting back onto the coach.

The man sitting next to him gave him a crude, assessing look, before starting to ask him questions.

"So you're English?"

John decided he'd better not give him a smart-arse answer back. But then, thinking better of it, he simply gestured with his head and muttered, "Yup."

The rain was starting to fall again – large, steady drops that would shortly turn into a downpour – and John hoped the bus would make it on time to the airport. He was short of money; all he had left was $4 and his return airplane ticket. He was desperate. To make matters worse, it was a really hot day and he was dying to get off the bus; the air-conditioning didn't work very well and the three days of sitting on that bus had become very uncomfortable and smelly. John wished he could have a shower.

Just then, he noticed a car come up from behind them, accelerating past the coach and then staying in front of them for hours. He couldn't stop looking to see who was driving the car – at the back of his mind, John was expecting Pedro to show up at any time.

Eventually, the car turned off, leaving the coach behind. John was still staring through the window, trying to come to terms with all of it. Every time someone spoke to him, his hands shook uncontrollably. He was sure now that all of this was a set-up. Maybe John had read Pedro all wrong. There weren't as many signals as there'd been at first, but he remembered well the full eye contact, the sidelong glances, the check-outs, all totally discreet.

When they finally arrived at the airport, the first thing he did was to clean himself as much as possible in a little sink in the toilets. Afterwards, he stared at his reflection in the mirror and questioned his sanity. He wasn't certain what or who he was looking at anymore. He went over the whole nightmare one more time in his head, and he immediately felt like crying. No, he thought to himself. He had to pull himself together. Nodding and taking a deep breath, he walked back into the terminal. He felt completely drained. He needed some food, a lot of sleep, and some silence to sort things out.

Suddenly, a wave of pain ran down the back of his neck and down into his back, and he grabbed the top of a nearby phone booth with his right hand until the pain slowly passed. Once he'd straightened himself up, he decided to try and call Sonia. He picked up the receiver and put his last few dollars into the slot, then punched in the number from memory. She answered on the third ring.

"Good morning, Sonia," he said as casually as possible. "How are you?"

She didn't reply for what seemed like an eternity. "I'm okay," she finally replied.

Her relief was obvious. She sounded so shocked to hear his voice. He told her he was coming back soon. "I can't wait to see you. I just wished it was today." He closed his eyes and hung on to the case of the payphone. The pain came back. "I have to go now."

He took several deep breaths and steadied himself before deciding to take a seat for a moment. Slowly, the throbbing pain receded. He noticed people staring at him and one person even tried to approach him. The man was about six foot three, and did not take his eyes off him. Looking straight ahead, John began to push through the crowd. What the hell is going on? he thought to himself. I need a break. How could anyone have known?

He fought an impulse to look over his shoulder. What if I've got it wrong? A shiver ran through him. He breathed in deeply and paused for a moment, then looked across at the airport bar where a group of young men stumbled out. Drunk and happy, and not a care in the world. He toyed with the idea of going in to have a beer, but shrugged the notion away. That would eat up the rest of his cash. When he looked back up, the man had gone, and relieved, he quickly got up and walked down the other end of the terminal until he was sure he wasn't being followed.

The plane was due to take off in two hours, so he sat down and picked up a newspaper. He wasn't really reading, just scanning through the headlines and trying to pass as much time as possible. His eyes were really somewhere else, scanning the terminal. He walked over to the vending machine and bought a black coffee, then placed it on the table in front of him. It took him a few attempts, but he finally managed to swallow some down. The words in front of him blurred together and all he could see was Pedro's face, all he could think about was how he'd allowed himself to get screwed.

When he next checked the overhead monitors, he saw that the flight was ready to board, and he was so anxious to go through that he was trembling. Trying to shake the stiffness from his limbs, he ignored the pulsing pain in his neck and walked through the check-in and then through security.

He was quite worried by now as he had to present his passport, and when the security man looked at it, he studied John's face carefully. Then he handed the passport back to him and said, "Have a nice flight."

John looked at him and smiled. He was shaking as he was walking, but he didn't care. In John's mind, the scales had just tipped in his favor. He was finally flying back home.

An hour later, he was on the plane and finally relaxing a little. The stewardess arrived with another large vodka, and he forced a smile as he thanked her. Reaching for his glass, he wondered if he was becoming just a little too reliant on the comfort of alcohol. It was only a temporary measure, John reassured himself, just a way of getting through this difficult time.

He knew for sure, of course, that all of this would affect him for a very long time, and couldn't help wondering what would have happened had he stayed. Was all of this just a string of coincidences? But coincidence could usually be explained by the laws of chance and probability. Realizing how dangerous his situation had become and how close he'd come to landing up in a cell, John knew he was a very lucky man.

He still remembered the conversation he'd overheard between Pedro and Drinda about him stealing Tony's identity. He was running down the list of questions and trying to put together the pieces. What was Pedro's intention? Was he trying to set him up? Was he trying to blackmail him? John realized he might never know. Sighing, he downed the vodka and leaned back in his seat, attempting to sleep.

Chapter 15

London

The Pan Am flight arrived in London an hour late, the plane landing on the tarmac with a gentle bump before going into what seemed to be an endless taxi. When it finally swayed to a stop at the gate, John stood up and retrieved his small carry-on bag. "I hope we'll see you again," the flight attendant said, smiling at John as he stepped into the jetway. He grinned back at her. The immigration line seemed to go on forever, and after a long wait, he stepped through the glass door and into the terminal. John was exhausted and drained, unsure what to do next.

He decided to check into a small bed and breakfast in Hounslow; thankfully, he still had access to his old UK savings account, so he had no problems paying for the room. He needed to get a grip and take it easy, and basically just try to relax.

When he was in his room, he lay on the bed for hours thinking about the last few months. Those hours turned into long, drawn-out days as the pain refused to subside. It got to the point when he realized he had a passionate dislike for himself, then the loneliness started to kick in. This went on for weeks.

There was one major problem with this: the owners of the bed and breakfast were prone to playing loud music, making it hard for him to think, and all he wanted to do was sit while struggling with his thoughts.

He stared out of the window at the scrap of a back garden, watching an empty plastic bag blowing aimlessly in the wind, occasionally catching on the scrawny branches.

He was brought out of his sulking by the sound of a knock on the door, which he reluctantly went to answer. It was the landlady.

"I need your rent," she asked, staring at him questioningly. The loud music he could hear before was even louder out in the corridor.

John hovered next to her, chewing his lip, tapping a foot. Even the room felt restive, and the noise was reverberating off the thick walls, making it hard to think, let alone hear what she was trying to say to him. "I can't hear you. What did you say?"

"Rent! I need your rent!" she said, as if he were stupid.

Sighing, he mumbled, "I'll have it soon" before closing the door in her face. It was all getting too much for him.

That night, he had this great feeling of emptiness. The room he was staying in was small, and it contained a three-seater sofa that converted into a double bed. The upstairs floorboards creaked, and you could hear footsteps as people walked from their bedroom to the bathroom. Then a flush, and the trill of water climbing up to refill the toilet tank. Then there was the muffled voice of the late-show host on TV.

He tried to tune everything out as he laid his head on the pillow and closed his eyes.

The next morning, his head didn't feel as bad as it had last week. Outside was still and quiet except for the infrequent hum of traffic, but John felt nervous and alone. Every time he tried to relax, all he could see was the girl lying on the floor. How could you clear your head from such a trauma? It was like she was haunting him.

John sat in his room all day until it was late, and then he became too scared to sleep. Deep down, he knew there was something wrong with him, but he didn't know what to do. It was a harsh, desolate place he inhabited, the only sound the pounding within his mind. John ignored the stinging by staring at the ceiling, listening to the rage that was trying to destroy him. When that failed to make him feel any better, he got up and tripped over his shoes on his way to the sink and looked down at them accusingly, as if anyone but he could have put them there. He looked up after kicking them across the room, and that was when he knew.

Behind some books was a bottle of vodka, half full. He sipped some straight from the bottle and kicked the words around in his mind. What was the proper way to word this letter? What was it that he really wanted to say? He sat down to write, but after a few hours, the wording was still not correct, and by now he was getting a little tipsy.

He lined the empty bottle of vodka up with the other empties, then made one last attempt to write the letter. When that didn't work, he got a tape recorder out of his case and started talking, telling Sonia – through his tears – that he loved her very much. He said that he felt she could do better than him, and then over and over John repeated the same phrase: "I love you."

When he was done, he turned off the tape recorder and dried his tears. He told himself that he needed to be focused if he was going to go through with this, so he placed his personal belongings in a pile and said a quiet prayer. Another five or ten seconds, and that would have been it if it hadn't been for his landlady pounding on his door, demanding payment.

This was no doubt the lowest point in his life, but eventually, after what felt like forever, he began to feel truly well for the first time in a long time – stronger and more able to see what should be done to lead a better life. After a long think, he decided to go to a hypnotherapist for help; knowing that his problem was inside his mind, he wanted to find someone who could change the way he thought. He hurriedly rifled through the yellow pages and found one quite close to where he lived. Once he'd plucked up the courage to make an appointment, he started questioning himself and debated just leaving it, but he quickly got irritated with himself for being so indecisive.

The next day he rushed out early, attempting unsuccessfully to wipe a coffee splatter off his tie. When he arrived at the nondescript suburban house and knocked on the door, a young woman answered and invited him in.

"You must be John," she said, smiling at him and only briefly looking at his scruffy tie.

"Yes," he replied, shaking her hand and entering into the hall.

They took over a small office room in the back of the house and got started. It felt good to be able to unburden all his fears and feelings onto her, to be able to talk freely about the things that he had to keep hidden from everyone else. After his first session with her, he felt pretty good.

John realized that he felt so food, in fact, that he kept going back to her. At each session they tried various exercises, some of which involved hypnotism that made him feel very relaxed and able to explore his own imagination. He started to gain more confidence, and the anxiety attacks and paranoia grew less intense.

After a few more sessions, he was starting to feel like a new man.

Chapter 16

The alarm went off at 7.30 a.m. and Sonia reached out to turn it off before sitting up on the edge of the bed and stretching. She grudgingly went downstairs, and she'd just started a pot of coffee when the phone started to ring. It was John.

Sonia's heart jumped at the sound of his voice. She hadn't heard from him since his phone call from the airport and had assumed he was still in the States. John had told her that he was flying back to London the following day and asked whether they could get together.

She broke down in tears. "What are you thinking? Why did you go and now you want to come back?" The hurt still stung, and Sonia knew it always would. She could pretend everything was alright, she could lie to her friends and tuck the hurt aside during the day, but at night her dreams were filled with what might have been: John's smile, his touch. Everything about him.

They had met three years earlier when she worked on the Terminal Four information desk at Heathrow Airport, and at the time she thought their relationship was solid – they'd even be planning to move in together – but one day he didn't turn up for their lunch date and then he simply disappeared. The next time she heard from him again was when he phoned her from Miami Airport.

"Hey, are you okay?" His voice was wobbly and something inside him hurt; he wished that she knew how much he cared about her.

"I'm fine," she insisted. "I'm not sure what to do. I'm scared..." She trailed off and after a moment she mumbled, "I don't know what you want me to say." She paused. "It's totally – I just don't know what to think."

"Okay, I understand, don't worry. It will all be fine. Let's just meet tomorrow."

Sonia thought for a moment before answering, and when she did, her voice was quiet and uncertain. "Okay."

A couple of hours later, John jolted like an invalid woken from an afternoon nap by sounds of movement in the bedsit above. He heard someone urinating, then flushing the toilet. A door closed, before whoever it was moved back across the creaky old timber floor. Then peace descended once more.

He lay still and tried to go back to sleep, but it was still too noisy upstairs. Getting up, he started to slowly get ready, pressing his shirt and shining his shoes. While shaving, he turned his cheek carefully to the mirror to ensure he hadn't missed a single whisker. He wanted to look as good as possible.

Later that day, from a distance Sonia saw his blue eyes flash as he gazed at her from where he was waiting outside the tube station. She took a deep breath, hoping to steady her nerves that were already fluttering to life in the pit of her stomach.

When he broke free of the crowd and headed straight for her, Sonia knew she was in big trouble. She should be running away from him, but all she wanted to do was throw herself into his arms. Then he was there, standing right in front of her, staring down at her. He opened his arms to her and raked his fingers through her dark curly hair. She seemed different, he thought, in her pretty dress and high heels. She was still beautiful, and one look into her eyes said that she was the same woman who had captivated him before. But damned if he didn't miss how she looked in tight jeans.

They went into a restaurant, just like those old days, and the waiter poured the wine, left the bottle on the table, and moved away. She took a sip of the wine. It was cold and crisp and eased the tightness in her throat. She gave that stare, just the way she used to. "I didn't start out intending to hurt you, Sonia. It wasn't some kind of plan."

After a long moment's silence, he leaned forward and kissed her. A curl of warmth wound around the pit of her stomach, but she mentally stamped it out. Could she trust him? she thought. He'd hurt her and lied before. Why wouldn't he do it again?

She shook her head a little and blinked away the burn of tears stinging her eyes. Hoping to steady herself, she kept her eyes fixed on the scene in the restaurant. The waiter approached with plates of food, and he was quick, efficient and gone in moments. Sonia only picked at her food, she wasn't hungry.

"At least eat something," John said, stopping the waiter and ordering her favorite dessert. "And please try and talk to me."

"I don't know what to say," she admitted, staring at her wine glass.

"I know it's not going to be like it was before," he said, "but I miss you. Will you come back to my place? We can talk more privately there."

Sonia was about to say no – no way was she going anywhere with him – when she looked up at him, up at those blue eyes she used to love so much. After a few more moments of hesitation, she nodded.

After sharing a zabaglione, they grabbed the unfinished half-full bottle of wine and went back to his new bedsit, where he fumbled in his pocket for the keys before opening the door. The room was about eight foot wide and twelve foot long, and it had just enough space for a single bed and a built-in desk and chair. He had rented a small television and put it on top of the refrigerator, and there was a sink under a large mirror in the corner behind the door.

He kicked off his shoes and shrugged off his shirt, and she watched silently. They then moved close to each other and held each other. It was such a comfort to feel her after all this time.

They whispered for a while – about the room, about how long it had been – and then she pulled his face towards her and kissed him. It felt just like it had before, and she climbed onto his lap, straddling him, her cotton dress slipping up around her knees, one of her shoes falling to the floor.

In that moment, all of her doubts just melted away.

They woke up early the next day and went for a coffee. Once they were seated at a corner table, he ordered a small espresso, while she just had a filter coffee. It felt good to be back, doing these normal couple things again.

"Listen," he said, sighing. "I was sort of hoping this would be our big reunion, the rebirth of our long-term relationship."

"Wait, John," said Sonia, frowning at her coffee. "Before you get all preachy on me, why don't you tell me what's really going on? By your own admission, you've been back for several weeks now and you've hardly told me anything about what you done."

John took a breath and held it. The guilt about lying was smallish. Nobody needed to know anything, and he definitely couldn't tell her what happened in America – it all still felt too raw. So instead, he smiled and took a sip of coffee before giving her just enough information to satisfy her curiosity.

The Sunday papers were on the coffee table but he moved them into a pile then poured her another coffee. They sipped in affable silence, broken only by the soft munch of little pastries.

"Work," she said suddenly, as if she'd only just realized she was on duty that morning. She stood up and gave his shoulder a squeeze. "I'll see you later."

Time went on, and they slowly put the past behind them. It soon became apparent that they wanted to spend the rest of their lives together, and in a whirlwind they got married and honeymooned in a hotel in Covent Garden for two nights. The hotel manager led them through the hall himself, pressed the elevator bell and unlocked the door of their room. Placing a bottle of Champagne onto the table, he smiled and pulled the door close.

"I can't believe we're married!" said Sonia happily as her husband handed her a glass.

Page 164

"Tell me about it," replied John, who clinked the glasses together and smiled at his wife. His life had really turned around, and his dark days after America seemed like years ago.

The next morning, Sonia woke up as the early morning light spilled through the windows. She pulled the duvet over them and turned to face John, who was debating with himself whether this was a good time for honesty. Sonia didn't know about the other stuff, his double life, the death – would it just ruin everything if he told her now? The truth was malleable. She could handle it, he thought. He just needed to pick the right moment and now was not it.

Sonia suddenly scratched her nail gently down his back. He thought about how much he wanted someone to do that, just a quick scratch, and he let out a gasp, one quick teary moan.

It was afternoon when they finally surfaced. She was dressed in a sensible black skirt and a white-striped blouse, with barrettes clipping either side of her hair. As much as they didn't want to, he had to drag her away back to Twickenham. They'd decided to open a new restaurant, the next phase in their new married lives.

The building had a tiny corner bar with a haphazard patchwork aesthetic, its best feature an oriental screen – an extravagant work in wood. The room was, in fact, shitty, a showcase of the shabbiest design offerings of an earlier decade, but the ultimate effect was strangely homey – it looked less like a restaurant and more like someone's benignly neglected fixer-upper – and jovial.

They named the restaurant Scott's, after his surname. Yes, they thought they were being clever, but most people thought it was a Scottish restaurant. They pictured the locals wrinkling their noses: Why did you name it after yourself? But their first customer, a red-haired woman, said she liked the name. They felt superior after that, which was a good thing.

Everything was starting to look up.

Chapter 17

1993

Life had only just got back to normal when they visited Sonia's mother one evening, and as the night wore on, everyone drank more and more, enjoying themselves.

Suddenly, the telephone rang. Sonia's mother answered and told John there was an American who wanted to talk to him.

John's stomach dropped and a sick feeling washed over him as he made his way to the phone.

"Hi there John, this is Pedro," came the voice on the other end. There was no mistaking the voice on the other end. It was Pedro, alright.

John went silent for a moment. "You know this isn't a secure line," he finally said, not able to completely mask the annoyance in his voice.

There was a frustrating sigh on the other end, then he said, "Listen carefully." Pedro's voice had a hard, I-mean-business-edge to it, which did nothing to soothe John's nerves.

"What is that supposed to mean?" John asked.

"You're smart, figure it out."

Confused, John froze. "I'm not in the mood for your games," he eventually said in an attempt to assert control.

John paused for another moment, asking himself, What does he want after all this time? before realizing that he had to see Pedro in the flesh. There were too many unanswered questions to do this over the phone.

"Okay, where are you? And what do you want?"

"I'm coming to London next week and I will contact you, we can talk then. Have a nice day."

Suddenly filled with anger, John flung the phone onto the couch, his fury enveloping him like a cloak. He stood there, jaw clenched tight, unable to speak, and after a while he sat down on the couch, resting his head in his hands.

Sonia was looking at him, wondering what was wrong. He'd forgotten that she wanted to tell her mum she was pregnant.

Reluctantly, he nodded at her and tried his best smile. She went and sat next to him, entwining his hand with hers.

"We have an announcement to make," she said, before bursting into tears and shouting out, "I'm pregnant!"

Having blurted it out, it seemed like she was happy – that it was a relief to tell everyone – and that was all that mattered. The far side of the room went silent for a moment, then there was a whoosh of collective breaths being taken.

Her dad aimed his unblinking eyes at John, then smiled, waiting for him to nod. Her mum just beamed at both of them. He took exactly two seconds to think before saying, "No more working as a waitress for you, darling," and kissing her gently on the cheek.

At home, the next few days were very stressful, and John worried constantly. His happy new life was turning into a nightmare. His mind was wrestling with all of the implications of what seemed to be the truth. How did Pedro know where to find him? What did he want, and why now? John sat on the bed for several minutes looking around the room, thinking of only one thing: that he'd liked the idea of being a father – in fact, he felt proud. But an uneasy feeling was starting to spread through his guts, and he didn't intend to spend the rest of his life looking over his shoulder. He was thinking, thinking, thinking. And coming up totally blank.

Walking into the living room, he eased his way onto the couch. Do I tell Sonia everything that's happened to me or do I go to the police and tell them? He looked around him, his eyes resting on the watercolor of a country house. He thought it best to try to act as normal as possible, at least until he had time to think this through properly. He didn't want to worry his wife.

Even performing simple chores was difficult at first, but after a couple of days it began to get easier. One morning, he took a deep breath and finally relaxed a little, once more looking at the painting. Sonia gave him that look again, and he tried hard as he stared at her – no anger, no arguments, the constant kowtowing, the capitulation, the sitcom husband version: Yes, dear. Of course, sweetheart. She was clever, he had to exert himself just to keep pace with her. She always thought ahead, and he got smarter being with her, and more considerate.

But John's mind was racing. He didn't know what Pedro wanted from him, but one thing he knew for sure was that he had to be strong and somehow hide his feelings, which was really difficult: he wasn't looking forward to meeting Pedro again, not one little bit.

He took a sip of his coffee, remembering what Pedro had told him in the States: "One day I will come to Great Britain to see you." In hindsight, it was as if this whole nightmare had been planned from the very start, and now John knew Pedro was serious.

He shook his head. He knew Pedro was up to something, but what? Why was he coming to London? He had to know!

In truth, John was losing it, and this was becoming an increasingly exhausting way to live. He was pretending – the way he often did – that everything was okay. He couldn't help it.

Finally, it got to the point when reality itself was confusing him – it was like this wasn't real. But life went on, and he had to work. On his way to the restaurant, his eyes roamed up and down the street, the panic clearly showing on his face – pretending he was calm and under control now was nearly impossible. Nothing could put him at ease, and even the thought of Pedro's name made him panic. He wanted to cry out with the pressure, but there was no one to cry out too.

Taking a deep breath, he carried on walking. Either way, it would be over soon.

Chapter 18

Pedro arrived on a Sunday afternoon and checked into the Master Robert Hotel in west London.

He crossed the hotel's small lobby before speaking to the man behind the desk, asking if his room was ready.

"I'm afraid you're a little early for check-in, Sir," was the response from the polite, smiling desk clerk, "but I expect it to be free within the next hour. If I could just get some ID from you now, you can go straight up once it's ready."

A little annoyed but trying not to show it, Pedro handed over his US passport. "Is your bar open? If I have to wait, at least I can have a drink."

The clerk nodded, smiling slightly. "Of course, Sir. If you'd like to take a seat anywhere in the foyer, we can take your order and I'll inform you when you can go up."

Pedro agreed, sitting down and ordering a whiskey as he took in his surroundings. When the drink came, he drank it quickly and ordered another one. A couple of hours – and a few drinks – later, the concierge made eye contact with Pedro, holding up a room key before handing it over to a porter.

"This way, Sir," the porter – a short, squat man – announced, before leading Pedro to the elevator and up to the second floor. Upon entering the room, the porter showed him around, then stood hovering for a tip.

Pedro nodded approvingly, slipping the porter a note before saying goodbye and walking into the bathroom. There was a mirror over the sink and he paused to study his reflection before brushing his hair back behind each ear.

Pedro had already planned out his day. He'd made certain contacts in London and he was aware that he was known by British Intelligence – as far as the British knew, Pedro was working for the C.I.A., which could be confirmed by the Bureau. Pedro had managed to get the Americans thinking that he was there to investigate bad bankers who had left the States, which worked well; the British didn't want to get involved in what Pedro was doing, and that was fine by him.

He was expecting his files and documents to arrive soon, and once that had happened, he could get on with things. After a quick lunch, he called the embassy and asked if he could attend the meeting taking place there later that day. Pedro knew that they were more than likely recording the call, so as usual he chose his words carefully and kept the conversation brief. "Listen, I can be there in twenty minutes." He was keen to make progress with his work in the UK, and with his contacts already established, there was just the matter of attending a few meetings. He had to answer to the American Embassy before he knew how far he could go.

He was deep in thought on his way to the embassy, so much in fact that he didn't hear when the taxi driver said, "Guv'nor, we're here." The man had to repeat the words and cough loudly just to get Pedro's attention.

As he stepped out of the cab, Pedro noticed police everywhere, something he didn't understand – why was security so tight? He strolled in with a buoyant air of anticipation, but as soon as he arrived he was stopped in his tracks. First he had to walk through the X-ray scanner and report to reception before being ushered down the corridor to sign in. There was an armed security guard on the door, with another guard sitting behind the desk opposite. He held up his hand, pointed up wards and said abruptly, "Please go up the stairs and turn right."

Pedro followed the orders, and upstairs he was greeted by another man who was sitting behind a desk. He continued down a long hall with ugly grey-coloured walls and linoleum floors and was finally met by David Jacob. He wasn't a tall man – only coming up to Pedro's shoulder – but he held himself as though he were much taller then Pedro. His skin was weathered and darkly tanned, his greeting enthusiastic. The hand he offered was rough from work. "Pedro, thank you for coming by at such short notice."

Pedro returned the smile as he shook his hand. "My pleasure, Sir."

David then directed him into a room – the floor made of rubber, the walls and ceiling covered in grey acoustic foam – and Pedro was asked to stand in the middle for twenty seconds while he was scanned. On the ceiling was a sealed glass light that came on and beamed a green flickering glow onto him, before moving in a circular motion around the room.

"All clear," said David, "and can you step this way." He went into another room, this one a soundproofed office with no windows – just a desk and two chairs. David motioned for Pedro to take a seat and asked if he wanted coffee.

"Please."

David went over to the desk and busied himself with the coffee machine as he spoke. "Pedro, we were informed by Washington late last night regarding your arrival, and we just wanted to let you know that if we can be of any help to you, don't hesitate to contact me directly. These are my contact details." He handed him a business card before going back to focusing on the coffee.

"Thank you. I'm sure I'll need your help some time; things can get rather unpredictable."

"What do you mean?"

"Well, I got to keep an eye on people, and who knows? It can all go wrong."

David nodded, keen to ask about relations between the US and Britain. "I suppose you share information?" he asked as he handed over a small cup of coffee to his guest.

"There are certain things I'm not at liberty to discuss."
Pedro's face showed no emotion. "I wish I could say more, but I
can't."

David nodded again. It was clear that he wanted to move the
conversation in a more serious direction. "Pedro, may I ask you
something?"

"Of course."

"From one man to another."

Pedro looked at him across the table for a moment, allowing
the words to sink in. The innuendo was simple.

"We are both gentlemen. We do not lie to each other,"
continued David.

Pedro inclined his head respectfully, signalling that he
understood.

"Do you trust your informers?"

Pedro was in the process of sipping his coffee, which was a
good thing because it helped conceal the grin on his face. He quickly
put on his poker face as he placed his cup down and said, "That's an
interesting question." Pedro wasn't sure what to say, but he wanted
to see where this was headed.

"I noticed that you chase a lot of bankers, so are your
informers reliable?"

Pedro gave a noncommittal nod. "Yes, it's difficult to know
who to trust these days," he added vaguely.

"Pedro, I suppose there are a lot of untrustworthy people in
that industry, but after all, a bank is a bank."

Pedro nodded. "I often find it necessary to remind myself of
a point that seems obvious, but that is often misunderstood by so
many, and that is that the World Bank is not really the World Bank
at all: it is rather a US bank, and as you know, occasionally there's –
how shall I put it – a certain degree of corruption."

"Absolutely." David pointed his cup at Pedro and extended
his forefinger. "My point exactly." He stood. "Here is your file with

the details of who you're interested in. Just keep us informed. Is there anything else?"

"No," answered Pedro. He didn't want to create any issues, and there were undoubtedly a few. Pedro wasn't willing to share, but he thought that in order to help improve his relationship with David, he should at least offer him something. He opened his briefcase and laid a plain file folder on the desk. "Have a look."

David sat back down, putting his reading glasses on before lifting the file's cover. His eyes widened with disbelief. He leaned back in the chair and scratched his scarred left cheek. "Oh, my God."

"What is it?"

"'Who' . . . 'Who' is it you mean." David shook his head. "This is someone I have not seen for a long time, but he is very dangerous."

"I heard he'd retired a few years ago. This is his address, he now lives outside Manhattan."

David nodded. "Tom MacGregor. Men like that only know one thing. They don't retire . . . they just simply die one day. So what's he doing in my home town?"

"That is a very good question," Pedro replied.

"They call him The Dog," continued David. "He started off in the trade, pulling off scams. The guy is bad and there are warrants out on him, for murder, extortion, you name it. Some of our people said he'd disappeared a long time ago." He paused, staring into his own coffee cup for a moment, lost in thought. "Thank you for that, and once again, Pedro, feel free to contact this office any time."

Pedro stood up and walked over to the door, assuming the meeting was over.

David had been born with a great sense of awareness, and he knew he had to take that awareness to another level. "Wait," he said.

Pedro shrugged. He knew the question was unavoidable.

"So how did you find out so much about Tom MacGregor? We've tried for years." David stared at him, willing him to answer.

Pedro reached for the door handle, and, with a satisfied smile, asked, "Anything else?"

He didn't argue the point with David.

Chapter 19

John lay on his back on the sagging mattress and stared at the ceiling, his thoughts unfocused. Used to being up much earlier, he was yawning and rubbing at his tired eyes. This was a very stressful time; Sonia was not talking much to him at the moment, and it was taking its toll. They lay side by side, close enough to touch, but not touching. He could hear her breathing. He was surprised to realize that she was wearing some kind of fragrance; she must have put it on before getting into bed.

"Just in case you're getting any ideas, don't," she said after a minute.

He paused for a moment before getting up, and as he stared at his reflection in the mirror, he made no attempt to deceive himself: the dark black eyes staring back at him were the look of a worried man.

Just then the telephone buzzed – a recorded message from Pedro to remind him that it had been a few weeks now and that he was still waiting for them to meet. John dropped the receiver onto the chair, feeling more exhausted than ever.

Sonia suspected there was something wrong with John: he was acting very weird, being all quiet and nervous. Meanwhile, John was just avoiding her questions, clearly hoping she would stop asking him things. She wasn't helping matters, though, forever asking him what was wrong and what was worrying him. It was a vicious circle.

Sonia curled her lip, glaring at him. John knew what she thought: that he was probably having an affair. How wrong she was.

He got out of the shower, wrapped a towel around his waist and made a decision – to sort things out with Sonia, one way or another.

"Look, I'm sorry, Sonia," he said, trying to keep his voice level. "I just didn't get much sleep last night."

"That's because you drink too much coffee," she said in a matter-of-fact tone. After a few minutes she smiled and nodded. "You caught me off guard last night," she admitted with a grin meant to put him at ease. She looked up at him wide-eyed, her mouth open to say sorry, but the word wouldn't come out. Getting fidgety now, she tucked her hair behind her ears before meeting John's gaze. He had a pleading look in his eyes. "You have to understand, John: you got to be honest."

John had to swallow, though he couldn't bring himself to say anything.

She licked her lips, taking a moment to pull herself together while John stared back at her. He slowly lifted his brows as the morning light dawned on his eyes, and Sonia's hands tightened in her lap. She stared at them for a long time before turning her whole body to face him and resting her face on his hands. He took a deep breath to steady himself and then held her tight for a moment.

He was still afraid that he might fall back into depression again, especially as he had to hide these dark secrets from Sonia, but the last thing John wanted was to upset her. How could he tell her what was going on?

There were times when he could understand why people who were backed into a corner just gave in, and this was definitely one of those times. In fact, this was the way he would feel every single day as long as he was carrying this horrible secret. But what could he do?

He knew this wasn't going to be a good day, and at the moment, John had bigger and more immediate problems to deal with; he would have to put off debating his salvation for another day. Right now he was more focused on finding out how Pedro would react to what he had to say – Pedro had opened a small office in town, and it appeared that his new line of work was beginning to keep him busy.

John jumped into his car and drove quickly, mulling over what he was going to say to him. When he got to the location, he parked near the entrance to the car park, beyond which sat an old brick house with advertised office space.

Without stopping to think – or talk himself out of it, maybe – he walked upstairs and banged hard on the door to the office, feeling quite angry about the whole situation. The insane grins and double thumbs-ups between both of them were, as far as he was concerned, now history.

He opened the door to find Pedro sitting at his desk, and surprising himself, John shouted, "Why don't you just fucking leave me alone?"

Pedro grinned, a smile devoid of humour. "Sorry, John, but you know very well I can't do that; I know what you've done."

"What do you mean?" John asked, his bravado slipping.

Pedro raised his eyebrows in surprise, then started laughing – something that confused John even more. "Just do what I say," Pedro said. "I suppose you'll be telling me next that it was all my fault!" he added sarcastically.

John nodded, not trusting himself to speak yet.

"What?" he shouted. "It was your fault. John, I would like us to be friends and get along. But first, tell me what happened to the parcel?"

"You mean when you set me up, and I was attacked?"

"That's right, and you killed the guy. Remember?"

"No. That was self-defence, and you know it."

"So why did you run away, John?"

"My hands might have been bloody but my conscience is clean. I had done the job you asked me to do." He tightened his jaw, forcing himself to control his anger. Pedro wanted him to react, but John was in control here, not him.

"I say it again, John. I want to be your friend."

John cocked his head, as a vein started to throb in his left temple. "Listen to me, Mr Clever: so where's the evidence? What evidence do you have that I killed someone?" He balled up his fist at his side; he would have loved to punch the little shit right in the face.

"Rock solid, I got all I need," Pedro said, his face pale but his voice firm. "There's no disputing it, and you don't seem to be taking this seriously."

"Oh, I'm taking this deadly seriously, I can assure you," John said.

"I'm disappointed in you; I thought we understood each other. Tell me where the parcel is, John."

The way John pursed his lips told Pedro that he wasn't following his line of reasoning, and he shook his head abruptly as if to clear his thoughts from what was being said.

"Well," Pedro prompted him to reply, "I know you have it."

"I would say it's pretty obvious," John said, folding his arms across his chest and letting his weight settle on one leg. "The fact is, I don't know. I must have dropped it when I was running. I hid behind the rubbish bin, so I could have dropped it there. Just be careful about what conclusion you draw."

"Conclusion? What conclusion?" Pedro stood up, stepping forward to within striking distance of John. "I think you should be careful with the tone you use with me," he said. He knew John was lying. "I'll tell you what you did." Pedro shifted his weight from one foot to the other. "You took it and put it somewhere, and now I want it returned." He took a step back and looked at him expectantly.

John's face hardened, and within a second he had closed the distance between them, before prodding Pedro in the chest with his right index finger. "Why don't you calm down and stop being such a dick for a second? What kind of asshole do you think I am? I'm telling you again: I don't have your parcel."

Naturally, Pedro didn't like the reply, and he stared at John with narrowed eyes, more than a hint of menace in them. He fished out a Marlboro, lit up, and let out a discontent sigh.

John's lips twitched a little. "I'm not lying."

Page 180

John could tell by Pedro's expression that he was deeply concerned about something: he easily picked up on the tone of hesitancy in his voice. John kept his eyes on him, fidgeting with his key ring as he asked, "What's bothering you?"

"What's not bothering me would be a more accurate question," replied Pedro. "For now the parcel can wait; we'll come back to that conversation another time."

Pedro was trying to read a document at the same time as talking, and he wiped a drop of sweat from his face with his forearm as he looked down at the paper.

John still felt uneasy. He thought back to the first time he'd laid eyes on Pedro: his gut had told him everything he needed to know. He didn't like him that much then, and he sure as hell didn't trust him now. Pedro was complex, calculating, and he always had that sly look in his eyes, like he was constantly planning how to get one over on you.

He stared at John for a few moments, until he could no longer hide the trembling of his lips or the way his eyes were stinging. He shook his head almost frantically, covering his mouth with a shaking hand before seeming to calm himself down. He looked John directly in the eyes and said, "Enough of this nonsense. What is done is done." He patted John on the shoulder. His tone was honeyed, meant to smooth over the situation, but it was having the opposite effect on John.

Tilting his head as though he had something to prove, Pedro mumbled, "Look, John, I'm going to look after you and you're going to look after me, OK?"

John found himself stepping closer as his voice lowered to an angry hiss. "Is this the part where you tell me you're a changed man?"

Pedro ignored his question. "Both of us are going on a journey together, and I'll be watching you all the time to make sure you don't try to double-cross me. I am here for a reason, so don't undermine me; I know what I'm doing and I am always one step ahead. Remember, you killed that man, and, as far as I know, the police are still looking for the killer. The best thing now is for you to just take it easy, and sign on with my agency." He actually had the nerve to smile as he added, "You're such a hard man, John."

John looked at Pedro with a blank expression, working his lips to try and frame his next words. Eventually, he nodded his head, sucking in a deep breath. "For God's sake!" he cried. "Are you even listening to me? Leave me alone!" He was breathing heavily now, beginning to lose his grip on the conversation.

"What is it you want from me?" John asked. He knew the question made it seem like he was considering giving in, so he countered it with harshness as he spat out, "I won't waste your time."

"We really need to be friends," Pedro said in between puffs of his cigarette, which he'd picked up while John had been talking.

John couldn't speak for a moment, but after a few seconds, he finally found his voice. "Is this some kind of a trick?" he stammered.

Pedro leaned forward, getting far too close for comfort as he whispered in his ear, "Nothing of the sort."

John recoiled away from him, taking a step back. "Look, I know you're being difficult with me, but can we just drop it?"

Pedro smirked at him as John took a moment to think. He was beginning to run out of options. He knew that Pedro wasn't a nice person, but if he were to accept that Pedro could change, then maybe he would change as well? John knew he just had to accept the way it was, no matter how much he didn't want to do it.

Just then, the phone started to ring. Pedro stared at him, then at the phone, then back at him before asking, "Is there anything else?"

John carefully lowered his hands to his knees. "If you don't pick up, you'll never get any business." The phone stopped ringing, and Pedro made a face, stabbing the cigarette in the ashtray as he let out a mortified growl. John stepped back in surprise, and during the stunned silence, the door to the office opened and a woman stepped in. John thought this would be a good opportunity to make a scene in front of his clients, but he decided it just wasn't worth it; the conversation had zapped all of his energy.

"Take a seat, I'll be with you in a minute," Pedro called out to her.

John was still standing by Pedro's side, throwing quick glances over his shoulder at the woman.

"John, I'll see you later."

The woman stood frozen to the spot, her fidgeting hands giving away her nerves. She was staring at Pedro with a look of desperation in her eyes.

"Forgive me," she whispered, grabbing Pedro's hands as she spoke. "I've been to the police, they won't do anything. It was all part of this drug culture," she said. "Look, my son, he's caught up in it too."

Pedro saw the frustration on her face. "This lowlife might have to learn things the hard way." He glanced at John, nodding at him in a way that made it clear: they were done here.

John slipped out of the room, his gaze remaining on the woman until Pedro closed the door behind him.

Later that day, Pedro was standing directly in front of the school, staring at the open space in front of the building. You could see the deals being done: it was evident by their dark, shallow eye sockets and fidgety behaviour that they had drug habits.

Pedro was sitting in the café opposite, pretending to read a newspaper while he studied the various faces. As he did so, he could feel the eyes of the dozen or so patrons on him – there was a hard edge to the cafe and its clientele. Pedro had been able to sense it immediately.

For the next hour, he took his time and watched the men and women who stopped by to visit the dealers, the practiced manoeuvres of quiet hands exchanging things under the tables. The pusher across the street was short and fat, and he wore dirty jeans with a long black coat. Pedro watched a few more transactions take

Page 183

place before standing up and placing some cash on the table. Leaving the cafe, he approached the man outside with a smile on his face.

"What can I do for you?" the dealer asked, while taking a drag from his cigarette.

Pedro nodded at him briefly, rubbing his palms on his trousers, continuing to fake nervousness.

The man began to mumble a short list of his drugs and his prices, but Pedro stopped him mid-sentence. "Let's walk over there," Pedro said, pointing at a nearby alleyway. The man agreed, grinding his cigarette butt under his heel.

Once in the alley, Pedro winked at the man and said, "I'm not a druggie. So, I'll make this simple for you: if you try and push your shit in this area again, they'll find you swinging from the rafters of that basement you live in on Tottenham Court Road. Do I make myself clear?"

Without warning, Pedro spun around to the left, a short metal pipe clutched firmly in his right hand. He swung it with such force that it broke the man's chin.

"So, do I make myself clear?" he asked again as he watched the drug dealer cower on the floor.

"Yeah," he spluttered, through the blood that was now pouring down his face and neck.

Pedro smiled. Things were going in the right direction, and he was on course to expand his business. In a big way.

Chapter 20

She was almost there. The industrial estate was a maze, but she had no difficulty finding the place she was looking for. She parked her Ford, got out, and forged a path through the crowd who were waiting for the fish-and-chip shop to open.

Opening the office door, she asked for Pedro, and he turned, folding his forearms across the top of his expensive high-backed leather chair. It swirled to the left until his weight settled.

She was a very tasteful-looking woman, at least in her mid-forties. She wore a tight, black, short skirt and a revealing white blouse, and she smiled in a way that made you look at her twice. She was here for a job interview and she clearly knew how to impress. Pedro couldn't take his eyes off her as she raised her hand to her face and brushed back her long, black, wavy hair.

"So nice to meet you. Welcome to my office."

"Thank you," she said, smiling at him warmly.

"Have a seat. Can I get you a glass of water?"

"Please."

She looked around the small office, finishing her survey at approximately the same time that Pedro poured them both a glass of water. Her eyes zeroed in on the old-looking leather briefcase on his desk.

"So, Sue, can you tell me what experience you have? I've read your CV and I saw there was a gap of nearly six months, so I'd like you to run me through the details."

After a conversation about a well-known pop star whom she'd recently had arrested for a drug-related crime, she went on to explain that the pop star had been set up by someone on the police force.

"I had an issue with one of my colleagues. Balls had been in the force for twenty years – that wasn't his real name, but it was what they all called him. His real name was Bradley Dowler. His most prominent feature was a hooded brow, that I once heard described as being 'hung like a cliff over a pair of cold black eyes'. He scared people."

Pedro took a swig of his water, chewed on his bottom lip for a second, and then in a quite voice asked, "So what happened?"

"I exposed him, and life became difficult. The other lads gave me a hard time, so I quit."

"Were a lot of people upset about what happened?"

"Of course. I learned a long time ago, Pedro, that you can't control what people say or do."

As they continued to talk, Pedro and Sue started to hit it off, and he was more than impressed. An hour later, he found that he really couldn't fault her. Sue's manner was both chatty and enthusiastic, and it was clear that she was a very intelligent woman.

She crossed her legs, then uncrossed them as she asked him, "What is your core business?"

"At the moment I'm doing little bits of work for the newspapers; mainly finding people, really. We don't check our watches or what day it is – we just get the job done. You know how it is… just because it's Sunday doesn't mean our enemies take the day off."

"Very true," Sue said.

Pedro unbuttoned his suit jacket, took it off, and draped it over the back of his leather office chair. He clasped his hands in front of his chin and seemed to consider where he should start. Inhaling sharply, he asked, "How are you when things get rough?"

"If you mean do I get sick at the sight of blood while on a crime scene, you don't need to worry about that; I've seen enough bodies in my time."

Pedro was keen to make contacts within the police to help him achieve what he had come to London for, and for this he needed to recruit Sue West. She was good at her job, and she had risen quickly through the ranks of the Metropolitan Police, both in spite of the fact that she was a woman and because she was a woman. Political pressures had ushered in the brave new age of women in positions of command, and Sue knew there were still plenty of misogynists around who thought the only reason she'd made it was that the bosses had had to reach their quota. She ignored all the whispers, focused on her job, and took comfort in the fact that she still had some friends who knew she was qualified and had earned her position.

"As I said, don't worry about me. I'm used to being in the middle of it." She smiled, and so did Pedro – this was exactly what he needed.

Her new role was to be forensic investigator. It was common for the Metropolitan Police to employ independent companies to help with forensics, albeit purely in the photographic area, and some cases required independent forensic advice. This was an excellent opportunity for Pedro to ease his way into the back rooms of the police, and to try to find as much information as he could about any key figures in the force.

Yes, Sue West would be perfect.

***

John was just about to enter the M3 when he realised that he'd left his keys at Pedro's office, so he continued on the roundabout and doubled back on himself. Traffic was light on the way back, and he got there in record time.

As he rushed up the stairs, he spotted the shadows of two people through the frosted glass of the door – it looked like they were huddled over, talking. John's mind was still trying to make sense of the events that had brought him here, as well as the one question he still couldn't answer: who could he trust?

The desire to flee is not always wise, he told himself, as he took a deep breath and opened the door. He stood there with his hands shoved deep in his pockets, and he cracked a smile as he quietly said, "Sorry to interrupt. I left my keys here."

Pedro nodded, as if the interruption hadn't rattled him in the slightest. "John, this is Sue. Sue, John."

"Really nice to meet you," Sue said, smiling at the newcomer.

"John just started working here today," Pedro said pointedly.

Pedro had spent a lifetime observing people, and John wondered if Pedro had noticed something about her that had caught his eye. It was nothing drastic, just the way she stared. John watched her carefully for a minute, and her expression never changed, not even once, not even when he looked directly into her eyes.

She seemed to have decided not to talk – she just nodded and smiled a lot as she listened to John and Pedro. She then continued the conversation she'd been having with Pedro earlier.

It turned out that she kept a notebook; John noticed Pedro's eyes as she ran her finger down the list of names and contacts. She raised her right eyebrow a fraction, just enough to make her point. John laughed.

"We were just about to have lunch," Pedro said. "Why don't you join us?"

"I'm a professional," she said, "I never mix business with pleasure."

"Golden rule?" Pedro asked mockingly.

A slight smile tugged wistfully at the corners of her lips as she wondered what Pedro would be like in bed – of course, that would never happen; she had to remain professional.

If she'd known how scientifically he was analysing her, she'd have got up and walked away right there and then. None of the women he'd dated had lasted. Maybe he was the problem; he just didn't have the urge to shop around, or make a concerted effort. Life seemed too short.

Sensing the tension in the room, John turned to Pedro. "I can't do lunch either; things to do, people to see." With that, he nodded at Sue and turned to leave.

"See you tomorrow!" Pedro called out to him as he closed the door.

The next day, Pedro called John on the telephone.

"I have a job for you."

"Please will you leave me alone?" asked John, getting a little desperate now. "If I help you…" he trailed off, sighing. "Actually, what is it you want me to do?"

"I just want you to sit in restaurants."

He paused, trying to get his head around the statement. "So you want me to eavesdrop?" He'd almost been hoping Pedro wanted him to do clerical work in the office, help with filing and answering the phones. Of course, that was too good to be true.

"That's right."

"On who?"

"Doesn't matter at the moment."

"Can I be the judge of that?" John asked sarcastically.

Pedro cleared his throat, his mind working fast. "If our relationship is going to work, I need you to understand certain things. When I tell you I want something to happen and I want it to happen immediately, it needs to happen."

John felt the hair on the back of his neck stand up. He cleared his throat and pushed his chair back a few inches, resisting the urge to just slam the telephone down.

"I understand, but there are certain complications."

"You don't need to worry about any complications, just do want I say." He paused, and John could hear him sighing. "You know what, John? You need to get off your high horse. You're not the only one who I look after here. You need to listen to me."

"Do I now?"

"You made a deal with me a long time ago and now I'm saving your ass – that is something you should never forget. If you're willing to step back and take an honest look at this relationship, you'll understand that it has been a very beneficial one for both of us. If you're not willing to do that, then let's end this thing right now, and trust me on this: a week from now, you'll be in a cell."

John couldn't remain silent for another second, and when he replied, his voice was razor sharp. "Oh, for Christ's sake!" He wanted to growl, to really let rip with a chest-vibrating, rib-cracking growl. Then he wanted to tackle Pedro and rub his face in the dirt – perhaps he'd do just that when he was next in the office. The all-knowing attitude – as if he could read everything about John – was irritating the hell out of him.

The next time John was in the office, Pedro acted as if it was no big deal, and the sheer stupidity of it all meant that John was tempted not to go through with it. What Pedro wanted him to do was to spy, there was no way to sugar-coat it. Spying. A crime that carried a long jail sentence. He asked again why Pedro wanted him to do it but just got back an earful of harsh words, none of which really answered his question.

John stared blankly at the desk for a minute, images of what he wanted him to do flashing through his mind. What Pedro was saying implied something pretty sick, and it worried him.

John was messing about with the zip on his jacket, zipping it part way up, then down, then back up again as he thought.

"Are you listening, John?" Pedro asked, impatience in his voice.

John glanced up from what he was doing and nodded. Before Pedro could say anything else, the phone rang and he took the call. John watched the emotions play across his face as he spoke to whoever was on the other end. It was a brief conversation, but it was clearly important.

When Pedro ended the call, he looked up with regret in his eyes. "I'm sorry, I've got to go. I have a meeting with a man called Samuel."

John was surprised to hear the frustration in his voice. It was as though he had a split personality, with one side of him working behind the scenes. He really didn't know which Pedro was the real Pedro, and that worried him. It worried him a lot.

"John, I don't think you take me seriously enough, so I'll say no more. I am losing faith in you. I'll call you soon." And with that, he left.

Chapter 21

John had been refusing to think of his reaction to Pedro's 'request' as anything other than a little curiosity, and he suddenly wanted a drink, very badly. He never normally reacted to stress this way.

Shit. Shit. He took a deep breath, trying to get his thoughts in order. Still uneasy about the whole situation, he'd decided to make some enquiries and find out a bit more about Pedro, but so far he was getting nowhere: it was as if this person did not exist and had no identity. When he'd met Pedro, Argentina was at war with Great Britain. Could this be the reason he was here, for a revenge attack? But if that were true, then who was he after?

Wanting to get out of the office, John had gone for a walk and had ended up at a local bookstore. While he was there he thought he'd look up reference books about leaders and dictators, but he was having trouble finding what he wanted.

After taking a lot of subtle but deep breaths, he made eye contact with the young man behind the counter who, when asked, nodded, said "Yes Sir," and then led him to the shelf where they were located.

Taking down some of the books, John pulled out a notepad and pen and started to take notes. After a while, he noticed that the young assistant was still loitering, apparently keen to say something. John looked up at him.

"We close at four," he finally said.

John nodded, before focusing back on the books. He wasn't even sure what he was searching for; maybe he thought he was going to find Pedro's name and photograph in a book. But then it occurred to him that Pedro probably wasn't his real name – it could be absolutely anything. He had no idea where to start, and he could feel the desperation building up inside him.

The young staff member lit a cigarette and headed towards him with a glint of purpose in his eyes, telling him, "We are closed now."

John squinted up at him. "Smoking'll kill you."

The young man just rolled his eyes and looked the other way.

Weird, John thought, before throwing him a skeptical look and walking out of the shop. Finding the nearest phone booth, he called his answering service – it sounded like he'd become pretty popular: two new messages. Well, it was more than he usually got. The first was from Pedro telling him they needed to meet again, which he deleted right away. His wife, Sonia, had left the second message. She was calling to let him know that the dinner party had been confirmed, and would he "please not throw a fit?" He owed her, but he wasn't sure he owed her quite that much. At the last dinner party they'd attended he'd been rude to her friend, and it had ended up with her going nuts – she'd never liked him, so it was a mutual feeling, but still… it hadn't gone down well with Sonia. John slammed the receiver back into the cradle, shot a quick look at his watch, and winced. Actually, he thought, I've only got ten minutes to get to the office.

Outside, he sat in the car for a few minutes to make sure no one was in the building. Then, certain that the office was closed for the day, he went around the back, walking quickly. As it was getting dark and as he really had to act quickly, the only way in was through the window, which he hurried over to.

John needed to get into Pedro's office so he could – hopefully – find something of interest, and after hesitating for a moment, he decided to break the window glass, careful not to let it fall on the floor. Instead, he put the broken pieces into a black rubbish sack before checking behind him, making sure that no one was watching him: the last thing he needed was for the police to come.

Fully aware that Pedro was too clever to believe that this was simply a burglary, he had to clean up after the break-in, and after measuring the size of the glass, he went over to the nearby glazier and bought a sheet of glass and a tube of silicone. He knew Pedro was going to be away for a few days, which meant that he had a bit of time to try to find out as much as he could.

Back in the office, he turned on one of the desk lights, aware that the overhead lights would be too bright. Pedro had this thing about really bright lights, which was good for when you were working, but bad when it came to covert operations.

Pedro always kept the key for the filing cupboard in the desk drawer, and John flipped through the stack of notes but found nothing of real interest.

After a few more minutes of fruitless searching, he sat at his desk, trying to think. Would Pedro keep anything here in his office? Leaning his arms on the table, he tried to think like him, studying the walls as though looking for some meaning in the plaster. After having a good look around, he methodically picked his way through various bits of papers that had been left scattered around the room. Most of Pedro's private paperwork wasn't there; John knew that Pedro carried it in his briefcase, but it was worth a look anyway.

He was getting towards the end of his search when his eyes widened. In one of the filing cabinet drawers was a cardboard box wrapped in brown Kraft paper. It was heavy, around ten pounds, and reinforced with filament tape. There was no writing on the paper. Mysterious. Very mysterious.

He removed the box, placed it on the floor between his feet, and then stared at it, so ominous in this new setting.

Suddenly, a sense of dread descended on him. Why haven't I found this before? I should have found it. Plus, if he opened the box now, Pedro would know that someone had been looking around his office. There was only one thing for it: he decided to place it back in the drawer.

He used the sleeve of his sweater to wipe the filing cabinet – just in case he'd left any fingerprints – and then continued with his search. He found nothing except for a piece of paper in the waste bin with a long-distance telephone number written in marker pen. On the back of the paper, the name of a café was written in black ink.

Could it be that the parcel was meant for someone at the address of the cafe? His skin crawled at the possibilities. Thinking that the number might come in handy, he took his pad and pencil from his pocket and immediately jotted it down. He then put the piece of paper back where he'd he found it in the waste bin. That was when he noticed something else: several timetables for the London Underground. He looked closely but found nothing of importance on them.

Just sitting at his desk, he experienced that sickening feeling people have after engaging in something deeply private only to find out that they'd been observed. To tell the truth, he was half expecting Pedro to walk through the door – maybe he was losing his cool or something like that.

Suddenly, the telephone started to ring, and John ignored it in case it was Pedro checking in. On the sixth ring, the answering machine kicked in, making him jump. He couldn't ignore the call altogether though, so John sat up, tapping his pencil against the table top. There was a crackle.

"Hello, this is Milan. Can you call me? I need to talk to you." The tone of his voice was laden with worry. The background noise faded on the line.

Not expecting any meaningful clues, John decided to keep an open mind and not jump to any conclusions. Whatever was going on with Pedro was his business alone; John just wanted to make sure that he wasn't involved. After a strained pause, he told himself for the hundredth time that he should be careful.

Eventually, John decided to call it a day; he wasn't going to find anything else in the office, and the more time he spent there, the more likely it was he'd be seen by someone.

Before he climbed out of the window, he cleaned up any remaining broken bits of glass from around the window frame, then set the silicone around the edge of the frame before gently pushing the new glass into its layer. It was getting dark now, which made it much easier for him to move around.

He walked around the front with the black dustbin bag, then threw it randomly in someone's front garden. Once he'd got back into his car, he sat there, thinking. John knew he needed to do something, but what? He could try to expose Pedro, which might be the answer, but how could he do that without exposing himself? He decided the best way was to play along with Pedro's plan and just wait for the right moment to make his move.

Chapter 22

Samuel was waiting at a small table outside a fast food joint when Pedro pulled in. The only reason he'd spotted him was because he was a slightly taller version of his father, right down to the grim lips and hard jaw. He looked just about as approachable, too.

"Samuel?" Pedro asked, extending a hand.

"Yeah, that's me," said the man, slowing coming to his feet and returning the handshake. He carried himself as though he was operating on too little sleep and too much stress. "I appreciate you meeting with me in spite of your busy schedule. Can I get you a drink or something?"

Pedro shook his head and sat down.

Samuel nodded. "Then let's get started. This is the new file. He will be coming soon, so expect him shortly."

Showing little emotion, Pedro raised his head and said, "Okay, leave it with me," then slid the file into his briefcase. He didn't want to say too much. Instead he shifted on his stool, as though he was rearranging himself.

Samuel got up, scratched his head, held his hand out to Pedro and said, "Yeah, nice to meet you."

Pedro cocked his head curiously. "Okay." The meeting over, Pedro got up and walked away. It had been a long wait – tens of thousands of man hours of prep – and the meeting was now done. If Pedro was going to complete his contract, he knew he'd have to get John on his side.

It was getting dark, and Pedro tossed his briefcase haphazardly onto the passenger seat as he sped off in his dark blue BMW. Parking quickly, he rushed up the steps to the office and sat down at his desk. He was in a dangerous mood, having spent the day considering his next move, and he was very much on edge.

Just then, Pedro heard the screen door slide open and Sue approached from behind, gently touching his shoulder. Over the last week she had opened up to him – had shared so much with him – and in return he had revealed almost nothing of his past, except that he had briefly worked for the Argentine Central Intelligence Agency. It had taken a considerable degree of craftiness and charm to get that much out of him. Pedro had begun his career as a young analyst, but it wasn't long before he found his way into the Operations Directorate. That was all she knew.

The traffic was bad and John was running late, his smile fading as he considered his situation. He looked at his watch, driving quickly as he weaved in and out of the constant stream of cars, passing under a glowing billboard that was promoting cigarette smoking. Coming to a halt, he turned the engine off and slammed the car door shut.

"I'm sorry I couldn't get here any earlier, traffic was heavy," John's eyes went watery, cheeks flushed. "Sorry again."

Pedro studied him, making John feel scrutinised; he reached up and self-consciously smoothed his ruffled hair.

Just after John had reluctantly agreed to work for him, Pedro had increased the team and brought in Reg Wright. At the time, Pedro had chewed on the right words to describe Reg: "He has spent over twenty-five years in forensics at Scotland Yard," was all he would say, and John had looked unconvinced. To this day, no one could understand why Pedro had employed Reg; he had to be ready to collect his pension, and his value and worth to the business wasn't readily apparent.

In the office now, Reg didn't look happy as he took off a pair of cheap reading glasses. "Listen to me, I can walk through a house once and know more about its occupants than a psychiatrist could after a year of sessions," he boasted.

Sue didn't even try to hide her smile; she even let out a tiny laugh. "Oh, really?"

"Sue! Take it easy," Pedro snapped.

Sue looked contrite. "Sorry, Reg. I shouldn't have teased you."

"As long as you do a good job, I don't care." Pedro took a deep pull of smoke, held it in his lungs for a glorious moment, then let it swirl from his nose.

Reg ignored her apology. "I can't believe you; I mean, this is me we're talking about." With that, he picked up his glasses and returned them to the bridge of his nose.

Sue was watching him. "I don't even know what I'm saying sometimes," she said quietly.

"As an example," continued Reg, "I like a house that looks lived-in – general wear and tear is a healthy sign. A house that's too antiseptic speaks as much to me of domestic discord as a house in complete disarray. Alcoholics, binge eaters, addicts, sexual deviants, philanderers, depressives – you name it – I can see it. I can see it all in the worn edges of their nest. You catch the smoky reek of stale scotch and cigarettes, a desperate abundance of smells. Normally I don't even have to go inside the house to make a diagnosis; the curb side analysis is usually enough."

Sue and John exchanged looks. Her raised eyebrow spoke volumes, as in, What's he talking about?

Pedro looked at Reg and said, "If you ever have a question, just ask me. I don't usually bite."

John's eyes flared and he turned away with a secret smile. "No, you don't. Not usually."

Pedro had to take a call, and after a few minutes he placed the phone down, stood up very slowly and took off his jacket. His expression unchanged, he coughed a quiet cough and told them all to sit down.

They had been asked to re-examine a crime scene where the police had discovered a decapitated corpse. "The medical examiner thinks that the blow was struck with a long serrated-edged blade into the mouth. He understands that there have been similar cases."

Sue glanced over at him. "How do you mean?"

"Three other deaths over the last three years. All stabbed in the mouth with a serrated-edged blade. What we have is a serial killer in London." He paused dramatically to let this statement sink in with everyone. "Let's take Reg with us. He might be able to help."

"Okay, I'll get the camera. Let's see what we can find – you never know."

"Listen you two, we cannot be too involved with the case. We just need to give a second opinion, okay?"

Sue nodded, before adding, "Let's go in my car."

They all walked out to Sue's car, and as soon as he'd got in, John had the thought that it was like sitting in a perfume boutique. She must have sprayed her car that morning, but it wasn't a bad thing – it was a cheerful surprise.

Reg shrugged out of his jacket, slumping down in his seat next to John while Pedro sat in the front. The traffic was bad, as ever, but soon they were very close to the crime scene, and as Pedro always said that was the time you had to keep your eyes peeled, they slowed down on approaching the traffic lights.

Sue eased back on the accelerator, pumping the brake in an attempt to stop, but the tyres on the car began to lose their grip and they felt the vehicle swerve across the road. Sue quickly remembered to steer into the skid to keep the car on track, and after the wheels had locked, they eventually came to a stop.

John shivered, but it wasn't just the cold that was giving him goosebumps: he thought they should have been more careful. He looked at Reg, whose mouth was quivering, his dentures clacking against his remaining teeth.

"I'm not feeling too great," said Reg, wiping sweat off his forehead.

"Easy buddy," whispered John, who had tilted his head back against the headrest, suddenly exhausted. When he leaned forwards and saw just how sick Reg looked, he grabbed a towel that had been lying on the middle seat and pressed it to his temple.

Reg's eyes shot open and he jumped a little, moving his head against the towel. "I'm sorry. I'm sorry. This is terrible." He sounded as though he was consumed by remorse and embarrassment; his mouth was tight as he spoke, his voice shaking with pent-up fury.

Pedro suggested that Reg should wait in the car while they went over to the crime scene, and everyone agreed. Luckily, the mobile flashing light on the roof of the car guided them through the darkness to the scene, where yellow crime scene tape festooned several brownstone houses, and where uniformed officers had taken up their positions on the corners. An ambulance was now on the scene, as were several vans from the local media.

"So what have we got?" asked Sue.

A group of men stood around the body: the fluorescent yellow of the ambulance men waiting to take it away, and policemen in black waterproofs and chequered hats who thought they had seen it all before. Until now.

They parted wordlessly to let Sue through, and the first thing she saw was the police surgeon crouching down, leaning over the corpse and delicately brushing aside the soil with latex fingers. He looked up, and as she loomed overhead, Sue saw the brown withered shin of the dead man.

"He's been dead for a few hours?" she asked.

"No more than that," agreed the man.

"How did he die?"

"Violently, by the looks of it. There appear to be several wounds to the throat and mouth, but it'll take the pathologist to give you a definitive cause of death." He stood up and peeled off his gloves. "Better get him out of here before the rain comes."

Sue nodded, but she couldn't take her eyes off the face of the young man. Although there was a shrivelled aspect to his features, they would be recognisable to anyone who knew him. The last victim had bled to death, and the thought made Sue sick. From the look of this one, she would guess the same. Thankfully, though, it wasn't her job to guess.

"Myuhmyuhmyuh." It was a thick-tongued noise, a noise she always made when she wanted to convey her indecisiveness, accompanied by a dazed roll of the eyes. It was all she could say at the moment.

A man had peeled off from the crowd and was now walking towards the crime scene. In his late thirties, he had dark hair and heavily muscled shoulders. Maybe another policeman, Pedro thought, though he didn't recognise him.

"Inspector Long," said the man, holding out his hand.

Pedro took his hand, his handshake tight but quick.

"As of this moment, we have uniforms securing the external perimeter. There are men posted here, here, and here," he pointed. "Uniforms have already evacuated the ground floor flat. We haven't had contact with anyone inside the residence yet, which, frankly, doesn't make me happy. Can you make yourself useful and have a look?"

"Perfect," Pedro replied.

He picked up his pace. Now charged with a task, he had choices to make, and he ran through them quickly in his mind. First off, he instructed Sue and John to look around the grounds while he checked the upstairs flats. Once that was done, he would think of what needed doing next.

After a while of searching, Pedro heard the distant sound of breaking glass coming from the direction of a window in the building across the street. He suspected it came from the balcony that overlooked the crime scene, but when he scanned each room, he couldn't find anyone. He had now been on the scene for ten minutes and he reported in the detail.

Sue took a deep breath and immediately regretted it: it was the smell that made it worse. The repulsive combination of spilled booze, urine, and the weird, almost metallic odour of blood. While holding a cup of coffee in one hand and desperately wishing she had a cigarette in the other, she was momentarily conscious of the fact that she wasn't wearing any makeup, and her hair, which she wore tied back, was probably sticking out in a way that made her look slightly deranged. She'd been to enough crime scenes over the years, however, to know it was a waste of time to worry. Instead, her eyes returned to the body of the victim where it lay, both humped and sprawling.

Trying to take over, she suggested that if you looked closely, you'd see that some of the blood had been sprayed back towards where the body was lying. "I suspect the killer did it to wash away his or her footprints," she added.

"Yes, I agree, and if you look closely, you'll also see that the killer must have moved the body – there is blood by this tree," John said. She looked at him with an air of astonishment. "No," she said. "The body was struck by the tree and he somehow must have wandered over and fallen."

Inspector Long, who was leading the investigation, interrupted. "Also, I think we may have a partial print to the right of the body along the fence." He pointed to a small patch of mud and the corner of what looked like a tennis shoe track. "Can we get someone to cast that before we step on it?"

"Thanks for the input, Inspector."

Inspector Balls was also at the crime scene, and he surprised the hell out of Sue by patting her on the back and offering a hand that was completely ignored until he eventually let it fall casually to his side.

For her part, Sue had hoped to get through the rest of her life without ever seeing Inspector Balls again, but tonight her luck had ran out. Balls had been one of the officers who'd turned against her when she'd worked on the pop star drug case. As her gazed shifted to the other side of the crime scene, Balls called out far too loudly, "A pleasure to see you. It's been far too long!"

Sue sighed and spat out her words, not caring who heard, "What are you doing here?"

"You know how things work," he replied with a broad grin. "We go where we have to." Balls laughed heartily, and when he was just one step away from Sue, he held out his arms as if he was ready to embrace an old friend.

Sue shuddered at the thought of touching him, and frowning, she stretched out her right hand, signalling him to keep his distance.

Balls began patting the pockets of his coat in search of something, and a moment later, he fished out a packet of cigarettes and a lighter. He lit one and extended it to Sue.

Disgusted by the gesture, she turned the other way. She had always prided herself on being professional at all times, but she was seriously struggling to keep her cool in front of the Inspector.

"Come now, my dear Sue. I know it ended badly between us, and I'm sorry for that, but surely we can be professional about this?" he asked with a smile.

Sue said nothing for a moment, before spitting out the words, "You're a prick." She stood there with a file shielding her right hand, and as she held two hidden fingers up to him she replied, "If you're so clever, how many fingers am I holding up?"

Balls just smiled.

Sue fixated her eyes on the inch-long piece of ash that was precariously dangling from the end of Balls' cigarette. "This is a crime scene. If that ash drops on the ground or on the body..."

"Sorry," Balls said, wide-eyed as he suddenly realised his mistake. He held his hand under the ash as he made his way to the kerb and flicked it into the street.

Watching him leave, Sue's eyes narrowed as he hissed through clenched teeth, "I'll be back in a minute, Sue."

Just then the forensic team arrived, and a photographer stood to one side of the body, clicking away. Balls shouldered his way back into the garden.

"Any idea who killed him?" She found herself asking the question before she could stop herself, and instantly regretted it because she knew that Balls was incapable of telling the truth.

This was definitely not one of those straightforward murders, like wife cheats on husband and husband goes on a killing spree. This was an entirely different scenario, and as Balls continued to analyse the obvious, Sue's eyes were busy noting the more interesting aspects of the crime scene. There were certain incongruities she had noticed, but she was keeping them to herself. For now.

As she was staring at him, she suddenly remembered something about Balls. His bravado was misleading, but the sudden case of the fidgets wasn't – the guy was so shifty.

Balls turned to Sue and smiled at her. "So, who are you working for now?"

"Just a private investigation agency," she answered vaguely. The less he knew about her, the better, as far as she was concerned. She gave him a reproachful look that was as beguiling as it was coy.

He called out to her again, intrigued, but she silenced him, her hand slicing through the air and cutting him off. "I can't do this right now. Get it? I can't."

He wavered where he was standing, for a second looking like he wanted nothing more than to come right back at her and pick up where they'd left off.

She stared back at him stonily for a few breaths and then finally glanced away.

The sweater Sue was wearing was clinging just a little too tightly to her curves, and it wasn't surprising that most of the male police officers were checking her out – when you didn't have much to do other than stand in position, the sight of an attractive woman was something you couldn't ignore.

John also gave her the nod, but she just shook her head and ignored all the attention she was getting.

It was a relief when she could finally step away from the crime scene again, and she gratefully drank in the air. It was hardly fresh, but even the traffic fumes were better than what she'd been breathing recently. Across the street, the crowd of onlookers had grown since she'd arrived – as usual, the news of a killing had spread rapidly around the neighbourhood, and everyone wanted in on it. It never ceased to amaze her how people liked to come and gawk, as if murder was a spectator sport, and there was always a dubious minority who wanted to share the experience. Some things never changed.

After what felt like hours and hours, Pedro suggested to Sue they should grab something to eat. "I can't guarantee we won't run into these people, though."

Sue nodded and picked up her bag.

Pedro was glancing around at the groups of people nearby as he waited for her to answer, trying to make sure he didn't put her in an awkward situation. She threw her bag into the back of her car and slid into the driver's seat. Buckling up his seat belt, Pedro suggested The Fig and Tree around the corner, hoping for some privacy so they could talk freely.

"I used to go there a lot when I worked at the station," Sue said in the way of an answer, and the conversation quickly turned to the time when she'd had issues with the other officers at the station.

"Balls seems like a top-drawer asshole," Pedro observed.

"He wanted to pin it on me, wanted to make himself look good," replied Sue bitterly.

They soon got to the pub, and upon entering, Pedro chose a door-facing seat in one of the booths. The waitress came over and took their drinks order, then Pedro turned to Sue. "As a general rule, when I'm in public places, I don't like sitting with my back to the door," he explained. "I want to be able to see who's coming in and going out, just in case."

Sue slipped in next to him, nodding. Sometimes she found people's habits strange, but this one she could understand.

The waitress – a plain brunette – set their drinks on the table, and Sue picked hers up while Pedro turned his face away from her; he'd noticed a tall, curious-looking guy staring at them from over in the corner.

"Is that the guy, the guy in the corner?" asked Pedro.

She glanced over, shaking her head. "No." She sipped her Diet Coke, flinching at the taste. "I don't know why I still order this stuff."

"Me neither," said Pedro. "Maybe we should get something stronger?" He ordered two large glasses of Scotch without waiting for Sue to answer, and when they arrived, she drank it silently.

Pedro studied her. She was pretty – prettier than he'd previously thought. He'd never really seen her this close up before, and he noticed with a smile that her face was covered in tiny freckles. Running a hand through his thick, black hair, he spoke under his breath, "I wanted t-to say..." he laughed at his flustered stuttering, then licked his lips nervously – it was obvious what he wanted to do.

"Come here," Sue whispered, reaching with one hand around Pedro's nape and pulling him close. "I've been wanting to do this since the day of the interview," she murmured, as she kissed him passionately. "Sorry."

"Don't ever apologise for that," he said, smiling, as he glanced at the illuminated face of his watch; it was getting late. "Sue, here's what I need you to do, and it's important that John knows nothing."

Pedro went on to tell her his plan, stopping occasionally to sip his Scotch.

"Okay," she said, after a slight pause. "I can do that. When?"

"Friday."

The next day, Sue was the first to arrive. She had forgotten that the decorators were due to repaint the office that morning, and Pedro had already suggested that the group gather at a new location to plan the day's questioning. First, however, he had to collect a package from the post office, and as he got in the car, Sue joined him.

"Will you let me speak to you a moment or two, Pedro?" she asked with an engaging but perturbed smile.

Pedro didn't answer. He seemed extremely unhappy, whatever the reason was. Perhaps it was the weather, she thought – it was early Tuesday morning, cold and still dark. A flurry of snow swirled across the windscreen.

Shivering, he rubbed his hands together before starting the car, and once he'd parked across the road from the post office, he turned to Sue. "The others are waiting over there at number forty-five," Pedro told her, pointing towards their temporary office.

"I'll get a coffee while I wait for you," she said.

Nodding, he went in to collect his package, and soon, they were all standing in the new location.

The murder was on every front page in the region. The reports were vague about the circumstances, but, reading between the lines, it was clear that the details were too gruesome to go into.

"Have a look," Sue said, gesturing at the paper in front of them.

Pedro sipped his coffee as he stared at the article. "This is what it's all about," he said after reading it carefully.

It so happened that Pedro had already read all the available evidence before, including the coroner's initial report. Earlier that morning, he'd heard back from the police medical examiner: apparently, the police had missed the blood by the tree and when they went to re-examine the scene, they found a business card – still in a plastic seal – which had been hidden in the grass near the tree. A forty-year-old male had been arrested.

Pedro looked very pleased with himself. "All in a day's work," he said.

Sue smiled. "It would be interesting to sit in on the police interview. I'd like to know what the man's motives were."

"I suppose that's one of the disadvantages of just being a private investigator," John said.

"Yep. I guess that put me back in my box," she replied, offering a little laugh. She turned to Pedro and smiled.

He stared back at her, his expression unreadable.

Chapter 23

Sue was in a bad mood.

"Fuck me. My fucking feet are fucking killing me," she said, sighing.

"Your feet are always killing you," said a rather annoyed-sounding Pedro. "You're a bleeding investigator, for God's sake – why the hell do you wear four-inch heels to work?"

"They make me look taller," said Sue, shaking her head and shrugging, as if that explained everything.

"How the hell can you afford such expensive shoes on the money I pay you, anyway?"

"Ha," she said, raising her eyebrows at Pedro before adding, "my phone's not working."

"Use mine."

Pedro passed it over, watching as Sue tapped in her number and waited. As her own phone sprang into life, Pedro flinched. "Sue, you need to calm down a little. I don't know what's going on – one moment you're like a real professional private investigator, and the next you act like it's all too much for you."

"I'm fine," she replied, though her shaking voice said the opposite.

Later on, Sue took her lunch out of her bag, ready to eat it at her desk. Taking the pre-made sandwich out of its plastic casing, she started picking out the cucumber slices one by one, before opening a packet of crisps and slipping in the ready salted snacks between the bread in its place. So much for trying to stay healthy.

Pedro watched her, concerned. After picking at the crisp sandwich for several minutes, she got out a plastic container and a fork, poking at its contents before shoveling a fork load of what appeared to be tuna mayo into her mouth. She sat like that – a gob full of the sandwich filling – for a few seconds, just staring at the desk.

Pedro was just about to say something to her – to snap her out of her strange paralysis – when she sprang from her seat, grabbed her car keys, and rushed from the office, leaving the rest of her sandwich and her bag behind.

John glanced at Pedro. "What on earth was that all about?"

Pedro shrugged his shoulders – he had no idea what it had been about. Sometimes, Sue was a mystery. An enigma.

Almost exactly one hour later, she returned, apologising as she sat in her seat. "Sorry, sorry… I've just been having a bad morning." She laughed quietly. "A bad day, in fact."

"That's not like you, Sue," said Pedro, trying to sound concerned. He didn't usually go in for all this touchy-feely stuff, but with Sue it just kind of slipped out.

"I'm fine," she snapped, before taking a deep breath. "Sorry, it's just my sister – I had an argument with her. The worst one we've ever had. It always happens – she sneers, sneaks, and tries to demoralise me."

"I suppose it's normal to fall out with your sister sometimes," said Pedro, nodding.

Sue laughed. "It's not sometimes; it's all the time."

"But why?" asked Pedro, intrigued as to why this seemed to bother Sue so much.

Sue sighed. "Let's just say we haven't got on for quite a few years. It started when…" she sighed again, as if suddenly tired of something, "I failed my university course. She laughed at me – humiliated me – and when she went on to appear on TV, and I was still the 'failure of the family', well… I haven't really liked her since."

"Sue, try to be a listening person rather than a talking one. Don't take this personally," Pedro added when Sue looked mutinous, "it's for your own good. And you must stop blowing your top – you lose dignity every time you raise your voice."

She just smiled back at him, unsure of what to say.

John watched the whole thing with interest. Pedro seemed to have got his act together since he'd started his agency. He'd got contracts, a good reputation, and what seemed to be – at least on the surface – a thoroughly thriving business. How he'd done it, John wasn't sure.

As Pedro swallowed the last of his coffee, he stood up and threw the empty plastic cup towards the bin, hitting the side of it. Staring at the cup – which was now on the floor – Pedro sighed and then, a few seconds later, started to shake. John could see in Pedro's eyes that he wasn't thinking straight. Had he detected a weakness? Whatever it was, John was determined to find out more.

The next morning, John arrived at Pedro's office early to collect his wages. They were finally back on the old premises following the redecorations, and Sue was already at her desk, looking through some paperwork.

As John only worked part time, he wasn't aware of all the cases they were working on at the moment, and to be honest, he didn't care that much, yet at the same time, the sooner he finished this investigation work, the better. The prospect of not having to see Pedro again certainly brought back the old smile. He wanted to tell Pedro how sick he was of the set-ups and the "Oh-my-goodness-look-who-showed up?" crap. Once he'd collected his money, he would be ready to leave the second he'd made his point, but he was furious to discover that Pedro wasn't in the office. There was no way he'd be able to endure another day of this crap.

On seeing John hovering around, Sue decided to make polite conversation. "So, how long have you known Pedro?"

John shrugged. "Oh, it doesn't matter. It's a long story."

"Come on, tell me. Why not? I can just ask Pedro anyway."

John sighed. "You do that."

Sue stared at him for a few moments. "You don't fool me, you know; maybe one day you'll tell me all about it."

He shrugged again, non-committal. "Maybe I will."

He'd never really spoken much with Sue, but now they'd broken the ice, he thought he'd make the most of it. "So you and Pedro… are you two… together?"

He expected her to answer – even if it was just to say no – but she just sat there, staring at him as the silence grew around them.

When he couldn't take her gaze any more, he looked off to the right, seeing the less-than-impeccable kitchen. There were dishes in the sink and half-eaten food still left on the plates – he guessed Pedro wasn't so neat in every area of his life.

Sue continued to observe John like he was a ticking bomb, which wasn't entirely wrong.

With there still being no sign of Pedro, and as he was no longer able to stand the silence, John mumbled goodbye and left.

A few days later, they were both called into the office for a meeting with Pedro.

"Listen, you two."

Still revelling in his success after helping the police crack the murder case, Pedro's intention was to praise John and Sue for their hard work, but the look on John's face told him that he must have found a chink in his armour. Had the stress begun to show?

Suddenly tongue-tied, Pedro decided to adopt a more assertive tone. "You did a great job on the murder case." He cleared his throat. "But let's not forget who's the boss here: you follow my orders to the letter, or you can look for employment elsewhere. No exceptions." He looked pointedly in John's direction.

Trying to appear calm, John ran his hands roughly across his face as he stared back at his boss. "Is there an issue or something, Pedro?" he asked.

"No," he answered, a half-smile on his face. I just like to keep the office in order."

Later that day, Sue also noticed that something was wrong. She noticed a lot of things – she was ambitious and was always looking for opportunities, so she kept her eyes open when others wouldn't.

Suddenly, she looked up from what she was doing and started questioning John: How long had Pedro been in the country for? Was he really an Argentinian? What was his deal?

"Don't ask me any questions," replied John irritably. "Pedro is my boss and that's just the way it is."

Sue stared at John. She'd never liked his attitude, and he wasn't doing much to change her opinion of him now.

When she came into the office the following morning, she found Pedro whispering into the telephone, and upon seeing her, he flushed red and quickly hung up.

Soon after, Pedro made his excuses and left the office – apparently he had a meeting to go to. John wasn't in yet, so as soon as her boss had left, Sue immediately went over to his phone and pressed redial. Going by the number, he'd been on a long-distance call to Argentina, but as John chose that moment to walk in, she didn't find out any more about it.

It was getting towards lunchtime and the office was dead – there was just some paperwork to tidy up. Bored, John went down to get the late post, and when he came back upstairs he caught Sue going through Pedro's filing cabinet. She sat back and shot him a look.

"What are you looking for?" he asked.

"Can I help you?" she retorted defiantly, completely ignoring his question.

John looked back at her. He wanted to say something, but the eye contact only lasted a moment. He wondered how he should proceed, and once he'd walked away from the situation, he decided that the best option was to call Pedro.

"Look, Pedro, it's not my business, but that girl wonder you've employed, you can't trust her. I just caught her going through your files."

There was silence from the other end for a moment, and then Pedro said, "It's fine. It's nothing for you to worry about."

He hung up before John could say anything else.

The next day the office was closed, but on Thursday morning John arrived early. Soon afterwards, Sue came in, humming and singing.

"You're happy," he said.

"Yes, John."

John shot her a meaningful look and her mouth snapped shut. He couldn't tell what it was, but he knew something was wrong – he could feel it.

Just then her phone rang, and as she answered her expression formed to one of shock. Putting the receiver down, her body stiffened as she stood up. She then opened the door and walked straight out without saying anything.

John watched her go, saying nothing. He knew of course that Pedro was an expert at detecting weaknesses in other people and manipulating them, and he had a feeling that this would be the last time he would ever see Sue. He wasn't at all surprised, therefore, when Pedro arrived an hour later and said that she wouldn't be back.

"So business as normal," Pedro added.

"So that's all it is for you – just business?" asked John, already knowing the answer.

"Yes, of course."

"Was it carefully planned? Or was it just paranoia?" John asked.

"What are you saying?" Pedro responded, a look of distrust on his features.

"Nothing. Just thinking back to the old days," said John, staring at his boss.

Pedro didn't reply.

Sue was woken early the next morning by the light spilling through her window. Feeling like an axe had been embedded in her skull, she drank some of the water from the glass she found on the floor and pulled the duvet over her head, before curling up and going back to sleep. She was feeling bad after yesterday – she'd really enjoyed working for Pedro, and she'd hoped it would be a long-term thing. Guess not.

It was afternoon when she finally surfaced, dragging herself off the sofa and stumbling into the bathroom. Now, two hours later, she was hunched over her fifth cup of black coffee and trying to make sense of the previous day.

The atmosphere in the office had been heavy and subdued – no one could quite believe what had happened.

Sue had only come in to clear her desk, but his words were still ricocheting around her head: "I didn't want to fire you because you do such a great job, but I had no choice. You broke the rule and that's it – don't show your face here again."

She told herself that Pedro was making a mistake. "Pedro, I know what I did was wrong and I'm sorry," she'd whimpered. There had been no reply.

"Thanks," She thought to herself that hopefully she'd fooled the office into thinking that she was fine, but she felt like saying, Hey! I have feelings too!

Oh, what was the point? She told herself to get over it. That was the only thing she could do.

But there was something else. She was an unusually attractive little thing, even now when her face was flushed, and in the past she'd used it to get jobs, and keep jobs. So why hadn't it worked now?

It was at times like these that you needed company, and she couldn't bear the thought of going home to an empty flat. Feeling the tears prickling her eyes, she quickly shuffled the papers in front of her and tried to concentrate on something else. Despite her best attempts, however, her thoughts kept drifting back to the empty flat.

She was almost forty-one and her love life was on the rocks. She really was a top-notch looker, but she'd never wanted a steady man. The nearest she'd got to any kind of relationship over the past twelve months was a quick fumble in the back of a taxi with a man who'd felt so guilty he wouldn't even take her calls.

"You okay?" John asked, turning to look at her over his shoulder as he walked in.

She just nodded.

John could tell she was hurting, and though he wasn't sure if this was such a great idea, he just went ahead and said it: "Why not call him again to apologise for what happened between you two?"

Sue gaped at him for a second before bursting out laughing. "I'd never call him, John. I swear. There's nothing I have to say to him, and if I did call – even to apologise – he'd take it the wrong way. That's why I'd never do that." Tears fell down her face then, and she looked down to try and hide them.

John shook his head in disbelief. Just what was he supposed to do with a sobbing woman?

Chapter 24

Still feeling a little guilty after complaining to Pedro about Sue and getting her fired, John decided to take the cabinet –which had been too awkward for her to move out of the office and put in her car – to her place. It was on his way anyway.

Sue didn't often go out, nor had she that many friends, and her social life had dwindled a lot over the last year. Her oldest friends were all in the Metropolitan Police Force, but she'd never minded; she was always busy and, with the new job, tired too.

It took John a while to find the flat – a Victorian three-storey purpose-built block near Fulham – and twice he got caught in the one-way system, in a long snarl of evening traffic, before eventually working out where she lived. He let out a sigh of anger – after a difficult day, the last thing he needed were more complications.

Eventually he parked his car in the multi-storey car park, turned off the engine, and walked down the cement stairs in search of the entrance. He made his way over to the house, pushed open the communal door, climbed the shallow flight of steps, pressed the buzzer, and waited.

A few seconds later, she opened the door and smiled warmly at him. "Hello there. This is a surprise."

"I brought your cabinet."

She smiled again, before walking back to the car to help him carry the piece of furniture to her flat.

She looked pale and strained, two dark smudges of mascara shadowing her eyes. "I'm sorry," she said. "If I'd known... but of course." If she'd answered his phone calls, or even checked her messages, she would have known John was coming. "Sorry," she murmured again.

He followed her into the communal hallway, along a corridor and then through another door to the right. Her main living space was small and sparsely furnished, and as he looked around the sitting room he saw several strewn clothes, a severely puckered rug, and a discarded glass on the floor. There were women's shoes seemingly everywhere – one here, one there, one over there by the dark blue Futon-type sofa bed. There were a couple of lamps giving some much-needed light to the room and the table at the side of the room was completely covered in piles of paper. In fact, the paper, as if making a bid for freedom, had migrated into every corner of the room.

"Welcome to the mansion," she said. "I'd apologise for the mess, but to be honest, that would suggest it doesn't normally look like this." Her speech was slightly slurred. He noticed a bottle of vodka – already a third empty – sitting on the table.

"Are you really okay?" It was a stupid question but he still felt obliged to ask it.

"Sure," she said. "I'm fine, thanks."

She scratched her head, causing her hair to stand up in jaunty spikes. She then started making little unnecessary noises as she moved around, clearing her throat, speaking to herself, lifting a pile of old magazines just to plonk them down on the coffee table. It seemed to be almost in preparation for something, and it was like a combination of self-reproach and possibly misplaced obligation that had brought her here. One thing was for sure: she had something on her mind. I just hope Pedro won't bully her, John said to himself. She's not as steely as she likes people to think.

He still wasn't entirely sure why Pedro made a big deal of her. But then again, that pretty much summed Pedro up: he was unpredictable in the way he handled people.

She picked an empty glass up off the floor and poured herself another stiff shot from the bottle. She forced a smile. "Well, I need one even if you don't."

She blinked once, twice, and then shook her head almost imperceptibly, as if to rid herself of the image: Pedro was such a shit. A huge air bubble formed at the back of her throat, and she looked as though she were either going to sob or laugh. She laughed.

"I don't blame you, John."

He shrugged, not at all fazed by what she said.

"I have to ask you, though," she continued, her voice dropping slightly. "I overheard a conversation that you and Pedro had a few weeks ago."

"What was that?"

"Sit down. I guess you could sit on my bed if you want? I'm sorry, that's pretty creepy but I don't have any chairs."

"Yes," said John, perching on the end of her bedspread. "So what did you hear?"

"Pedro said that now was a good time to tell you that he knew you better than you could ever imagine. And that you thought you were moving through this world alone, unseen. But you shouldn't believe that for a moment. He'd studied you and knew what you were going to do before you did it. He knew where you'd been and he knew where you were going. So what was that all about?"

"Look, Sue," he said, exhaling deeply, "I mean..." he paused, staring at the ceiling. "Ah, what the hell." His voice wavered on the last word.

"Mm-hmmm," she said, seemingly deep in thought.

John was both shocked and confused, and he was beginning to feel like he was being used. Why? And why was she still asking questions after what had happened to her? If she just wanted to keep him distracted for a while, if she was trying to get him to reveal something, it wouldn't work. It seemed fairly obvious though that she was up to something.

He took a deep breath and gathered his thoughts. One key thing about Sue was that she was brilliant. Her brain was so busy, it never worked on just one level – it was whirring away all the time.

The second thing about Sue was that she was one of those people who were never wrong.

She knew exactly what he wanted to hear: "You are one of the good guys," she whispered with a smile.

He responded with a no-problem flick of his hand, before looking around at the empty walls and the posters rolled up on the floor. "What's happened?"

She raised her eyebrows. "Well, I wanted you to know before you heard it from someone else," she said brightly. "Everything is all packed away. I've decided to move to Manchester."

"What?" he asked, more than a little surprised. He honestly thought she'd stick around, at least for a while.

They sat for a while then in a semi-companionable silence. He felt like cracking a joke to clear the air, but she never really laughed a lot, anyway. In fact, she'd rather that he never laugh either, or be funny. Silence was fine.

After a minute he stood up, unnerved, undecided. Before he could do anything else, however, there was a bang on the door.

Sue cursed under her breath as she walked over to it then flung it open: it was the elderly woman who lived in the flat next door.

Ever since Sue had first met Mrs O'Brian six months ago, the old lady had been regularly knocking on the door with her homemade shortbread biscuits or lemonade, telling her that she should be married by now. Every time she brought this up, Sue would get irritated. "I don't miss it; I don't miss men. It's a relief just to walk into a shop and have no one look at you." She was married to her job, but if she was honest with herself, deep down she would have liked to be in a relationship. Not that she'd ever admit that to her neighbour.

Today, however, Mrs O'Brian just looked distressed. "Please can you help me?"

"Calm down, Mrs O'Brian, tell me what's happened," said Sue, concern growing on her features.

"Sue, I'm sorry, I don't know what to do." She began to cry but quickly wiped away the tears, clearly furious at herself for crying. She paused then, clearly trying to think of something to say.

Mrs O'Brian nodded at her door, and John followed them both into the next-door flat. The place smelled of old shoes and stale mattresses.

What John saw next made his stomach drop: Mr O'Brian was lying face down in a pool of blood.

Sue looked like she was in shock – she was staring at the corner of the cabinet, chewing her lip, thinking that it looked as though he had fallen and banged his head: he was lying on the floor next to a stool which was sitting on its side.

Sue glanced sideways at John, her eyebrows raised in a silent question.

"We need to call the police," he said.

"I don't like this," Sue said. "Something doesn't look right – we have a lot of uncontained issues here, and I won't call the police until they're contained."

"Come on, you can't be serious," said John, as he looked at his watch. It was late – he was late. He was supposed to be meeting Sonia, and he couldn't wait there any longer. "Look, I can't hang around," he told Sue.

"It's okay, John, I'll take care of things here, you go."

He stood up and wiped his hands on his jeans. "I'll see you later, Sue. I'm sorry about your husband," he said to the neighbour.

Sue nodded, and with that he walked down the stairs and towards the car park. Several streetlights suddenly flickered to life at intervals along the bridge, just as it started raining heavily. He walked on, his head tucked down against the elements, and when he glanced up again, he saw that he'd nearly reached the steps at the other end of the bridge. By now he was soaked. He took a deep breath, pulled open the car door, and flung himself into the leather seat.

Now that the events of the past couple of hours started to sink in, they sent a shiver down his spine, and he was wondering whether Sue had set him up. Had she befriended him purely to manipulate him? She was certainly difficult to read: friendly sometimes, and other times distant. She was brilliant and charming, and she wanted you to believe she was perfect – but she wasn't: John suspected she was controlling and a bit of a liar, to say the least.

Right now though, his main concern was getting home. What reason would he give Sonia for being late? The restaurant normally gave him the perfect cover: busy with their daughter Cassandra, Sonia assumed he worked there all day as they served both lunch and dinner, but John had employed a head chef so that he could cover his own shifts at Pedro's agency. Usually that worked, but it was now well after closing hours, and she'd know that.

He turned the engine on and pulled out of the car park, but after five minutes the damned car broke down on the M3.

* * *

It took a few moments for the bedside clock to come into focus, and Sonia stared bleary-eyed at the numbers. Two minutes past 11 p.m.

"What the hell?" she cursed.

Miserable after spending her birthday alone, Sonia had gone to bed early – at 9 p.m. to be exact. It had taken her a while, but eventually she'd nodded off and had fallen into a deep sleep.

Now, her muddled mind was more than a little confused. 'Who the hell would be ringing at this time?' she wondered. A terrifying thought suddenly shot through her groggy mind, making her very alert: John! Fearful that something had happened to him, she snatched the phone and answered it. "What's wrong?"

"It's me, look, I'm sorry, the car broke down on the M3 and I'm at a service station waiting for the recovery service." Instinctively, her hand flew to her chest in relief, as she told him not to worry. Once she hung up the phone, she lay back in bed, trying to get her heartbeat back under control. At least he was safe.

John had to leave the keys with the recovery man, only realising that his house keys were on the same ring when he arrived home an hour later. He banged loudly on the front door, causing a worried Sonia to jump out of bed. She pulled on her dressing gown, flicking on lights as she went through the house before making her way downstairs to the front door. Her shadow could be seen through its mottled glass panel.

"I'll be with you in a sec," she called out. She undid the latch and opened the door.

John was waiting patiently on the darkened doorstep, doing his best to shield himself from the rain that was coming down by the bucketful.

"Let's get you out of those clothes and warmed up," said Sonia. "I'm gonna put the shower on for you; that'll help." She wandered off into the bathroom, waiting a few moments for it to heat up. "It's ready for you now – take those wet things off and get in."

Sonia pulled fresh towels from the hallway cupboard and laid them on the tiled floor outside the shower cubicle. "I'll leave these towels here for you," she called through the shower door. "I'll go and make you a hot drink for when you get out."

While he showered, Sonia picked up his discarded wet clothes, and inspecting them carefully, she noticed some bloodstains on his shirt and trousers.

She paused in her tracks. Bloodstains?

Her heart hammering in her chest, she tried to think of all the possible scenarios – attack, murder… accident? Anything could have happened, and while she tried not to jump to conclusions, it was easier said than done.

* * *

The next day, back at the office, John had just finished telling everyone about his experience the night before.

"Oh my God, John, that's terrible," one of the office girls gasped.

"Are you okay?" Pedro asked.

"Yes, it was all very shocking and messy, but I'm fine. Understandably, the police want to question me about it."

"Apparently they think he could have been murdered," Pedro said, nodding. He already knew all about it, of course.

Pedro caught the look of concern in John's eyes before he turned away and dug back into his sausage roll. His jaw clenched forcefully with every bite.

"What? That's not possible," said John. "He fell off a stool, it was lying on the floor."

"Did you stay until the police arrived?" Pedro asked.

"No."

This instantly got John thinking: What was Pedro trying to say? He thought about his clothes. They had a little blood on them, which he must have picked up from the corner of the cupboard as he stared at the spot where Mr O'Brian was lying. Did something bump against his back? He must have banged his head on the cupboard. Wait, he thought. My handkerchief. I used it to try to wipe some of the blood off my jacket. Did I leave my handkerchief at Sue's flat?

His stomach churned as he realised he couldn't actually remember.

* * *

It was the following morning, and John had barely got up when the door bell rang.

He opened the door, hiding half of his body behind it as he was still pretty dishevelled; his spiky hair and creased boxers told their own story.

A D.C. Nolan was at the door, who had been waiting to interview him at the local police station: John had overslept. Nolan pointed at his watch and, when John attempted to apologise, raised his index finger and made the "uhp-uhp" sound that grown-ups make when children try to interrupt. Slowly, his index finger lowered, then landed on the watch face.

Sonia had overheard the conversation – if you could call it that – and came rushing down the stairs. "What the hell?" she asked, trying to figure out what had happened. "Oh boy." She rolled her eyes at her husband, then looked angrily up at the ceiling.

"Mr Scott, we could do this down the station, if you prefer?"

"No, please come in, take a seat."

"Just a few questions. The night of Friday, 27th April 1997, you and Miss Sue West found Henry O'Brian's body on the floor of his flat. Is that correct?"

"Yes."

"Did you notice anything strange?"

"No."

Nolan raised his eyebrows before jotting something down in his notepad. John desperately wanted to lean over and see what he'd written, but he restrained himself. He had to keep calm.

The interview carried on, and after half an hour of questioning, D.C. Nolan was coming to the end of his questions. John got the impression there were no suspects and nothing for him to be concerned about.

"Just one more question: is there anything you want to tell us or add?" asked Nolan, staring at John.

After thinking about the question for a moment, John thought he should have mentioned that there was a stool lying on the floor but he decided that this could lead to a different line of questioning, and he was far too tired of all this rubbish as it was.

"No," he replied.

Chapter 25

Pedro swung his legs out of bed, shaking his head and letting out a loud, deep yawn. He wasn't feeling as bad as he should have been, but there were a few cobwebs to shake loose. More than a few, perhaps.

An hour later he was on the treadmill at the gym, and after the workout, he took it easy for a while, relaxing before he left for the office.

Last week, Pedro had read in the papers that the Argentinian Latin Dance Studio was coming to town, something that very much interested him. Saying he was keen to show him something, Pedro called John into his office and asked him to join him at the opening the following Thursday. He arranged to pick him up at 6.30 p.m.

John had never seen Pedro this excited before. "Why do you want to go to a dance studio?"

"It's a long story," was the reply. "And we haven't got time."

John nodded, knowing when to leave things well alone. "I've got a couple of things to take care of tomorrow; do you want me to do anything else?" he asked Pedro. It was getting late.

"Yeah, John. I got a Mrs Low, she wants to hire me to find her husband. He took large amounts of money from their business account and joint credit card and has left his wife to face the music. I talked to her last week and she said she'd told the police everything, but they didn't take her seriously. Something about her story doesn't add up, though. I smell a rat."

"What did you say to her? Are you going to help her?"

"To be honest, I just stood there with my hands in my pockets and gave her a funny look. Then she turned on the water works: 'I'm deeply ashamed it's all come to this. I truly believed he loved me.'"

"You didn't fall for all that, did you?"

"No." Pedro shrugged. "But the money is good."

She'd pulled out her notes and bank statements, fanning them in front of his face like a card trick. She'd then begun to sweat while he read them. "Okay, I'll look at these later." He had taken some more details from her and explained that if he helped her, he'd need to know everything. For starters, which bank accounts and credit cards did she share with her husband? Did she know that the money her husband had taken from their company account was clients' money? She'd just shrugged. Useful.

John looked at his watch. "Well look, if it is okay, I'll go now and see you tomorrow."

Pedro just nodded, his thoughts elsewhere.

The next day was normally a paperwork day, unless there was something big on, and the only assignment they had on the books was Mrs Low: Pedro had decided to take on the case. He wanted John to follow her husband, but he knew it could be a long stake-out.

"I guess a little cash would just make me feel more comfortable. Should something happen. Should I need to get out of there quickly," John suggested.

Pedro opened his wallet and pulled out two twenty-pound notes, pressing them gently into his hand. "There you are," he said indulgently. He scrambled around for a pen before writing the address on his notepad. He then ripped the page out, folded it over, and handed it to John.

When asked about her husband's normal daily routine, Mrs Low said that he often had lunch at the Institute of Directors in Pall Mall. On the off chance, John sat in the car outside the IoD, watching the building all day. After an hour or so, to seem less

Page 232

stalkerish, he got out of the car and made his way to one of the empty tables outside the shop from where he could see the front door of the club.

Mr Low never showed, but his assistant did: John recognised her from the extensive file Pedro had already compiled. He followed her to a hotel in Croydon, his car bumping along the narrow lane of the hotel grounds before he steered it on to a secluded verge in the car park and shut down the engine.

He leaned back in his seat, crossed his fingers behind his head, and sighed. He had not touched the flask of coffee he had made for staking-out purposes; these days he wanted to piss all the time, but nonetheless at some point he would need to relieve himself behind the boot of the car. Getting out of the car, he looked up at the hotel, an attractive building dating all the way back to the eighteenth century. Heavy clouds had settled, which made him sigh – he thought the day was supposed to clear up, not get worse.

He tucked in his chin, shoved his hands deep in his pockets, and mumbled to himself, "it's freezing." He patted his pocket; his flashlight was there. Good – the sky was darkening rapidly. As he unlatched the gate to walk across the mini golf lawn, he quickly checked the car park again. There was no one there. Spotting the hotel entrance, he decided to go inside and wait.

After a couple of hours of sitting in the bar – and much to his surprise – he saw Mr Low enter and sit down in the hotel's restaurant. He ducked his head slightly, trying to be discreet as he watched him. Strange. John folded his hands and sat up straight, before jotting down some notes in his pad. Time: 12 to midnight. Tall woman, believed to be his assistant, waiting to meet Mr Low. John couldn't really write any more than that, and in any case, he felt that he'd seen enough. He did a lot of pacing up and down before he slipped outside, got into his car, and drove back to the office.

After writing his report, John looked up from his desk and glanced at the clock on the wall; it wasn't quite straight, but at least it was correct. It was clean and still new-looking, but something about it was slightly off – just like his desk, a smart modern curved wood chip veneer with a box shelf on one side. The computer screen was just too big, so that the edge ended up being hidden by the box shelf. And the arms on the chair prevented him from getting close enough to the desk, so instead he had to lean forward to use the keyboard. Still, he shouldn't complain: it was a vast improvement on the last office.

He opened the bar cabinet, took out a tumbler, and poured himself a large Vodka. After a couple of hours he felt a headache coming on, and deciding to call it a night, he shuffled outside and down the cement steps into the car park. Opening the car door, he slid into the leather seat, before driving slowly back home.

Pedro arrived in the office just after 3 p.m., as always smelling of some expensive lunch, this time devoured with one of the directors of a new security company. On his way back he'd gone to the hotel in the hope of interviewing Mr Low. After a successful meeting, Pedro was satisfied that Mr Low was telling the truth. When Pedro called John with the news, he answered in his usual way, sounding like he'd been drinking all night.

"Hello, who is it?"

"It's me," Pedro replied.

John pushed himself up against the headboard of his bed and flipped on the light. "What is it?" He asked, rubbing his hand over his face to cover his yawn. "What did he say?"

"Her husband thinks she's behind it. She's trying to frame him for fraud in revenge for his affair with his assistant."

Pedro thought back to their meeting. "Fuck," Mr Low had said. "That's why she changed the alarm code at our house – she forced me to leave her. Not only did she dupe me into believing she still loved me, she actually wanted to put me behind bars." He almost laughed. "Good Lord, I hate her, but you have to admire the bitch. She set me up.'"

"Excuse me, Mr Low, but I think a lot of people will find it hard to believe you just said that," noted Pedro.

"It's the most awful, horrible feeling in the world to have to say something like that to someone you shared your life with for over twenty years. I still love her, I just can't live with her." He shrugged. "All I'm saying is that it's been the most brutal eye opener for me. How can you love someone who only cares for money? I've tried all my life to be a decent guy, a man who loves and respects women. And there I was, thinking nasty thoughts about my wife. And let me say it, let me say it right now: I cheated. I disrespected my wife. I didn't want to be the man that I had become. But what else could I do?"

Pedro pulled a card out of his wallet and passed it over. "If you think of anything that might help, call me. Thanks again for taking the time to meet with me."

Mr Low looked almost delighted to end the interview and took the card with a smile.

When Pedro confronted Mrs Low, she replied, "Shit, what's new? Anything bad happens, I'm responsible. That's bullshit." Then she shouted, "What are you talking about? That's crazy. You hear me!" She was extremely agitated and nervous, as if her husband was in the next room.

"It would have taken, what, six months to set all this up. You must have hated him a lot," Pedro said, thinking that she was obviously hiding the money. "Why not just divorce him? You could have taken him for everything he had."

"Not so simple," she replied.

"Yeah, you got greedy and stole the clients' money, didn't you?"

"No."

"We have it in your husband's own words: 'I think she is trying to set me up.' Seems you knew he was having an affair, so you wanted him to suffer."

She asked in a quiet, measured voice filled with disappointment, "So what are you going to do?"

"You look very, very calm," Pedro said. "All along, you've been acting inappropriately. You've been unemotional, flippant, and you've tried to play me."

"That's just how I am, don't you see? I'm stoic. He cheated on me, not once, not twice, but three times. I've had enough."

Pedro knew she'd had a hard tome, but his voice was stern as he asked her, "So where's the money?"

She just stared at him, thinking – she could tell that she'd been found out. It took a second, but she finally decided that the sooner she answered, the sooner she could leave.

"Okay, look, I really want to go back to my old life. Or my old life with him. I've had a lot of time to think and daydream, and what I've been daydreaming about is him, in those early days. I thought I would daydream more about him getting what's due to him in a tiny prison cell, but I haven't so much, lately. I think about those early days, when we were so good together, and it feels nice."

Sounding more patient than he felt, Pedro replied, "I don't think the two of you have anything left to say to each other."

She stayed quiet for a moment, then wiped a hand nervously over her mouth as she sat up straighter. She let out a sigh, stood up, and wrung her hands. "I think I should go now." She felt a wave of nausea coming on. "I can't do this anymore. Waiting to be arrested, I can't stand it."

"She doesn't sound like an angry woman, Pedro," John said when Pedro told him the details outside the office later that day. "Seems like she desperately tried to explain her actions to you. She's worried." He gave a tut. "Jesus Christ, Pedro, aren't you tired of all this? Just let it go."

"John, I don't like to be used. You might have a different perspective on people, but where I come from we don't."

John leaned against the railings at the bottom of the steps that lead up to the office, looking thoughtful. "You can't tell the police everything you learned; without Mr Low's statement, it's just an accusation. The evidence you have is circumstantial, if that. You couldn't very well tell the police assigned to her case that she admitted taking the money. The fact is, we don't know where she put the money."

"I know, I know." Pedro thought for a moment, then said that he'd give her one day. That was it – if she hadn't returned the money by the same time tomorrow, he would drop everything and pay the police station a visit.

When he hadn't heard anything the following afternoon, he informed DC Evans of the whereabouts of Mrs Low.

* * *

The next morning, John wheeled his chair away from his desk and grabbed the protein milkshake he'd left in the tiny refrigerator in the office, tapping his foot in time to the beat. Pedro was constantly playing Latin American music these days, and while sometimes it got too much, John quite enjoyed the sound today.

Just then, there was a knock on the door, a loud, furious bang that made them both look over. Annoyed at the interruption, John flung it wide open, greeting fury with fury. It turned out that Pedro had employed a new office boy: a young, overweight, spotty-faced fellow called Edward. He was breathing heavily and sweating, his shirtsleeve torn and his hair wild. He pushed past John and marched straight through into the back office without a word.

As far as John was concerned, Edward was "just a tea maker." The boy didn't appreciate the humour in that remark, and he turned to look at John, giving him that arrogant, pug-like stare. John just stared back at him. He thought Edward was a bit strange, but Pedro liked him – he said he was just a daydreamer.

Page 237

"Let's not worry too much about that; the boy's just going through a growing-up period. I'm keen to train him," he said.

John wasn't so sure, but he was curious to see where this was headed. Here's where things get a little dicey, he thought. Not quite sure how to take the next step. Still, he decided to play along.

Unbeknown to John, Edward's father was the head of some major security firm, and his appointment was no coincidence...

Much to John's surprise, Pedro walked over and gathered the two of them in a giant hug, John's face ending up scrunched on Edward's neck. He really didn't want to deal with Edward's armpit, and he tried his best to wriggle away.

"Come on, you two," Pedro said.

"Okay, Pedro, I wish I could say more but I can't. I think you're crazy to keep him on. I think there's something disturbing about him," said John, after Edward had wandered off.

"You're just going to have to trust me on this," said Pedro. "Can you do that?"

John nodded, watching as Edward started inching towards the door, "Thanks, but I have to go now, I'm meeting my father." Pedro was about to say something when John piped up and asked, "Is he here to work or not?"

Pedro nodded. John took two box files from one of the shelves by the door and dumped them in front of Edward. "Read these, and cross-reference them on the computer," he commanded. "It will give you an idea what of we do here." John checked his watch. "Give me a brief on these names. I'll give you an hour," he added.

He could almost feel the heat from Edward's anger rising, the tips of his ears now a bright red – a sure sign he was on unsteady footing. Crap just started to pour out of his mouth, completely unstoppable, while John was still shooting questioning glances his way. When Edward noticed he was being observed, he flicked his head and gave them a sideways glance. The hint of a grin spread across his lips, but he was clearly very nervous.

Page 238

With his eyes looking down at the well-worn tile floor, he mumbled, "What's the problem?"

Edward was really fucking John off – he could feel him looking over his shoulder all day, smirking. It was just the way he sat there, dull as shit. What annoyed him most, however, was the way he talked, all softly and gently, as though he'd been on a course to deal with retards. John clenched his jaw even more tightly, thinking that his skin must be bubbling as it seemed to be the only thing holding back his rage. This was really bad. With so little distance between them, John had to call on patience in order to keep from dragging him across the table top and tying the boy in knots.

He finally made it home after an extremely long day, too exhausted to do more than brush his teeth and flop down on his bed. Once his eyes closed, however, it was as though his brain awakened from his stupor, taking the opportunity to curl around for a depressing walk down memory lane.

It was going to be a long night.

Chapter 26

After looking after his busy restaurants for the next few days, all John wanted to do was go home and rest. He was daydreaming and nearly falling asleep on the chair in his office when he was interrupted by a gentle tapping on his door. It sounded hesitant, from someone respectful – someone reluctant to disturb him, unlike Edward upon his arrival.

All the same, because his line of thinking was broken, there was a second round of tapping. Sighing loudly, he got up and pushed his chair backwards with such force it caught on a temporary cable on the floor and nearly toppled over. He flung the door open.

There, in the hallway, stood Pedro.

"What?" John growled.

"Have you forgotten that you are coming to the dance studio?"

"I'm sorry," he sighed, "I totally forgot. What? You think I did it on purpose?"

"Of course not," Pedro replied.

"Anyway, I can't see the point of watching a dance. Why do you need me to come?"

Over the years, John had realised that it was easier to comply with orders, but it still got him thinking a little as it all seemed a bit strange. This person he had been treading very carefully with over the last five or so years had a hidden passion? Call it his intuition or whatever, but one thing was for sure: this was not Pedro, or at least not the Pedro he knew.

It was a spring day – John would later remember it as it was the first day of the month that there was no rain – and in a sort of strange way, there was a feeling of good vibes in the air. A good mood. When Pedro was happy, everyone was happy.

"John, listen. When I was a child I used to love to dance like this. My love of dance started when I was young. I wasn't a good dancer, but my mother was amazing."

The polite conversation carried on for a minute or so and was only stopped by Pedro glancing at his watch every few seconds.

"I can't imagine you as a dancer, but I suppose it explains your personality," noted John.

"What?"

John shook his head. "Nothing. Just give me a minute, okay? I'll see you downstairs."

"I'll wait in the car," Pedro told him.

They arrived at the studio on time, climbed two flights of stairs, and pushed open the brass door. As you entered, you could feel the vibe of the Latin sound swaying through the air, the whoosh of bodies moving around you. There were a couple of old ladies in the corner nodding their heads along to the music, and John and Pedro took seats nearby.

John glanced towards the parlour, which was partially concealed by a red velvet drape. Pedro could hear the sounds of the piano, and a young woman singing while a couple rehearsed a dance. The room was spacious; it had once been a small gym. Over on the other side of the room the dancers all took their partners. It was so tense, and yet relaxing, just to watch. Their hands remained joined, so tightly clasped, as they turned their heads at exactly the same time to the sound of the violin. There was a constant hum coming from the ceiling fan, adding to the atmosphere of the sound of the music.

"So everyone, listen," Rosa, the instructor, said. "A good dancer is one who transmits a feeling of the music to his or her partner." Rosa was a short, slim, and very sexy girl – she had that Latino look.

The class continued, and John and Pedro watched in fascination – everyone was so good, and the beat was so infectious, it was incredible to see.

Soon John realised that the class was about to come to an end, and that it was time to leave. Standing by the exit, a redhead introduced herself as Anne and tried to engage Pedro in conversation, asking whether he was there to dance. She seemed a bit keen, but all the while, Pedro could only think of that other girl, the short girl in charge, with her dark long black hair. John noticed that Pedro had kept his eyes on her throughout the class.

"Look, I'm going to get off now. See you later," John said.

"Yeah, John. I'm going to stay a bit longer," said Pedro, staring at the woman.

* * *

Outside the office, there were a couple of elderly women talking at the bottom of the steps, and when John said good afternoon, they both looked up and smiled, while nodding insincerely at the same time.

John walked across the concrete-and-weed car park and climbed into his car. He had to collect some paperwork from Pedro's accountant and then the plan was to meet him later.

After waiting for what appeared to be an eternity in the crappy waiting room, with its dirty windows and bent plastic seats, the papers were finally ready, and he stood up to leave. As he walked out of the office, the bakery next door was getting its powdered sugar delivered, funnelled into the cellar by the barrel-full as if it were cement. He stood and stared at it for a while, fascinated.

He met Pedro an hour later in the bar – an Irish bar in a not-so-Irish place – and gave him his papers. The bartender, a big bearded guy, grinned when he saw them come in and poured them both whiskeys.

Page 243

"What's up with you?" Pedro asked. "You look a bit nervous."

John huddled over his glass. I need to sit here and drink a few more, John said to himself, while out loud, saying: "Just been one of those stressful days." Then, after a pause: "And Pedro, I don't always get why you make these unpredictable decisions."

Pedro told him not to worry. "I had several agendas when I asked you to meet me today, but one of them is certainly for the two of us to be friends again."

"Give me an example," John said.

"Oh, for God's sake," Pedro said, raising his hands in protest. "This is not a debating contest. You know exactly what I mean."

After a few more minutes of awkward conversation, Pedro put his coat back on, saying he was running late. Neatly folding his newspaper, he left it on the bar top with his empty glass, a five-pound tip tucked underneath it. Afterwards, John realised that they were spending more time in the bar than they needed to, and that it was becoming a bit of a bad habit.

"Look, John, I'll see you in the morning," Pedro said, before rushing out.

John still couldn't understand the sudden excitement in Pedro – he would lie awake at night, wondering if Pedro was just getting old and forgetful, which could mean that their mutual secret would just disappear. Somehow, however, he didn't think so. None of this made things any easier; it just dredged up the past.

It was nearly 9 a.m. and he was supposed to be at work. Grabbing his jacket and keys off the coffee table, he drove to the office, his foot itching to slam down on the gas pedal.

"You're late."

"Bullshit." Then, "I didn't mean to say that, sorry – it just came out."

Pedro growled at him and told him not to be so disrespectful. "If you can't control your tongue, you should leave."

John could have thought of several creative ways to end the conversation, but he knew that Pedro would probably bite back, and he didn't have the energy for that right now. "That's enough!" he said instead.

John thought to himself, One whisper to the right people that there is more to Pedro than they might think, and he would become the biggest pariah in his field. He would be ostracised by his colleagues and hated by every friend he's ever made over his professional career. To John he was just a man with a nice head of hair, thinning just enough to give him the seasoning of a man who had seen the world and who knew the differences between right and wrong. Unfortunately, insecurity came with the job, and John knew he would always be looking over his shoulder.

They had a lot on at the moment, and when a guy came into the office, John overheard Pedro saying, "We couldn't really take it on right now. We are too busy."

After the guy had left, John asked Pedro what he wanted, as he knew they could have fitted him in somehow.

"Oh, it was definitely going to be a time-intensive case to take on. If I decided to, it would probably turn out nothing more than a girl who'd got mad with her parents and had run off with the money."

John told him that he had a bad feeling about today.

Pedro cleared his throat, looked over his shoulder, and asked, "What is it?"

"I don't know, it's just a bad feeling I'm getting."

"You might want to keep your feelings to yourself," Pedro suggested, clearly annoyed.

"That's why I usually keep my mouth shut."

Pedro sighed. "You ask too many questions, John. Maybe today you should give it a break – just sit there and listen for a change, and stop complaining about Edward."

Edward didn't know how he kept managing to show up during personal conversations between Pedro and John, but he'd done it again. He wasn't even halfway up the stairs when their voices reached him, and he could tell that both of them were fired up about something. He thought the knock on the door would be loud enough to bring Pedro to the door, but with the way those two were yelling, he wasn't surprised they missed his arrival.

He debated going back home, but decided against it when it occurred to him that John might be persuading Pedro to fire him. If that was the case, he wanted to get his two cents in.

He lifted his hand to knock again and then opened the screen door. The room immediately went quiet. John swivelled around in his chair, and the way the blood drained from Edward's face, John knew he'd been standing outside like a jackass, listening to them argue. Edward shoved his hands deep into his pockets and got busy staring at his feet. John watched him, and he didn't miss the way he bit down on his bottom lip as if he was trying to hold something back. What, John didn't know, but it was something, alright.

Pedro looked over at him. "Edward, just the man! Can you move those files back into the cupboard?"

Pedro smiled at Edward, then got back to studying some old paperwork. John noticed there was a long list of names, some of which were highlighted. He tried to look at the other papers but Pedro caught him looking and closed the file. He stood up to go and put the file back into his briefcase, and there it was under his chair, staring John right in the eye: Pedro's diary.

John quickly bent down and grabbed it, then asked Pedro if there was much he wanted him to do as he couldn't stay long that day.

"It doesn't matter now, it can wait until tomorrow," Pedro replied.

John nodded and left, wanting to get out of there as quickly as humanly possible.

John needed to telephone Sonia – desperate to spend a bit more time with her, he was hoping for a bit of a night out. He picked up the phone, shaking a tumbler filled with ice near the receiver so she could guess that he wanted to go out that night. "Hey Sonia, I'll be home at seven."

It was a thirty-minute drive – straight west, down the M4. Once again the motorway was closed due to the usual road works, and the diversions through the new housing estate made him shiver a little: the sheer number of gaping dark houses that had never known inhabitants, or homes that had never known owners. The thirty-minute drive turned into an hour, then longer, and it was close to eight thirty when John finally pulled into the driveway. He unlocked the front door and dropped his keys on the mirror table in the hall.

"Well, well, well, guess who's back?"

"I'm sorry. You're not angry, are you?" He sank down onto the couch and rested his head in his hands.

"I was, but now I'm not," she said. "Let me set the scene: tonight is a really nice night, not too cold. Tonight you can actually walk to the High Street, and tonight is the opening of the new Italian restaurant. So why should I be angry?"

He hadn't eaten and his stomach was seriously protesting the lack of breakfast and lunch. And now it looked as though dinner was a pipe dream… He learned back into the couch and tried to get comfortable. Sonia stared at him – she was all dressed and ready to go.

"So let's go," she said eventually, sounding resigned.

He stood up, mumbling something in vague agreement before closing the door behind them. I have too much to think about at the moment, he thought to himself.

Over dinner, the same questions came up time and time again, and afterwards, they slowly walked back holding hands, like lovers do. Her eyes shot to the clock tower across the road – it was nearly midnight. She smiled up at him, both of them finding the exact same things worth remembering. They had the same rhythm, the same wavelength – they simply clicked, and they knew each other inside out. He would just look at her reading in bed, laughing at nothing, and then his mouth would be on hers. It was their way of life, and it happened just like that when they got back to the house.

The next morning, he told Sonia about the strange man who'd been hanging around outside the pub as he drove home the night before. Two policemen had approached him with an end-of-shift weariness, and John had noticed that the man was thin, and that he had a dishonest look about him. For some reason he suddenly ran into the road and John's car had very nearly hit him. Remembering the incident now, John sighed – he had to take a second to get his wobbling voice under control.

Later that day, Pedro called John and suggested that he wait outside the Latin dance studio with Edward. He asked him to follow Rosa and simply log everything she did, in case she wasn't at the studio. Pedro also gave him her Queensway address and asked him to wait outside her house.

Reluctantly, John called Edward and arranged to meet him near where he lived. He drove into town, through his old estate, roaring past the street he used to live in, and as he parked, he saw Edward leaning against the doorway of a shop. Like a fly trapped in a corner, John thought. Okay, he didn't really like him, but he had no choice but to work with him.

Leaning against the railings at the bottom of the stairs, he called out to the boy. "Get in the car!"

"That's a nasty dent you've got in your door," Edward said by way of a greeting.

The remark made John think about the man who had run onto the road last night – there was no way he'd hit him. Reminding himself that he had to keep focused on the job, he lay down a few rules to Edward. "While we're watching, we must try to act normal," he told him. "And stop fucking mumbling."

Edward had that stupid grin on his face again, making John think – not for the first time – that the guy was a total nut job.

"I don't want to hear you speak yet; I'm still trying to figure out if you're worth the risk."

Edward was rolling his eyes while John was talking to him, and that pissed him off even more. In fact, John was fighting the urge to grind his face into the floor. They sat in silence for a few moments before he grabbed hold of him and pulled him towards his face, saying clearly, "I'm not trying to be a dickhead." Then, "Alright, alright, let's stop before this gets more stupid than it already is. Don't fuck with me."

This seemed to do the trick, as Edward nodded and said, "Yeah, John, fine with me. To be honest, I haven't been feeling all that well, and it's put me in a bad mood."

"Mood has nothing to do with this. This is serious shit, and while I know you made a deal with Pedro, you should open your mind to the possibility that you can get hurt."

Edward nodded, wisely saying nothing.

They drove towards number forty-five Queensway, and John looked around as he passed the houses. Pedro had told him that Rosa lived in an avenue – wasn't an avenue supposed to have trees? There wasn't one in sight. It was as if the local council had decided to ban anything with an inclination to turn green; most of the front gardens – small mean squares – had been concreted over. Grey was the only enduring colour, from the sky to the ground. Miserable.

He eventually parked his car and they trudged across the road so they could get a good view of her house. When Edward pushed open the low chain-link gate, a big German shepherd dog started to growl, and it took John just half a second to realise that Edward wasn't comfortable.

He cursed and took an airborne Heisman step. "Sorry," he was breathing hard. "I'm working on it, but most dogs scare the hell out of me."

Edward wasn't a tall man. In fact, he was short, only coming up to John's shoulder, but he held himself as though he were taller than he was. Shifting his weight from one foot to the other, Edward noticed John staring at him. "What?"

John shook his head, and they waited for a while in silence before a Hispanic girl – her hair in a long dark braid – and a black guy with the stance of a marine walked out of the block of flats. John was beginning to wonder if she was going to show, but Edward suggested they keep watching the door. Just then it opened, and she stepped out wearing her hat pulled down so it covered her ears. Her hair was also pulled back in a ponytail, making it hard to recognise her. It was 9.00 a.m.

They followed her down Queensway Road, waiting as she stopped at a second-hand shop. They noticed she was looking through an old record collection, before handing money over to the shopkeeper. John called Pedro and told him that there was nothing unusual about her day so far.

Later that day, Edward sat down with Pedro. John had dropped in to collect his keys and was caught off guard by a wave of loneliness – John didn't like the vibe he'd been getting from the two of them all weekend. Whenever he'd enter a room, hushed conversations would stop abruptly, making him paranoid and irritable.

Edward shook his head when John wasn't looking and Pedro grinned. Embarrassment was a multi-headed beast, and as Edward went through the motions, he swallowed up another wave of mortification. Still, he was keen to tell Pedro everything.

Edward shook his head, then spat out a curse. "I need to talk to you – to explain." He was beginning to wonder whether this was the best time to tell Pedro that he had seen John pocket his diary, but he knew he had to tell him.

Pedro stepped closer to him and lowered his voice. "This is not the time or the place to hash out your chicken shit ways. As far as I'm concerned, you are becoming a waste of time and space." The twinge Pedro felt as he watched hurt and embarrassment flood Edward's features was the exact opposite of what he expected to experience. Edward's hands fell away and he ran a hand over his mouth uncertainly.

The movement triggered something in Pedro's memory and he fought his rising shame. "Okay, let's start again."

"He's not a nice guy."

"Stop worrying about what your colleagues think of you," said Pedro. "A few of them might be your friends, but most of them would just as soon see you fall flat on your face. I made a deal with your father a long time ago, and if you're willing to step back and take an honest look at yourself, you'll understand that this has been a very beneficial time for all of us. If you're not willing to do that, then let's end it now. Here's what you're going to do, Edward. You're going to go downstairs and get some fresh air, have a smoke, and then you're going to come to one of two conclusions. Either you're right – we're all wrong, and you have all the answers – or you're going to figure out that you've become an insufferable ass whom no one can work with."

John – who had been listening – had never wanted to punch anyone so badly. "I can't be bothered with all of this," he said, before slamming the door in anger. Edward shook his head.

In Pedro's world, everything boiled down to a matter of black and white. Those under his command followed his orders precisely and flawlessly. There were no exceptions: rules had to be followed to the letter. But John had many questions and no answers. Who was this man? And what did he want?

John was keen to go somewhere quiet to read Pedro's diary, and sitting in a nearby coffee shop, he sipped his latte, just to give himself a second to think. He opened the first page, and thanks to the basic Spanish he'd managed to pick up during his years drifting around the world, he quickly realised that this little black book was mostly an official record of events in Pedro's past, back in Argentina

during the Dirty War. John still didn't know what to say, or think –
too many things were swirling around in his head. He sat back,
looking just the littlest bit pleased with himself. He knew the
answers were in the book.

Pedro's Diary
1976, Buenos Aires

I couldn't tell you how many times I've passed that house
without giving it a single thought. It doesn't possess any remarkable
qualities. It has no side entrance, no life, and no real history. Just its
own dark secrets. I know of the suffering in its basement.

That day, my hands grasped the edge of the solid double
metal gate, shaking hard. Releasing my grip, I stood back and drifted
into my own thoughts. Uneasy, unpleasant feelings lingered in the
air.

In front of the crowd in the square was a strong-looking,
well-dressed man in his late sixties, snugly attired and in a grey silk
scarf, thick gloves, and a dark felt hat. His eyes looked hardened,
framed by a web of deep wrinkles. He raised his arm and gestured
purposefully. I respect this man and have done so for a long time –
ever since I was a child and during the revolution, I remember him
helping my family when money was tight.

Practically every building of any size had been seized by the
workers and was draped in the red or black flag of the anarchist;
every wall was scrawled with hammer and sickle and with the
initials of the revolutionary parties; almost every church had been
gutted and its images burnt. Churches here and there were being
systematically demolished by gangs of workmen. There were no
private motor cars. They had all been commandeered, and all the
trams and taxis were painted red and black. The revolutionary
posters were everywhere. The town had a gaunt, untidy look; roads
and buildings were in poor repair; the streets were dimly lit at night.
The shops were mostly shabby and half-empty. Meat was scarce and
milk practically unobtainable. The old man was once a powerful,

well-respected and tough person in the community, always making sure my family were well looked after.

I always talk about this man, and tell my friends that I have become the person I am today because of the old man. Everyone used to think he was a spy, but he is a retired police officer with whom I've become friends.

I helped him walk down the gravelled path, the soft pebbles crunching noisily beneath our feet. Only when we were away from the crowd did we speak.

'Papers wouldn't be hard for me to acquire,' I told the old man.

'Oh, yes, Pedro! It's getting to know the right people that matters, and of course, having the right papers in place. If you need any more help to become a policeman, just give them my card,' he said while knocking out his pipe against the heel of his shoe.

I saw something in his face then that deeply moved me, and I wondered whether I would always be grateful to the old man.

I joined the secret police in the working-class neighbourhood of La Boca. The entrance to the headquarters – a splendid stone building in the middle of the town with a cobbled courtyard to the rear – is through two tall wooden doors. Crimes are investigated, information dug up on the criminal in the hope of gaining money. Bribery is common. The world stinks of corruption and I have my nose in every crevice. I've quickly climbed the ladder and become quite a figure in the underworld of the secret police. Most of all, I've gained respect. Wherever I go in my local neighbourhood, people look up to me. Corruption leads to situations which attract power, and this was something that some of the secret police aspire to: announcing discovery of incriminating files, 'proving' that the communists are on the brink of a long-planned revolution. Women and children are sent in front of the terrorist groups. It scarcely matters that there is no proof of such allegations. Suspects are rounded up in military-style trucks.

More and more now, I am casting covetous eyes at the ever-growing strength in the southern corner. The last barrier has been broken, and now anything might happen. People waste no time on meaningless goodbyes, no need for pockets, or huge suitcases, or fashionable clothing. Surveillance is crucial: people want order. It is estimated that a new administration would need between six and nine months in which to achieve major changes; if it does not seize the opportunity to act decisively during that period, it will not have another such opportunity. The threat of violence or simply non-compliance is always lurking in the background, threatening the life of one brittle government after another. Doorbells ring harshly, echoing from one side of the stairwell to the other.

A letter has arrived assigning me to advise on the situation in Chile. I have been ordered to travel immediately, so I have packed what I can and am about to overnight. I have been put in charge of Operation Sebastian.

* * *

John looked up, rubbing the rough stubble on his chin as he said to himself, My God. His eyes shot to the clock. It was nearly five. He hurriedly rifled through the last few pages. For a moment he couldn't focus on anything, and he swallowed past the lump in his throat. Pretending he was calm and under control was nearly impossible for him.

John stared ahead of him, completely dumbfounded at what he had just read.

Chapter 27

Pedro stayed close to the phone throughout Tuesday morning, and even if he knew it hadn't made a sound, he kept picking up the receiver every few minutes as though he were yanking it from a holster. He just wanted to check it was still working.

A few hours later, Rosa called and suggested they meet at her school next Thursday. The call was a welcome distraction and, excited to hear from her, he agreed to come at 6 p.m.

On the day, he put the car into gear and whipped it around – causing gravel to spit out from under the tires – but he still arrived a little late. Today was not a day for second-guessing or regret; it was a day for action. And he was ready for it.

There was a couple sitting in the corner of the room. The man was rangy and thin, with a face that tapered severely into a dribble of a chin. The woman was just ugly – brazenly, beyond the scope of everyday ugliness: with tiny round eyes, a long twisted nose, and pale skin speckled with tiny spots. She told Pedro, "This is my partner; we used to dance like this."

Carefully considering his answer, Pedro finally replied, "Just a guess of mine, but I'd say you were the best."

"Over here, Pedro," Rosa called – she had spotted him.

She pulled him onto the dance floor, taking his coat and putting it on the chair. Her nimble fingers arranged his tie into an expert knot: she knew that presentation was important. Rosa laughed like an impressionable schoolgirl and Pedro realised that there was more to her laugh than she revealed – though nothing bad. She didn't drink, smoke, or do anything to harm her health.

Pedro was jittering from one foot to another, desperate to do something, but moving slowly as though his bones hurt. It was easy to tell he was definitely out of practice.

"Now we'll find out what you all know." Rosa started to click her fingers, then clapped her fingers rhythmically in the air and to the sides of her leg.

Pedro nodded mechanically. He didn't really know what she meant, but he wanted to seem as cooperative as possible.

"What does the clicking of the fingers mean?" he asked.

"Counting and clicking the fingers is a way to get into the world of the living rhythm," she replied.

He smiled. She really was an impressive creature. "Shall we go for a drink after we're done?" he suggested.

She smiled, her fingers still clicking away.

They walked down the high street and into Restaurant Triangle, which had a nice little bar at the back. After the waiter took their order, there was a long silence broken only by the sound of someone in the kitchen, throwing pots and pans around in either a fit of temper or in extraordinary clumsiness.

They smiled at each other, laughing at the noise and breaking the ice, and they sat there all night, drinking glasses of wine and talking.

He refilled her drink once more and sat back on the hard wooden chair, thinking how wonderful it was to speak in his mother tongue again, and how lovely she was. The bar seemed to cheer her up, but he knew she must be hungry after all that dancing. He asked if she would like something.

"Most of the time I'm far too busy for things like this. I eat at my school," she replied.

"Would you like some Bayonne?"

"Bayonne, that's like ham, right? We should get some," she said. She raised an eyebrow at him, "I'm intrigued."

He brightened a little more and reeled off a rather lame line: "How long have you danced for?"

"Eh, so what?" Rosa said shrugging her shoulders, her usual way of beginning a conversation. "All my life I have only cared for my music and my dancing, especially when I was at school. I used to dream of one day becoming a famous dancer." Her eyes glazed over a little as she pictured her old dream.

Heavy black kohl framed her tiny brown eyes, presumably to make them appear larger, and he couldn't stop staring at them – they were fascinating. They talked mostly about Latin music and a little about the history of the tango, and several hours into their discussion, his mobile phone rang.

"Not, now." He tossed it back on the table top, and it made such a racket that the girl at the next table jumped. She blushed and smiled at his apology, flicking her hair over her shoulder in a way that she must have thought was alluring.

He nodded politely and looked away, figuring she'd get the picture. In fact, Pedro didn't have the urge to date around. It seemed like a waste of energy to get a relationship going only to realise that it wasn't working and that he'd jumped the gun. He didn't really care that much. As far as he was concerned, this was work.

"Actually, did you know, Rosa, that the origins of the tango are related to brothels? And that it was danced between men and prostitutes but in a marginally lower class area?"

"It's most certainly a sexy dance," she said, smiling.

He shrugged a yes; she scanned his face for his reaction, both their elbows on the table.

He waited a moment, then looked her in the eye as he asked, "Do you have a boyfriend?"

She blushed. "I have many friends who are married – not many who are happily married, but many married friends. The few happy ones are like my parents: they're baffled by my singleness. A smart, pretty, nice girl like me, a cool job, money not an issue. They sit with their cups of hot chocolate and try to think of men they can set me up with. So the answer to your question is yes and no. What I have is my dancing."

"I understand."

What she didn't tell him was that she had been in a pretty serious relationship not so long ago, for a year. But she began to find him alarming: there was a problem Rosa had that put her off men for a while.

"Sometimes I do feel lonely, and I go home and cry for a while. I am almost twenty-eight. That's not old, I know – especially in London – but the fact is, it's been a few years since I've even really liked someone. Sometimes I wonder whether there's something wrong with me. I smile a lot to make up for my face, but this works only sometimes. In college I even wore glasses for a bit, fake ones with clear lenses that I thought would lend me an affable look."

"Oh," Pedro said, with real concern in his voice. "You're beautiful, and don't let anyone tell you any different. I know, it's hard to come to a new town and it's hard to make friends."

"Sometimes I think that there is something wrong with me, perhaps unfixable," she whispered, casting her eyes down.

Pedro stared at her, arms crossed. "Look, you have to move forward."

She shrugged, looking up at him again. "Actually, all the stuff I don't like about myself has been pushed to the back of my mind. To be honest, I feel naturally happy."

It was getting late, and the waiter, who had pale blue eyes that jittered like an unnerving tic, stood next to them, hoping they would ask for the bill. For a while he shuffled around clearing empty glasses, then he started to move in all the chairs and tables from outside.

Rosa said that maybe it was time to go, but also that it was a shame as they were having a good time. They laughed. The waiter looked over again. They were running out of things to say; it was Monday night and tomorrow would be a long day. They exchanged silent smiles as they walked out into the cold, into the great 'What next?'.

"Can I give you a lift home?" Pedro asked.

She nodded, and they walked down the high street to find the car. His hand on the small of her back, their faces stunned by the chill. They got in, and the music whispering in the background changed to something mournful right on cue, filling the interior of the car with an invisible weight. Pedro shifted into gear and stared straight ahead.

As he started driving, he brought up the dance school again. "How do you raise money to support the school?" he asked.

She seemed very relaxed now; they were really hitting it off and they felt comfortable in each other's company.

"My grandma back in Miami used to send me money each month."

"I see. Rosa, where do your parents live?"

"I haven't seen them since I was a very little girl," she replied. "I remember my mum – she had long wavy hair – but I can't really remember my dad. My grandmother doesn't talk much about my parents."

"Do you have any pictures of them?" he asked, hoping he sounded casual.

Mellowed out from the drink, Rosa didn't find the question odd at all, and she opened her purse to take out a little photograph of a woman.

"This is my mother."

"She is very pretty," Pedro said, glancing quickly at the photo. "What happened to her?"

"All I can remember is that when I was little, my mum would take me to the park every week. There was a small group of people there every time. It was the first time that I listened to Latin music – they had this old-fashioned record player that they kept playing. Ever since it's been in my head, even now. I remember people used to pass by and watch what I was doing. They would meet every

Page 259

week and just sit around having coffee, and sometimes they danced a little to the music."

Pedro said it reminded him of when he was a little boy back in Argentina: of Sunday afternoons at the Plaza Dorrego in Buenos Aires, in his neighbourhood of San Telmo. "We would all go there and watch the people dancing the tango. Sometimes it's nice to remember those good times, though there's something disturbing about recalling a warm memory and hoping you feel good afterwards."

"I know what you mean," Rosa agreed. "They're mostly sad memories for me, though. I remember a man who would keep talking to my mum. He was in his thirties, with long wavy black hair, and he always wore a short black leather jacket. He drove a brown Mustang car. As he would drive away, he would wave to Mum."

She remembered sometimes that her mum would cry as they walked back home. One morning, she'd got up late for school, and when she came down the stairs, her grandma was in the kitchen baking bread. "Rosa, you're up," she'd said.

She asked her grandmother where her mum was; she had a really bad feeling that something was wrong.

"Rosa, Mama has gone away for a couple of days."

She burst into tears straight away, knowing deep down that something had happened. "Where's she gone?"

"Rosa, please don't worry, I am going to look after you," Grandma said.

Rosa looked over at Pedro. "There was another person sitting with my grandma: a tall man with glasses. It looked like he had one leg shorter than the other when he stood up – it was as if he was standing at an angle. He just smiled at me and told me not to worry, that everything would be alright. Grandma told me to go and wait in the other room, and I could hear her asking how long it would take. The man said he would have to wait at least five to ten years before he could do anything. I have always wondered what they meant, but my grandma always used to say to me that one day I would be proud of my mama and papa. This always used to make me feel happy, as it meant that one day my parents would come back."

Pedro nodded slowly. "Rosa, how did you manage to come over to Britain?" he asked.

"My grandma helped me a lot to become a dancer; she made me join the local dance club, where there was an opportunity to enter competitions. She used to say to me that one day I would be a great dancer. She told me I should go to Europe as the best of the best were there, and I was incredibly excited at the thought: I loved dancing, and I started thinking that maybe I could fulfil my dreams there."

She sighed, smiling at Pedro. "It was my eighteenth birthday party, I remember it well. My grandma gave me an envelope, and all my friends were sitting around the table. They all watched as I opened the letter and took out a shiny blue form, which turned out to be a one-way ticket to London. I didn't know what to say, I just smiled and said thanks to grandma. Her friends cheered, and Max, my boyfriend, just smiled and nodded his head. The next week I was on the plane to London. I've lived in London for seven years now, and I still love every minute of it. I thought my dreams were ridiculous, and never imagined they could come true, or that I could feel this way." She smiled again, shrugging. "I tried not to worry too much, but it was hard."

They had got to Rosa's house a while ago, and had been sitting in the car and talking for nearly two hours. When Rosa moved to get out, Pedro leant forwards and gently kissed her on the cheek.

As they parted, she looked down at him with giant stunned eyes, studying his face, certain that he was studying hers. It was silly but incredibly sweet, she thought, Pedro spending so much energy trying to figure her out.

Just as she was about to open her front door, she called out and waved. "See you soon."

Pedro nodded. "Soon."

Chapter 28

Rosa woke up early. Feeling happy, she tossed her pillow to one side of the bed and kicked her feet out from under the sheets. Dangling her foot from the side of the bed, she knew she'd have a busy day ahead of her at the studio. She pushed aside the white louvred closet doors and ran her hands over the rainbow of clothes, the bright pinks, the summer whites. And then without thinking, she reached out her arms and went for the black suit. It made her think to herself how different it had been a year ago and how her life had become a little boring. The break-up of the relationship with her boyfriend had been bad. It was difficult to explain how ordinary your life could be, even when extraordinary things were happening around you. She felt sick, as though she had stomach flu. She lost weight during those weeks. She couldn't keep any food down. Every few days there was a message on her answering machine, and the voice as all too familiar: "Rosa?" her friend Lisa would say. "If you're there, would you kindly pick up?" After a lot of help from her friend she began to feel more confident, and her dancing helped too. During those weeks, much of her life was predictable.

Today, she was keen to get to the studio. She wasn't walking, doing a sort of shuffling run instead while trying to keep her upper body still.

Later that day she had her favourite student. Marcos was a young boy, perfect for the dance she had in mind.

She told him, "You must start a movement and step at the exact moment the sound appears, or instantaneously follow it. In this composition, the movement must correspond perfectly with the music. You must rehearse, more, and more."

"Okay, I understand," he replied.

"Reacting to the music is not the same as dancing with the music."

Marcos nodded. Exhaustion was licking at his muscles, and although he smiled he looked tired.

"When you react to a sound you hear there is a time delay, as if the movement is not inside the music. A dancer is more than an organism that merely reacts to sensory information. You are also interpreting the story of the music by telling it. You have to catch the spirit of the music."

Life could not have been better for Rosa right now.

The office telephone rang. Anne, the office clerk, trotted across the room towards her.

"Rosa, there's a call for you from a guy. He won't give me his name."

Rosa picked up the receiver in the office. "Hello?"

A deep, thick voice replied, "Hello," and then, after a brief pause, "I am a friend of your grandma and she told me to give you a call if I ever came to London. And well, I am visiting London next week."

He sounded American with a distinctive Spanish accent, and his pronunciation was familiar. There was something about the way he said "Rosa" which was bugging her: She knew his voice.

Her grandma had died a year earlier. Rosa wondered whether this was an old friend of hers who wanted to share something important with her.

She was under a lot of stress at the moment: The dance school was busy and she was spending a lot of time trying to get the dance event right. She decided to check the guest invites, with Anne sitting beside her on the couch. The ancient, much abused cushions sank severely under their weight until they ended up pushed up against each other, arms touching, which was fine with her; she just wanted everything to go well. By the time Anne was done, the whole room buzzed with efficiency. Rosa was lucky to have her working alongside her. Rosa patted her on the shoulder and shuffled the invites. "That's it, yup." She nodded.

Knowing she was far too busy, Pedro didn't call for a while. Unbeknown to him, she really wanted to be intimate with him and hoped that one day they could be together.

When her phone rang, she flicked a glance at the display and quickly shut it off, telling herself that she needed to concentrate.

"You should pick up, Rosa," Anne said.

When it rang again, she answered. It was her grandma's friend.

"This is Santiago."

"Who?" Her body stiffening immediately, a concerned look on her face.

Then she realised who it was. He sounded much friendlier this time. She felt giddy for a moment and had to clear her throat before agreeing to meet Santiago sometime next week. She thought, I don't know what my reaction is supposed to be: shocked, consoling, disappointed? My grandma never confessed any troubles. The fact of the matter is, something is not right.

***

She was on her way to meet a friend after a busy day. Lisa had called Rosa and asked to come round. She was funny and always made her laugh but the only thing was that she had a tendency to get a bit bossy and liked to take charge. Rosa wanted to tell Lisa all about Pedro: He was so sexy, so gorgeous and handsome. He was one of those guys – good looking in a way that was impossible not to notice. He made her feel so much like a woman every time she saw him. He'd be fumbling with his pen or something, and it made her feel really excited every time she looked at him. But the thing with this guy was that he was more than good looking:. He was stupidly handsome. And he'd somehow moulded attractiveness into the belief that he wanted to achieve the best for everyone. Women didn't just want him: They saw him and decided that he was the source of their future happiness. He was the perfect combo of bad boy and knight in shining armour.

"When I first met him I thought he had to be Italian with all that black hair."

"He sounds like my kind of guy." Lisa nodded.

She poured Rosa a glass of wine and told her to drink only one glass; she didn't want her to have a hangover tomorrow.

"Aren't you worried that some guys only use women?" Lisa asked.

"No," Rosa replied, "This feels different."

She told her friend that the other day they'd had dinner at a restaurant in Soho: sea bass and Chablis. During some dates she'd been on in the past she'd run out of things to say, felt dull-witted, bored. But no, not this time; they'd talked all night.

Lisa's Pete was due home soon, sweaty and salty and beer loose from a day at the football. They would hear the key turn in the lock, and Pete would wander in. Lisa would curl up on his lap and ask him if he'd take her out. "A really stressful week," he would say. "Wear this, don't wear that. Do this chore now and do that chore when you get a chance", and by that he meant there and then. Her mum had a few things to say about him too, such as, "He can't even be home on time." Lisa would hold up her arms, as if to say, "Stop there. I'm not having this conversation again, Mum. It's a waste of time."

Even though she was enjoying their chat, Rosa felt like she shouldn't be there. She looked at the clock on the wall.

"Hey, I've got to go, it's past midnight.

Chapter 29

The following week Santiago arrived in London. He had a car meet him at the airport which took him to the London Hilton on Park Lane. The doorman opened the car door and welcomed him to the hotel.

His room overlooked Hyde Park. Santiago was tall and very well-dressed. His thick dark hair was just beginning to turn grey at the temples. The first thing he did was sit down and open his packet of Marlboro cigarettes. He had a habit of inhaling deeply and for much longer than other people did, and usually finished his cigarette after four to five puffs.

Room service arrived with his club sandwich and a bottle of whiskey. He had an old-style briefcase which had leather straps and a buckle used to fasten them. He opened it and took out his diary before lighting another cigarette and writing down an account of his movements as well as his plans for the rest of the day. After just one long puff, he left his cigarette in the ashtray to burn itself out. He seemed calm, untroubled in a serenely peaceful manner.

He picked up the phone by the bed and dialled a number. "Can we meet?"

Rosa suggested they meet for a coffee but not that day as she was trying to open up a dance show.

"Yes, that's fine, there's no rush. We'll have time to get better acquainted later. But I want you to know I've followed your career closely and I'm a big fan."

Santiago was generally a very calm person and took his time to do anything, so it wasn't difficult for him now to just sit in his hotel room or in the park writing in his diary. On Tuesday morning he contacted Rosa again and they agreed to meet at a coffee shop on Kensington High Street the following day.

It was 6.30 a.m. on a chilly Wednesday, and the birds could clearly be heard chirping. It was daylight when Santiago left his hotel, and the traffic noise was getting louder. He decided to walk to Kensington as there was plenty of time; Rosa was going to be there at 9.30 a.m. He stopped to buy an English newspaper, rolled it up in a tube and just carried it in his hand rhythmically tapping it on his leg as he walked slowly down the high street. He was clearly deep in thought.

He arrived at the coffee shop a little early. He sat down and ordered a small coffee and lit a cigarette while he waited for Rosa. By 9.45 a.m. Rosa had still not arrived. Santiago just sat there waiting patiently and had another coffee. When she arrived, she just stood by the coffee shop door looking at him, as if trying to figure him out.

"Over here, Rosa," Santiago called out. He met her eyes, his jaw tense all of a sudden, before his smile turned into a full grin.

"Please sit down, very nice to meet you."

When she met his gaze, the jaunty, almost amused light started to drain from his eyes.

"How was your flight?" she asked.

"It was terrible," he replied, "But I hate flying, so unless it's a particularly smooth flight I always complain. Do you mind if I smoke?"

"That's fine," Rosa said. "So, Santiago, what brings you to London?"

"I was a friend of your grandma. In fact, when I was a young man she used to look after me. I was really upset that she passed away last year. She was a special woman."

"I know," Rosa said. "So why are you in London?"

"I made a promise to your grandma that I would watch out for you."

"That's very kind of you, Santiago, but I really am fine."

Page 268

His order was ready. "Excuse me," he slid the cash across the counter and returned with a plate of muffins and two coffees balanced in his hands. He sat back down.

"Tell me," Rosa asked, tearing off a large of blueberry muffin and putting it into her mouth. "I feel as if I know you from somewhere else. Have we met before?"

"Maybe when you were a tiny girl." He wiped his mouth with a napkin and burned a path down his throat with his swig of coffee.

"Where are you staying?" she asked.

"The Hilton on Park Lane. You should come and see me one night. We could have dinner and talk properly."

The waitress brought over two more coffees. Santiago was keen to get to know Rosa a little more.

"Have you got a boyfriend?"

"No, I am put off by boyfriends. Plus I don't have any time." When he pressed her for more information she continued, "I trusted someone once and he lied to me. A few months into the relationship, my credit card balance had gone from £5,000 down to zero. Yes, I had been showered with attention, diamond rings, flowers; I just didn't know at the time I would be paying for all of it, and that was only part of the problem. I discovered that he had lied about his educational background, credentials, status, profession. Then I found out my diamond ring came from his ex-lover's dead body. When I went to the police, they just said 'Lying is not a crime." Rosa paused for a little while and took another bite of her muffin before continuing. "Look, I would really love to talk more, and to hear more about grandma."

Santiago drank some more of his coffee and shook his head as though simply mentioning what had happened to Rosa had upset him.

"I take it you disapprove." Rosa shot him a questioning look.

Santiago brushed back his hair with his right hand and shrugged. "Listen, I know I don't know you that well, although I would like to. I know you're a private person - I am, too; I get that, it's just that you have to be careful in this world, you just don't know."

He'd suddenly tensed up as he tried not to think about how terrible it must have been for her. He wondered how she'd coped.

Rosa noticed that his expression and smile had lost a little of their energy.

Her hazel gaze was a heartbreaking combination of pain and hope. Santiago opened his mouth to say something, but whatever it was was left unsaid.

It was 11.30 a.m. and Rosa had to get back to the studio. Santiago stood up first and held out his hand to her.
"There is something very familiar about you - it's as if I've known you for years," she said.

Leaving the shop, she waved to Santiago and said she'd see him soon. From the bus stop, she could see him walk out of the coffee shop. Only now did she realised that one of his legs was shorter than the other. Walking seemed to cause him pain as he was shifting weight from side to side and the shorter leg had to be dragged up from behind. She paused for a moment, a little nervous and unsure of what she had just realised. This was the person who was with her grandma the day her mama went missing. She started to shake a little and felt really strange. She knew that she had to stay focus to make sense of it all at this pivotal time in her life.

On her way back to the studio she felt baffled. Thinking over and over again, I really do know this guy. She had no idea where this left her. Would they see each other again? She'd hoped for clarity but still didn't have any. Instead she was confused about what to do next.

Chapter 30

By the time Friday night rolled round, Rosa was so nervous she could barely think straight. The entire day she'd been trying to carry on conversations with people while her heart was beating in her throat.

She rifled through the closet until her hands latched onto a tight black Amanda Wakeley outfit. She didn't mean to spend so much time on her hair, but everything had to look just right tonight.

The doorbell rang. God! Rosa zipped into the closet and grabbed a pair of black heels. The car was waiting to take her to the opening night of her dance, and despite her nerves, she was relieved that it was finally here, and rejoiced in the achievement.

When she arrived at the studio, she noticed her fingers were shaking slightly. The turn-out was great – a quick look around confirmed that plenty of journalists were in attendance as well as representatives from the Council and a large group of Latin American ex-pats. She truly hoped this was it. She had only been standing there waiting for a minute or two but it felt like an eternity. Trying to keep her shaking hands under control, she walked up to the stage to welcome her guests and introduce the first dance. From the corner of her eye, she saw Pedro watching her and giving her a little encouraging wave. This was it, it was now or never.

The evening was fabulous and all the dancers were immaculate. They looked wonderful and the main dancers were spectacular. When they ended the dance in a great dramatic finale, all the guests cheered. The press were loving it, and one journalist even called Rosa over and said that it had been wonderful: "I loved how poetical the dance was, and how you used Latin character in the choreography to tell a story."

The reviews would all be glowing and praise the "mesmerising" choreography; with one in particular pointing out that the main male dancer was "a talent to look watch out for."

It was true that the performances had been exceptionally moving. Looking around the room after the finish, Rosa noticed that people were crying, and even she had tears in her eyes. The main lead's style was unique, and not something seen before; it was clear that he had put his whole heart into sharing a compelling, engaging story, and this was what had kept everyone glued to their seats. It was not because of personal stories or struggles, it was about the dance that told a story. The dancers moved about the stage without ever saying a word, choreographing a full arc, from exposition to climax to denouement, and you could feel it all the way into your soul.

Pedro didn't know how the rest of the evening was going to go, but he was wishing with every fibre of his being that it would all go to plan.

He said to Rosa, "I hope you're going to take things easy now, and have a break."

She told Pedro that she'd find it hard to rest. She'd worked all her life to get to this point. Pedro told her again she should take a break. He beamed at her, then surprised her by leaning forward and kissing her on the cheek.

Pedro's eyes lit up. Standing up in slow motion, he wagged a mocking finger at Rosa. She gave a wolfish smile. "Please can you introduce me to that journalist over there as I recognise him and would love to chat to him." Pedro fell back into his seat, glowering. His smile was wide and bright, and a rare pleasure. There were no nerves, not even when she seemed surprised. Pedro had so many sides and each one was more confusing then the next.

"He is one of the most famous people I know. He is a journalist and writes for a well-known newspaper. He specialises in royal gossip and has a reputation for supplying juicy royal stories to the tabloids."

Pedro already knew that, but didn't say so. Rosa introduced him, and the journalist complimented her on a wonderful performance.

This man was feared and adored. He knew who used to be married to whom, how they made their money, what schools they'd gone to - and, most of all, who they were sleeping with. Little wonder that when he arrived at a function, a frisson of discomfort swept the room. He set about deflating the egos of the idle rich and pricking the pomposity of the powerful.

When asked, he would say his revelations were never motivated by personal vendettas but by his belief that the public had a right to know.

Pedro told him that he admired his work and always read his articles with great interest. The two of them stood in the corner for a couple of hours drinking. When the waiter Rosa had hired for the evening offered the journalist a glass of champagne, he declined. "No. I dislike the stuff."

Pedro called the waiter back and asked for two glasses of Chablis. He had done his homework and knew that this man had a camel's thirst for Chablis. Pedro was one of those affable sorts to whom you are drawn the instant you meet. Inevitably, their talk turned to royal gossip and then to wine.

"I have a good story to tell you," Pedro said. "You should know that a friend of mine recently got married. He has a pretty good wine cellar. It gives him and his wife a lot of pleasure. Anyway, he decided that they would have their wedding at a resort in the lakes. Naturally, they decided to take some of the wines with them, better to enjoy the moment. So, on the morning of their wedding day, they started loading up the car with wine for them to drink over the weekend. Before he put the wines in the trunk, he showed them to his wife. 'I thought we were saving those for a special occasion?' she said. 'Well, unless you have plans for the waiter that I don't know about.' The wife explained that she wasn't thinking." The journalist burst out laughing, and Pedro joined in.

Desperate to make this contact, Pedro offered his services to the journalist.

"What do you do?"

Pedro explained,

"If a situation is so bad as to seem impossible, I can help. Or if you ever need to find anyone I can help too. My contacts can provide a little more focused information and attention than the police can offer."

The journalist gave his warm approval and they exchanged business cards.

"One of the best nights of our lives, don't you think?" Rosa said. The room had slowly been emptying over the past hour or so, with only a few stragglers left. She'd handled the journalist with perfect poise and charm, but she was also clearly star-struck after meeting the great man in person.

"To be honest, so was I. I just didn't let on." Pedro said when she confided in him, "And yes, definitely in the top ten or so."

He was teasing her. Pedro knew exactly what he was doing, calculating every possibility and risk. He was a consistent chap. He had such an exact mind that he would fold the same strip of card in exactly the same way he had been doing for years, or place his Parker pen pointing in the same direction on his desk every day. He would never change his habits, and always reacted in the same way to certain situations, both physically and mentally.

***

Pedro was aware of Santiago's arrival in London, and the reasons behind his trip. What Rosa didn't know was that Santiago's real name was Jorge Zaffaroni: He was her father.

Zaffaroni was here for one thing, and one thing only: revenge against the British government. A government which he blamed for the Dirty War and his enforced defection to the US.

Zaffaroni had checked out of his hotel. He called Rosa. "Hey, where are you?" He sounded nervous. Rosa's voice was too loud when she answered and she quickly dialled down the volume "Yes. What?"

"I have to go away for a few weeks, and would very much like to give you a present before I leave."

She agreed to meet him later that day at her studio.

It wasn't easy for the taxi driver to find a place to park; the large studio was surrounded by cars and the usual detritus. Zaffaroni crossed the road and paused on the porch steps to give the street a discreet once-over before pulling the door open. He looked around for Rosa.

"Over here, Santiago! Very nice to see you again."

Without preamble, he replied, "Rosa, I have this letter I would like to give you. It's something your grandma wants you to do. When you have your next live performance, I would like you to give this letter to the journalist who was at your dance evening last week. I know he comes a lot and he enjoys your dancing."

"But why?" She looked puzzled.

"As I said, Rosa, it's one of the reasons you are here. Your grandma has arranged this moment for you, and she would expect this of you. Please don't ask any more questions."

Searing pain shot through her head at hearing his words, and she wondered whether she should sit down for a minute to catch her breath. How was it possible that less than a week ago she'd felt that she could trust this person, even felt responsible for him? She felt like she wanted to say something, but kept silent, glancing around the room, alone with her thoughts. She was confused, but knew this was important. She put the letter in her safe.

"Once again, Rosa, in one week you have another dance night. Please give the letter to the journalist as soon as he arrives." Then, after a pause, "Rosa, I am going away tonight but I will call you soon."

Chapter 31

Feeling a little lonely and sad, Rosa called Pedro but he was busy explaining details of a case to one of his staff and had his mind on other things. And yet, he couldn't get Rosa out of his head. There were people you met whom you made a connection with, and such people were just too hard to let go of. Rosa was one of those: She'd got under his skin and he couldn't stop thinking about her. But he knew that he had to stay focused on his cause.

Later that day Pedro called her back and they met for dinner at a local French restaurant. Rosa was not her usual happy self. They sat and drank champagne but she was quiet and didn't say much.

"What's wrong?" Pedro asked.

"It's nothing. I just feel quite embarrassed."

"Don't feel like that."

The waiter was hovering near the table.

"Are you ready to order, Sir?"

"Just a salad for me," she said.

"I'll have the sea bass."

The waiter brought a nice bottle of wine. Rather annoyingly, he kept topping up their glasses every two minutes. Aware that Rosa wanted to tell him something, Pedro told the waiter to please leave the wine to him.

Rosa started to feel a little more relaxed now, and she started to smile like she used to. He asked her if she had any more dance nights planned.

"Yes, I have, next week."

"Actually, sorry, Rosa, you did tell me. I just forgot. Maybe we can dance together again."

She was still not completely herself.

"Come on then, what's wrong?"

"It's something that happened the other day. A friend of my grandma came to see me and it was strange. It all seems so secretive, and like it's a mystery. I've met this guy, his name is Santiago, and I think I remember him from many years ago. I was a little girl and he was sitting with my grandma, but the really strange thing is that it was the day my mother disappeared. Santiago has asked me to look after a letter for him, and to give it to that journalist – the one you were talking to at the dance evening."

"Now I understand why you're down. But look, maybe there's a reason for everything and maybe it's all meant to happen this way."

"I don't know, Pedro, it's just a funny feeling I have."

He took her hand. Both felt as though there was an electric shock shooting down their arms: They had not even shaken hands before. Pedro paused to get control of himself; he was a little too tempted to grab her and just hold her tight. Suddenly, Rosa burst into tears. Pedro gritted his teeth.

"Do you need some water?" He grabbed a glass from the bar and skirted the edge of the table to place it in her hand. Instead of taking it, she shot to her feet and threw her arms around him, sobbing for all she was worth, and spilling the water over his forearm. Pedro patted her hair and her back with a rough hand. She was latched on so tightly that he was experiencing every quivering breath she took.

"I'm so sorry," she cried. He patted her again.

Pedro knew exactly how to manipulate and mislead her. When Pedro wanted to, he could win anyone over with his charm. "I'm going to tell you something important. Santiago is your father."

Rosa went very still. It took a few moments before she responded.
"What do you mean he is my father? How do you know this?"

"Listen, Rosa, I don't know all the details but I know for sure that he is. And I really think that you should just follow his instructions. I am sure there must be a good reason."

"But?" she asked, biting her lower lip furiously, starting to look a little scared.

Pedro needed to calm her down.

"There may be days when you get up in the morning and things aren't the way you hoped they would be. That's when you have to tell yourself that things will get better. There are times when people disappoint you and let you down. But those are the times when you must remind yourself to trust your own judgement and opinions, to keep yourself focused on believing in yourself. Look, Rosa, this is what my mum would say to me whenever I was down."

Pedro just couldn't tell her all the details about her father. It would have been too risky. It was important to accomplish what he needed to do.

"I don't know where to start. I've just found out that everything I ever believed is a lie and that my parents are the ones who started the lie."

"You're probably angry. But think about how hard it must have been for them."

Pedro suggested they leave now. Walking slowly towards the car, he grabbed her hand tightly and told her not to worry. Rosa asked Pedro if he could stay the night as she felt very lonely and afraid.

He inched the car slowly into the driveway. When they got to the front door, Rosa was shaking hard and couldn't remember the entry code.

"Calm down, Rosa."

She cried, and Pedro hugged her and told her not to worry, that everything would be fine. Rosa tried again and this time she keyed in the correct numbers. The inside light was not working. She held Pedro's hand and guided him up the narrow staircase. Inside her flat, she switched on the living room light and wished she'd cleaned it up. She hadn't counted on Pedro visiting her.

"Please have a seat, can I get you a coffee?"

Safe in the knowledge that Rosa had now fallen for him, Pedro was sure that she would do whatever he wanted.

His eyes rested on the pictures of Latin dancers on her wall. There was also a picture of her grandma, a tiny old lady with a little girl. Presumably Rosa.

"She used to have an old violin. She said it was a very special violin and she told me that I should look after it forever. She used to say to me. 'Fifty years ago, nobody wanted old instruments because everybody thought modern ones were better than the old ones. Like a camera - the modern version is better than the old. But if you find a camera from 1870, and you see the photographs of that time, they are fantastic, and you cannot take those great portraits in black and white with the best modern camera. You cannot make these pictures.' This is the reason why she told me I should look after this old violin."

"Your grandma was a very good teacher."

"I never thought that I'd ever be in your room," Pedro whispered solemnly, slicing through Rosa's memories, his eyes still flitting from place to place in the room.

"I didn't see this coming, either." She had to clear her throat to get the words out. She lifted her hand and gently clasped the side of Pedro's neck, giving him time to back away if he needed to.

He put his arms around Rosa and gently kissed her on the lips. She responded. Pedro was exploring the silken skin of her back upward to her shoulders. Seeming to remember where they were, he slowed, reluctantly pulled back and touched his forehead. "I'm sorry," he said hoarsely." . . Got carried away."

"It's okay, really."

Pedro stayed the night. In the morning Rosa said, with a smile on her face, that she just couldn't sleep. But a man like Pedro

Page 280

was well-trained in treating intimacy with the same glib attitude with which he treated every thing else.

"I've always been able to turn myself off like a light. I usually tell myself, 'I'm going to sleep,' my hands in the prayer position against my cheek, but not last night," she said.

"Try to go back to sleep," Pedro suggested.

"Are you coming on Friday?"

He leant forward to kiss her cheek and whispered in her ear, "Good luck." She looked back at him with a cheerful smile on her face.

***

The second dance night was a sell-out again. The cars rolled up to the door with their VIP guests. A couple of the press had arrived, and they were taking photographs of the dancers, and the who's who of the entertainment world. Trays of champagne and canapés were on offer. Looking out for the journalist, Rosa finally spotted him in the crowd.

"Excuse me, I was asked to give you this letter."

He thanked her with an astonished look on his face and went into the corner of the room to open the letter. When he'd read it he looked as though he had seen a ghost.

The letter announced that an especially prominent member of the establishment would die on a certain date, and that it would not be an accident.

As far as the journalist was concerned, this was sensational news, but of course nothing had happened, as yet.

In the meantime, Pedro was carefully watching what was going on. He knew that the journalist would try to sell this information to a newspaper, but what Pedro really wanted was to expose the British Government for what they were.

The journalist understood the importance and the significance of the letter only too well, but he worried about what to do as he did not want to cause any unnecessary issues in case the content proved to be untrue.

For the next few days Pedro had the journalist followed wherever he went, and he had his house bugged. He knew that if something bad happened, and this information was leaked to the public, there was no way the government would take responsibility. Which meant that the very fact that this information was being hidden would be proof that the government had a dark secret to hide.

The journalist booked a table for two people at a well-known restaurant in St James's Square. His guest was going to be a well-known politician. Pedro hoped he would be able to record their discussion about the impending high-profile death. The fact that it had not even occurred yet did not matter – that they would do nothing to prevent it despite the warning that it would not be an accident was enough to implicate them. And the perfect opportunity to expose the British and show the world that they'd withheld the evidence.

Chapter 32

Pedro kept calling John, keen to meet him again, but this time in a well-known restaurant in St James'. The number of phone calls were beginning to worry John: He was still trying to keep Pedro a secret and hoped that none of his family overheard the conversations he had with him.

"John, I would like you to help listen in on a conversation in this restaurant."

"You mean eavesdrop. On who?"

"It's not important, just some royal correspondent for a daily newspaper. He's doing a story on the royals, if you come down to the office I can wire you up."

John was up early. When he faced the mirror, he couldn't look at himself. Eventually, he forced himself to open his eyes and found those brilliant hazels staring right back, filled with uncertainty. He knew the sooner he got on with it the more quickly he could get back to normal. His eyes shot to the clock on the wall. He had an appointment to sign a contract for the purchase of another restaurant in Twickenham as the lease on his current one was coming to an end, and had to be in the West End soon.

He crossed the walled courtyard and knocked on the ironbound front door. A dark-suited man took his name and left him in the reception hall. It was an enormous two-storied room. Mr Lawrence ushered John into his office, and offered him the brown-leather chair facing him across his desk. Then he opened the bottom right-hand drawer of the desk and pulled out the contract for him to sign. John finished the coffee Mr Lawrence's secretary had brought him and stood up. He looked at his watch, remembering that Pedro was expecting him. He'd have to get a cab from Grey's Inn to Chiswick.

He hurried down the corridor to Pedro's office, knocked and walked in simultaneously, catching Pedro whizzing his model globe round on its axis with his right foot. Part of the reason why John found talking to Pedro so exhausting was that he never knew the right answer. There was always a right one and a wrong one – he was very black and white – but he gave no clues and was disturbingly unpredictable about everything. His views were fixed. It must have been something to do with his brilliant, original mind, and he made life hellishly hard for anyone who tried to cross him.

"So, tell me again," John asked him.

"I will make sure you're well paid."

"I'd like to be well off, I don't know about well-paid. There's only so much money I need – a lot more than I've got now, that's for sure. But what I want is not so much the money. And that's something we both already know."

There was a potent edge to their meeting; an inescapable sense of involvement that told John he was either going to go crazy or fall in too deep. He did not trust Pedro. He did not trust himself to make the right decision.

There was a sort of calm to the room. In the kitchen to the left you could hear the gentle drip of the coffee machine, and the only movement came from the gentle floating of a million specks of dust suspended in the air, highlighted by the slits of sunlight that penetrated the louver blinds.

A little later, John went to the toilet and was about to open the door when he overhears Pedro talking on the telephone in Argentinian Spanish. This was the first time he'd heard him speak in his native language. John stopped in his tracks and listened. When the name 'Diana' was mentioned, John was startled: Things started to make sense now. And all of a sudden, he understood the real reason why Pedro had come to Britain.

As soon as John pushed open the door, Pedro stopped talking and looked up at him, clearly shocked to see him.

"Come in," he said.

He had the ceiling fan on full power and was playing his usual music in the background. It suddenly occurred to John that behind Pedro's vivacious facade, he was nothing but vulgar.

Pedro shook his head and held his hand up to John, telling him, "One sec" while he began searching for some paperwork in one of the stacks of folders. John waited in tense silence to hear what he had to say. He could not help but notice the brown leather briefcase with the letter T engraved on it, and next to it a sheet of paper with a list of names and times. He could just make out one of the names which looked like Princess Diana. John ran his hand over his mouth, a sure sign and that he was extremely upset, and something he only did that when he was freaking out. Overcome by dread, he looked around the room for some kind of inspiration, for a hint of what to say or do.

"Look, Pedro, I'm fed up with this, with the phone calls, everything. You're causing me a lot of stress. I feel that you're just playing with me. Just tell me what you want, and let's get on with it; let's get it over and done with so I can lead my life."

"Don't worry, John, we're very close to the end."

Hearing those words "very close to the end" sent a chill right through his body. Pedro then repeated himself and continued,

"Just one more job and both of us will be free. Here's the wire, let's test it. See if we can record at the other side of the window." Pedro gave him a hard stare. "Yes, John. We've been friends a long time and we know a lot of heavy shit about each other." John paled but didn't make a move to speak. He didn't want to come across defensive, even though he felt every defensive wall inside him clicking into place.

"Let's be realistic here. I trusted you, but I'm more than a little scared here. Why should everything be different now, or as you say, 'Just one more job and both of us will be free.' I find that hard to believe."

Pedro's throat tightened and he tried to loosen it with a gulp of warm water left over on the office desk. The silence that followed was heavy.

"What do you want to hear?" Pedro snapped, I told you it's going to be over, now come, on let's take this forward."

Pedro hooked up the tape recorder and stuck a bent paper clip to its metal frame to hang the microphone down on his side of the glass window.

"Perfect. You must keep it facing outwards. We must be ready as we won't get another chance. I would like you to meet me at this restaurant tomorrow night at 7.30 p.m. and take your wife. I have already reserved you a table, but be sure to be seated by the window, or close to it. I'll be on the other side of the room, in case the reporter moves tables. Here is the small tape recorder which must be connected to the transmitter."

"What if it goes wrong?"

"It won't. Just try to keep close to him and when he talks, don't you talk."

Increasingly scared, John began to head down the hallway without saying another word, but Pedro slid in front of him, blocking his way and slamming the door shut with his body.

"I don't know why you're running away." The anxiety was now bleeding into his words and Pedro took a couple of deep breaths to control it.

John stared at his shoes and mumbled something that Pedro couldn't hear before lifting his eyes.

"I'm not running, I'm tired." But John knew he had no choice.

He was sweating and his hand was tightly clenched his fingers were going numb. If Pedro disowned him, then so be it. There was no relief in the telling - no weight coming off his shoulders. He just knew the next few minutes would determine whether or not he would be able to handle it. Pedro clipped the receiver to John's hip and ran the wire up the inside of his jacket. After wrapping the coil around the back of his ear, he wedged the little flesh-coloured earpiece into position. He turned up volume and did a quick radio check.

John cleared his throat impatiently. "Okay."

Chapter 33

"Home, sweet home..." John mumbled as the taxi drove away thirty pounds richer. He wanted to be with her even more now, and tell her everything, but he knew that would probably be a mistake. Whether or not John told Sonia everything about himself, this was something he had to do in his own time. He was hurting pretty bad at the moment.

Sonia was still half asleep and seemed shocked to see him tonight, she thought he was working at the restaurant.

He'd brought her a bunch of roses and left them at her bedside. She didn't have time to dwell on the generosity because he closed the door quietly behind him. Several hours later he gently opened it again. "Would you like a cup?" She smiled sleepily. "I'd love one."

Downstairs, the heels of her shoes were clicking gently against the polished floor tiles. They were both proud of their house, the warm colours of the intricately woven rug and the extensive use of delicate moulding. The room was a masterpiece. It resembled the cover of a fancy magazine. It was elegant and warm. She loved it.

"By the way, do you fancy going out for dinner tonight?"

"Hmm. That's why the flowers?"

"What are you implying?" he asked impatiently.

After a long silence she looked at him with compassion and honesty.

"I mean what on earth do you need to be sneaky for? If you want to go out, just say so."

"Actually, I call it being romantic."

* * *

Page 289

When they arrived at the restaurant dead on 7.30 p.m., the room was already starting to fill. The restaurant was very upmarket and there seemed to be more waiters than customers. Pedro was seated at the bar. His clothes were immaculate: his suit and shirt as pristine as if he'd just bought them at Savile Row. John tried to avoid eye contact with him but it wasn't easy - he was constantly looking at him from the corner of his eye.

John had told Sonia that they were here for an early birthday meal. There was an awkward pause in their conversation: It seemed she wanted to say something but couldn't push out the words, and he was trying to think of things to say to her, but it was difficult to stay focused. They talked about the time he'd left to work on the cruise ships and Sonia had met another man. He told her that he didn't blame her: She just fell in love with someone else. But just because he didn't blame her didn't mean he didn't feel it. He told her that he wasn't angry with her, but somehow he thought that she wanted him to be. She always told him that he never showed enough emotion, that he never got mad. He didn't feel mad, just sort of deflated. Like when you let the air out of a balloon really slowly. Usually it went in circles if you let it fly around on its own. That was sort of what his head was doing.

They were seated near the window. Three tables across, Terence Conrad was sitting with a well-known actor whose name John couldn't remember. Along came the wine waiter.

"Sir, here is our list."

It was like a book – at least five hundred different wines in its contents.

"Could you direct me to the white section?" Sonia said pointedly. "You know the wine we drink."

"Do you have the Meursault 79?" John asked the wine waiter.

He was so deep in thought it took him a moment or two to realise that Sonia was squeezing his hand.

As they waited for their wine, the reporter and his guest arrived and were seated at the table right next to theirs. He could just catch Pedro's movement in his eyes telling him that it was him. He had connected the device to his leg and it was set to high volume, so anything that was being said would be picked up.

Their first course arrived, but John was barely registering what he was eating. He couldn't help but try and listen in on the conversation at the next table. Predictably, it was mostly about recent newspaper stories, including one about the Royals.

"Apparently she drinks a lot," the journalist said.

John froze when he thought he heard that "they" didn't want any individual of "Middle Eastern" origin in the family.

"Look at this letter."

Discreetly glancing over, John could see shock on their faces. He knew this was something big.

It was getting late and the conversation was still recording. As the two of them were still deep in conversation, John picked up the odd well-known name. He was a little concerned that the tape might not last, but luckily the reporters seemed to have stopped talking.

He noticed that Pedro had asked for his bill and paid. As John and his wife got up to leave, the two journalists did the same. Pedro was waiting outside. The journalists had already got into the first taxi waiting, and the doorman asked if John and his wife would like the second. John could see Pedro in his mind's eye, waiting for him to find him and hand over the tape. Something inside him told him not to. He told the cabbie to take them to Waterloo Station.

When they arrived at the station, Sonia told him she needed the Ladies, giving him the opportunity to duck into the Gents and remove the listening device. Back in the terminal, he found a locker and deposited the device inside it. When Sonia met him back outside the Ladies to complain about the long queue, she stopped in her tracks and remarked that he was sweating profusely and looked a bit nervous.

Page 291

"I think the wine has gone to my head."

Realising that they had less than four minutes to board the train, they hurried to their platform. On the way home, he silently stared out of the train window pondering what had just happened, and wondering whether he should have given Pedro the tape.

That night the phone rang. Sonia answered.

"Hello, who's this?"

There was a rustling at the other end. She turned over to John and shook him awake. He slowly came to, blinking as he opened his eyes.

"Pass it here."

It was Pedro.

"I have to go."

"Where? Why?" Sonia sounded alarmed.

She grabbed his hand and looked up at him with her big blue eyes. He gently extricated his hand from hers, got up and put on his trousers, looping the belt round and clipping it into place. Thinking too himself that surely she must have noticed that he'd changed a lot over the past couple of years.

He went outside to the telephone box and called Pedro to tell him not to call any more. But Pedro was having none of it, all he was interested in was the return of the tape. He threatened to report John to the police for what happened in the States.

"Why don't you get a life and leave me alone!" John shouted down the phone.

Everything Pedro did was strategic planning, always outthinking his opponents, especially when it was a question of life or death.. Every move, every variation of each move would be analysed. John knew that this would not be easy. But how could he be sure that once he'd given Pedro the tape he wouldn't report him to the police?

Safe in the knowledge that Pedro wouldn't do anything to him while he still had the tape, he decided not to give in.

That night Zaffaroni flew to Paris. Two days later, on the way back to the airport, he read the French papers and was satisfied with the results of his work.

Chapter 34

John was having breakfast with Sonia and reading the newspaper.

The papers were still dominated by the news about Princess Diana's tragic death in a car crash in Paris, just after she'd left the Ritz Hotel with her companion Dodi Al Fayed, the son of Harrods owner Mohamed Al Fayed.

"Have you read this?"

"What, the Princess Diana story?" Sonia looked up.

"It's a conspiracy," John said. "Look? There are doubts over the accident, and questions over whether the establishment did not want any Arab connection."

"Don't believe everything you read, John."

"They feared that Diana would convert to Islam."

"It doesn't bear thinking about, imagine the implication that would have on the church and state."

"My theory: one or more rogue cells in the British Secret Intelligence Service hatched and carried out a plot to kill her, or some offensives were in operation as Diana was a threat to the throne, and therefore the stability of the state."

John had another theory, but wasn't saying.

The phone buzzed. He looked over to Sonia and nodded, picked up the receiver from its holder and walked into the other room. He already knew who it was. The line went silent for a few seconds, then the voice at the other end spoke. John slumped down into the chair and took a deep breath before dropping his head into his hands and swearing. "What the . .?"

"I need that tape, John, and I will be there tonight to see you."

He told Pedro to calm down, and that the tape was safe. He was happy to hand it back, but he wanted to make a deal with him.

"I want you to leave the country and not come back."

"John, be careful what you say. Remember I know what you have done."

"Pedro, I'm not afraid of you any more. There's no proof that I did what you say. Anyway, you seem very desperate to get your tape."

"I will hound you forever, believe me."

"I know what's been happening, Pedro," John said. "And I know you had your reasons."

"You don't know the half of it! What happened to you was awful but it had to be done," Pedro said.

"I know more than you think."

"Do you?"

But John laughed and told him that he really didn't know anything. Pedro sounded a little upset now - he must have hit a nerve.

"I knew about you and that false name you went under," he said.

Then he laughed. It was a brittle sound. And he went on to tell John that even Drinda had never cared one bit for him.

"Actually, I knew that." But all this had made him think: Was this the revenge Pedro was talking so much about? John had never seen him so desperate to get hold of something.

John left the restaurant early that night. As he was getting into his car he got a feeling that someone was behind him, and within a split second he was pulled back by his hair onto the ground, and kicked on his leg. His head throbbed, he felt as though someone had punched him really hard. Pedro was standing over him.

"John, this is your last chance, I need that tape now."

"Pedro, hear me now - why don't you just piss off?"

"Yeah, piss off," Pedro said.

"Leave the country," he told him, "and it's yours."

"You have by midday tomorrow to hand it over. I tried to be nice to you, John. Would it help if I begged?"

He needed a moment to let that sink in, with Pedro just staring, waiting for his answer.

"No."

He walked back towards the car, but Pedro followed him, got in next to him and said, "Look we used to be friends."

John gave a laugh, the kind that wasn't entirely sympathetic. "You're completely out of your mind if you think I'm going to let you get off scot-free doing what you did to me."

There was another worrying silence. Eventually, John expelled a short exasperated breath.

"Where are you?" A voice in the darkness.

John breathed a sigh of relief. "Over here!"

It was one of his waiters. He was supposed to meet him that night to give him his wages.

Joe approached the car. "John, do you know how long you'll be?"

Pedro hissed, "Tell him to go away." He didn't want any witnesses. Finally he got out of the car, turned around and walked away. John was fighting against the urge to chase after him, to slam him hard against the wall and shove his weasel teeth right down his filthy Argentine throat. The slightest movement hurt.

While he was waiting for Joe to return, he rolled up his trouser leg and examined the damage. There'd be a mighty bruise by tomorrow but he didn't think anything was broken, and the damage to the rest of his body was only superficial.. There was an ache in his shoulder and in the eye, caused by what he regarded as a lucky punch. Joe returned.

"Are you okay?" he asked. "Your face..."

Now that Joe had mentioned it, he became aware of a harsh stinging sensation along the left cheek and forehead. His left eye wasn't feeling so great either. Wiping his face with the back of his hand, he glanced down and saw the smears of red. He peered into the rear window. "The little shit has drawn blood. Great! By tomorrow I'll look like I've been in a goddam cat fight."

"They've done a damn good job on you," Joe said.

But that was the least of his problems. His right leg felt like it had been put through a crusher. And there he was, thinking that Pedro always played by the rules. Perhaps he didn't know him as well as he thought.

Joe put out his hand.

"Give me the car keys then?"

When he had the keys, he jiggled them between his fingers for a moment, gazing at the dashboard.

"You can drive, can't you?" John asked anxiously.

"No, I just thought I'd come over and play dodgem with your bright red Golf," Joe said.

"Just put the key in the ignition," he told Joe, "and switch on the engine."

"There's no need to look so worried. I'm only savouring the delights of being behind a wheel again. My motor spent so much time in the garage I had to scrap it."

"And you haven't got another because . . .?"

"Because waiters get paid a pittance in wages and I figured it was cheaper to use public transport."

"Maybe it's because you like a drink or two."

"Right," he said.

He told Joe to drive straight on and head towards the exit.

"Are you sure you wouldn't like me to take you to hospital?"

"No, thanks."

Joe glanced down towards his leg.

"It's not broken is it?"

"No."

When he snatched his hand away, the abrupt movement increased the ache in the shoulder. Joe started to ask questions.

"Who was he?"

"Just a poor bastard who is really a good guy. That's the problem."

Joe suggested that someone was sending out a warning.

"You call that a warning?"

"So, some bastard just tried to kill you."

John shook his head.

"If he wanted to kill me, he could have."

They sat in silence for a while. There was a Chinese takeaway across the street. Joe wanted to get out, saying he was hungry.

John was late getting home. He limped to the bathroom and stared at his face in the mirror. It wasn't a pretty sight. His left eye, half closed, was swollen and bruised. Only a year ago he'd been faster on his feet. The episode had left him badly shaken. The guy means business, he thought.

Sonia was standing at the bottom of the stairs with her arms folded across her chest. He dreaded what he thought was coming next – more than likely a barrage of questions - , but she surprised him by making a statement instead.

"You've been attacked."

His throat felt suddenly dry. "Yeah," he croaked.

She ran her hand gently across his leg.

"And it would appear you have not seen a doctor."

Her expression remained neutral.

"I don't suppose you are going to tell me how this happened?"

John rolled his eyes.

"You know me and my feelings . . . they don't really go together."

"That maybe true with other people, but not with me. I am not judging you. You should know that by now, I don't know everything you do, but I have a pretty good idea. Have I ever complained?"

"No."

He gently kissed her on the cheek and told her he was sorry. In an effort to redirect the conversation he told her she was handling this pretty well.

"What do you mean?"

"I thought you'd be mad."

"I'm not exactly thrilled but I don't see how getting angry would help."

John froze in his seat and tried to swallow the lump in his throat. This was it. His opportunity to tell her everything. He opened his mouth, eyes glued to Sonia's back were she stood looking out of the kitchen window. Tell her. Say it.

It was the right moment, but once again he lost it. He stood up and kissed her on the forehead and then went into the bathroom and closed the door. He looked in the mirror, took a deep breath, and tried to figure out how much he could tell her. But the words would not come. A crippling vice had settled over his vocal chords.

Back in the living room, Sonia ran a patient hand over her hair. Then she sighed and left the room without saying another word. He watched her go, part of him madly trying to gain control of his voice and call for her to come back. Afterwards he felt angry and sullen. He took a shower to relax himself.

Early next morning, John was sitting on his back steps, ready to rip off the Band Aids and reassess the cuts on his leg when he heard the phone buzzing in the kitchen. He rushed inside, picked up the phone and clicked the answer button. It was Pedro.

"Yes," he said.

"I'm going to take care of you, John."

John slammed the phone down. He thought again that this had to be really important for him to want it so badly. It wouldn't be safe for him to collect the tape he had hidden in the locker at the train station – Pedro was sure to be watching him.

******

He stood and looked at himself to take inventory of his pains and aches. After waking once during the night to use the bathroom and take a handful of painkillers he was surprised that his leg didn't feel worse. He took some solace in the fact that it was slightly better than last night, but the whole situation weighed on his mind, and he could see that he wouldn't get any rest until he'd sorted it.

He decided to go and see Pedro to try to come to some sort of a agreement. Driving up to the office, he spotted Pedro walking towards it. John stopped and called out to him. He got out of the car and looked him straight in the eye. Pedro just smiled and gazed up towards the sky. The clouds were low and grey. A few flakes of snow were starting to fall again and the smile faded from Pedro's lips.

"Hey, I wasn't casting aspersions. I know you're a man of thoroughly upstanding principles," John said sarcastically.

"Don't be rude."

Pedro realised that he was being mocked and wasn't really in the mood for it.

"Before we get into the finer detail," Pedro continued, "I think there's something you should see."

"I've seen as much as I need to. I think all I want to see is for you to leave me alone." John raised his eyes and smiled.

"Okay, so what if I offer you something that money can't buy?"

"And what would that be exactly?"

"Your freedom."

"No, forget it."

"Admit it," Pedro said. "Tell me there isn't a niggling doubt. Tell me that it hasn't crossed your mind, even for a second, that I could just be speaking the truth. Are you really going to let this opportunity slip through your fingers?"

"Give me one good reason why I should believe you! So what are you saying – that I will lose my freedom? Pedro, I really think you should step back for a moment, you're not thinking straight."

Pedro seemed to think about this for a moment before responding with an empty laugh.

"Okay," he said. "Just give me the tape and we can part as friends."

John replied impatiently. "I'm not really in the mood for a long conversation about what you want."

"Time is running out, so do the right thing."

"Face to face and hand to hand, it's ugly and it's been messy, and you never forget. So how do you expect me just to take your opportunity, when we don't have the trust?"

"If you're not ready to deal with that, it can eat you up," Pedro replied.

Eyes on the floor, John took a deep breath.

"It's not always that cut and dry. In fact, Pedro, it's rarely that way. You have to get comfortable with uncertainty. Can you do that?"

"To tell you the truth, John, I don't know. I can't give you an answer. But I know that's not the right answer."

"But actually, that's the right answer! Pedro, you know it is the pretence as much as anything."

"All that hypocritical crap makes my guts turn over. Good or bad, take your pick, but you can't have it both ways."

Deep down, John wanted to sort things out but found it hard to make an effort to be pleasant.

"I need to know what's happening," Pedro said brusquely. He was getting really angry now. "Don't fuck me about, John. I don't like it. I don't like it one little fucking bit."

John told himself to stay calm. His life was already overburdened and he could hear the familiar self-pitying whine in Pedro's voice now.

"We've all got our problems. Just leave the country first and the tape is yours."

Chapter 35

Pedro had a lot of contacts within the police, but he didn't want to go tipping his hand. At the moment, everything he had was based on gossip and rumour. A little tip off-now and again would earn him a little more respect with the local CID.

Jones let out a moan that said, You have got to be kidding.

"Don't worry," Pedro said. "I'll make sure you're compensated. You get your head back in the game and get me what I need and I'll make sure you walk away with enough cash."

John had a call from the police on Saturday morning asking if he would mind attending an identity parade.

"Well, I do mind."

His voice turning more brusque, Jones made it clear that this was an order, not a request. "You fit a description."

When John arrived at the police station about 2.00 p.m., he was kept waiting for two hours in a holding room together with another man, who clearly noticed his unease.

"Don't worry," he said. "They might detain you for a while to scare you. That's all. As for me, I'm in and out of jail all the time anyway."

After what seemed like an eternity, an officer opened the door and introduced himself as PC Thomas. He explained that all he needed do was simply stand in line next to these other men. Realising he had no choice, John agreed, certain that this was Pedro's way of getting to him. He stood in line and turned up his collar, immediately regretting it as it was bound to make him look guilty. The trouble was that once this thought entered your head, you really did think you were guilty. He started to feel as if he had something to hide; being under pressure from Pedro started to grind him down. The guy next to him was tall and had a dark complexion. This was puzzling – John had always thought that all suspects are supposed to look alike when on an identify parade. PC Thomas politely called out "Okay that's it!"

The room alone made John feel faintly nervous, especially not knowing why he was there. Let's not jump to any conclusions, he thought as he was leaving the police station.

Pedro was waiting for him outside. He was standing near the revolving door looking like a child obediently waiting for the grown-ups to collect him.

"I'm sorry to make you go through all of that. I know how difficult it must be. I'm not the bad person here and believe me, I'm not making any presumptions or passing any judgements. I'm only here to help, John."

Staring him straight in the eye, John took a moment to consider Pedro's words. He forced his mouth into a quivering smile before clenching his fists, his knuckles turning white. He stormed towards him, but then decided to keep his cool.

"So this is what you think will make me hand over the tape? It will never work."

Pedro shouted after him as John walked away.

"Can we settle this?"

"I can't make any promises."

Pedro called out to him again and said "Thanks." But John ignored him and just kept on moving. Although he was anxious to rush home, he eventually slowed his pace, thinking. Rows of semis formed long alleyways. Each one was a potential escape route. He could run right now. It all felt so impossible. He stopped at a shop; through the window he could see a large TV set hanging from the ceiling. A woman standing next to him reeked of cheap perfume and cigarettes. I don't know, he said to himself. All of this seemed so normal: the woman, the man in the shop, how would they react if they were him? He'd lost track of his body. He was full of forward movement. Terror was his fuel. But all he wanted to do was just stop.

By the time he returned home he knew he had to try to sort this out soon. He even considered going to the police to explain what happened. Probably not a good idea, he thought.

Chapter 36

When he walked through the door and found the house empty, he remembered that he was supposed to meet Sonia for a drink at the local pub. It was his night off; the children were with Sonia's parents, and he hoped that an evening out would do their relationship the world of good.

John arrived a little early and sat by the window. Sonia was running late. He ordered another pint and stared dolefully out of the window. His thoughts started to drift; it was difficult to make sense of everything that had been happening lately. Sonia was already ten minutes late. He looked down at his watch, deciding to give her another ten minutes. It was possible that she'd got held up somewhere.

After nearly an hour and on his third pint, he was beginning to get a little upset: It was clear that she wasn't coming. He tried her mobile for the third time but was put through to voicemail. His heart sank – he'd really hoped that they would be able to resolve a few issues in their relationship.

When he walked through the front door, Sonia came down the stairs and made her way to the coffee pot, ignoring him as she passed.

"Hello," he said, wondering if she'd speak or if this was fully-fledged silent treatment. Grabbing the milk from the fridge, she shot him a pointed look and turned away. "We should talk." With a huff, she spun to face him, planting her hands on the edge of the kitchen table.

"I hope it's about you how sorry you are, I was waiting for an hour." He was in a stinking mood and told her that he'd had a really bad day waiting in the police station, which had got to him.

"Poor you," she mocked.

"You should try working for a living," he snapped.

"Oh yeah," she said, "and you should try going to school twice a day to take the kids and collect them."

He shot her another look, a veneer of calm suddenly settling over his bubbling temper. He grinned at her, realising that Sonia was right and he was wrong. He'd been so wound up in all this cloak-and-dagger stuff that it was really affecting his relationship with Sonia.

"What is it? If you're going to have another go at me, go right ahead."

"Not at all, sorry about that. I was out of order. And you were right."

Most of the time they were getting on, and he had to admit that it was usually his fault when they didn't. She hated when he had to work late, and probably suspected that he wasn't always at the restaurant when he said he was. He was still keeping his work for Pedro a secret from her, and had no idea how to remedy this. He shouldn't blame her. She went on a bit at times, but that was just her way of dealing with the situation: It made her feel like she's doing something instead of simply sitting at home.

"I'm sorry."

"You've said that at least a hundred times now," she said.

Relieved, John shut his eyes after having avoided another explanation of where he had been last night.

Sonia sank into the armchair in the living room. "Is there anything you're not telling me?" She huffed impatiently.

"Sonia, now is not the time."

He pulled her to her feet and gave her a big kiss on the cheek. She grunted and walked towards the mirror over the mantelpiece to stare at herself with a critical expression.

"You look fantastic," he told her.

Sonia dissolved right in front of him. There were no wracking sobs, just quiet breaths and a steady flow of tears that

Page 310

smashed the hell out his heart. He started to move towards her, but she held up her hand, waving him off. John latched onto her fingers anyway and sat down in the chair next to hers.

"No. Honestly. I'm just stupidly emotional." She smiled a little, got up and went into the kitchen, and asked if he wanted a coffee. She stopped talking so she wouldn't lose count as she spooned the coffee into the filter. They sat silently for a few minutes. The caffeine eventually kicked in. He told her he'd have to be at the restaurant early the following day but he'd try not to get back too late. Then came more questions. He realised he couldn't give a sensible answer to a single question. He blew her a kiss and went upstairs.

***

The traffic sucked, as usual, so when John finally pulled up beside the entrance and turned the engine off, he was already frazzled. The restaurant smelt of smoke and stale booze. Last night had been busy with a loud crowd. John had to do some food preparation, and after lunch he had a meeting with the bank manager. He was trying to raise money to expand the business. He was a little behind and had to finish off his projections and cash flow accounts.

When the restaurant door opened, he turned and came face to face with trouble. Drunk again, Joe stumbled through the door, wearing a button-down shirt with the sleeves rolled up. After a few seconds of tense silence, John crossed his arms and shot him a pointed look. "Go home." His mind was still racing and it was hard to concentrate. Some days were good but today was already starting to get to him. It was difficult to run a business with all of this going on at the same time. There were times when he thought about just running away.

Right, he thought. When you're going downhill, slow down 'cause it'll be dark and you won't be able to see. This had always been his motto.

It was after 7 p.m. by the time he ploughed back through the evening traffic and arrived home. What they needed was a stiff drink, a good Chinese takeaway and a few hours in front of the TV. "Grab some plates," Sonia pointed to the cabinet. "We can eat on the patio."

The children were still at her parents', and the neighbouring gardens were quiet. It was oddly cosy. Sonia brought out the food and set everything down on the table.

"What would you like to drink?"

"Beer?" John said hoarsely. He was very off balance, as though his emotions couldn't decide where to settle. Should he still be angry? Should he be friendly? He didn't know how to proceed, and decided simply to hug her.

"Now you're suddenly all over me, I don't understand and I don't know what's going on," she said.

"Nothing's going on."

"I can't," she said, abruptly pulling away from him.

He stood back, confused.

"Can't what?"

She shot cursory glance towards his groin before gazing up at him with a sigh.

"I mean I can't just turn it on and off whenever you feel like it," she said.

"It's been months since we've ... and now. I just thought –."

"I'm perfectly aware of what you thought. So why can't we just sit down and talk," she suggested.

Sonia slowly raised her eyes. He loved her, but no matter how much he wanted to repair the relationship, he just couldn't have that conversation and tell her everything that had happened and was still happening.

She flounced angrily into the kitchen and grabbed her bag.

Page 312

"Fine, I'll see you later."

He wondered if it was something he did – or didn't do – that might make someone behave like that towards him. What more could he do? You try this, that, anything. You cry. Shout. Beg. Threaten. Plead.

Pedro turned up at his house, unannounced as always.

"Give me the tape. I certainly am not going to harm you, if that's what you're so wrongly worried about. Then we can part ways."

John was upset that he had turned up at his house. And Pedro knew it. He told him just to go and to give him more time.

"Who was that?" He heard Sonia shout from the kitchen as he shut the heavy front door in Pedro's face. He didn't know how long she'd been standing there. "Why aren't you answering me? Don't tell me you're drunk again." He was annoyed at the accusation, but relieved that she hadn't overheard their conversation. The old wooden door must be thicker than he'd thought.

Chapter 37

It was an early sunny morning in July. John opened the door of the restaurant to let in fresh air. The night before one of the diners had been sick all over the carpet after one too many neat whiskeys. John decided to close the restaurant for lunch.

It was midday by the time the postman handed Joe a recorded letter, addressed to a Tony. Joe took it over to John.

"Who is this Tony? Shall I open it"

"No, give it to me." John's voice sounded tense.

He shook his head as he opened the letter and said to himself, Here we go. His stomach seized up. He didn't know what this meant, but he started to fear the worst. Joe gave him a suspicious look and tried to peer over his shoulder to read the letter.

John read it again, a wave of angst surging through him as the realisation that Pedro would stop at nothing hit him. Sure enough, the letter was addressed to the FBI.

I wish to inform you of the whereabouts of Tony A Lester whom I believe is wanted for the homicide of Del Carlos on 21 March 1982. He now resides at the above address and his real name is John Scott.

Joe looked surprised as he watched his reaction.

"John, you've gone all white."

"Yeah, mind your own business and get on with your job." John sounded angry now.

Joe was a funny little short Irishman, and always drunk. He took a swig of his Scotch and swallowed hard. The trouble with people like him was that it was hard to know if they were drunk or not: He would reach a certain alcoholic level and he stay at that point, simply by constantly topping himself up with more booze and never sobering up

Page 315

"John, I'm sorry, let's go out for a drink."

"No, thanks, it's okay."

Joe wouldn't take no for an answer, and eventually John gave in. They pulled up at the first bar and took their drinks over to an empty table. Joe said in his simple manner,"Boss I love working for you."

John stopped him there and said the drink was going to his head again.

"You don't like me much, do you?"

The next day Joe would oversleep. His head would be banging, a harsh persistent throb that would set his teeth on edge. The only thing he would be able to think about would a large cold beer. It would be the fourth time he'd be late that month. It had only been a few drinks – he did not need much to top himself up. Joe would stand just inside the door to the restaurant, his head in his hands, waiting for John to let him come back to work again. There was no doubt in John's mind that Joe was a liability, but he had a charm about him which was both simple and hard to resist.

John had to go back to the restaurant to collect some paperwork. It was 3 p.m., and Joe was still in the pub leaning against the bar with his eyes trained on the back bar with its display of whiskey bottles. John stopped on the way out to tell him he'd better be in work tomorrow. The barmaid squinted at Joe, her eyelids heavily lined with black mascara.

"You have a cigarette?"

"Smoking'll kill you. I've already got plenty of other options if I decide a slow death is right for me."

The barmaid rolled her eyes. "Fucking weird."

John thought to himself that the barmaid was right. Joe had a creepy way of saying things. He was wound up tight, jumpy and defensive. Joe slammed his hand down on the bar, making the

Page 316

barmaid jump. John almost felt sorry for him, he'd never had much luck with women. He didn't think he'd ever had a steamy glance across the room or anything. He pulled Joe out into the street bar and told him to go home. His eyebrows raised now; he hadn't even realised himself how angry he was.

"Get a grip." He grabbed Joe by the scruff of the neck.

John knew it was just a matter of time before he'd get another threat from Pedro. His time was up, Pedro would hit again, and John was feeling increasingly anxious. Sure enough he got the call. Pedro simply said that it was just a matter of time before he'd give back the tape before hanging up.

John had always known that sooner or later his past would come back to haunt him. Something like that was impossible to hide, and every single word had led him closer to recovering the tape. Now escape no longer seemed an option. Just give it to him, he thought. Walking around, John could feel his heart pounding with worry. His thoughts were swirling round and round in his head. Nothing was what it appeared to be. This was all wrong. It still felt wrong to give him the tape, and yet it seemed right.

John was surprised when he didn't hear from Pedro over the next few days. He checked with his office, and one of his staff whose voice he didn't recognise said that Pedro had gone back to the States.

John didn't know what to think. Was this the end? Should he celebrate?

Chapter 38

Their meal at the local bistro was a nostalgic and unhurried ritual. The delicate little chocolates which came with the coffee were divine, the ambience timeless. Back at home, John turned the TV off, left the empty wine bottle on the glass table, and they headed upstairs for bed. It must have been 1.30 a.m. After a few drinks, the ticking of the clock always drove him crazy. John had just dropped off when he was woken by a loud thumping noise on the front door.

From the bottom of the stairs, he could see two shadowy figures through the glass door. He called out, "Who is it?"

"Police."

He opened the door. The taller man took his wallet from his pocket, showed him his badge and asked if he was John Scott.

"Yes, I am," he replied.

"We have reason to believe that you have committed a crime, and must ask you to accompany us to the station."

"I haven't done anything."

"You're under arrest for the murder of Henry O'Brian. Anything you say may be taken down and used in evidence against you."

"What are you talking about?"

Sonia came rushing down the stairs. He told her not to worry, that it was all some kind of mistake. But he knew exactly what was happening, and who was behind it. Sonia began to cry and clung to his arm. The policeman took hold of his other arm and guided him out of the door and into the unmarked police car.

At Twickenham police station, he was taken into a room and told just to sit on the bench seat for a moment. Ten minutes later, the door opened and the desk sergeant called him over to the desk. The arresting officer who'd brought him in came back into the room and told the sergeant,"J Scott is charged with murder." Later he was booked in and escorted to a cell down the corridor. He watched the officer's face as he slammed the door shut. A feeling of emptiness hit him as if his whole world had just fallen apart.

DC Nolan turned on the recording device and stated the date, time and place.

"John Scott and his solicitor Peter Brown from Dunn & Co are present with myself, DC Nolan, and Sergeant Dower. I would like to ask you some questions regarding the death of Henry O'Brian on 27 April 1997. Do you understand?"

"Nothing to do with me."

"Please just answer yes or no. I ask you again, do you understand?"

"Yes."

"Mr Scott, let me ask you this: Did you hit Henry O'Brian?"

"No."

"Mr Scott, did you push him off the chair or stool?"

"No."

"So you never hit him or you never pushed him, which is it?"

"Both. I never done anything to hurt him, I found him lying on the floor."

"Stop. Just answer the question I ask you."

"Mr Scott, let me ask you this: In the last statement you gave us at this station on 29 April 1997 we asked you if there was anything else you wanted to tell us, and you said no. Is that still the case?"

"Yes. That's still the case."

"Mr Scott, we have reason to believe that you pushed Henry O'Brian from the stool which he was standing on, and that you then picked up the stool and removed it from the scene. Is that correct?"

"No. Well, yes, I did pick up the stool as it was lying next to him, but only to push it slightly to one side."

"Mr Scott, where exactly in the flat was the stool and where did you move it to?"

"I didn't move it as such. I sort of gently pushed it to one side."

"So let me get this right, Mr Scott: Now you're telling me you sort of pushed it, but earlier you said you picked up the stool. So which is it? Let me also put it to you that the stool was not found by the body, it was found in the kitchen, and we have your prints all over that stool."

"This is not so. Okay, you may have my prints on the stool, but I never moved it."

"Mr Scott, I have heard enough. We are charging you with the murder of Henry O'Brian."

John's solicitor interrupted. "I need to speak to my client in private,"

Left alone with him in the interview room, Peter Brown told John that he felt they didn't have enough evidence, and that they would try to make their case stronger by showing the judge that John was a danger to the public. They would probably try to hold him on remand. It could be weeks or even months before an application for bail would be granted.

"But I didn't do it," John protested.

"Look, as far as I know they had a tip-off, and apparently there's a blood-stained handkerchief at the crime scene. They are searching it again now as we speak. If they find something... Well let's hope they don't. The first thing is to make a bail application and try and get you out of here."

"What about Sue? And Mrs O'Brian?" John suddenly perked up. "They'll be able to corroborate my testimony!"

Brown shook his head sadly.

"Mrs O'Brian died of a suspected heart attack shortly after her husband's death. And Sue West has disappeared without a trace." He sighed. "I'm sorry to be the one to break this to you, but there's no way you're going home today."

A wave of shock surged through John's body as he struggled to understand the full meaning of these words. It felt as if all his blood had drained away, leaving him feeling limp and dazed. Was he going to prison?

"No! No!" He shouted. "I have a house, a family. I'll lose everything."

"Calm down, John," his solicitor said.

"How long will I get?"

"Six years, if you behave yourself, but that's if they find you guilty."

He felt tears welling up. A door opened behind him and a security officer took hold of his arm and guided him out. He had to stop crying now and face up to the situation. He was walked to a desk where his details were given, forms filled in. His solicitor came to tell him that the room where he was to meet Sonia to say his goodbyes was out of order, so he wouldn't be able to see her before he was taken away. Dejected, John sat alone in his cell for a couple of hours.

Around dinner time the door opened and he was led into a corridor where there were others already waiting to be escorted into a yard surrounded by high walls. There was a security van with tiny windows waiting for them. They climbed in through a low door in the back, each of them placed into one of the tight cubicles which lined both sides. The seat was hard. Although no one could see in through the windows, they could see out. Once everyone was seated, the door was locked behind them and the van made its way around London. On the way to the prison it stopped twice to pick up some more passengers. Once they arrived at Wormwood Scrubs, they were checked in. All the other prisoners were given prison uniforms of denim trousers and white T-shirts, but as the only one on remand, John was allowed to keep his own clothes on. After a shower they were escorted to B wing, where John was put in a cell with a guy who was in for arson. They exchanged a few words but he didn't feel like talking. He had the lower bunk. The walls were bare, and the glass on the small windows was broken. They lay on their bunks, doing nothing for a few hours, until they were asked to leave the cell for exercise.

Inside a prison your nightmare begins on the first day. He woke up as the early morning light came through the window. Feeling like a hammer had been dropped on his head; he was sure he'd crack up if he stayed here too long, locked up for twenty-three hours a day. The guard would close the cell door with a smile on his face.

After a sleepless night, he heard the rattle of the keys on the door at 7.30 a.m. They got dressed and went for breakfast. They would spit in your food if they didn't like you. There was a cell right beside the queue which held a young man who had been accused of child rape. All the inmates knew this and while queuing they would constantly yell abuse at this man: "We will kill you, you sick bastard." This would happen three times a day, at breakfast, lunch and dinner. John could hear the man crying in his cell like a child. They knew it would only be a matter of time before they would have to move him. John suspected that the prison had deliberately put this young man in this cell, so he would receive constant mental abuse from the inmates.

When they came down for breakfast one morning, John noticed no one was banging on the cell door any more and wondered whether they'd moved him to another cell. The guy in front told him that the child rapist had hung himself last night. What kind of place was this? John was horrified. If the young guy happened to have been innocent, then this was a gross injustice.

After breakfast, John was taken to see the doctor.

"Will you be getting any script?" another inmate asked as they waited their turn.

"No," John replied, thinking he meant medication.

"Tell them you're on heroin, and they'll give you a dose of methadone each day, and they'll give you tablets you can use as currency."

He ignored the advice and told the doctor he was fine.

The whole prison system was corrupt. Somehow the guards, or the screws as they were commonly known, would constantly be party to bribes: They simply turned the other cheek. The whole prison system was riddled with drugs. On visiting days it was easy to spot the wives and girlfriends smuggling them in: They would kiss them and transfer a little packet of foil between the lips. If he could see this, John was sure the prison system knew this too. It was all designed to keep the peace and prevent the inmates from riots, and this in turn gave some of the guards power and respect while small groups of inmates, who each had their leaders, would push the drugs within the system. Meanwhile, the outside world was blissfully unaware of the full extent of any of this.

Anyone expecting a visit was rounded up and taken to a room with about thirty chairs around the walls. He just sat there and tried not to breathe in too much of the smoke from the cigarettes everyone else seemed to be smoking.

The door opened, a few names were read out and the prisoners who'd been called stood up and walked out. Finally, after about half an hour, his name was called. As he entered the hall, there she was: Sonia was waiting for him. She stood up and he hugged her. As he was kissing her he forced himself not to let the tears well up in his eyes. He held her hand tightly, and she said everything was okay, the children were fine and she had made arrangements to go to court again on Monday to apply for bail. When they were told that visiting was over, Sonia got upset. It felt as though both they worlds had come to an end.

* * *

Jack Dallies was one of the hard nuts on remand you would not want to cross. He reminded John of those big bouncers they had on the doors of East End London clubs. He'd been charged with

GBH after attacking and almost killing another man. The whole prison system was full of people like Jack.

Once a week Jack would get his stash sent in. One day John was in Jack's cell having a chat when Dennis, who was a few cell doors down the wing, came in and closed the door. He lowered his trousers, bent down and pulled a small packet from his asshole which he handed to Jack.

"John, give it a wash."

"Must be joking. It's full of shit."

However, seeing as he might be in there for a while, he decided to do it.

As it turned out, Jack was actually a highly intelligent and resourceful guy. Somehow he was always able to get whiskey and other drinks brought in.

John asked Jack what had happened with his wife and how bad the guy was he'd beaten up.

"Yeah, don't mind telling you what happened."

It had been 8.40 p.m. when Jack limped into the Cork and Whistle. It was raining.

"I sat down and ordered a pint of Guinness. By rights I should have been getting home but I really needed a drink first."

Jack continued to tell how he'd had a massive row with his wife which started over breakfast, and had been simmering all day. It had been over six months since Jack had made love to his wife and he was feeling angry. Nothing had been the same since he'd walked into his office and caught the two of them together. Jack had just watched and tiptoed across the hall and back downstairs. That morning over breakfast, Jack said he knew that she was still seeing Dev Stagg and if he caught them again he would kill both of them. She was a woman in her early forties, slightly plump, with dark long brown hair. Jack flapped the newspaper he was holding in her face, but she just giggled and waved him away. He left the kitchen before could do something he would later regret.

The next few weeks seemed normal and they didn't argue. Until one night. Jack was supposed to be away in Manchester, but the trip was cancelled. It was 7.08 p.m. when he got home and opened the door to find his wife and her lover in bed together. Jack felt angry, sick, disgusted. He wanted to confront them, but his pride held him back. There was only so much humiliation a man could take.

His wife looked up at him and said simply,

"Yes, I am having an affair and I wanted you to find out."

This was when Jack lost it. He ran towards them, pulled her out of the bed and threw her against the door. Then he dragged Dev Stagg from the bed, picked up a chair and started to hit him on the head. Trying to defend himself, Stagg repeatedly punched him in the stomach, making his head spin.

"I can still see the scene now," Jack told John. "Then I noticed he'd stopped moving."

He was in a bar the next day, on his second pint of Guinness, when the police arrested him for assault.

"Has your wife gone?"

"Of course she's fucking gone."

The last thing John wanted to do was to upset Jack. So he tried not to stare too hard at him. There was a screw heading towards the door, a set of keys jangling in his hand.

"You better go now," said Jack.

John got his first wage, £1.50 per week. The next day he was surprised to wake up to something most unpleasant: a splash of warm water through his cell window. No one had warned him about this: Those inmates who did not have a toilet in their cell, rather than queuing to slop out, threw urine out of their window and straight into another one.

If it hadn't been for Jack, John would have had a very hard time in prison. Jack looked after him, almost treating him like a boy.

Can you imagine a bowl of yellow-brown liquid, a slop of lumpy watery mashed potato and a spoonful of lumps of mince meat on top of the pile, and a quarter of a carrot? Believe it or not, this was supposed to be a cottage pie. But actually, it wasn't that bad. It just looked as though someone had used their hand to scoop it onto the plate. They didn't use salt in the food for some reason. Luckily the inmates were allowed to buy little packets of salt and sugar from the shop with their £1.50 wage. Okay, he was a chef, so yes, he was fussy. Prison food was bland and it did not need a sophisticated palate to recognise slop.

A few weeks later, he was back in court. His solicitor told him not to worry.

"Why?"

"They never found the blood-stained handkerchief, so I don't think the prosecution will object to bail."

John flashed his lawyer a lopsided grin. He didn't feel so confident; looking in the mirror in the morning, he'd thought, That's it. His moustache was trimmed short but he'd skipped the razor today, so he had the sort of scruffy stubble which looked like it could be used to sand wood.

A young uniformed police officer told him to stand right at the entrance of the door into the court. The lawyer said,

"Yes, we really need you right here, I will try to call you to the stand as soon as possible."

The police officer told him to sit on the bench by the door. He leaned forward and rested his elbows on his knees. He stroked his moustache with both hands and folded them under his chin. The room, small to begin with, was cramped by a rectangular wooden table that filled almost the entire space. The police officer was friendly, and he could see that John was nervous. "Try not to let it get to you."

John limited his response to nods and friendly grunts.

There was a knock on the door. When she unbolted and opened it, Sonia was greeted by a sturdy looking woman in a dark grey overcoat. Sonia thought it was a saleswoman trying to sell door to door.

"Hello. Can I help you?" she asked politely.

"No, but I can help you," the woman replied. "Get your coat. I'm from Dunns: Your husband is in court this morning."

Traffic slowed to a crawl at the junction of Holland Park. Then it stopped completely as two lanes became one. There were road works all over town. The driver checked her watch.

"Twenty minutes."

"Be patient."

She smiled apologetically as she moved through this crowd outside the courtroom, repeating "excuse me," turning this way and that to shuffle by. People stared curiously. Someone said, "That's his wife." The press were there; shouting questions and snapping photos and generally being their irritating selves. They were not interested in the details of the investigation, only in the raw fact that an innocent person was dead. Sitting on the other side of the courtroom were the dead man's grief-stunned family: They sat still and quiet, talked softly, and stared. The face of one of the girls was tear-smeared by mascara. A trio of energetic elderly ladies arrived in the galleries, one looking at her face in the mirror, all wearing sleeveless tops that revealed their wobbly arms. They nodded at Sonia respectfully, then flicked a glance of disapproval when the defendant was called up from the cells below.

"Don't worry," said the woman who'd brought Sonia to court. "Mr Brown is a good lawyer. He identifies with the crowd, and somehow gets them on his side."

"All rise for His Honour, Judge Barnes," the court clerk called.

"Good morning, Your Honour," said Miss Davies, the court prosecutor. "Your Honour, Mr Scott is charged with murder and is on remand. If I can begin firstly by handing over the documented evidence so far, and I would like to point out that the case does not have a date for a committal hearing as yet."

"Thank you. Mr Brown, do you have a copy of this?" the judge asked.

"Yes, Your Honour, we have."

"Your Honour, we're here on behalf of the defendant John Scott and we would like to make an application for bail. It is our belief that this case would fail in a crown court, because of the lack of evidence. After discussing with Miss Davies we are in agreement that this case should never have been brought before you. We therefore ask if this case could be heard today, if there are no objections."

"Thank you Mr Brown. This is certainly an unusual request. Are there any objections from the prosecution or the police?"

"We have no objections," Miss Davies replied.

"I'm happy to hear the case," Judge Barnes declared. "So if we can keep it precise and brief. I expect decorum at all times. No outburst. No one leaves until I dismiss the court. Are there any witnesses, Mr Brown?"

"No."

Brown never flinched one bit. He simply stood very still and was entirely focused on the judge. When he sat down he looked over his shoulder and said quietly to his assistant,

"I will call Mr Scott on the stand and start with a few questions. Can you have a chat and bring him up to speed."

"Mr Scott, I would like to take you back to 27 April 1997. In your own words, can you tell me why you entered the premises."

"Yes, Sir, I had to go and see a work colleague who had lost her job. Her name was Sue West."

"So what happened afterwards?"

"There was a knock on the door and it was the woman from the other flat. She was upset. I entered the room and found the body lying on the floor, I thought he might have fallen off a stool."

"What made you think he had fallen from a stool?" Mr Brown asked.

"I'd done something very stupid. The stool was lying on its side next to the body, and I pushed the stool with my left hand to one side so I could pass by the body."

"Mr Scott, I refer to the statement of DC Nolan, which confirms that the stool was found upright at the other side of the room. Can you explain how that could be?"

"I'm very sorry, Mr Brown, I can't explain that. While I was in the room the stool was lying beside the body."

"Thank you, Mr Scott. No more questions." Brown paused for a moment before addressing the judge.

"Your Honour, as I referred to earlier, this case should never have been brought to court. The evidence is weak and there is no real proof that my client has done anything wrong, any more than what he has already omitted to. Yes, he pushed the stool to one side. Yes, his fingerprints have been found on the stool. That does not make him a killer."

"I would like to adjourn for one hour," Judge Barnes said.

After one hour of waiting, the judge was still in conference.

"Why is he taking so long, how long will I get?"

Just as his lawyer opened his mouth to tell him not to worry, the court clerk emerged through the large heavy wooden door.

"All rise for Judge Barnes."

The judge closed his eyes and let out a deep, satisfying sigh.

"After careful consideration, I don't think there is sufficient evidence to prove that the defendant is guilty. Not only is there a distinct lack of forensic evidence, but the key witnesses have either passed away or disappeared. In view of these facts, I have no choice but to find Mr Scott not guilty."

In the gallery, Sonia cheered before breaking into tears.

Feeling emotional himself, John rolled up his pinstriped shirt sleeves, walked over to her and kissed her all over. "Can it really be all over?" His voice was muffled. The exhaustion, the stress, the sleepless nights, the scrutiny, the time away from Sonia and the children. The whole event had felt like being plunged with a weighted belt into a dark and weedy pond. You managed to scramble up for air, but the rest of the world didn't matter. And you were constantly thinking you were drowning.

They both knew it would take time to get back to normal. Money was tight. He had to keep focused, keep busy. When he got into the car, the fuel gauge was showing less than a quarter full, something that he would barely have noticed a month ago. Now it was a more serious matter. Before, when he needed fuel, he simply pulled into the station, filled up and paid with his credit card. His restaurant had to close when he was arrested. Gone were the credit cards, gone the bars and nights out, the restaurant dinners. They had to tighten their belts for a while.

Chapter 40

John hadn't heard from Pedro since his arrest, and believed he was out of the country, called back to the States for whatever reason. But it seemed unlikely he'd never hear from him again. This was far from over.

Not long after John's release, Pedro flew in from Boston and landed at Heathrow at 7.30 a.m. The rain was torrential, and the plane was not allowed to taxi to the gateway. The passengers were forced to wait patiently on the plain, as the cabin staff brought out the carafes of steaming hot coffee and Danish pastries. Finally, the captain announced,

"We are very sorry for the delay as we are waiting for a gate to become available, but we should be able to move very shortly."

Security was very tight. Pedro managed to get off the plane at 9.30 a.m. and rushed down into the baggage hall to get his bags. Approaching passport control, he muttered to himself that he probably be delayed another two hours, but thankfully, he was waved right through after showing his documents.

He urgently needed to contact John to complete his mission and was under great pressure to end the matter quickly.

Pedro was the last person John wanted to talk to. By now he was hoping against hope that he had gone away for good. But that was not to be.

As soon as he'd checked into his hotel, Pedro called him.

"I'm back and we must talk. Can we meet at the Wolseley Bar tomorrow?"

"Alright." John hesitated.

Page 333

He arrived before Pedro and sat in the corner. The waitress came over to ask what he would like. He ordered a small beer, feeling increasingly apprehensive: You never knew what to expect from Pedro. Having to wait for thirty minutes did little to calm his nerves.

Pedro arrived carrying the same leather briefcase the man had given him at the bar in San Francisco all those years ago. He avoided eye contact with John and ordered another beer for him and a glass of white wine for himself. Sounding deceptively casual, Pedro mentioned that he remembered coming here just over a year ago and the same waitress serving him, something which seemed to make him feel uncomfortable. He reached into his pocket to touch the one-way ticket back to the States which he was going to show John, but decided to wait. He always arranged the smallest details in his life so he could move on at a split second's notice. It was an obsessive habit. He owed nothing and cared for nothing.

John was surprised how civil they were towards each other, considering their shared past and how much he had learnt to hate him. Pedro seemed less demanding today.

After silently looking at him for a long time, Pedro suddenly spat on his fingers and wiped the side of his face.

"John, you know I need this tape. Let's make a deal, I am willing to leave the country and say nothing."

John recognised the look on his face: One side of Pedro's mouth twitched as he attempted a smile. A body language expert would probably be able tell you his life story from that look.

"I'll let you know."

"No, John. You misunderstand me: 'I'll let you know' won't do."

He watched Pedro's eyes narrow as he was trying to keep calm.

"John, you're a second-rate man, not the shining star required for hard core, high-risk intelligence. So don't play with me."

Page 334

"Can I ask you something, and will you answer honestly?"

"Yes," Pedro replied evenly.

"Why did you try to set me up?"

"What do you mean?"

"I'm talking about the old man who fell and banged his head and died. Did you call the police and tell them it was me who killed him?"

"Why do you ask, when you already know the answer. Yes, I did, I have the handkerchief with your blood on it. You notice things," Pedro shrugged his shoulders. "And I notice things. We're two of a kind."

"Answer this: Was Sue part of the set up?"

"Yes. She gave me the handkerchief, and I did not give it to the police."

"Do you still have it?"

"Of course. But you don't have to worry, I have no intention of handing it to the police. At times we have to play dirty, but I am hoping that we can avoid any more unpleasant situations."

The gall of this man, John thought to himself. When he'd met him fifteen years ago, he had been drawn to his confidence, but now he realised that what looked like confidence was actually the façade of a cold, calculating, manipulative bully. Whatever was going on inside his head was starting to feel freakish. He had to wonder what made this guy tick as there was definitely more to him than you could ever imagine.

Pedro had wordlessly placed the one-way ticket on the table, and for a split second John was tempted: Like everyone else, he was flawed. But not as flawed as the man opposite him whose self-deprecating manner and melancholic conversation he was now starting to find defeatist in ways he didn't like or understood.

He asked him again why he couldn't just be honest and tell him why he needed the tape, but in reality, it did not really matter that much to him. Pedro had already tried his hardest to hurt him and his family, and very nearly caused the break-up of his marriage. Deep down, John knew that if he really wanted to, he could just keep rooting around until he found out for himself. And he would find out eventually.

With a wry smile, Pedro said, "You're very persistent." Was he starting to trust him a little, let him in even?

There was something very strange about all of this. It was not in Pedro's nature to back down. Something about his pale face told John that his nerves were frayed to the breaking point. Sensing the questions in John's eyes, Pedro put his fingertips together and placed his elbows on his knees before he explained the situation to him again.

John used to see Pedro as a genius, a philosopher, an abstract thinker, but right now he looked almost defeated as he started talking. His story sounded like something from The Killing Fields.

He would be standing still blinking, his ears ringing and his brain failing to immediately register the carnage around him. The scene was littered with arms and legs and unidentifiable chunks of – who? He would just drive around and see people lying on the ground. One man had had his leg cut off and was lying there screaming in agony. All Pedro could do was keep going, although it was difficult. Some people just got used to the pain, the anger. There was one child running around who'd lost his parents, running through the crowd, a baby really, although he must have been five or six. People were just running around aimlessly, all they cared about was their own. It was hell, but then one day, it got even worse.

By now tears were running down Pedro's face.

"You know, the first thing I saw was a butchered male body. The fellow's torso was twisted horribly and partly submerged in water. I had seen plenty of gore before, but this was possibly the worst."

But the full extent of the massacre, the carnage, was much worse than thought. A second corpse was cut and ripped open with the mother's baby still attached inside her.

"I shouted, 'Who the hell can tell me what happened?' But it was just mayhem, and everyone was confused."

"Somebody must have witnessed these murders," John said.

"Look, John, I don't mean you any harm. I come from a country where you have to do what you have to do. I have spent the better part of my life keeping secrets – state secrets, even family secrets, emotional secrets. Moving between the extraordinary and the ordinary, and now it's wearing me out. Believe me, my time has come and I don't want to do this any more. I would rather we part as friends. Just let me do what I need to do and I am gone."

John's mind struggled to take it all in. What was he talking about? Was it really possible?"

"I'm offering a truce."

"And if I say no to your offer?"

"Please don't. I too, at times, have felt great hate for those that have taken so much, with no sorrow for what they did. But hate wears you down, and does not hurt your enemy. It is like taking poison and wishing your enemy would die. I have struggled with these feelings many times."

After a brief pause, he continued,

"It is as if there are two persons inside me, John. One is good and does no harm. He lives in harmony with all around him and does not take offence when no offence was intended. He will only fight when it is right to do so, and in the right way. But the other person inside me, ah! He is full of anger. The smallest thing will send him into a fit of temper. He fights everyone, all the time, for no reason. He cannot think because his anger and hate are so great. It is hard to live with these two people inside me, because both of them try to dominate my spirit."

"Odd."

"That is another one of your odd notions," said Pedro. "You have a fashion of calling everything 'odd' that's beyond your comprehension."

John sensed deep-seated anger in Pedro, but should he feel sorry for him?

"I'll let you know."

"Please, you must bring this tape to me."

"Okay, I'll meet you."

Pedro let out a sigh of relief. But John hadn't quite finished.

"The only thing is: How do I really know that it will be over?"

"Look, John, there's only so much I can tell you, but please trust me. It will be over."

"If only that was true, " John mumbled.

"Why is everything so difficult with you?" Pedro sounded angry again. "Come now, my dear John. I know things did not end well between us, and I am sorry for that. Surely we can be professional about this."

Pedro closed his eyes for a moment and clenched his fist. John still was not sure he could trust him. Accuracy and truth had no sanctity to Pedro. For him they were devices to be used to advance his agenda and schemes.

"Let's end this now." Pedro stood up and straightened himself while looking directly into his eyes.

"Okay." John suggested they meet outside Euston Station the following day. "I now know why you want this tape. It's something to do with the death of Princess Diana."

For a while, Pedro just looked at him and said nothing.

"John, I really think it's best for both of us that we part as friends and end this now."

"Maybe you're right, but all of this does worry me a bit. And why do you need the tape? To take revenge? On who, and for what?"

"John, you know what I am capable of. All I want to do is expose an injustice, uncover a liar. That's all I ask."

"I don't know how you managed to pull this extensive masquerade off, Pedro, but I suppose we're going to find out soon."

"I'm in a position where I think – call it arrogance, if you must – that I know what's best. I know what's damaging and I know what's not damaging, and I know what the British are really all about, and I know what's best, and I'm going to act on that."

"You are totally without principle. There's no right or wrong, no morality or immorality in your eyes. You only want. You manipulate people and you don't see yourself as different from others."

"Only smarter. And in my view everyone is corrupt."
"No, you are wrong. Can you overcome the dark, brutal secrets of your past you talk so much about?"

Pedro stared coldly at him while the words sank in. John was going along with this. But oh, was he worried what would happen to his family. He didn't want them hurt by vicious accusations against him. No matter how ridiculous and untrue.

Before long, he was pounding the pavement. He had to see his wife and daughters, and hold them in his arms, tell them he loved them, try to explain that whatever wicked stories they might hear weren't true. Or at least, that there had to be some reasonable explanation for what could affect their lives. He toyed with the idea of going out for a few drinks but he shrugged the notion away. He had to be up early next day, he needed to have his wits about him. Too much was at stake.

He got up early the following morning, worried about this meeting. It just did not feel right. Clearly suspicious, Sonia questioned him,
"Why are you leaving so early?"

It was awful having to lie to her all the time, but he had no choice. That was the trouble with lying: Once you started you had got to keep doing it.

He wondered whether he should he leave a note explaining what was happening, just in case it all went wrong. But what would she think of him? He considered himself to be a very proud man, and if there was anything Pedro had taught him it was "Never give up and never show your weakness." But honesty was difficult.

He had a very quick coffee before he left the house through the back door. Rather strangely, it wouldn't open until he yanked it really hard. It felt like a warning not to go, but he told himself not to be stupid, the door was just a little stiff. It was about 5.30 a.m. and still dark.

Pedro could be waiting for him, or maybe he was following him. John drove to the station and took the train to Knightsbridge. He did not want to be observed or mistaken for any reason. Although the street wasn't busy, he was checking behind him every second. He needed to stay focused. Usually the traffic would be streaming past, but this morning there was only the odd car, headlights reflecting off the surface of the road as people set off early for work, or returned from night shifts.

He quickly got off the train and walked swiftly up the escalator. He went into a coffee shop, bought an espresso and sat down for five minutes just to calm himself. This also gave him the opportunity to make sure that nobody had followed him. He walked out of the shop and carefully checked, but all seemed to look clear. He passed Harrods. It was a sunny day. He walked down to Green Park where he stopped a taxi and asked to be taken to Waterloo Station. Getting out of the cab, he observed a tall well-dressed man watching him. He was pretending to look the other way, but kept looking from the corner of his eyes. John started to feel nervous; maybe he should abandon today's mission and give up completely. He stood for a moment with his hands shoved deep in his pockets, kept his chin tucked in and his eyes uninterested as though he were just another labourer heading off to work.

Maybe he should walk around the corner and wait a little. The clouds turned grey and it started to rain. Everyone in the street rushed to take cover. Wearing only a light, short jacket, he quickly ran towards the station.

He still didn't trust Pedro. There was a possibility he was being followed. When he was sure that no one was watching him, he entered the station. More questions started to go through his mind: What if the items had gone from the locker? How long did they wait before they reopen a locker? And what about hidden cameras in a major train station like Waterloo?

The terminal was getting busy now with hundreds of people milling around. He felt himself losing it for a moment, but he knew this was it and he had to try to keep himself together. There was the locker - it was located near the gents. He purchased an espresso from a vendor and used his wait to casually determine if anyone was watching him. Unable to spot anyone suspicious, he slowly walked over, all the while checking around him. He took the key from his pocket and pulled open the door: There it was the little carrier bag with the recording equipment and tape. He picked up the bag quickly and looked around before making sure that nothing was missing. He decided to take a seat for five minutes just to settle his nerves before he went down to the Underground.

Not normally someone to panic, he started to feel increasingly anxious now. At that time of day you noticed people more, and started to imagine them watching you. He very nearly got on the wrong tube. Keep calm, he kept telling himself, and eventually he got on to the correct train. It picked up speed and as it went into the tunnel the lights dimmed and it became dark. Euston station was only two stops away, but it seemed like an eternity.

He wondered whether Pedro would be there or not.
He finally arrived at the station and walked outside to check if he was there. He had not seen him inside the station, so he supposed he was waiting outside. There he was.

He was standing near the kerb, seemingly aware of a man nearby on his left-hand side who was regarding him with some amusement. He looked like your average businessman of thirty or so, neatly dressed and standing in the queue waiting for a bus.

For a moment John thought that Pedro was going to abandon this meeting. But he was wrong - this was his only chance. Nothing could have been better. And Pedro seemed to think so too. He turned away for a few seconds, then composed himself. John noticed he was panting frantically as he fumbled hurriedly in his waistcoat pocket and then raised his hand to his lips. There was something furtive about this movement, but immediately afterwards his bearing changed. His laboured breathing lent him the appearance of a man who had just run a desperate mile, but a curious air of detachment, of sudden and profound indifference, replaced the strain of the effort. He still hadn't spotted John.

He decided to cross over and face Pedro directly. He'd spotted John now and nodded to him, just about making eye contact before looking sharply at the carrier in John's hand. John paused for a moment and looked at his watch. He hesitated now: Was he doing the right thing? He started to cross the road, Pedro's eyes fixed on him in case he changed his mind. John walked slowly, looking out for traffic.

Suddenly, Pedro stepped out into the road, presumably to meet him half way. Before John realised what was happening, he heard the sound of a speeding car breaking, the sound of a tyre screech, then a thump. Pedro didn't stand a chance, he'd been so focused on John and the carrier bag that he didn't look out for traffic. Just walked out and bang! He was knocked over by a car.

Stunned by the impact, John wondered whether he was dead.. The car had hit him on one side of his body and he was knocked headlong across the road. For a moment he could not recollect what had just happened. Then things came to him slowly. There was havoc, a police car racing to the scene. Pedro started to shake all over. It felt as though he'd been shot. You felt that you had died, but were not sure. He started to see things differently very quickly. And, what felt so good at that moment was knowing that it could really be over.

Would life ever get back to normal? What should John do with the tape?

He leaned over Pedro to check him out. He lay there, his eyes half open. Pedro realised John was standing over him. He felt so dismayed and confused. He raised his hand and clutched John's jacket with all his strength, pulled his face close to his own. His eyes accusing him of voyeurism. John held his breath in disbelief of what had just happened. His eyes were drawn to something he had not spotted before: a scar just below Pedro's left cheek, barely discernible amongst the blood which covered his face. Pedro whispered into his ear,
"Put the tape in my hand."

John hesitated. No, he thought. It was as though he were against a wall and there were a side entrance for him to escape through. It felt like a way out. Hooting horns, backfiring engines were overwhelming, the traffic was building up. The weight of all of this began to impact on him physically. For a moment he felt mentally assaulted and defeated.

He heard the paramedics shouting," Out of the way!" He just stood there. A sudden pat on his shoulder made him jump. "Come on lad, move it." He could see that Pedro's body had gone into convulsions. The paramedic gently lifted him on to the stretcher and placed him into the ambulance. He asked if he could go with him in the ambulance, said he was a friend. Who had done this? He was overcome by a vague but powerful feeling of dread. He was physically run down. He didn't look too good. He started to breathe heavily, but after a few minutes it steadied and seemed to be under control.
"Stay with us, Pedro!" he called out.

Pedro opened his eyes a little, just for a second, before closing them again. His body started to shake a little. One of the paramedics started to talk loudly to him and tapped him gently on the cheeks.

"You're a very lucky man, just relax, try to breathe slowly. We're just going to give you a small injection, try to keep still."

He was told that there was nothing he could do, as Pedro needed to rest. He went home, and early the next day he called the hospital and was told he had three broken ribs and a head fracture. But all he could think about was his missed opportunity. John was suddenly struck by the realisation that this had all gone wrong and that at this precise moment, he had to accept personal responsibility. He had to acknowledge the possibility that he should now stop all of this. The stark reality was that he was faced with a dog-eat-dog world. His family had to come first.

He decided to visit Pedro. There he was: tubes and intravenous lines penetrating his body. He could hardly move, and was clearly in a lot of pain.

"How are you?" John asked.

Minutes, hours, days could have elapsed for all he knew, because time had no relevance in an intensive care unit. Only one of his eyes would stay open. He realised that his head was swathed in bandages, and that that was why he couldn't move it. The lower portion of his face seemed to have solidified slightly. He told John he was in a bad way and lucky to be alive.

"Your nose was broken. So was your cheekbone and the other cheekbone was pulverised. That's why your eye is bandaged."

Pedro took a deep breath before making a brief sound of pure terror.

"Look, John," he whispered. "I just want to get out of here, just give me what I want and I'll be out of your life forever."

Pedro looked at John as though suggesting that he was being unreasonable. John decided to hand it to him - he knew any other action would be futile.

"You won't be going anywhere for a while. You can't even move."

Page 344

After he handed the tape to him, Pedro seemed relieved and just stared for a moment. Had John walked into a trap? He actually felt good, thinking that this could be the end. He said his goodbyes and told Pedro he'd look in tomorrow.

The next day he strolled towards the hospital with a buoyant sense of anticipation. But as soon as he arrived in intensive care, he was stopped in his tracks. Pedro was not there. He searched frantically, but there was no sign of him. He asked the nurse,

"Do you know where he went? Has he been discharged? Or moved to another ward?"

He ran his hands through his hair and shrugged, and took a deep breath waiting for her reply. She told him that two men had arrived that morning and wheeled him out.

"Did you not think to ask where he was going?"

"Sorry, looked normal to me. The two men had long white coats on, so I thought nothing of it."

He felt a layer of sweat coating his skin. He was tempted to just give up. Then he reminded himself that he had endured all of this – for what?

* * *

The leather-jacketed, thuggish man appeared to take some time to realise what he had said.

"Either you're thick, or you're in shock," Pedro told him.

The man wore one of those strangely popular black plastic fedoras. He reached into the pocket of his jacket, took out a packet of Marlboro and lit a cigarette. He took his first deep puff, tilting his head back slightly. As he exhaled he offered the pack to Pedro, who waved it away.

"So where do you go from here? Why not use it now?" The man asked.

The mere idea that he would dare question his authority upset Pedro a great deal. He had chosen each man for his discipline and skills, and above all else absolute obedience to his orders. They were told upfront many years ago that this mission would require a great deal of patience.

"I know the risk. It's my plan, remember. We just have to keep it safe for now. Just because you helped break me out doesn't mean I owe you. Just take me to the port," Pedro told the man.

"You can hardly move," he replied.

He studied Pedro while narrowing his dull porcine eyes until they were mere slits. Then he shrugged and took another drag on his cigarette.

"That's enough. You try spending years like I did. It's a rat hole here. And if you're not cool with the way I do things . . . Don't worry, just walk away. If you stick to the plan, my plan, it will be successful." Pedro shrugged.

The leather jacket man smiled derisively.

"Okay, this will work. Just don't take unnecessary risks," he said sharply.

They waited till night-time. He helped Pedro get into the back of the car which was parked by the embankment's main gate. As he ducked down and slid onto the seat, he was overwhelmed by a stabbing pain in his hand. Pedro cursed under his breath. Using his teeth, he tugged glove from his right hand, finger by finger, and dropped it onto the seat. His hand was swollen like a golf ball. A wave of pain peaked as he sat in the back of the car, but after a few moments the surge passed and Pedro breathed a sigh of relief. The leather jacket man was restless; before starting the engine he turned and checked if there were police around; even in the darkness several people were walking, some with dogs. They had to be careful. After a long drive, Pedro was keen to keep moving further.

"Seeing as you seem to know the plan, how are we on time?" Pedro asked.

"Perfect. Look," the man pointed to the ferry employee lowering the chain which blocked access to the boat.

The ferryman waved the BMW, first in the queue, to come forward. Pedro checked and watched in the side mirror as the car rolled forward. By the time it stopped at the bow of the boat, another glimpse in the mirror showed a yellow Lada pulled up right behind them.

"This is where I leave you."

The leatherjacket man opened the door and twisted his bulk out on to the cobblestone ramp.

"Happy journey, my friend," he flexed his forefinger and flicked his cigarette away.

A man got out of the yellow Lada, opened the driver's door of the BMW and sat down. Pedro almost jumped in his seat when he heard the tapping of metal on glass next to his ear. It was the toll collector using the back of his ring finger. Pedro rolled down the window and handed the man a ticket. As the fellow moved down the row of cars behind, Pedro stretched his left arm out of the window. His right arm hung limp, although he found that he could at least move his fingers and make a fist now. He tried to shake the stiffness from his limbs, ignored the pulsing pain in his shoulders and just focused on the ferryman. The BMW was in line to be the first off on the far shore.

The crossing took ninety minutes. Finally the ferry tied up on the north-east side of Jersey. The car wheels slipped and churned on the cleats of the wet metal decking as it rolled forward onto and up the cobblestone ramp. Pedro was due to catch a flight late that day to Athens.

Chapter 41

Athens

"I'm Malcolm Webb, welcome to Athens."

Malcolm stood straight and stretched his neck to one side, then to the other. He was somewhere in the reach of five feet ten inches tall. There wasn't an ounce of fat on his perfectly sculpted frame.

"It was a long trip. Longer than I thought." Pedro replied.

"Let me help you." Malcolm explained that he had a car waiting outside. He was based in Budapest. "I got back the day before yesterday and I have to go back there when I'm finished here. It's too much goddamn travel. This is the end of their summer in Athens, but I understand it never gets really cold."

Once outside the terminal, Pedro seemed to wilt before Malcolm's eyes.

"The apartment stays cool," Malcolm assured him. "There are fans and you take a rest before we get started."

"I assumed headquarters told you what I have."

When Malcolm didn't reply, Pedro spoke again. "Maybe I assume too much."

"No, they told me, just not very much."

Pedro now felt perspiration forming on his forehead and had to wipe his hand across his hair line. Malcolm said that all he had been told was that he had to collect a package and get it to Budapest as soon as possible. Pedro wondered whether he could be trusted. Until he had answers, his survival instinct told him to do what he was trained to do - operate on his own. Suddenly searing hot pain shot through his shoulder and down his arm. A wave of nausea hit him and for a second he thought he was going to throw up. Ten seconds passed and then twenty, until finally the pain subsided.

Pedro took a couple of deep breaths. He knew he was walking a very thin line and could only try to anticipate what Malcolm had in mind.

"I'll be back around lunchtime tomorrow. I'll let myself in with the key in case you're asleep, so don't put the chain on the door."

Pedro knew that this was it: It was nearing the end of the line for him. The room smelled - it was a brew of sweat and other odours given off by men crowded together in close quarters, tinged with a hint of fear. It began to make Pedro feel uneasy, and less than certain about Malcolm. Groaning in pain, he dropped to his knee and reached around the back of the bed stand. The fingertips of his left hand had just found what he was looking for when he felt the floor beneath him tremble. The vibration was intense enough that he knew that it could only be caused by one thing. He withdrew his hand and rose just enough so that he could look over the bed towards the door. There, in the thin strip of the light under the door, Pedro saw a shadow pass, then another. He cursed to himself, seriously worried now.

After a few hours he decided to take a walk around the city. Up ahead he sighted a low-slung bridge with curved stone arches. The crunch of the dirt and gravel under his feet made it difficult to walk. He was still in a lot of pain from the accident, and now that the painkillers were starting to wear off, he needed something quickly to relieve the agony. Aware that he was almost certainly under surveillance, he stopped in a Jumbo supermarket and asked the sales assistant for painkillers. Next, he stopped at a newsstand and bought a copy of a major Brazilian paper, O Globo. He had chosen this route because it would force any surveillance team to move from crowded areas into empty streets where they would be easier to spot.

A car stopped next to him and Malcolm called out to Pedro.

"Yes, is there a problem?" Pedro smiled.

But he didn't react to the prompt. Instead, he watched Malcolm take out a pack of cigarettes from his pocket, and light up and inhale. Smoke poured from his nostrils as he talked.

"Let's start again," Malcolm said.

When Pedro just smiled in response, he continued,

"You have all the time you need; as for me I have two hours max. They sent me for two reasons. Firstly, I need the tape from you now."

Then he paused and took a second puff of his cigarette.

Pedro's deep brown eyes were fixated on the inch-long piece of ash which was precarious dangling from the end of Malcolm's cigarette.

"Secondly, my orders will be to dispose of you if you don't hand it over now."

Malcolm trained his grey eyes on him, waiting patiently for his response.

That last comment had touched a nerve, and Pedro didn't know whether his discomfort showed through. He was too weak to offer any other option. Malcolm looked at him with an expression which seemed to border on amazement. He spoke slowly now and stared at him. His tone wasn't hostile, but it was measured.

"You may not see it, but I'm taking care of you," Malcolm said, sounding like a sympathetic therapist. "This double life you've been living is not healthy. The mental strain can be too much, you should think about retirement."

Pedro felt a twist in his gut.

Malcolm went on to explain the psychological "toll" he had planned. That it wasn't enough to simply kill. He wanted his targets to lie awake at night and wonder who was after them. He wanted them to spend their entire waking day glancing over their shoulders, he wanted to drive them insane. Malcolm wanted Pedro to experience this fear.

"You need to listen to me," he told him.

The problem, Pedro knew, was Malcolm's maverick streak. The little shit was clever, and Pedro knew he couldn't underestimate him, but the law of averages told him that sooner or later, something would go wrong, and he would end up in a jam which could cost him his life. One of Pedro's assets was the ability to slow things down in his mind's eye. He could calculate what other players were going to do and how they would react. When things were tense, he could block out the fear and focus on what was important, and slow things down before acting. But right now Pedro felt vulnerable and exposed for the first time. Panic-induced decisions had a nasty way of leading to a bad, or in this case, fatal outcome. Pedro's cover was as good as he could hope for, considering how he felt.

Malcolm was excellent at what he did, and he had already proven his penchant for autonomy. He bristled against control, and so far, Pedro had been willing to ignore all of these transgressions because the man was so damn unique in how he operated.

"Pedro. Our country, as well as our beloved employer, has a glorious history of throwing those men who are at the tip of the spear under the proverbial bus when things get difficult."

"You can't be serious?" Pedro was genuinely shocked by his theory.

Malcolm folded his hands under his chin and leaned back in his chair.

"Justice is blind, and if you train a man to be judge, jury, and executioner . . Well, then you shouldn't be surprised if he some day fails to see the distinction between the terrorist and corrupt. Unsuspecting fools who thought themselves safe after years of United States help have gone bad." Then, after an uneasy silence, "Get in the car."

Pedro thought about it for a moment before replying,

"I'm not sure I'm buying it. But okay, I will give you the tape. Later."

Malcolm shrugged. "Only time will tell."

Pedro began to shake with a mix of fear and white-hot rage: These people wanted to kill him, no matter what. He'd been betrayed,

Pedro walked away. From a distance, there was the sound of a click, then a thump and an explosion. There it was. Pedro had been shot in the back of the head.

* * *

Back in London, John was not sure what to do. He was trying to get his life back to normal – but what was normal after all these years of living in fear? Pedro had disappeared, and Reg Wright and Edward of all people had taken over his office, for reasons John failed to understand. One evening, he waited for Rosa outside her dance studio. She looked pale and considerably thinner than when he'd last seen her. When he questioned her about Pedro, she politely insisted that she had no idea where he was, and was clearly keen to get away from John.

He knew that he should be relieved, but driving home, he couldn't help wondering whether he would ever see Pedro again.

THE END

Printed in Great Britain
by Amazon

35062755R00202